RAMAGE AND THE FREEBOOTERS

LORD NICHOLAS RAMAGE, eldest son of the Tenth Earl of Blazey, Admiral of the White, was born in 1775 at Blazey Hall, St Kew, Cornwall. He entered the Royal Navy as a midshipman in 1788, at the age of thirteen. He has served with distinction in the Mediterranean, the Caribbean, and home waters during the war against France, participating in several major sea battles and numerous minor engagements. Despite political difficulties, his rise through the ranks has been rapid.

In *Ramage and the Freebooters*, his third recorded adventure, Lieutenant Lord Ramage is given command of the brig *Triton*, whose crew is in the throes of mutiny, and a mission to the West Indies.

DUDLEY POPE, who comes from an old Cornish family and whose great-great-grandfather was a Plymouth shipowner in Nelson's time, is well known both as the creator of Lord Ramage and as a distinguished and entertaining naval historian, the author of nine scholarly works.

Actively encouraged by the late C. S. Forester, he has now written thirteen 'Ramage' novels about life at sea in Nelson's day. They are based on his own wartime experiences in the navy and peacetime exploits as a yachtsman as well as immense research into the naval history of the eighteenth century.

Available in Fontana by the same author

Ramage
Ramage and the Drum Beat
Governor Ramage, R.N.
Ramage's Prize
Ramage's Diamond
Ramage's Mutiny
Ramage and the Rebels
The Ramage Touch
Ramage's Signal
Ramage and the Renegades

DUDLEY POPE

Ramage and
the Freebooters

FONTANA/Collins

First published by Weidenfeld and Nicolson Ltd 1969
First issued in Fontana Paperbacks 1977
Fourth impression February 1983

© 1969 by Dudley Pope

Made and printed in Great Britain by
William Collins Sons & Co. Ltd, Glasgow

For Barley Alison

CHAPTER ONE

As Ramage's carriage rattled along Whitehall he was surprised to see the long and wide street was almost deserted. A file of red-coated soldiers swaggered past the end of Downing Street with the white plumes of their shakos streaming in the wind, boots gleaming black and cross-belts white from carefully applied pipe-clay. A brewer's dray drawn by two pairs of horses and heavily laden with hogsheads precariously balanced, pyramid fashion, approached the Admiralty from Charing Cross.

A pieman pushing his handcart, corpulent from tasting his own wares and obviously tipsy from sampling those of a brewer, stopped outside the Banqueting House of Old Whitehall Palace and as he mopped his brow bellowed, 'Buy my plum pudden!' A pedlar, sitting astride his spavined horse and trying to persuade the occasional passers-by to look at the remarkable bargains in lace and brocade displayed in his large leather pack, glowered at the pieman and moved on another few yards.

On both sides of the street a few people dodging puddles left by a heavy shower of rain looked from a distance as if they were performing some complicated dance.

Ramage sat back, squashing the upholstery which exhaled a smell of mildew, picked up his cocked hat and jammed it on his head and—as the driver swore at the horses, swinging them over to the middle of the road for the sharp left turn under the narrow archway and into the forecourt of the Admiralty—wished he felt more like the naval officer he was than an errant schoolboy summoned before a wrathful headmaster.

The wheels chattered over the cobblestones before the carriage stopped in front of the four immense columns dominating the main entrance. The carriage door creaked open and a hand pulled the folding steps down. The doorman coming out of the entrance hall as Ramage alighted, stopped when he saw the visitor was a mere lieutenant and went back into the building.

Telling the coachman to wait, Ramage walked up the steps into the spacious entrance hall where a large, six-sided glass lantern hung from the ceiling and his footsteps echoed on the marble floor. On his left the large fireplace was still full of ashes from the night porter's fire and on each side of it were the curious hooded black armchairs which always reminded him of a widow's bonnet.

From one of them a liveried attendant rose with calculated languidness and, in a bored and condescending voice, asked:

'Your business . . . sir?'

The 'sir' was not an afterthought; from constant practice it was carefully timed to indicate lieutenants were the lowliest of commission officers and that this was the Admiralty, of whose doors the speaker was the lawful guardian.

'To see the First Lord.'

'I . . . let me look at my list.'

Ramage tapped the floor with the scabbard of his dress sword.

The man opened the drawer of a small table and, although the list was obviously the only thing in it, he scrabbled about for some time before taking out a sheet of paper. After glancing at it he looked at Ramage insolently before replacing it and closing the drawer. 'You'll have to——'

'I have an appointment,' Ramage interrupted.

'Quite . . . sir. I'll try to arrange for you to see one of the secretaries. Maybe even this afternoon.'

'I have an appointment with Lord Spencer at nine o'clock. Please tell him I'm here.'

'Look,' sneered the man, all pretence at politeness vanishing, 'we get lieutenants in 'ere by the gross, captains by the score and admirals by the dozen, all claiming they've appointments with 'is Lordship. There's only one person on the list to see 'is Lordship this morning and 'e ain't you. You can wait in there'—he pointed at the notorious waiting-room to the left of the main doors—'and I'll see if I can find someone to see you.'

Ramage was rubbing the lower of the two scars on his

right brow: an unconscious gesture which a few weeks earlier would have warned a whole ship's company that their young captain was either thinking hard or getting angry.

Suddenly turning to the doorman—who was obviously enjoying the episode—Ramage snapped: 'You! Go at once and tell the First Lord that Lord Ramage has arrived for his appointment.'

The man was scuttling for the corridor at the far end of the hall before Ramage turned back to the liveried attendant who, by now looking worried and rubbing his hands together like an ingratiating potman, said reproachfully:

'Why, your Lordship, I didn't realize ... You didn't tell me your name.'

'You didn't ask me and you couldn't be bothered to see if I was the person on the list. You merely hinted that a guinea would help arrange for me to see a clerk. Now hold your tongue.'

The man was about to say something when he saw Ramage's eyes: dark brown and deep-set under thick eyebrows, they now gleamed with such anger the man was frightened, noticing for the first time the two scars on the lieutenant's brow. One was a white line showing clearly against the tanned skin; the other pink and slightly swollen, obviously the result of a recent wound.

But Ramage was still shaken—as was every other officer in the Royal Navy—by the latest news from Spithead and felt a bitter rage not with the man as an individual but as a spiteful personification of the attitude of many of the Admiralty and Navy Board civilian staff.

By now impatiently pacing up and down the hall, Ramage thought of the dozens of assistant, junior and senior clerks, and the assistant, junior and senior secretaries now working under this very roof, all too many of whom administered the Navy with an impersonal condescension and contempt for both seamen and sea officers amounting at times to callousness.

It was understandable because of the system; but it was also unforgivable. Many—in fact most—of these men owed their time-serving, well-pensioned jobs to the influence of some well-placed relative or friend. They filled in forms, checked and filed reports, and at the drop of a hat rattled off the wording of regulations parrot-fashion, unconcerned that

9

the seaman they might be cheating out of a pension was illiterate and ignorant of his legal rights, or that the captain of a ship of war suddenly ordered to account for the loss of some paltry item might be almost at his wit's end with exhaustion after weeks of keeping a close blockade on some God-forsaken, gale-swept French port.

An inky-fingered clerk was, in his own estimation, far more important than a sea officer; ships and seamen were to him an annoyance he had to suffer. No one ever pointed out that he existed solely to keep the ships at sea, well-found, well-provisioned and manned by healthy and regularly paid seamen. No, to these damned quill-pushers a ship of war was a hole in a gigantic pile of forms and reports lined with wood and filled with convicts.

Most of this shameful business at Spithead was due to men like this, whether a junior clerk at £75 a year humbugging the distraught widow of a seaman killed in battle or a senior secretary at £800 a year ignoring the sea officers and telling ministers what they wanted to hear. The Devil take the——

'My Lord...'

The porter was trotting alongside him and had obviously been trying to attract Ramage's attention for some moments.

'My Lord, if you'll come this way please.'

A few moments later he was ushering Ramage through a door saying, 'Would you wait in here, sir: His Lordship will be with you in a few minutes.'

As the door closed behind him Ramage realized he was in the Board Room: in here, under the ceiling decorated with heraldic roses picked out in white and gilt, the Lords Commissioners of the Admiralty sat and deliberated.

Their decisions, jotted down by the Board Secretary on scraps of paper as they were made, resulted in orders being sent out to despatch a fleet half-way round the world to the East Indies, or the 128th captain in the Navy List commanding a frigate off Brest receiving a reprimand for failing to use the prescribed wording when drawing up the report of a survey on a leaking cask of beer.

Large or small, right or wrong, it was here in this room that the decisions were made that governed the activities of more than six hundred of the King's ships whether they were cruising the coast of India or the Spanish Main, blockading

Cadiz or acting as guardship at Plymouth. If the ships were the fighting body of the Navy, he reflected, here was its brain, working in a long room which had three tall windows along one wall and was panelled with the same oak used to build the ships.

And Ramage saw it was an impressive room which had absorbed something of the drama and greatness of the decisions Their Lordships had made within its walls during the last five score years or more, sitting at the long, highly-polished table occupying the middle of the room.

The high-backed chair with arms at the far end was obviously the First Lord's, and the pile of paper, quill, silver paper-knife, inkwell and sandbox in front of it indicated he probably used the Board Room as his own office.

Ramage, intrigued by several long cylinders looking like rolled-up white blinds and fitted on to a large panel over the fireplace, walked over and pulled down one of the tassels. It was a chart of the North Sea. A convenient way of stowing them. Then he noticed the whole panel was surrounded by a frieze of very light wood covered with carvings of nautical and medical instruments and symbols of the sea.

The instruments were beautifully carved, standing out in such relief it seemed he could reach up and use any one of them. An azimuth overlapped an astrolabe; a set of shot gauges hung over a pelorus; a cross staff used by the earliest navigators was partly hidden by a miniature cannon. And, emphasizing the importance of good health in a ship, especially on long voyages of discovery, the snakes and winged staff symbol of Aesculapius and a globe of the world.

There was what seemed to be the face of an enormous clock on the wall opposite the First Lord's chair, but instead of two hands it had a single pointer, like a compass needle. Instead of numbers round the edge, there were the points of the compass, while the map of Europe painted on its face had the axle of the pointer exactly where London was.

He saw the pointer was moving slightly, ranging between 'SW' and 'SW by W'. It was the dial that his father had long ago described to him and which, by an ingenious arrangement of rods and wheels, showed the direction the wind vane on the Admiralty roof was pointing.

And it was very old—that much was clear from the map

which showed the North Sea as 'The British Ocean'. Calais appeared as 'Calice' while the Scilly Isles were simply labelled 'Silly I'.

Each country was indicated by the arms of its royal family, and even a casual glance showed Ramage that some of them had long since vanished, removed from their thrones by death, intrigue, revolution or conquest.

As he reached for his watch he noticed the tall grandfather clock beside the door through which he'd entered. Ten minutes past nine. The figure '17' showed in a small aperture carved in the face—the date, 17 April. Ingenious, yet the clock was obviously very old: the wood was mellow, the metal of the face—which was surrounded by elaborate gilt work—had a rich patina, the mirror on the door was dulled with age, like old men's eyes.

Ramage remembered something his father had told him about the clock: it was made——

'Good morning!'

Ramage spun round to find Lord Spencer had come through a door at the far end of the room which had been indistinguishable against the panelling.

'Good morning, my Lord.'

Ramage shook the proffered hand.

'Your first visit to the Board Room?'

'Yes, sir.'

'I guessed as much, though your father knew it well enough. Were you admiring the clock or bemoaning the unpunctuality of the King's ministers?' Spencer asked banteringly.

Ramage grinned. 'Admiring, and trying to remember what my father told me about it. And admiring the whole room.'

'I love it,' Spencer said frankly. 'I use it instead of my own office. I'll be your guide before we sit down to settle your business.'

The words were spoken lightly, but for Ramage they had an ominous meaning. Certainly the first Lord was being affable enough, but the family had suffered enough at the hands of politicians for him to be wary.

'Let's start with the clock. Made by Langley Bradley, the man who made the one for St Paul's Cathedral. It's been telling the time and date for nearly a hundred years, so the mirror'—he bent down to grimace at his own image—'has reflected every Board meeting since this place was built in 1725.

'These carvings over the fireplace—pearwood, by Grinling Gibbons, as you've probably guessed. He did them in the 1690s and they were probably taken from Wallingford House, which was knocked down to make room for this building.

'And how do you like our wind dial? I can glance up and see if a nice west wind is keeping the French shut up in Brest, or if there's an east wind on which they might slip out. In fact until I became First Lord I never realized what danger an east wind brings to this country, giving every enemy fleet from the Texel to the Cadiz a chance of getting out of port. Or what an ally we have in a west wind, penning them in like sheep!'

Because of his father, Ramage had known the Spencer family since boyhood. Never very well, but enough to allow the First Lord to relax with a lowly lieutenant for a few minutes.

And now he was impressed with the older man's obvious enthusiasm for his job as First Lord of the Admiralty. But for all that he was a politician; any day a Government reshuffle might promote him to some other post or demote him to some well-paid sinecure like the President of the Council for Trade and Plantations. Or to complete eclipse if the Government fell—which he guessed it might do over the Spithead affair. Yet since Spencer was appointed First Lord three years ago he'd become both popular and respected: an unusual combination.

If the Board Room was about seventy-five years old, Ramage reflected, it meant members sitting at that table had given the orders which sent Anson on his great voyage round the world in the *Centurion*. And Captain Cook on three voyages revealing the extent of the Pacific Ocean. And sent Admiral Byng—much too late and with a small and ill-equipped squadron—to defeat off Minorca. Then, as the resulting public outcry threatened to topple the Government, had obeyed its order to make Byng the scapegoat and brought him to a mockery of a trial which led to him being shot by a firing squad on the quarterdeck of the *St George* at Portsmouth.

And, he realized with a shock, from here had gone the orders sending his own father to the West Indies in command of a similar squadron in similar circumstances. Following the inevitable defeat, similar orders for a court martial had been

13

given and for similar reasons—though his father had been disgraced as the price of the Government staying in power, not shot ...

Spencer must have read his thoughts because, his face expressionless, he said casually: 'Yes, some great and some shameful decisions have been made in this room. I can't claim credit for any of the former nor undo any of the latter.'

Ramage nodded, since no answer was needed, but he felt a considerable relief because Spencer had said more than mere words. The trial of Admiral the Earl of Blazey had been a cold-blooded political manoeuvre, but it had also split the Navy.

That had been inevitable because many officers were active in politics or linked by family ties or patronage with leading political figures. They had been quick to strike at the Government of the day through his father—and not a few took advantage of an opportunity to satisfy their jealousy of a young admiral already famous as one of the Navy's leading tacticians. Although several of these men were now dead or superannuated, there were still many in high positions who carried on the vendetta against the Earl's family—helped in turn by the younger officers who looked to them for promotion—and the vendetta had extended to the Earl's son and heir, Ramage himself.

'Sit down—here, in Lord Arden's chair.'

Arden, second senior of the Lords Commissioners, sat at the First Lord's left hand.

As Spencer unlocked a drawer in the table, Ramage thought of the brief and peremptory letter in his pocket ordering him to report to the First Lord. It gave no reason, but as far as Ramage was concerned there could be only one.

Spencer put several papers on the table and, patting them with his hand, remarked: 'Mercifully there are few lieutenants in the Navy List who've had so many contradictory reports on them forwarded to the First Lord.'

And here we go, Ramage thought bitterly. First the honeyed words: now the harsh judgement. Well, it wasn't unexpected. He'd been back in England for several weeks since the Battle of Cape St Vincent. For the first three he had been recovering from the head wound, and as soon as he wrote to the Admiralty reporting himself fit he'd expected the summons to

London or an order to report to some port for a court martial.

His father hadn't tried to comfort him; in fact the old Admiral insisted he didn't accept any reprimand and, if necessary, demanded a court martial. But the days had gone by without anything more than a bare acknowledgement of the letter. While it meant no reprimand it also meant no employment.

Turning the pile of papers over so the bottom one was uppermost, the First Lord said:

'Let's just run through these. Then you'll see my predicament. Here's one from Sir John Jervis—as he then was—dated last October and praising you for your bravery in taking command of the *Sibella* frigate after all the other officers had been killed, and going on to rescue the Marchesa di Volterra from Napoleon's troops. He encloses one from Commodore Nelson—as he then was—which is even more fulsome, saying you literally carried the Marchesa off from beneath the feet of the French cavalry.

'Now for the next one. This, from another admiral, refers to the *same* episode and says you should have been condemned by a court martial for cowardice, and that the trial he'd ordered was interrupted.

'What am I to believe? Well, I take the word of Sir John, since he's the senior officer.

'Then we have the third report, again from Sir John, telling me how you captured a dismasted Spanish frigate while commanding the *Kathleen* cutter. As Sir John says, he admires your bravery but cannot possibly overlook that in making the capture you flatly disobeyed Commodore Nelson's orders.

'Well, all that seems clear enough—until I open the enclosure from Commodore Nelson which is full of praise and doesn't mention a word about disobedience.'

He put down the two pages and picked up the remaining ones.

'I received this shortly after the despatch describing the Battle of Cape St Vincent. Sir John gives due credit to your action but makes it quite clear that he's not sure whether it was due to bravery or foolhardiness, and that you acted without orders and, much worse, lost the *Kathleen* cutter, into the bargain.

'Now,' the First Lord said flatly, 'that's more than sufficient grounds for a court martial. However, since Lieutenant Lord Ramage is involved, it's not as simple as that. Do you know why?'

A puzzled Ramage shook his head.

'Because on the same day I received a private—and, I might say, quite irregular—letter from Commodore Nelson pointing out that had you not deliberately rammed the Spanish *San Nicolas* with the *Kathleen* cutter and slowed her down, he would never have been able to catch up and capture her and the *San Josef*, and he ends his letter with a request that I should "look after" you.'

'Well sir, I——'

'And as if that wasn't enough,' Spencer said with a show of anger, 'no sooner does Sir John receive an earldom for his splendid leadership in the battle than he tells me that if any occasion arises where a resourceful young officer is needed, I could make use of you—as long as I didn't expect you to pay any heed to my orders!'

'But, my Lord——'

'And another very senior officer present at the battle writes to a friend—who sent me a copy of the letter—saying that you and another officer ought to be brought to trial at once in case other captains take it into their head to ignore the Fighting Instructions and quit the line of battle.'

'But Captain Calder's known to be jealous of the Commodore——'

Spencer lifted a hand to silence him and said grimly, 'I didn't mention Captain Calder's name, and I recall that the Commodore received a knighthood and the nation's admiration for capturing two Spanish sail of the line.'

Numbed and resentful, Ramage stared down at the table, trying to guess the reason for Spencer's long recital. It sounded more like a prosecutor reading the charges. Warily he waited for the judgement since he obviously hadn't been summoned to see the First Lord for a social talk.

'How is the Marchesa?'

'Well enough, thank you, my Lord,' mumbled Ramage, taken completely by surprise and wondering if he'd murmured his thoughts aloud.

'She looked very lovely at Lady Spencer's ball the night

before last. In fact we both remarked what a splendid pair you made. You're an appalling dancer, though.'

'Yes, my Lord.'

'I believe she's very grateful for the risks you took when rescuing her.'

'So I'm given to understand, sir,' Ramage said stiffly.

'And obviously prepared to run risks herself by dancing with you.'

Ramage remained silent.

Spencer suddenly slapped the table and laughed.

'Ramage, my boy, every other lieutenant in the Navy List would give ten years of his life to sit where you sit now with the First Lord. At every opportunity they'd say "Yes, my Lord", "No, my Lord". They'd laugh at my poorest jokes. They'd agree with everything I said. They certainly wouldn't sulk, because they know one word from me would put them on the beach for the rest of their lives.'

'Quite, my Lord.'

Every word was true and Ramage knew it; he was sulking like a schoolboy: like a child who kept crying long after he'd forgotten what caused the tears.

'There's a slight difference in my case, my Lord.'

'And that is . . . ?'

'Since I knew before I came into this room I was going to be put on the beach for losing the *Kathleen*, sir, I've nothing to lose—or gain—by laughing, saying yes or saying no.'

Even as he spoke he regretted the words: they were—discipline apart—unnecessarily offensive to a man who was clearly trying to do in the kindest, most tactful way, whatever the Board had decided. And Ramage suddenly realized he'd misunderstood Spencer's earlier remark about the great and the shameful decisions made in this room. The Board must have outvoted Spencer, who'd probably spoken up for him. Spencer had been giving him advance warning, not apologizing for the orders given years ago to his father.

Yet the First Lord said nothing in reply to his outburst; no anger showed in his face; instead it was bland. He looked down and opened the drawer again, bringing out several flat packets, all sealed with red wax. He sorted them out and slid them along the table towards Ramage.

'Read out the superscriptions.'

'Rear Admiral Sir Roger Curtis, K.B., off Brest...Admiral the Earl St Vincent, off Cadiz...Rear Admiral Henry Robinson, Windward Islands Station...Lieutenant the Lord Ramage, Blazey House, Palace Street, London...Lieutenant the Lord Ramage, Blazey House, Palace Street, London...'

Ramage glanced up to see Spencer's sardonic smile.

'You can open those addressed to you. Here——' he pushed across the silver paper-knife.

Nervously Ramage slit open the first. He recognized the once-folded piece of parchment and his eyes immediately picked out the relevant word—'Lieutenant the Lord Ramage ...His Majesty's brig *Triton*...willing and requiring you forthwith to go on board and take upon you the charge and command of captain in her...Hereof, nor you nor any of you may fail as you will answer to the contrary at your peril...' It was signed, 'Spencer, Arden, Jas. Gambier'—three of the Lords Commissioners.

His commission! And what a command—a brig! *Triton, Triton*...? He searched his memory.

'Ten guns, two years old, fresh out of the dockyard after a refit,' Spencer said.

'Thank you, sir,' Ramage said humbly, holding up the commission. 'I didn't expect quite...'

'I know. Keep your gratitude for a moment: you've another letter to read.'

Unpleasant orders, no doubt. He broke the seal and unfolded the paper.

By the Commissioners for Executing
the Office of Lord High Admiral
of the United Kingdom & Ireland

Whereas by our Commission bearing date this day we have appointed your Lordship to the command of His Majesty's brig *Triton*, you are hereby required and directed to proceed without loss of time in His Majesty's brig *Triton* under your command to Rendezvous Number Five off Brest and deliver to Admiral Sir Roger Curtis the packet with which you have already been entrusted. You will then, without loss of time, proceed to Rendezvous Number Eleven, off Cape St Vincent and having ascertained from whichever frigate is stationed there, the posi-

tion of the squadron under the command of Admiral the
Earl of St Vincent, you are to deliver to His Lordship the
packet which has already been delivered to you, taking
particular care that neither you nor any of your ships company shall inform any other person or persons in Lord St
Vincent's squadron of the state of affairs at Spithead.

Upon reporting to His Lordship, you will answer any
questions put to you by His Lordship as freely and truthfully as is within your power.

As soon as His Lordship permits you will leave the
squadron and proceed without loss of time to the Windward Islands Station and, immediately upon finding Rear-
Admiral Henry Robinson or, should he be absent, the
senior officer upon the station, and deliver to him the
packet of which you are already possessed, and answer any
questions put to you as freely and truthfully as lies within
your power. You will take particular care that neither you
nor your ship's company shall inform any other person in
Admiral Robinson's squadron of the state of affairs at
Spithead.

You will then place yourself under the command of
Rear-Admiral Robinson, or if he is absent, the senior
officer upon the station, for your further proceedings.

Given the 16th day of April 1797.

Spencer, Arden, Jas. Gambier.

As he was reading the time-honoured phrases, Ramage
knew there was a 'but'. Giving him command of the *Triton*
brig was obviously the Admiralty's way of privately approv-
ing his recent behaviour and equally privately rewarding him
for it; but there must be a special reason why he had been
selected. The task seemed more appropriate to a frigate commanded by a post-captain.

'Well?' demanded Spencer.

'Seems straightforward, sir.'

'The *Triton*'s at Spithead.'

But every ship of war at Spithead had mutinied: when
Admiral Lord Bridport had made the signal to weigh anchor
a few days ago, the seamen in some fifteen sail of the line had
refused to obey, run up the shrouds and given three cheers.
The officers had been sent on shore and ropes had been rove

from the foreyardarms, warning that anyone who did not support the mutiny would be hanged.

At this moment, Ramage reflected, the Admiralty which administered the most powerful fleet the world had ever seen couldn't tell a dozen men to row a boat with any hope of its order being obeyed. He laughed involuntarily at the absurdity of it.

Immediately Spencer's hands clenched, the knuckles white.

'You find the fact His Majesty's Fleet at Spithead is in a state of mutiny and complete anarchy a laughing matter, Ramage?'

'No, sir!' he added hastily. 'It's just that I seem doomed to get commands in—er, unusual—circumstances. The *Sibella* was under attack and sinking when I had to take command as the only surviving officer. My first task after being given my first official command, the *Kathleen* cutter, was to rescue the crew of a frigate aground and under enemy fire. Then I lost the *Kathleen* at the Battle of Cape St Vincent. Now—if you'll forgive me for saying so, my Lord—my next command is a brig whose crew has mutinied!'

Spencer smiled and for a moment said nothing. Yes, the lad was like his father. Face on the thin side, high cheekbones, eyes deep-set under thick eyebrows, nose straight, not quite aquiline. By no means handsome but, as his wife had remarked a couple of evenings ago at the ball, there was something about the lad that made him stand out among the hundred or so men present. Hard to define why—he wasn't tall; in fact he was quite average. Slim hips, wide shoulders and an arrogant walk. No, Spencer thought, not arrogant as much as confident. Habit of rubbing that old scar over his brow—as he was doing this very minute—when he was worried. Had trouble pronouncing the letter 'r' when he got excited—he'd just say 'bwig' for 'brig'.

Spencer forgot the mutiny as he studied Ramage, realizing a lot would depend on the lad's character over the next few weeks. Next few hours, in fact. No, it wasn't the face or the stance, nor the physique or the voice . . . At that moment Ramage glanced up nervously and Spencer saw that part of it was the eyes. He realized they could express the same menace or defiance as the muzzles of a pair of pistols. And looking into them you could no more guess his thoughts than you could see the lead shot in the pistols' barrels.

Yet you didn't see those eyes across the length of a ball-room. What was it then? It was like glancing up at the night sky—a few stars out of the millions visible caught the eye, for no apparent reason. Spencer finally admitted he couldn't define it, though it was clear why Ramage's men were devoted to him: he combined a decisive manner with a dry sense of humour and, like his father, he combined a highly developed, even if arbitrary, sense of justice with an uncontrollable impatience with fools. Well, no harm in that—as long as he never became a member of the Board and had to persuade the rest to adopt some policy they were too stupid to understand.

Realizing he'd been staring at Ramage for some moments, Spencer smiled and asked:

'Why do you think you were chosen to command the *Triton* and given these orders?'

'I've no idea, sir,' Ramage said frankly.

'Since you've already given the reason yourself without realizing it, I'll tell you—and I'm speaking to the son of an old friend, not to a young lieutenant!

'The Board know full well that to get the *Triton* under way at Spithead is going to need ingenuity and quick thinking by her commanding officer; perhaps even highly irregular methods which might lead to violence and which, if it resulted in a public outcry, the Board would have to disown.'

He held up his hand to stop Ramage interrupting and continued:

'The Board also know it's easier to persuade fifty seamen than a couple of hundred, so they chose a brig rather than a frigate. Selecting a lieutenant to command her—well, there was only one man known to them who was the junior lieutenant of a frigate when he was rendered unconscious in battle and woke to find himself her commanding officer and behaved with great initiative and bravery; and only one lieutenant who was quick enough to spot that the only way to prevent several Spanish ships of the line from escaping capture was to ram the leading one with the tiny cutter he was commanding.

'That the lieutenant happens to be you is a fortunate coincidence,' Spencer added.

But Ramage had already spotted the potential trap.

'If anything went wrong at Spithead, then I'll make a convenient scapegoat,' he added bitterly. 'And the son of "Old Blazeaway" into the bargain.'

'Scapegoat, yes—if you fail,' Spencer said blandly. 'And no public credit if you succeed, because no one but the Admiralty knows the problems you'll have overcome.'

'Exactly, my Lord.'

'You have a poor view of politicians, Ramage—and in view of your family's experience, I can't blame you. But you'd be wise to give the Board a little more credit. For a start, the Board chose the man they thought would succeed. That's their prime interest. But the man they chose might fail and might become a scapegoat.'

He wagged a finger as he said slowly, emphasizing each word, 'Don't forget any public outcry brings the Navy into disrepute. Just suppose a public outcry forced us to bring you to trial. What better defence can the Admiralty have for their choice than citing your record so far—omitting your tendency to ignore orders? Who else could call witnesses to his character ranging from Lord St Vincent and Sir Horatio Nelson down to seamen who were on board the *Kathleen* when you rammed the *San Nicolas*?'

Ramage was almost persuaded and grateful to the First Lord for his frankness. He was just going to reply when Spencer said quietly:

'We're putting a lot of faith in you, Ramage. It's vital that the three admirals are warned of what's happening at Spithead. Supposing the mutiny spreads to Admiral Duncan's fleet watching the Dutch, or Sir Richard Curtis's off Brest, or Lord St Vincent's covering the Spanish off Cadiz, or Admiral Robinson's covering the Windward and Leeward Islands, or Sir Hyde Parker's at Jamaica . . .

'The Royal Navy's all that stands between us and defeat,' he continued. 'You realize that. The price of bread is rising, the people are restive with empty purses and often empty bellies, Parliament is more than restive with a Government that can only announce defeats and the defection of one ally after another on the Continent. And every damned merchant in the City of London is screaming that he's ruined. Sometimes, Ramage, I wonder where and how it will all end. I daren't even think of *when*.'

Since his only knowledge of the mutinies came from the newspapers, Ramage asked: 'What exactly are the men asking for, sir?'

'More pay; leave to visit their families when in port; better provisions and issued at sixteen ounces to the pound, not fourteen; vegetables to be served with fresh beef instead of flour when in port; better conditions for the sick; wounded to be paid until they're fit or pensioned . . . It's a long list.'

Hard to judge Spencer's attitude from his voice, but Ramage wondered if the First Lord knew the views of many of the junior captains. For sure he'd have heard the views of every admiral with enough wind left to express them; yet did he realize that quite a number of officers had for years felt the men's conditions should be improved? Well, now was the time . . .

'I think many officers feel some of the grievances are justified, sir,' he said quietly.

'I daresay,' Spencer said, 'but we can only spend the money Parliament votes us—and that's already well over twelve million pounds a year. Why, the Secretary's calculated that it'd cost over half a million a year to meet these demands.'

'But granting the men leave after they've been at sea for a year or so——'

'Out of the question!' Spencer snapped. 'They'd desert in droves!'

'Not the good men,' Ramage persisted. 'They only desert because they desperately want to see their families.'

Then, seeing Spencer was tapping the table impatiently, he decided to make just one more point.

'Purser's measure, sir—I can guess that's one of the men's main grievances. Before they went to sea, these men always considered a pound weight consisted of sixteen ounces. Yet when a sixteen-ounce pound of meat is sent to a ship, only fourteen ounces are issued to the men and they're called a pound——'

'Ramage, you know as well as I do about wasting. Meat goes rotten, bread gets stale, beer leaks, weevils eat the flour. If the purser wasn't allowed the difference between the two measures he'd never balance his books!'

Ramage then knew it was pointless to argue. Spencer was

surrounded by clerks with their ledgers. He'd never seen a dishonest purser at work; never seen the wretched fellow altering his books the moment a seaman died, debiting him with clothes and tobacco he'd never had, so that there was nothing left of the man's pay for the wretched widow ...

Spencer's next question caught him unawares.

'Do you think you can make sixty mutineers get the *Triton* under way?'

'No, sir,' he answered, suddenly realizing this was his chance to lessen the odds. 'I don't think anyone could board a brig which had a mutinous crew and *make* them do anything, even if he had fifty Marines to back him up.'

He might just as well have flung an inkwell into the First Lord's face.

'My God, Ramage! You realize what's at stake? You, of all people, now saying you can't do it when a minute or two ago you said ...'

He began pushing his chair back, obviously intending to leave the room.

'Sir——'

Spencer paused. 'Well?'

'I'm afraid you misunderstood me: I meant I couldn't force a ship's company I *didn't know* to do what I wanted. But if I may ask a favour ...'

'Go on, man!'

'Well sir, I was thinking of my Kathleens——'

'—But she's sunk! They're distributed among Lord Vincent's squadron.'

'No, sir, Twenty-five of them were sent to the *Lively* with me—she was short of men—and came back to England.'

'Good men?'

'The best, sir! I chose them myself.'

'But the *Lively*'s at Portsmouth or Spithead; she's probably affected.'

'I know, sir,' Ramage persisted, 'but if half the *Triton*'s present complement could be exchanged for the twenty-five ex-Kathleens in the *Lively*, at least I'd have halved the odds by having nearly half a ship's company who've—well, who've——'

'Followed you because you're you ...' Spencer said with a grimace. 'Very well, a messenger will take the orders to

Portsmouth within an hour. That'll give the men plenty of time to settle in before you arrive.'

'May I ask one more favour, sir.'

Spencer nodded.

'The Master, sir. I'm sure the *Triton*'s present one is a good man, but the former Master of the *Kathleen*, Henry Southwick, might help me turn the trick with the men.'

'Very well. Anything else?'

'No sir. The rest is up to me.'

'Good. But look here, Ramage, I must make one thing clear. You know as well as I do that until you reach the West Indies and come under Admiral Robinson's command, you'll be a private ship. But don't go chasing after prizes just because there's no admiral to take his eighth share.'

Ramage's resentment must have shown in his face much as he tried to control it, because Spencer said coolly:

'You're a deuced touchy youngster. I didn't mean you'd go after the money; just telling you the Admiralty can't and don't approve of your habit of going your own way. I'd be a poor friend of your family if I didn't warn you not to make a habit of it. It's like duelling. Someone challenges and wins a duel. Very well—perhaps it was a matter of honour. But sometimes a man develops a taste for duelling: before long he's constantly looking for an imagined insult to justify a challenge. By then he's no better than a murderer.'

'I understand, sir.'

'Good. Now, you'll leave for Portsmouth tonight. We'd better spend half an hour going over the details of what's been happening at Spithead and how the Admiralty and Parliament view it, so that you can answer any questions from the admirals. Here, pen and paper and ink: make notes as I talk.'

CHAPTER TWO

Dusty and weary after a night's journey in the post-chaise from London to Portsmouth, Ramage walked through the great dockyard after visiting the Admiral Superintendent's office with as much enthusiasm for the task ahead as a condemned man going to the wall to face a firing squad.

Normally there was more bustle in the streets of Portsmouth than in the City of London; normally the dockyard was busier than Billingsgate Fishmarket, and the language riper, and one had to keep a weather eye open for fear of being run down by an exuberant crowd of shipwrights' apprentices hurrying along with a handcart of wood.

There'd be the thudding of a hundred adzes biting into solid English oak, shaping futtocks and beams for new ships of war; the sharp clanking of blacksmiths' hammers shaping red-hot metal in the forges; the grating of two-handled saws cutting logs into planks in the sawyers' pits.

Groups of seamen from the various ships with a cheery 'One, two and heave!' would normally be hoisting sacks and barrels of provisions on to a cart, while the masts and yards sprouting from ships in the docks between the buildings would be alive with men bending on new sails and replacing worn-out rigging.

Marine sentries guarding the gates and the buildings would be saluting smartly, muskets clattering in a cloud of pipe-clay.

But today the dockyard was deserted as though abandoned before an approaching enemy army. Not one adze, blacksmith's hammer or saw was at work; not one forge had its furnace alight: the mutineers had frightened the craftsmen into staying at home. The masts and yards were bare—indeed, few yards were even squared.

Although there were plenty of seamen about, they slouched,

some of them insolently walking out of their way to pass close to an officer without saluting.

For the first time in his life Ramage felt he didn't belong; neither to the dockyard nor the ships. All were alien, things of brick or wood through which malevolent ghosts walked.

And the Port Admiral . . . He'd cursed and sworn with well-nigh apoplectic vigour about the mutineers and the disrespect they'd shown him; but he'd been quite unable to tell Ramage what was going on. In fact Ramage ended the interview with the uncomfortable feeling the Admiral considered him an odd fellow for being so inquisitive and was far more concerned that, as a new commanding officer joining his ship he took a copy—and signed a receipt for it—of the bulky 'Port Orders' which outlined in considerable detail how the port's daily routine was to be conducted.

Ramage seethed as he recalled the interview. When he'd asked whether the *Triton* was provisioned for the West Indies and ready for sea, the question had been brushed aside, the Admiral drawing his attention to the first of the Port Orders and reading it out—'The receipt of all Orders or Letters on Service is to be immediately acknowledged in writing . . .'

Like a naval Nero fiddling while the Fleet mutinied, the Admiral reacted by ignoring it, apart from a tirade against the men in the *Royal George* who'd dared to hoist a red flag —the 'bloody flag'.

However, he'd finally managed to discover that Southwick had already gone on board the *Triton*. That was something, even though the Admiral added with gloomy relish that the mutineers had by now probably put him in irons and would do the same to Ramage the moment he set foot on board.

Recalling Lord Spencer's reactions when he'd attempted to warn him that many captains felt some of the seamen's grievances were justified, Ramage suddenly understood why the First Lord showed so little interest: he relied on his admirals to advise him; men like the Port Admiral. Men who, when they went to sea, took their own provisions, own cook and own servants; who, by the very nature of their high position, had to remain remote from the seamen. Little wonder the First Lord showed little sympathy for the men.

And suddenly he guessed that the mutineers' leaders must have realized all this long ago; realized that open mutiny was the only chance of getting better conditions. Since the men had already announced their loyalty to the King and vowed they'd sail at once if the French Fleet put to sea, there was no question that the mutiny was fomented by revolutionaries.

But why, he mused, couldn't people of Spencer's calibre understand that conditions *must* be bad for thousands of men to risk hanging to secure a few pence more pay, another two ounces in a pound of provisions, occasional shore leave and better treatment for the sick and wounded? The only possible explanation was that the admirals, unwilling to be the bearers of unpalatable news, had forgotten they had a loyalty to their men and told the First Lord what they thought he'd want to hear . . .

Who on earth was waving from that doorway? Suddenly Ramage recognized the lanky figure of Thomas Jackson, an American seaman and his former coxswain in the *Kathleen*: the man who'd helped him rescue the Marchesa and helped him escape, using false papers, after being captured by the Spaniards. Each had saved the other's life more than once; between them was the bond of shared dangers, failures and successes.

Glancing round to make sure none of the seamen was watching, Ramage walked over to the building, with apparent casualness, noticing Jackson had disappeared through the open door.

The building was a cooper's store, full of empty barrels and casks, with thousands of staves and hoops piled on top of each other in great stacks.

'Morning, sir: sorry to be waving like that but——'

'Good to see you, Jackson: you're mustered in the *Triton*?'

'Aye, sir: all the Kathleens exchanged into her from the *Lively* and Mr Southwick's joined. That's why I'm here.'

'How do you mean?'

'Well, sir, us Kathleens didn't think anything about the exchange because the *Lively*'s due for a refit soon; but when Mr Southwick arrived alongside one or two of us began to wonder. The original Tritons were all for keeping him off, but we got him on board. I tipped him the wink and as he knew you were due he thought I'd better stay on shore to keep a weather eye open.'

'Good. Now, how are things on board?'

'Bad, I'm afraid, sir.'

'The Tritons?'

'They support the mutiny, every one of them. There's no violence, though. They're good enough men at heart.'

'A particular leader?'

'O.e man—the rest follow him.'

'If he wasn't on board?'

'Don't know, sir, to be honest. Someone else might take his place.'

'Any likely candidates?'

'No, I don't think so. But I've only been on board a short while, sir: it's hard to be sure.'

'The Kathleens?'

Jackson looked embarrassed.

'Come on, speak out, Jackson. The whole damned Fleet's mutinied, so nothing else can surprise me!'

'It's difficult to explain, sir, because the men's claims are——'

'We're not discussing conditions in the Navy, Jackson, because I can't change them. Now, how do the Kathleens stand?'

'Well, sir . . .'

He understood only too well Jackson's dilemma: those twenty-five men were among the finest in the Navy: cheerful, loyal and well-disciplined. After the *Kathleen* had been sunk he'd hand-picked those sent to the *Lively* and it had been difficult to choose them.

And how ironical—here's Jackson, an American and in law neutral, explaining away the disloyalty of Britons to the Royal Navy!

'It's like this, sir,' Jackson finally began, running a hand through his thinning hair, then pinching his nose. 'The delegates from all the sail of the line have told the smaller ships to stay out of the mutiny, but they're being ignored, because all the men think the Fleet's claims are reasonable. So the Kathleens—well, in the *Lively* we were just a small group and with everyone else in favour—well, we agreed.

'Everything's being organized by the delegates in the big ships: they're doing all the running around, shouting and cheering, sending the officers on shore, and hoisting the "bloody flag". In the frigates it's different; it just means no one doing any work. Just playing cards and so on——'

Ramage interrupted: 'Stop backing and filling! Get to the point!'

'Well, you couldn't have done anything with the Kathleens in the *Lively* because whatever they thought they were outnumbered five to one. In the *Triton* there's thirty-six originals and twenty-five Kathleens. It's a question of whether the Tritons threaten to stop the Kathleens doing anything.'

'You think they will.'

'Yes. At least, this fellow I was telling you about will.'

'And the Kathleens would obey him?'

'I'm not sure.' Jackson said frankly. 'Stafford, Fuller, Rossi, Maxton—all of them would do anything for you personally, sir. But—well, this mutiny's the only chance the Fleet has of getting an improvement.'

'What you mean is,' Ramage said bluntly, 'they think they've got to be loyal to the mutineers, and it'd be unfair to ask 'em to be loyal to *me* as well.'

'That's more or less it, sir,' Jackson admitted.

'I wonder if the mutineers realize that if the French Navy mutinied Bonaparte'd shoot every third man.'

'I know,' Jackson said soberly. 'That's why I'm . . .'

He didn't finish the sentence, and Ramage knew there was nothing more the American could tell him.

The task was simple enough; the execution was so complicated he doubted if anyone could do it. Who, with nothing to offer, could talk honest men into dividing their loyalty?

'Go back on board,' he told Jackson, 'and pass the word to Mr Southwick that I'll be out within the hour. But don't tell anyone else.'

*

The boatman at the tiller of the little cutter slicing its way through the choppy sea to take Ramage to the brig at anchor near the Spit Sand outside the harbour was as talkative and inquisitive as his mate was silent and uninterested.

'The *Triton* you said, sir?'

'Yes.'

'Nice little ship. Just finished refitting, they say.'

Ramage nodded.

'You'll be the new capting, I suppose, sir?'

Ramage dodged the question in case the man was in the

pay of the mutineers, and asked: 'What happened to her present one?'

'Put on shore by the mutineers he was, like a lot of the officers from the ships of the line. An 'ard man, they do say.'

Ramage nodded.

'Took the new Master out to her last night.'

Ramage nodded again and, tapping the leather bag he held on his lap, said, 'I'm merely a messenger.'

The boatman eyed his trunk stowed under a tarpaulin to protect it from the spray.

'Aye,' he said, with all the insolence of a man who carried a Protection in his pocket, exempting him from the attention of a press gang, 'I guessed you must be.'

With that he spat to leeward and, jamming his hip against the tiller, dug into his pocket for a knife and a quid of tobacco. He sliced off a piece, stuck it in his mouth and began chewing.

The *Triton* was at anchor off Fort Monckton and just clear of Spit Sand, the big shoal on the Gosport side which almost sealed off the V-shaped entrance to Portsmouth Harbour. The shoal left only a narrow channel for large ships and it ran close in along the Southsea and Portsmouth side. Ramage noted grimly, as an idea began to form in his mind, that at half-ebb and half-flood the tidal stream there was very strong.

At first the Gosport shore sheltered the harbour entrance from the brisk west wind, but as the cutter slipped across the shallow Hamilton Bank the waves were short and high and spray blew aft, and Ramage wrapped himself in his boat cloak.

As the cutter beat down parallel with the coast he could see the *Triton* more clearly. Finally, with the brig bearing north-west the boatman growled:

'Mind yer 'ead, sir: smartly with them sheets, Bert.'

He pushed the tiller over and the sail swung across, filled on the other tack, and the cutter sped directly towards the brig.

Outlined against flat land to the south of Haslar Hospital the little brig looked trim and warlike. Her two masts were exactly the same height; her hull gleamed black with a broad white strake sweeping along a few inches below the top of her bulwarks and a little wider than her gun ports, which showed as five black squares. She was floating low on her marks—showing she'd been provisioned for several months—and her yards were hanging square.

Ramage realized the boatman was steering to go alongside on the larboard side, a deliberate insult since the other side was used for officers.

'Starboard side, dam' you,' Ramage growled without looking round. 'That's cost you your tip.'

'Sorry sir—no offence meant; just wasn't thinking.'

'Don't lie: d'you think I don't recognize a former man o' war's man?'

It was a long shot but, from the way the man lapsed into silence, an accurate one.

The mate went to the halyards and, as the boatman luffed up the cutter, let go the halyard. Both of them grabbed the sail and stifled it and a moment later the mate had hooked on alongside the brig.

After paying the boatman Ramage slung the strap of his leather bag over his left shoulder and climbed up the brig's side battens.

There'd been no hail from a sentry on board the *Triton*, but Ramage knew many pairs of eyes had been watching his approach.

A few moments later he was standing on deck just forward of the main mast. A score of seamen lounging around were doing nothing, but Southwick, his hat unsuccessful in its attempt to contain his flowing white hair, was standing there saluting, a broad grin on his red face.

'Welcome on board, sir!'

Ramage returned the salute and at once shook the old Master by the hand.

'Hello and thank you, Mr Southwick: I'm glad to see you again. Are there any other commission or warrant officers on board?'

Realizing the significance of Ramage's words, Southwick said quickly: 'No, sir, only myself.'

'Very well.'

Unhurriedly Ramage opened the leather bag, took out and unfolded a large sheet of paper and, turning so the men on the deck could hear, began reading it aloud, the wind snatching at his words.

'By the Commissioners for Executing the Office of Lord High Admiral of the United Kingdom and Ireland...to Lieutenant the Lord Ramage...His Majesty's brig *Triton* ...willing and requiring you forthwith to go on board and take upon you the charge and command of captain in her accordingly; strictly charging and commanding all the officers and company of the said brig to behave themselves jointly and severally in their respective appointments, with all due respect to you, their said Captain...you will carry out the General Printed Instructions and any orders and instructions you may receive...hereof, nor you nor any of you may fail as you will answer to the contrary at your peril...'

He folded the paper and put it back in the bag. By reading to the officers on board the commission appointing him captain, he had 'read himself in', lawfully establishing himself in command. In happier times the ship's company would also have been mustered to hear it and he would have concluded with a speech which would have given them all a chance to size him up.

Jackson, Stafford and Fuller were now standing by the gangway, and Ramage was thankful for the American's foresight which ensured that his first order, to be made through the Master, would be obeyed. First impressions...

'Mr Southwick, would you have my trunk hoisted on board from the cutter—the boatman has been paid. Then join me in the cabin.'

With that he walked slowly aft to the taffrail, turned and looked forward along the whole length of the deck.

Every object and every person he saw was under his command: he was the king of all he surveyed. Legally, he had more power of life and death over these men than the King himself: he could order any of them to be flogged, which the King could not. He could order them into a battle from which they couldn't possibly return alive, and since the King didn't command a ship he couldn't do that either.

But, Ramage thought ruefully, just as no king was safe from revolution, no captain was safe from mutiny; and for all the good it did, his commission could have been a cook's recipe...

Walking forward the fifteen feet that brought him to the

companionway, he clattered down the steps and turned aft into the two cabins which would be his home for the next few months. Stretching the full width of the hull, one abaft the other, they formed the stern of the ship. Forward of them were three small cabins on either side, against the hull, the space in the middle forming the wardroom. Each was about six feet square and in them lived Southwick, the surgeon, purser, and other senior men.

Ramage glanced round at the main cabin. It was larger than he expected and he needed to bend his neck only slightly to avoid banging his head on the beams. The door was in the middle of the bulkhead and there was a similar door in the other bulkhead leading to his sleeping cabin.

The main cabin was well furnished: a desk to starboard against the forward bulkhead was lit by the skylight above; next to it a sideboard fitted the ship's side and had a glass-fronted cupboard over it.

On the larboard side a well-padded settee made three sides of a square, its back against the forward bulkhead, the ship's side and after bulkhead. A table was fitted in the middle so that four or five people on the settee sat round three sides of it, leaving the fourth clear for the steward to work.

Walking aft into the sleeping cabin, Ramage found it was small and dark and airless: the hull was curving into the centre-line so sharply (the rudder was hung only a few feet farther aft) that there was less than five feet headroom.

The long, open-topped box that was the cot, slung at head and foot by ropes secured to the beams above, had just enough room to swing with the ship's roll without banging the larboard side of the hull. On the starboard side there was a chest of drawers and an enamelled basin with a mirror above it. But the only light came through the open door: the skylight did not reach over this cabin.

Ramage returned to the main cabin and went to the desk, opening the leather bag and emptying out its contents as he sat down.

His commission, a new copy of the *Signal Book for Ships of War*, the letters for Admiral Curtis, Lord St Vincent, and Admiral Robinson, a small flat parcel, and the copy of his orders from the Admiralty.

After locking the *Signal Book* and letters—the most secret

items on board—in the top drawer of the desk, he opened the parcel. It was a small portrait in a plain gilt frame, and a good likeness—the artist had almost caught the unpredictability of Gianna's expressions—one moment so patrician, the next so impudent. And the way the light glistened in her jet black hair. And the small nose, high cheek bones and warm, expressive mouth.

Although the portrait was simply a head and shoulders, one could see the subject was small—barely five feet tall; and even a stranger could sense she was accustomed to rule. How long, he mused, before she ceased being a refugee and could return to her tiny kingdom of Volterra, with its 20,000 inhabitants, all of whom were now part of Bonaparte's empire?

She might be the ruler of Volterra and a wave of her hand might have dismissed her chief minister; but Ramage relaxed for a few minutes to relive their parting a few hours ago at Blazey House, in Palace Street. Since Gianna was living with his parents, she'd insisted on nursing him while he recovered from the head wound. Neither of them had been over-anxious to speed his convalescence.

The door of his bedroom would be flung open; a moment later Gianna would come in carrying a tray of food. She'd set down the tray, shut the door and run into his arms. He grinned to himself as he thought of the cold meals he'd eaten because the tray had remained on the table for so long before they remembered the ostensible reason for her visit to the sickroom.

When the time came to write to the Admiralty reporting he was fit for duty she'd been full of secret plans to prevent him getting an appointment; in fact his father had eventually —unknown at the time to Ramage—warned her not to meddle. But, like Ramage himself, they loved her deeply; she'd become the daughter his mother always wanted. Yet when his mother had once hinted, when Gianna was out of the room, that she would make an excellent daughter-in-law, the old Admiral had pointed out that Volterra would be a turbulent state by the time Bonaparte was driven out of Italy; the spirit of revolution would linger. The people might be unwilling to return to the old, almost feudal system. Gianna might have a struggle to regain her place as Volterra's ruler, and a foreign husband would be a handicap. Grunts and the scuffling of feet on the companion ladder beyond the bulkhead interrupted his thoughts and told him the seamen were bringing down his trunk.

Stafford backed in first, holding one end, followed by the lanky Suffolk fisherman, Fuller, who was holding the other. Jackson brought up the rear with sharp but good-natured exclamations of 'Mind the table—steady, Fuller, you clodhopper!'

Ramage pointed to the after cabin. He'd have to find out if the captain's steward was on board; but for the moment, until he was sure of the man's loyalty, he didn't want him rummaging around.

After putting down the trunk both Stafford and Fuller returned grinning, reminding Ramage of a pair of eager spaniels.

'Well, you two, I'm glad to see you again.'

' 'Twas a surprise, sir,' said Fuller; and Stafford's cockney face showed he meant it when he said, 'Never guessed we'd 'ave the 'onour o' servin' wiv you agin, sir!'

'From what I hear,' Ramage said dryly, 'it's an honour the rest of the ship's company don't wish to share.'

'Well, sir...' Stafford began, and Fuller's bony hands clenched and unclenched with embarrassment, the few yellowed teeth he still possessed showing as he opened his mouth to speak, but no words came.

'Very well,' Ramage said, and grinned. 'Carry on, Jackson, pass the word for Mr Southwick.'

'He's just coming, sir.'

Ramage heard shoes clattering on the ladder and as the three men left Southwick burst into the cabin.

'Heavens, I'm glad to see you, sir!' He shut the door. 'What a mess it all is!'

Ramage nodded. 'You've had an enjoyable leave?'

'Fine—though I'm glad to be back afloat again. And you, sir?'

'The same.'

'The Marchesa?'

'She's very well and enjoying England. She asked me to give you her best wishes.' He pointed at her portrait. 'She's still with us in a sense!'

Southwick grinned with obvious delight. 'It was good of her to remember me, sir. And that's a splendid likeness.

36

Your father, sir?'

'Very well. He enjoyed the tale of our scrap off Cape St Vincent.'

'Thought he would—and wished he was there with us, no doubt.'

'Now,' Ramage said briskly. 'Thanks for sending Jackson. How do we stand here?'

'Jackson was the only one I could send who'd be any use. That's how we stand...'

'As bad as that?'

'Well, that's how we stood a'fore you came on board.'

'How's my arrival affected the situation?'

Southwick ruffled his hair, obviously choosing his words carefully.

'Put it like this: the Tritons look to me like good lads who've just followed the rest of the Fleet, just as the Kathleens followed the *Lively*. What matters is that the thirty-six Tritons don't know you, and the twenty-five Kathleens do. They'd be a poor lot if they ever forgot what you've done for 'em.'

'I've merely tried to kill them from time to time.'

'Now, now sir,' Southwick chided, surprised at the bitterness in his captain's voice. 'You always take on so. In war some's got to get killed, and the men know that. Still...'

'Still what?'

'Well, you'll be wanting to know if the Kathleens will get this brig under way, even if the original Tritons won't lift a finger.'

'More than that: would the Tritons try to stop them?'

'I've been trying to find out, and to be honest I'm not sure; nor is Jackson. The Kathleens are torn between loyalty to the mutineers—you can understand that, though I'd like to see all those dam' delegates dangling from the foreyardarm —and their loyalty to you.'

'And what happens when the strain comes on both loyalties at once?'

Southwick, looking at him directly, said in a flat voice:

'It's entirely up to you, sir. That's Jackson's opinion—and he's a seaman among seamen—and it's mine, too.'

Ramage had known that only too well, even without the First Lord saying it. But coming from Southwick so bluntly it jolted him. *It's entirely up to you!* This was the loneliness of command. From the First Lord of the Admiralty to the old Master of the *Triton* came the same verdict.

'Any idea what my attitude should be?'

'None, sir, more's the pity. I was talking half the night with Jackson on just that point.'

'But you must have some idea: harsh and threatening, friendly and appealing to their loyalty, just laughing at the whole thing?'

'I'm not backing and filling to avoid the responsibility of advising you, sir. I simply don't know. None of us has *ever* seen open mutiny before!'

'True . . . Jackson mentioned a ringleader among the Tritons?'

'Well, not exactly a ringleader; there's one of them who's a sort of spokesman.'

'What's his name? An out-and-out mutineer?'

'Harris. No, not a real mutineer; in fact the sort of man I reckon you'd probably rate a petty officer after a couple of months. Just intelligent and literate. The rest of the men turn to him to read and write their letters and so on.'

Ramage grinned. 'Very well, Southwick. Now, do you know anything about my orders from the Admiralty?'

The Master shook his head and Ramage quickly explained them, concluding: 'We must get under way tomorrow morning: high water is six o'clock. I want to weigh an hour before and we'll get the most out of the ebb. I'll spend the rest of today wandering around. Make no attempt at enforcing discipline; just leave the men alone, so I can take a good look at them. How about the Marines?'

'No sergeant: just a corporal and six men. They're all right, but they can't do anything even if they wanted to because they've no arms: the seamen have taken the keys to the arms lockers, though not for those in my cabin.'

After the Master left the cabin, Ramage went to the sleeping cabin, unlocked his trunk and took out a pair of half boots. He checked the right one, which had a sheath for a throwing knife sewn inside, and pulled them on in place of his shoes.

There was much to do: before sailing he should go through all the papers left by the previous captain. There were inventories to check and sign, letters and order books to read, a dozen and one other things a new captain had to deal with as soon as he took over command to satisfy the voracious appetites of the clerks at the Admiralty and the Navy Board.

And then, with Southwick, he'd have to check over the ship: masts, yards, sails, hull, stores, powder, shot and provisions... small wonder the poor old *Triton* was floating on her marks: she was carrying enough food and water to feed more than sixty men for half a year; enough powder and shot to fight a couple of dozen brisk engagements; enough spare sails and cordage to keep her at sea despite wear, tear and damage from battles with both Nature and the enemy.

He went to bed early that night. It was obvious, after a couple of hours spent on deck, that there was little to be done while the ship was still in sight of the rest of the Fleet. His steward was too terrified even to unpack his trunk and stow the contents; the Marines dare not resume their duties, so he slept without a sentry at the door. By nine o'clock, after half an hour spent giving instructions to Southwick, Ramage was lying in his cot going over his plan once again.

It was all or nothing. If it failed he'd be a laughing stock and, since he'd received his orders direct from the First Lord, he might just as well resign his commission since any chance of further promotion—or even employment—would be nil. He'd be the comic hero of the saga of Spit Sand shoal.

CHAPTER THREE

Southwick woke Ramage long before daylight. Holding a lantern in one hand and tapping the side of the cot with the other, the Master whispered, 'It's half-past three, sir. Wind's fresh, north-west. Glass has fallen a bit, but nothing significant. Jackson's bringing your shaving water and a hot drink. Everything you mentioned is hidden away ready.'

The old man's cheerfulness was contagious, almost comforting, but, at this time of the morning, tiresome as well. His flowing hair and plump features lit by the lantern reminded Ramage of a genial Falstaff seeing if the Prince was still sober.

Scrambling out of his cot as the Master hooked the lantern on to the bulkhead, Ramage realized sleepily that the *Triton* was rolling quite heavily and the cot swung, catching the back of his knee joints so his legs almost jack-knifed.

'Last of the flood, sir,' Southwick said. 'There's quite a sea running.'

'Good. Blast this cot. And a north-west wind ... couldn't be better.'

'Let's hope it holds, sir: don't want it to back or veer for another hour.'

As Southwick left, Jackson came in with a jug of hot water and a large mug of tea.

'How are things, Jackson?'

'Our crowd were quiet, sir, but there was a lot o' chattering among the Tritons. I daren't seem too interested ... If Harris suspected anything, I'd wake up with a knife in my ribs. You can count on Stafford, Evans and Fuller, sir: I've had a chat with them. Rossi, too, after what you did for the Marchesa. He told all the Tritons a long story last night about how you and I rescued her. Then he told 'em how we rammed the *San Nicolas*.'

'How did they react?'

'Impressed. Very impressed. I think that's what started them all chattering. If you'll excuse me saying it, sir, my feeling is—well, it all depends on you now, sir.'

With that Jackson was gone, leaving Ramage stropping his razor, the American's sentence echoing again and again in time with the slap of steel against leather. He sipped the tea, poured water into the basin and lathered his face. Wiping the steam from the mirror he stretched the skin and was agreeably surprised that the reflection showed the hand holding the razor was trembling only slightly.

It all depends on you now, sir.

Blast Jackson for the reminder at this time of the morning. Did anyone ever feel brave before dawn—apart from Southwick? He'd said almost the same thing—*It's entirely up to you.* Jackson, Southwick and the First Lord . . .

He began shaving and found himself glowering into the mirror as the features emerged from the anonymity of the lather. As he wiped steam from the mirror again, he realized that in the next half an hour everything would depend on the impression that face made on the thirty-six Tritons.

He wasn't worried about the former Kathleens because, as Jackson had made clear, each of them had to sleep with a Triton in the next hammock. Each was realistic enough to know his captain couldn't save him from being knifed in the dark.

So, he told himself mockingly, it all depends—he pushed up the tip of his nose to shave the upper lip—on this face and this tongue. He stuck it out for a moment like a rude urchin, then cursed as he tasted soap in his mouth.

Ten minutes later, shaved, dressed and with the rest of the tea warm inside him, he pulled on his boots, making sure the strap over the throwing knife was clear. Then he took a mahogany box containing a pair of pistols, powder, shot and wads from his trunk and put it on the table. Leave the lid open or closed? Closed—it mustn't be too obvious.

He looked at his watch: fifteen minutes to four o'clock. Fifteen minutes to waste. Well, he might as well start writing his new log and journal, which should have been done yesterday. He took a large, thin book from the bottom drawer, unscrewed the cap of the inkwell, and wrote boldly across the front cover in letters a couple of inches high, 'H.M.S. *Triton*' and in smaller letters underneath, '*Captain's Log 18 April*

Under the Admiralty's 'Regulations and Instructions' the log had to be sent to the Admiralty after two months and a new one started. If he kept his command that long.

Opening the book and glancing idly at the first page, which was divided vertically under several headings, he began by filling in the blank spaces in the lines of print across the top of the page:

'Log of the Proceedings of His Majesty's Ship *Triton*, Nicholas Ramage, Lieutenant and Commander, between the 18th Day of April and the 19th Day of April.'

Since the nautical day was measured from noon one day to noon the next, the Navy afloat was always half a day ahead of the folk on land, and as far as the log was concerned, it was still the same day that he had joined the *Triton* and would be for another eight hours. He inserted the date and wind direction in the appropriate columns and, under 'Remarks' wrote: 'Joined ship as per Commission. Read Commission on quarterdeck. Ship's company apparently in state of mutiny.'

He shut the log impatiently, reflecting this would be a daily task for many months ahead, and took out a similar volume, writing on the front *'Captain's Journal, H.M. brig Triton'* and the same two-month period. On the first page he filled in the blank columns under the 'Date', and 'Wind', and drew a line under such headings as 'Course', 'Miles', 'Latitude' and 'Longitude'.

In the end column, headed 'Remarkable Observations and Accidents', he wrote:

On first boarding ship, read commission. Master reported to Captain that ship's company in state of non-violent mutiny. Captain's only order, to hoist his trunk on board, obeyed by three men transferred to brig the previous day from the *Lively* frigate. During evening Captain gave certain instructions to Master concerning getting the ship under way next morning. No Marines on duty but their basic loyalty reported to be not in doubt. Appears they (six in number and corporal) and the twenty-five men transferred from the *Lively* frigate fear reprisals from the original ship's company.

As he wiped the pen and closed the inkwell, Ramage glanced at what he'd written. If anything went wrong and his plan failed, the paragraphs he'd written in the log and in the journal would be chewed over by a court martial as carefully as a hungry dog chewed over a fresh bone.

Every word, every comma, would be questioned; every possible construction put on every phrase. It'd be no excuse to say they'd been written before dawn, before he was fully awake. And his plan—well, even though it seemed the only one that had a chance of success, it'd be treated as madness, because six captains sitting in judgement on him would never understand it.

Whereas they would expect him to wave the Articles of War and breathe fire and brimstone, he was going to gamble on men—on the intelligence of one in particular, Harris, the *Triton*'s spokesman whom he did not know, and on the sentiment of the former Kathleens, all of whom he did.

His bet was that he could guess the reaction of all of them, Tritons and Kathleens alike, when their captain sprang a surprise on them; did something they could never have expected and wouldn't know how to deal with . . .

He slipped his sword belt over his right shoulder and looked at his watch. Three minutes to four. He took the lantern from its hook and went up on deck.

★

The wind was fresh, not yet strong enough to sound shrill in the masts, yards and rigging—which he could just make out as black webs against the dark night sky—but sufficient to moan like a man in pain, unreal and almost ghostly in the night and already starting to sap at the confidence Ramage was just beginning to feel.

It should be light enough to aim a pistol in ten minutes or so since there was a hint of cold greyness about him. Soon Southwick came over with a lantern and reported:

'I'm just going below now, sir.'

'Very well; start from aft so you can see what's happening as you walk back again.'

As the master disappeared down the companionway it was almost uncanny on board the brig: it needed only an owl making its weird call to complete the illusion he was standing

43

in a graveyard: not a man on deck apart from himself. It was the first night he'd ever spent in a ship at anchor without men keeping an anchor watch, a Marine sentry at the gangway with loaded musket, and an officer, midshipman or warrant officer pacing the deck.

However, since the *Triton* had been anchored for nearly a week without even a cook's mate keeping the deck by day or night, he'd decided it was pointless for Southwick and himself each to lose half a night's sleep when both would need all their wits about them by dawn. Their Lordships would not approve; but since they had to administer the Navy, they could never admit a man ever needed sleep or had to use unusual methods in carrying out their orders.

Suddenly from below came Southwick's stentorian voice bellowing: 'Wakey, wakey there! Come on—lash up and stow; show a leg, show a leg, look alive there! Lash up and stow, the sun's burning your eyeballs out!'

Every few moments, sounding fainter as he walked forward, the Master repeated the time-honoured and time-worn orders and imprecations—normally bawled by the bosun's mates and punctuated by the shrill notes of their bosun's calls —to rouse out the men and have them roll their hammocks and bedding into long sausage shapes and lash them up with the regulation number of turns.

Then the men would troop up on deck to stow the hammocks in the racks of netting along the top of the bulwarks. There—covered with long strips of canvas to keep them dry —they also formed a barricade against musket-fire when the ship went into action.

'Lash up and stow, lash up and stow...'

The voice was very faint: Southwick must be right up forward now, turning to retrace his steps and see how many of the sixty-one men were obeying. This was the first of several crucial moments he and Ramage had to face in the next twenty minutes.

Then the Master was back on deck, swinging the lantern. He said quietly: 'All the Kathleens and the Marines are lashing their hammocks. The rest haven't moved. Harris's hammock is the nearest as you go forward.'

'Better than I expected. We'll wait a couple of minutes.'

The first half dozen of the seamen came up the ladder,

running to the bulwarks amidships and placing their hammocks in the netting. Normally it was done by orders; but there were no petty officers to give them. Although more men came up from below Ramage did not bother to count—Southwick would be doing that.

The Master murmured: 'Twenty-nine still below, sir.'

There was no chance those men were being slow.

'Give me the lantern.'

'Go carefully, sir. Let me come with you.'

'No, stay here, and get those men working—unrolling the hammock cloths, or anything that keeps them occupied.'

Now Ramage felt the cold of dawn and the more penetrating chill of fear. The black of night was fast turning grey; in a few minutes there'd be no need for lanterns on deck.

He stepped down the companionway and turned forward past the little cabins. As he went through the door in the bulkhead which divided off the officers' and warrant officers' accommodation from the forward part of the ship where the seamen slung their hammocks, he held the lantern higher, so it lit up his face. He had to crouch, since there was a bare five feet of headroom, but he'd learned long ago to walk with his knees slightly bent and back arched so he could keep his head upright.

The air was fetid: it was air breathed too long and too often by more than sixty men, and stank of sweat and bilge water.

Then he was abreast the first hammock which, its shape distorted by the body of the man in it, cast weird shadows as it swung to the roll of the brig.

'Harris,' Ramage said quietly.

The man sat up quickly, carefully keeping his head low to avoid banging it on the beams above him. He was, as Ramage had planned, in an uncomfortable and undignified position.

'Sir?'

'Harris, I can remember when I was a midshipman ...'

He paused, forcing Harris to say:

'Yes, sir?'

'Yes, Harris, I remember one poor midshipman cracked his skull. Died five days later. There'd have been trouble if he'd regained consciousness and said who'd done it. He didn't though, and we managed to change a new hammock for the one cut down ...'

Again he paused, and he sensed each of the other men in his hammock was feeling the same tension as Harris who, because Ramage's voice tailed off, was yet again forced to say:

'Yes, sir?'

Suddenly metal rasped against metal as Ramage drew his sword: the noise was unmistakable and, watching Harris's eyes following the blade as it came out of the scabbard, Ramage felt more confident.

'You've probably guessed the trick, Harris—we'd cut the hammock down. Only we made a mistake in the dark—instead of cutting it down at the feet end, we cut it at the head end, so the poor mid landed on his skull—not his feet . . .'

Harris said nothing: he was watching the sword blade glinting in the light of the lantern as Ramage waved it as though it was a walking stick.

Ramage judged that this was the moment, and said suddenly and harshly:

'Lash up and stow, Harris—and all the rest of you. If you're not on deck in three minutes I'll cut every hammock down. Bring the lantern with you, Harris.'

Putting the lantern down on the deck, he strode back to the companionway. He'd given the order to Harris about the lantern on the spur of the moment but for a particular reason. And the tone of his voice showed them all—he hoped —that it didn't occur to him they'd disobey.

On deck it was now light enough to see men moving along the top of the bulwark, paler grey patches against a dark grey screen, tucking in the hammock cloths.

Southwick came over.

'Most of these men are sullen, sir, very sullen. Jackson, Evans, Fuller an' Rossi are doing their best, but they've got to watch their step. How are things below?'

'We'll know inside a couple of minutes.'

'The lantern, sir?'

'I left it for Harris to bring up——'

'But——'

'Damn the *Regulations*, Mr Southwick; I have a reason.'

'Aye aye, sir.'

Snapping at Southwick hurt the old man's feelings, but Ramage was under too much of a strain to explain what seemed to him so obvious. No lanterns without a sentry was a necessary standing order to guard against the danger of fire; but for the moment the risk of fire was of little consequence weighed against getting Harris and the rest of them on deck.

He moved to one side so the mainmast did not obscure the forehatch, which he could just pick out as a square black hole in the deck forty or fifty feet away.

He watched until his eyes blurred. Was—he blinked a couple of times—yes, surely there was a square of faint light framed by the hatch coamings. Southwick tried to see what his captain was watching so intently.

Ramage blinked again and now he wasn't so sure: the hatch looked as black as ever. Suddenly it lit up, showing the shadow of a man with a hammock slung over his shoulder.

Of course it had darkened for a few moments because the man's body blocked out the light as he started up the ladder.

'Here comes Harris.'

'He's got some brains then,' Southwick grunted, 'and wants to keep 'em inside his skull. Was that yarn you were going to tell 'em about the midshipman dying true, sir?'

'No, but I nearly believed it myself as I was telling Harris!'

The lantern swung as Harris walked to the other bulwark and Ramage saw the rest of the men following. One by one they scrambled up and put their hammocks in the netting. Harris said something inaudible to the seaman next to him who edged along the bulwark and pulled out a rolled-up hammock cloth.

'So far so good,' Southwick muttered.

Ramage waited until the cloth was tucked in along its whole length, covering all their hammocks against rain and spray, then said:

'Muster everyone here if you please Mr Southwick.'

The Master bellowed the order and the men shuffled aft. The shuffle told Ramage what he needed to know and what he feared: the men had stowed their hammocks, they were obeying the order to come aft to hear what he had to say, but that was all: they were still mutinous—the majority anyway.

He scrambled up on top of the capstan and said loudly: 'Gather round, men.'

And, he thought grimly, this is one of the moments for which all the years of training are supposed to have prepared me.

They grouped themselves in a half-circle facing aft. Apart

from the faint moan of the wind, the rattle of halyards against the mast and the slop of waves against the hull, there was a sullen, brooding, menacing silence that could come only from a mob of discontented and potentially dangerous men: a silence like fog soaking cold and damp right through to the skin of the man facing them.

Ramage hadn't rehearsed a speech because his memory was so bad he usually forgot the words. Instead he usually memorized the main points he wanted to make. This morning there were just five.

'Well, men, you know by now I am your new Captain and Mr Southwick is the Master. I know some of you because we sailed together in the *Kathleen*. The rest I'll get to know very soon. And I have some news for all of you: news the Fleet won't be hearing for a while.

'Two days ago I was at the Admiralty receiving my orders from Lord Spencer, the First Lord. He told me I could tell you the Government has considered very sympathetically the delegates' requests for better pay, provisions and conditions in the Fleet. Because Parliament has to approve any changes, the Government is drawing up a new Act as quickly as possible.'

End of point one, and no reaction from the group, but they were listening intently.

'As far as all you Tritons are concerned, the Fleet's delegates will have to look after your interests—and I'm sure they'll do it well enough—because this ship is under orders to sail at once for Brest and Cadiz with despatches.'

End of point two and the men began murmuring: an angry murmuring, like disturbed bees. Ramage realized that in a moment someone—this fellow Harris for example—would take a pace forward and start haranguing the men. Then, as had happened in the rest of the ships, the officers—he and Southwick in this case—would be bundled on shore. Quiet words weren't working. Very well, now the gambler's bluff was being called.

'In the meantime,' he continued, his voice only slightly louder but the change of tone indicating the importance of his words, 'in the meantime, I want to remind you the discipline and conditions to be maintained on board this ship are those laid down in the *Regulations and Instructions* and in the Articles of War. No more and no less. But apart from them, let no one dodge his duty—it just means more work for the next man. And remember this: if you'd been in Bonaparte's Navy, every single one of you would've been hanged by now.'

That was point three. No reaction—nor did he expect any.

'Oh yes,' he added, as if it was an afterthought, 'hands up those of you who can swim.'

Hands were raised and Ramage counted them aloud.

'Nineteen out of sixty-one. Hmm . . . forty-two of you can't swim. Very well. Harris!'

He snapped out the name, and years of prompt response to discipline could not stop Harris taking an involuntary step forward.

'Harris—I want to speak with you alone. Go below and wait in the cabin. Take a lantern with you.'

It took Harris a couple of minutes to collect the lantern and go down the companionway, every man on deck watching him and wondering.

Ramage guessed—was gambling, rather—that Harris, by himself, was no threat: he was almost certain—but not quite —that Harris had become the men's spokesman simply because he was better educated and more articulate: he was not a trouble-maker nor a revolutionary.

He'd learned a lot in the few moments he'd watched the man in his hammock, and Harris was probably sensible enough to realize by now that Ramage unofficially acknowledged him as a spokesmen, and sending him below at this moment indicated there was something to talk about.

Suddenly Ramage said sharply to the group:

'Right: every man to his station for weighing and making sail.'

This was the crucial moment: he stood poised above the men, trying to will them to move, the words of Lord Spencer, Southwick and Jackson echoing and, as he watched, mocking.

Eight or nine men—all former Kathleens—turned and walked forward. But everyone else stood firm, many of them muttering to each other, a muttering which increased to excited talk. A dozen or so—again, they seemed to be Kathleens—remained silent.

'Very well,' Ramage snapped, a harsh note in his voice.

'Just remember this: forty-two of you can't swim, the tide's falling, and over there, dead to leeward, you can see the sea breaking over the end of Spit Sand...'

The muttering stopped abruptly, the men puzzled by his words, unsure what he meant, unsure whether or not they'd just heard some fearful threat whose significance they did not understand.

Ramage knew he had the initiative again and promptly jumped down to walk forward through the group, forcing men to step aside.

Then, stopping abreast the mainmast, he turned and said: 'Mr Southwick, the axe please!'

Southwick, who had been waiting unnoticed to one side of the men, walked over with a large axe in his hand: an axe used on wooding expeditions, when a boatload of men were sent off to some deserted beach to cut wood for the ship's galley.

Slipping his sword belt over his head, Ramage gave it to the Master in exchange for the axe, moving so he could look at the group of men as he turned. They might have been carved from stone—an impression increased by the grey morning light. But Ramage felt as if he was made of wet bread.

Axe in hand, Ramage walked forward, suddenly feeling almost sick with disappointment, apprehension and too much weak, oversweet tea. Talk had failed, but he knew talk was always dangerous—seamen interpreted soft words as weakness; hard words as a challenge. They judged a man by what he did, not what he said. As he'd half expected, his speech had proved a compromise and suffered the fate of all compromises, simply delaying the moment for action. Parliament and bureaucrats please note, he thought sourly, and wished he hadn't drunk the tea, which was slopping around inside him.

And then he was standing beside the anchor cable which, taut with the strain on it and three feet above the deck, was made fast round the solid H-shaped wooden bitts before being led below to the cable tier. The largest cable in the ship, it was a massive piece of cordage, thirteen inches in circumference. (More important, there were four others of the same size, each 720 feet long and weighing more than two tons, stowed below.)

Ramage took a firm grip of the axe, noting the wind hadn't changed direction and, if anything, was blowing stronger, so the Spit Sand shoal was still dead to leeward. He changed his stance, placing his feet wider apart. Had the men guessed? Hard to believe they hadn't, but like some wretched actor he had to make sure he was building up to an effective climax.

Turning to look over his shoulder he called:

'All well aft there, Mr Southwick?'

'All well, sir.'

The Master would shout a warning if they tried to rush him. Surprising how quickly the time was passing: it was light enough to recognize the men's faces. And, more important, light enough for them to see every move he made, and to see the waves breaking white on the shoal.

He raised the axe over his head and swung down hard on the cable where the first turn went over the broad and solid top of the bitts.

The thud almost numbed his hands, but the bitts made a solid chopping block. The blade cut perhaps a quarter of the way through the rope, but there was such a strain on it that already the severed strands began unravelling. A second stroke, then a third and fourth. The cable hummed as the whole strain of holding the ship against the wind came on the remaining strands. Stepping back a pace, clear of danger for the final blow, he swung the blade down again.

As if some giant plucked an enormous harp string, the severed end of the cable twanged and shot away from him, whiplashing the width of the deck before snaking out through the hawse like an escaping boa-constrictor.

A moment later a splash told him the cable, with one of the *Triton*'s bower anchors at the end of it, was now sinking into the murky water of Spithead.

The *Triton* was adrift: already, even as he turned aft, the wind began swinging her bow round to leeward. Since it was high water, with no tidal stream, the *Triton* had been wind-rode, lying with her bow heading to the north-west. Now she was swinging broadside on to the wind and in a minute or so the wind would be driving her down on to the eastern end of the shoal. Few if any of the men would know there was a channel, the Swatchway, cutting diagonally across the shoal just to the west of where the sea was breaking.

Ramage flung down the axe and began walking aft, his face cold with a perspiration brought on by fear, not physical exertion. It was done now: the challenge had been flung at the mutineers' feet: obey the order to make sail or drown when the *Triton* hit the shoal and either heeled over and then filled on the rising tide or was lifted up and down by the waves until she pounded to pieces. There was only one flaw and he hoped they'd be too excited to spot it: boats from other ships in the Fleet might rescue them in time.

The men began shouting at one another and gesticulating —not at Ramage but at the two boats stowed on deck between the two masts. Three or four men began hurrying towards the boats but Southwick was beside him holding out a musketoon, a musket with a very large bore and the muzzle belled out like a trumpet.

Ramage took it and shouted: 'Still!'

The sudden shout combined with the equally unexpected single word 'still'—which normally brought everyone on deck to attention—stopped every man and every tongue for five seconds, during which Ramage promptly cocked the musketoon, the click in the silence sounding as loud as a blacksmith's hammer hitting an anvil.

'If anyone moves towards those boats I'll fire through the bottoms so they won't float anyway. Now, you've three minutes to make sail before we hit the shoal.'

Touch and go: would they have the wit to rush *him* instead? There'd be plenty of confusion anyway because it'd been impossible to prepare a general quarter, watch and station bill which would have described every man's post for manoeuvre, including weighing anchor and making sail.

But no one was moving. Frightened or still defiant? Hard to tell, but he must assume the former. Plenty of confusion gave anyone with definite ideas or orders an opportunity to get control.

'Carry on, Southwick, this is our chance!' he said quietly. 'Walk aft—detail the first dozen you meet as foretopmen, second dozen maintopmen, then half a dozen afterguard and fo'c'slemen, and we'll sort the rest out as we go. Jackson and Stafford at the helm.'

Southwick gave him back his sword and walked through the group, gesticulating as he went. Still holding the musketoon Ramage watched, his body rigid with tension.

Yes! A dozen men were walking forward now, six of

them going to the larboard side and six to the starboard—
the foretopmen. A dozen more split up to go to the main
shrouds as maintopmen. A small group headed aft and another turned to the fo'c'sle.

Keep the initiative, he muttered to himself; but there's
not much time. A glance over the larboard side at the wide
area of waves breaking grey and white showed that even if
he got through a crisis with the crew, another of his own
making was looming close to leeward in the shape of the shoal.

'Away aloft!' he shouted.

At once two dozen men began scrambling up the ratlines
of both masts.

With that he began walking aft to the quarterdeck, the
traditional centre of all orders and discipline where Southwick was waiting anxiously.

'Going to be touch and go whether we can get into the
Swatchway!' the Master muttered.

'It'd better go—if we touch we'll never get off!'

Southwick's laughter, louder because of the strain he was
under, boomed across the deck. Men stopped for a moment
and looked aft nervously. Ramage, realizing it might ease
the tension, also began bellowing with laughter at his own
joke. Then the men carried on, obviously puzzled but probably reassured. The shoal was a couple of hundred yards
away: six ship-lengths. He'd just weather the western end
if no one made a mistake.

'Jackson, Stafford! Take the helm. Speaking trumpet,
Southwick.'

Handing Southwick the musketoon, he put the black
japanned trumpet to his lips and methodically began shouting the string of familiar orders which would get the *Triton*
under way. Quickly the triangular-shaped jib snaked up as
men hauled at the halyard, and the sheets were trimmed.

Almost at the same moment the foretopsail was let fall
from the yard, hanging down like an enormous curtain, followed by the maintopsail.

He could see the men were working swiftly now: the instinct for self-preservation was swamping any mutinous
ideas ...

Swiftly the yards were hoisted and braced round and the
sheets hauled home so the sails caught every scrap of wind,

but for many long moments the brig was dead in the water, the wind on her hull simply pushing her sideways down towards the end of the shoal.

Then, at first almost imperceptibly, the *Triton* gathered way and Ramage began passing orders to Jackson and Stafford at the helm. Once she was making a couple of knots or more the rudder would get a bite on the water; until then she'd continue moving crabwise to leeward.

Ramage watched the buildings on the shore at Gilkicker Point and saw the *Triton*'s bowsprit gradually stop swinging towards them, then begin to head up to starboard. Steerageway at last!

A glance over the larboard side showed the end of the shoal was less than forty yards to leeward; but even as he watched the flurry of waves breaking over it began to draw aft. Another glance round to get his bearings and see where the Swatchway Channel began.

Now the brig was beginning to heel in stronger gusts of wind and slowly Ramage managed to work her until, with the entrance of the channel broad on the larboard bow, it was safe to ease sheets and braces and bear away to pass through it.

Leaving Southwick to give the final orders to trim each sail to perfection, Ramage watched the bulky line of battle ships anchored to the south at Spithead, beyond the Spit Sand. The Port Admiral had been sure they'd open fire as the *Triton* passed, but Ramage hoped he'd taken them by surprise, unexpectedly cutting through the Swatchway instead of using the main channel and then, by hugging the shore under Gilkicker Point, keep out of the arcs of fire even if they could get the guns loaded and run out in time.

There was no sign of the alarm being raised; no flags being hoisted or a gun fired to draw attention to them.

'There's a little cutter flying our pennant numbers and trying to catch up, sir,' called Southwick.

Fresh orders? Or the surgeon, midshipman, bo'sun and sergeant of Marines the *Triton* lacked and the Port Admiral had been trying to find for him? Well, they'd have to chase for a few more minutes, until he could wait out of range of the Fleet's guns. Finally he said:

'Heave-to and wait for 'em, Mr Southwick; I'll be in the

cabin.'

As he went down the companionway to his cabin it was broad daylight but the thick, grey rolling cloud coming over the Porchester hills would hide the sunrise in a few minutes.

Well, he'd won every trick so far—although, he told himself bitterly, he'd had to do it by force: he'd failed to persuade the men to obey his orders from the beginning. Still, the effect was the same.

But winning the final trick depended on the cards held by the seaman Harris, waiting in his cabin. That one man might have it in his power during the next few hours to stop the *Triton* delivering the despatches to Admirals Curtis and St Vincent and then crossing the Western Ocean to warn Admiral Robinson in the Caribbean.

It was a crazy situation, he reflected, that the success of the First Lord's orders, the intentions of the Board of Admiralty, the desperate need to warn these admirals at sea without a moment's delay that the Fleet at Spithead had mutinied, probably depended at this particular moment not on storms in the Western Ocean, good navigation or Lieutenant Ramage, but on a man called Harris, rated able seaman in the *Triton*'s muster book.

He was standing by the table as Ramage entered the cabin and he stood to attention. Ramage nodded and hung his sword on a hook beside the desk. Pulling the chair round he then sat down and took the muster book out of the drawer.

The daylight shining down through the skylight was cold and grew, stronger now than the yellow, warm light of the lantern whose wick gave the cabin a stuffy, sooty smell.

Turning to Harris, Ramage asked quietly:

'When did you join the ship?'

'July last year, sir.'

Ramage turned back a few pages and found the entry.

Alfred Harris, age thirty-one, born at Basingstoke, Hampshire, volunteer, three years in the Navy.

Ramage chose his words carefully. Harris had been down here in the cabin for some time: he knew only that the *Triton* was under way, and that the whole ship's company had apparently obeyed Ramage's orders. Any reference to mutiny must, therefore, be in the past tense.

'Harris—were you the ringleader of the mutiny in this

55

ship, or just the men's spokesman?'

'Spokesman, sir.'

'Who was the ringleader?'

He knew Harris would never reveal a name; but he might reveal something much more important.

'There wasn't a ringleader, sir. You see, after the sail o' the line refused to obey the Admiral's signal for the Fleet to get under way, the delegates came on board and told us the Fleet had mutinied. We could see that anyway—men cheering, the bloody flag flying, an' all that.'

'Yet you were the spokesman for the mutineers in the *Triton*.'

'Not quite like that, sir.'

'Like what, then? The men had mutinied and they regarded you as their leader.'

'Well, sir, we hadn't really *mutinied*. We'd been—well, doing nothing, like the rest of the small ships of the Fleet, for several days. The delegates were all from the sail of the line: they told us in the small ships to leave it to them. Then when Mr Southwick suddenly came on board the men just left it to me to explain how—well, how things stood.'

'And before Mr Southwick came on board?'

'I was just one of the men, sir.'

Deciding bluff might help, Ramage asked:

'Why did they choose you? There must be a reason. In fact I heard you made yourself the leader.'

'No, sir!' Harris exclaimed. 'Whoever told you that's a liar!'

'Have you any enemies on board?'

'No, sir.'

'Then why would anyone tell lies about you?'

'I don't know, sir. All I——'

'Well?'

'—All I do is write the letters for them that can't write, sir, and read letters from home. The men—well, they sort of rely on me.'

It was so simple and so obviously true. To the men Harris would be 'educated'; an obvious choice as a spokesman. They hadn't so much chosen him as left it to him. Yet if the Admiralty acted harshly, interpreted the Articles of War literally, it could——

56

'You realize you can be hanged for what you've done?'

'Hanged, sir? Me, sir? Why, I . . .'

The man was stockily built, with a round and cheerful face, and fair hair that refused to grow at any normal angle from his head. He was the man in the shop helping the butcher, the baker or the grocer serve the customers: quietly-spoken, honest, well-meaning . . . And now the cheerful face was frightened: perspiration forming on the upper lip, hands clasped tightly behind the back, a slight sagging in at the chest, the shoulders coming forward, as if half-expecting a blow. And Ramage knew the man was hurriedly recalling the dozens of times he'd heard the Articles of War read aloud by the captain—at least once a month all the time he was at sea.

Ramage let him think for a full couple of minutes, then said quietly:

'I'll refresh your memory. Article Three, for instance: anyone who "shall give, hold or entertain intelligence to or with any Enemy or Rebel . . ."'—punishable by death. Article four: failing to tell a superior officer about any letter or message from an enemy or rebel within twelve hours—death or such punishment as the court awards. Article Five: endeavouring to corrupt—same punishment. Article Nineteen: making a mutinous assembly, contempt to a superior officer —same punishment. Then there are numbers Twenty, concealing "any traitorous or mutinous practice or design"; Twenty-one, any complaints about victuals to be made quietly to a superior officer, not used to create a disturbance; Twenty-two, disobeying the lawful command of a superior officer; Twenty-three, using reproachful or provoking speeches or gestures——'

'But sir, all I——'

'The delegates are rebels, Harris: they are rebels against their officers, captains, admirals and King . . . You "entertained intelligence" from them: you listened to what they said and obeyed them by joining the mutiny. You didn't tell a superior officer within twelve hours. By talking about the mutiny with the rest of the men you "took part in a mutinous assembly". You told the twenty-five men who joined from the *Lively* that the *Triton* had mutinied, and you and your shipmates scared them into joining you . . . Harris you can be hanged under half a dozen of the Articles of War: you've done things where the Articles don't even give a court an option—it would have to condemn you to death ...'

'But I only told Mr Southwick——'

'And the men from the *Lively*.'

'—Well, yes, I just sort of told them—they knew already, though.'

'Knew what?'

'That the Fleet had mutinied.'

'They didn't know the *Triton* had: you told them. Article Nineteen—you're guilty under both parts, and death the penalty for each. Twenty, Twenty-one ...'

'But I just *told* 'em, sir. I didn't make 'em join in. Anyone could have *told* 'em: it just happened to be me.'

'Harris,' Ramage said quietly, 'on the table beside you: the mahogany box.'

'Yes, sir?'

'Open it.'

Warily the man opened the lid.

'What do you see?'

'Pair o' pistols, sir. Bag o' shot, powder flask an' all that.'

'Take out a pistol and load it.'

The man was trembling now but fascinated by handling the most beautifully made pistol he'd probably ever seen. He poured a measure of powder down the muzzle, took a wad from a fitted box and rammed it home, then put in a round lead shot and rammed that home.

'The priming powder is in the smaller flask.'

Harris poured a measure from the flask on to the pan and closed the steel.

'Now load the other one.'

He'd gained more confidence and loaded it faster. Just as he finished and before he had time to put it down Ramage, still speaking quietly, said:

'Now pick up the other one.'

The man stood there, slightly hunched, a pistol in each hand.

'Cock them.'

A click from the right hand; a click from the left.

'Now, Harris, as you've probably guessed, those duelling pistols have hair triggers. The most accurate pistols ever made.'

'Yes, sir,' Harris said, bemused and puzzled by what was happening.

'Now raise your right hand—higher—point the pistol at me, Harris. Come on!'

The man's hand was shaking so much Ramage hoped he'd remember the warning about the hair triggers.

'Now Harris—you can shoot me, and use the other pistol on Mr Southwick. Then you can take over command of the *Triton*. You could sail her over to Boulogne or Calais—or Cherbourg, even Havre de Grace. Bonaparte'd pay you prize money for the ship—you'd all get a share: enough to live in comfort in France for the rest of your lives. Providing Bonaparte wins the war, of course.'

'But, sir,' Harris wailed, the pistols dropping to his side. 'Sir, none of us want anything like that.'

'But Harris,' Ramage said coldly, motioning him to put the pistols down on the table, 'if you shot me and Mr Southwick you'd be no guiltier than you are already. You can't be hanged more than once. Mutiny, intelligence with rebels, treason—a couple of murders won't make matters much worse.'

Even in the chilly light Ramage could see the man was almost fainting.

'Sit down!'

Harris sagged on the edge of the settee behind him, head between his hands, his whole body trembling.

Ramage was sickened by what he'd been forced to do; but now the most intelligent of the original Tritons fully understood the significance of the Fleet's action. And Harris sat there realizing, for the first time, how close his neck was to the noose at one end of a rope rove from a block at the foreyardarm.

Even now Harris was probably imagining the coarse rasping of the rope on his skin, the knot jammed against one side of his neck; imagining a shouted order and the sudden crash of a gun firing on the deck below where he'd been standing. Then the garrotting while his body soared straight up in the air as men ran with the other end...

Ramage said: "Harris, my precise orders are known to very few people: the First Lord of the Admiralty, the Port Admiral and Mr Southwick. But I'll tell you this much: this is going to be a long voyage. You already know nearly half the ship's company have served with me before. Only a few weeks ago I had to give them orders which they knew should have resulted in them being killed by the Spaniards. Even before that several of them risked death many times at my side. They've never flinched and they've never refused. In fact they carried out those orders cheerfully. You know all this?'

'Partly, sir; they was telling us last night.'

'Well, I command a different ship now. More than half the crew haven't served with me. The point is, Harris, I may have to give similar orders again . . .'

'Yes, sir?'

'Those orders will have to be obeyed.'

'And they will be, sir, if it's up to me!'

'Yet my first order—to weigh anchor—was not. Hardly a good start.'

'But sir——'

'That's all, Harris: carry on.'

The man wanted to say something but Ramage waved him through the door.

How many such men were there in the Fleet, in those great sail of the line, each with a ship's company of seven or eight hundred? Perhaps barely one in a hundred was a real trouble-maker, which left ninety-nine Harrises, all equally guilty in law but in fact guilty only of putting their trust in hot-heads; of being led astray; of believing they had a just cause of complaint and that once the Admiralty knew of it, they'd put it right . . .

Ramage took off his coat. It was a chilly morning but the coat was sodden with perspiration. And watching his own hands trembling he knew he wasn't a born gambler. He could sit back and plan the gamble, work out the odds and place his bet. But he lost his nerve just before the card turned face up and, more important, there was no thrill, no pleasure in it; just fear.

And the fear was like a fogbank: it penetrated everywhere and extended an unknown distance. It could last an hour or a week, and no man caught in it could drive it away.

CHAPTER FOUR

Southwick watched Ramage's hand. Both men were bending over the chart spread on the table in Ramage's cabin and the *Triton* had long since picked up the men from the cutter and got under way again to pass the entrance to the Beaulieu River, where four years earlier, the brig had been built under old Henry Adams's supervision at Buckler's Hard.

As he waited for Ramage to speak the Master wondered if old Adams was still alive. In view of some of the rubbish they were hammering together these days and calling ships, he reflected, it's a comfort to be in one that old Harry kept his eye on. Planked with oak cut from the New Forest, her ironwork wrought at the works at Sowley Pond just near the shipyard—aye, there wasn't much to worry about as far as the *Triton*'s hull was concerned. And give him another day or two with the masts, spars and rigging and there'd be no worry on that score either.

Ramage's hand moved to pick up the dividers. After opening them against the latitude scale he 'walked' them across the chart from the Needles to Ushant, the island just off the northwestern tip of France. He held one point of the dividers on Ushant and as he spoke Southwick noted the hand was rock solid: not a tremor to reveal nervousness or excitement.

'It's a hundred and eighty miles from the Needles to Ushant.'

'Aye, sir, and I'll put my money on the wind staying northwest.'

Ramage nodded. 'The cloud's well broken up now, and we carry the ebb for another four or five hours.'

That hand *ought* to be trembling a bit, Southwick thought enviously. The lad's been given orders tough enough to challenge an experienced frigate captain, and has just got under way in circumstances that'd daunt an admiral backed up by half a dozen companies of loyal Marines.

Who'd have thought of forcing a crew to make sail by cutting the cable and giving them the option of drowning or carrying out his orders? Now he's starting off on a four-thousand-mile voyage with a sullen and still mutinous crew. Why, he can't even be sure he'll see the night out: there's precious little to stop them from slitting his throat as soon as it's dark and running the ship across the Channel to Cherbourg or Le Havre—neither's more than about sixty miles away, and they'd have a soldier's wind . . .

'It's just as likely to veer as back,' Ramage said. 'So we'll take a chance it stays northerly, and make our departure from the Lizard, which is . . .'

He walked the dividers again.

'. . . just about a hundred and fifty miles.'

'Seems a pity to lose all that southing since the wind's fair.'

'I agree; but it'd be madness to round Ushant too close. Privateers, a couple of frigates . . . there's bound to be Frenchmen hovering off there to snap up something like the *Triton*. They know despatches for the squadrons are sent by cutters and such like. And they know small vessels like to cut the corners, instead of keeping well out.'

'Suppose so,' Southwick said gloomily. 'But the Lizard to Ushant's nearly ninety miles: we have to sail that much extra —more if the wind backs south-west and heads us.'

'Since we've more than four thousand to cover altogether, logging another ninety shouldn't be too much of a strain.'

'No, I didn't mean that,' Southwick said hurriedly. 'I was thinking of the time. Could cost us a day; make us a day late finding the squadrons off Brest and Cadiz.'

'Well, trying to save a day might end up with us in Brest as prisoners, and the *Triton* a French prize.'

'There's that to it,' Southwick admitted.

'And by the time we're off the Lizard,' Ramage said casually, 'we'll know a bit more about the crew . . .'

'You mean, if they're still mutinous we could put into Plymouth?'

'Yes—and they're less likely to do anything mutinous while they know the English coast is just to the north, and as far as they're concerned there's more than a chance of us meeting a frigate—or even a sail of the line—coming over the horizon bound for Plymouth or Spithead. But if they knew the French coast was only a few miles to leeward . . .'

'Quite so,' Southwick agreed, 'but if I was a mutineer I'd have a go tonight: I'd sooner make for Cherbourg or Le Havre than Brest . . . Still, I admit I never did like taking Ushant too close. With gales springing up in a couple of hours, that's the most iron-bound coast in Christendom. Just look at it.' His finger jabbed the chart where, between Ushant and Brest, dozens of crosses marked shoals and individual rocks.

Ramage snapped the dividers shut.

'Watch and watch about for you and me tonight, Mr Southwick. You can have the Master's Mate with you. I'm glad Appleby managed to catch that cutter in time.'

'You'll have Jackson, I hope, sir?'

'Yes. And I must get down to making up the general quarter, watch and station bill. I wonder how many ships have gone through the Needles without one?'

Southwick laughed as he took some courses off the chart. 'So far we haven't needed it, thanks to your axemanship!'

'I'm glad they didn't fell me,' Ramage said as he left the cabin and went up the companionway. Walking up and down the weather side of the quarterdeck he was glad of a few minutes of peace: it was good to be at sea again.

The *Triton*, helped along by the ebb, had been making all of ten knots as she surged past Hurst Castle at the western end of the Solent and began to butt into the swell waves from the open sea. But the wind was offshore and the sea did little more than kick up a popple on top of the swell so the *Triton*'s bow only occasionally sliced off the top of a crest and sent it showering up in a cloud of spray.

Looking around him—nodding to Appleby, who tried to disguise his nervousness at being left alone at the conn while the captain and master went below, and did not bother to hide his relief when the former came back on deck—Ramage could sense rather than see the men were sullen. Most of them, anyway. The former Kathleens no, they weren't sullen; more likely they were frightened. Poor devils—the Tritons could murder the lot of them in the dark.

Soberly he counted up the men he could rely on, whatever happened. First came Southwick, then Jackson, the cockney Will Stafford, the Suffolk fisherman Fuller . . . yes, and the

Genoese, Alberto Rossi, and that sad Welsh bosun's mate, Evan Evans. And probably Maxton, the West Indian. The young Master's Mate, Appleby, had only been on board a couple of hours and seemed nervous, but since he was only waiting for his twenty-first birthday to take his examination for lieutenant his loyalty was certain. Eight men...

And the more he thought about it, the more he thought Southwick was right. Tonight the French ports of Cherbourg and Le Havre would be to leeward: mutineers could find either without being able to read a chart...If he was a mutineer, it'd be tonight or never...

★

Forward on the larboard side, standing casually between the first and second carronade, Jackson and Stafford were looking over towards the English coast, talking in low voices and without moving. To an onlooker they were apparently just taking a last look at the land before the sun set.

'Wotcher fink, Jacko?'

'If they try anything, it'll be tonight.'

'Why t'night? Blimey, we ain't 'ardly clear of Spit'ead. I fink they'll wait 'til tomorrer night, or even later, when we're clear o' the chops of the Channel.'

'Tonight we're closer to good French ports; Cherbourg's less than seventy miles dead to leeward. Easy to find; easy to enter. No blockade. And Le Havre. After that it'd have to be Brest and they'd never get in without running up on some rocks.'

'But they can't think Mister Ramage won't be on guard t'night, surely?'

'Doesn't make much difference, does it? Just him, Mr Southwick and the Master's Mate. Appleby's only a kid anyway. The new surgeon'll be drunk—he's a soak; he'd got the shakes when he came on board. Three against nearly sixty.'

'What'll we *do*, Jacko?'

Jackson saw the knuckles of the cockney's hands whiten as he spoke. 'I don't know. I've been thinking all day and I just don't know.'

'Had the chance of a word wiv Mister Ramage?'

'No—and I daren't risk being seen trying.'

The cockney swore in a flat, hard voice.

'What about the rest of us Kathleens?'

'Rossi's sound, but not much use because they know he won't stand any nonsense: he's already told 'em that. That means if they rise Rossi'll be the first to go. Evans, Fuller, Maxton—I'm sure of them.'

'An' me 'n' you.'

'Yes: six of us if Rossi stays alive. Nine with the Captain and Mr Southwick and the Master's Mate.'

'Count the kid out: he don't know nothink about nothink. What'll we *do*, Jacko: this is our last chance to talk a'fore they pipe "Down hammicks"?'

Jackson said nothing and Stafford continued: 'So help me, what a bleedin' mess. Never thought I'd ever see a ship mutiny, let alone the 'ole Fleet. The claims are fair—no arguin' against that. But 'ere we are on the side of the orficers ...'

'Not the officers, the way you mean it. Just Mr Ramage and Mr Southwick. If it was anyone else it'd be different.'

'Yus, s'pose that's it. But wot abaht the rest of the Kathleens—why the 'ell can't they make up their pudden minds?'

'They have,' Jackson said shortly. 'They're for Mr Ramage —but they can do arithmetic, too. They just look at the few men on one side and three dozen on the other. I'll bet everyone of 'em is thinking of the chap in the next hammock, if he's a Triton. Every one of 'em knows a Triton's only got to reach over in the dark with a knife in his hand ... If it was just a question of those for Mr Ramage lining up on the larboard gangway and those against him on the starboard, then you could count on 'em coming out in the open.'

'Well, looks as if you an' me and Rossi and the uvvers'd better stay aft ternight.'

'Can't—they'd see we weren't in our hammocks and know a mutiny was expected. We've got to avoid bloodshed.'

'Well then, fink o' sumfink else,' Stafford said impatiently.

'I'm trying to, but you keep nagging at me. Hey! Remember what Mr Ramage always says—"Use surprise". Like he did with the *San Nicolas*—and today, cutting the anchor cable?'

'Yus, but 'e'd got a haxe—aye, an' 'e knew 'e 'ad a cable to cut. Where's *our* cable? Wot've we got fer a haxe?'

'I don't know, but we're thinking the wrong way. We're thinking of *defending* the quarterdeck against these mad bastards. We've got to attack first.'

'Ho yus, I'm all fer that. One glorious charge from one end of the lower deck ter the uvver, choppin' all their big toes orf wiv a tommyhawk an' smacking their 'ands wiv the flat of a cutlass blade an' tellin' 'em to be'ave. Yus, that's a real good plan, Jacko. Extra tot fer you, me lad.'

'Oh stow it,' Jackson said wearily. 'As a crowd they don't count; they can't even talk without leaders, let alone *do* anything. One leader, anyway; that fellow Harris.'

'Two others as well.'

'Oh? Who?'

'The cook's mate and the captain o' the foretop.'

'I've been wondering about them. Any others?'

'I'm not sure, but they're the ones that matter. I saw 'em clacking away at dinner. They're all in number six mess.'

'Three of them,' mused Jackson. 'So the odds are on our side—unless we wait too long.'

'What the 'ell you talkin' about? Odds are on our side? That's as likely as rum comin' from Aldgate Pump!'

'Six of us against three of them.'

'Three of—oh, I see. We gets 'em on their own. Cor, Jacko, you've——'

'Keep your voice down—and keep still!'

'Yes. Listen Jacko, maybe it's even easier'n you think. That Rossi, he moves like a cat an' he's diabulolical with a knife——'

'Diabolical.'

'S'wot I said. An' Maxton, 'e's the same. If 'e luffs up to weather o' bruvver 'Arris an' Rossi to loo'ard, an' each of 'em gently tickles 'is ribs wiv a knife, an' makes 'im swear he——'

'What? That won't stop 'em mutinying tonight, will it? Making Harris and his two mates swear to be good boys! You think they'd keep their promises?'

'Yes,' Stafford muttered dejectedly. 'No, I mean, yer can't trust no one, an' that's a fack.'

'Fact.'

'Fact,' Stafford repeated automatically. 'Orlright, Jacko, what's 'appened to our odds, then?'

Jackson looked at his fingertips and then scratched his head.

'Put yourself in the Tritons' places. They suddenly find out the three men who're supposed to lead the mutiny when it gets dark have disappeared. Like that. Magic. One minute they're there, next minute they've gone. Vanished. Not even a puff of smoke. What'd you do?'

'Stay in me 'ammick an' keep me bleedin' 'ead down,' Stafford said promptly.

'Me too. So brother Harris and the other two must vanish. No noise, no puff of smoke. Just vanish.'

'Over the side?'

'There's got to be no bloodshed, Staff. This is going to be a long voyage. Once we're over this bit o' trouble, we've got to mess with these jokers. They'll forget all about it, once they're down south in the sunshine. No, they've got to vanish just long enough for us to get the rest of the Kathleens out in the open—so the Tritons can see it's no go.'

'But they'll get another chance unless we make 'Arris into shark bait.'

'No—after that we leave it to Mr Ramage.'

'What'll 'e do?'

'I don't know. He'll do something, though.'

Then, keeping his voice low, the American explained his plan.

★

While Southwick was on watch Ramage sat at his desk with a large sheet of lined paper in front of him which was divided into many columns, and the muster book was open beside him, giving the name of every man in the ship. He'd written 'General Quarter, Watch and Station Bill' across the top of the page and now, without knowing anything about more than half the men, had to fill in the rest of it.

It took more than an hour to complete because each man had several different tasks, depending on whether the ship was weighing anchor; setting, reefing or furling sails; going into battle or going into harbour.

Each man was given a number, and the completed Bill listed all the tasks to be carried out in the course of various evolutions with a number beside each of them.

To make sure he hadn't made any mistakes, Ramage chose a number at random and checked it on the Bill. Number eight —he was in the larboard watch; in battle he was one of the two loaders at number five carronade on the larboard side; he was one of the boarding party, and under arms had a cutlass and tomahawk; when furling or reefing sails he worked on the fore-topsail, but when the order was given to loose sails—which needed fewer men—his post was at the capstan ready to weigh anchor. When the brig tacked or wore, he would be down on deck, hauling on the bowlines, trimming the sail . . .

Ramage's eye ran across the line. No, number eight was not expected to be in two or three places at once—the usual mistake made when drawing up a new Bill. He chose other numbers, checked them, and found they were correct. So Southwick could read it to the men before evening quarters.

No—on second thoughts there'd be no evening quarters! For the moment he wanted to avoid giving any orders to the whole ship's company because it gave them a chance to defy him. Orders to a few men at a time, yes; to a group, no.

In the meantime copies of the Bill could be made, ready to be pinned up where the men could read them.

He called for his clerk, gave the instructions, and then sat back in the chair, his feet up on the desk, rubbing the scar on his brow.

Southwick *was* right: if the men planned anything, it'd happen tonight. It'd be silent and swift. He, Southwick and Appleby would be killed—the mutineers wouldn't dare let them stay alive. Even handing them over to the French authorities as prisoners would be too dangerous because prisoners were often exchanged. Mutineers might get caught —serving in a French warship, in a privateer, maybe in a fishing boat. And an exchanged prisoner would give damning evidence at the court martial . . .

He, Southwick and Appleby could—no they couldn't; there was no way of training a carronade forward so the recoil wouldn't hurl it through the transom into the sea. And it was the wheel, the quarterdeck, that had to be defended. Not because they could steer the ship if the mutineers wanted to prevent them—all they had to do was cut the tiller ropes, brace the yards round or even furl the sails. But as long as Ramage could himself destroy the wheel and compass, he could stop the mutineers steering for France until they'd completed lengthy repairs. But, but, but . . . he was fooling himself. The three of them could do nothing that mattered much; nothing the mutineers couldn't make good in a few hours. And there was nothing he could do beforehand. He was checkmated by pawns.

Ramage sat up with a start, then recognized Southwick's characteristic rat-tat-tat, rat-tat knock on the door. As soon as he came in Ramage pointed to the chair by the table.

'Trouble, sir,' the old man announced, running his hands through the white hair which, freed from the confines of his hat, sprang out over his head like a new mop. 'I don't know what it is but...'

He stood up and opened the door suddenly, looking to see if anyone was outside eavesdropping.

He sat down again. 'Sorry, sir. But Jackson's passed me a weird message for you. As near as I can recall, tonight he wants you to keep people away from the companionway, keep the wardroom door shut, and keep everyone—including yourself, sir—clear of the breadroom scuttle because there'll be three guests in the breadroom tonight. Oh yes, and he'd be glad for you to find 'em there in the morning an' take the necessary action. It sounds balmy,' Southwick added, 'but he isn't drunk sir—leastways, I don't think he is. And that reminds me, he said could you leave a bottle or two of rum by the breadroom scuttle, and a lantern.'

'That's all he said?'

'That's all, sir,' Southwick said, pulling his nose. 'When I eased over close to ask what he was talking about—there were several men around—Stafford whispered something about the cook's mate keeping too close under their lee to say any more.'

'Pour yourself a drink if you wish,' Ramage said, waving at the sideboard.

'I'll join you in one, sir.'

'Not for me, thanks.'

'Don't think I will, then: we've got to keep our wits about us tonight. Oh yes, sorry, I did forget something. Stafford said they'd be obliged, begging our pardon, if we'd please get the surgeon tipsy and making as much noise as possible from the time "Lights out" is piped.'

Ramage picked up the pen and scratched the scars on his forehead with the end of the quill. Wardroom door shut—that'd be so no one from forward, where the Marines and ship's company slung their hammocks, could see into the wardroom (or see the scuttle, which was in the wardroom). Guests in the breadroom...a bottle or two of rum by the scuttle? Maybe Jackson and Stafford were going to hide there for the night. But why the rum? No—it couldn't be those two since whoever they were, they had to be found in the morning and he had to 'take the necessary action'.

Southwick suddenly thumped the table with his fist and growled: 'Why the hell can't they tell us straight cut what's going on?'

'Those two have a reason all right, though I can't think what it is. But it all points to me not doing or knowing anything until I find the "guests" tomorrow morning. It could mean that if the mutineers suspected I knew anything tonight, Jackson and Stafford would be in danger. Or couldn't do whatever they're planning.'

'Well, I only hope the reasons are good. Good grief, four or five men in the breadroom would pack it tight. And bottles of rum—they going to have a party down there?'

Ramage laughed. 'I think Jackson's using the word "guests" loosely. And one or two bottles can't mean many "guests".'

'Why the breadroom, though?'

'Where else could you lock up men where their shouts wouldn't be heard by the ship's company? Both the bosun's store and for'rard sailrooms are just below where the men sleeping forward sling their hammocks. Same goes for the dry room and coals stowage. The big sailroom's amidships and everyone would hear. Shot locker's too small, you can't lock it up, and it's right under the Marines. Spirit room—hardly appropriate. Magazine—not a very safe place from your point of view, most of it's under your cabin! But the breadroom—well, that's right under here.' He pointed downwards. 'No one who's been planning mischief and was locked in there would want to shout too much and wake the captain, would he? And the advantage is that you can only get to it through the wardroom, where the scuttle is. And both scuttle and the breadroom door can be secured. And with that blasted surgeon serenading his bottles, none of the ship's company would hear . . .'

'Hmm. Yes, that's a point. Why the rum, though. Reward?'

'I don't understand that. Jackson hardly drinks. Nor does Stafford. A couple of bottles—well, it's worth it.'

The Master stood up ready to go back on deck.

'By the way, Mr Southwick, no evening muster. Supper'—

he looked at his watch—'at the usual time, in half an hour. Pipe "Down hammocks" at seven, an hour early, and "Ship's company's fire and lights out" at seven-thirty.'

'But—no evening muster, sir! Is that wise? I mean, the——'

'For the moment, I don't want to give the men an opportunity to make a mass refusal to carry out an order. Lights out earlier than usual may upset any plans they have. Anyway, it'll leave them puzzled about what *we* might be up to. Particularly since we're up to nothing.'

'Aye, there's that to it,' Southwick admitted. 'Any special night orders?'

'No, just the usual—sharp lookout; all changes of wind, alterations in course and so on to be reported to me. But I'll be on deck with you until the "guests" have arrived. Don't wear a brace of pistols too obviously . . . And I'd enjoy your company at breakfast. Ask Appleby too. The invitation doesn't apply to our heirs, though, should anything go wrong . . .'

CHAPTER FIVE

Rossi and Maxton listened carefully in the darkness as Jackson explained the plan. The three men were sitting on the coaming of the forehatch with Stafford below at the foot of the ladder beside the dim lantern, stitching a tear in his shirt and, to an onlooker, standing there to catch the light.

'A pleasure,' Rossi said when Jackson finished. 'Much pleasure. But this much I know; it's better to make the finish. Dead men make no troubles; live men make much unhappiness.'

'Yes, Rosey, I know,' Jackson said patiently. 'But we've got to treat 'em like drunks—you know, as soon as they sober up they're sorry.'

'Drunks? Who say they is drunk? They's as sober as I is —was—I am.'

'No, I mean once we get clear of the Channel they'll forget the mutiny. We've got a long way to sail with these men; better not to antagonize them.'

'Antagonize? I don't understand this word—but——'

'Look, Rosey,' Jackson said quietly, using the one argument he knew would convince the Italian, 'this way is better for Mr Ramage. You understand?'

'All right, all right,' Rossi said reluctantly. 'Now Maxie, you are understanding?'

The West Indian grinned as he nodded.

Jackson said, 'All right then, that's settled. You take care of Harris and the second one—what's his name? Yes, Brookland—as soon after the change of watch as you can. Remember, Harris is the lookout at the starboard chains and Brookland's the same to larboard. We'll just have to wait for the cook's mate, Dyson, to come up on deck to talk to 'em. I'll make sure the top of the companionway's clear.'

'Yaas, Jacko,' Maxton said in his smooth, sing-song voice.

'We'll keep a watch for Dyson. The advantage of being a coloured gennelman is no one sees me in the dark.'

'Unless you open your mouth,' Jackson said. 'Those teeth of yours show up like a couple of rows of white marble tombstones.'

Below them Stafford swore violently as though he had pricked a finger and the three men stopped talking at this pre-arranged warning.

Jackson glanced down and, seeing Dyson pass Stafford and begin to climb the ladder, stood up and stepped back quietly. Pointing down, he hissed:

'Dyson! Get him now!'

The American hated sudden last minute changes in plan, but as an 'idler' who kept no watch, working only during the day, Dyson had no reason to come on deck after dark and this might be their only chance.

Before the man's head was level with the coaming Jackson was sauntering aft, his slow gait belying the tension that gripped him, making sure there were no seamen between the forehatch and the companionway.

Hell! The two men at the wheel! They were Tritons and they'd be standing not more than a dozen feet from the companion. Jackson quickened his pace, praying that the Master or Mr Ramage would be near the wheel. As he walked he eased out the belaying pin which had been tucked down the side of his trousers.

There were two shadowy figures forward of the wheel. Seamen or—no, he recognized Mr Ramage's cocked hat outlined against the slightly lighter horizon.

'Captain, sir!' he said loudly just as he was abreast the capstan.

Ramage recognized Jackson's voice at once, guessed there was a particular reason why he called while several feet away and at once began walking towards him with Southwick following.

'Captain here—that you, Jackson?'

'Aye, sir. Thought I saw something over there on the star-board bow...' As he reached Ramage he pushed him gently backwards. '...A fishing boat or something.'

Ramage clutched Southwick's arm and pulled him back, too, letting Jackson position them where he wanted.

The Master was quick enough to recall Jackson was not on watch.

'Lookouts haven't reported it yet,' he growled. 'Suppose you were just leaning on the rail thinking o' some doxy in Portsmouth. I can't see anything.'

Both Ramage and Southwick felt Jackson give them a warning touch and saw him turn away towards the approaching group.

'Damned fellow's probably drunk.' Ramage commented loudly, nudging the Master again. 'I can't see anything either.'

'Disgraceful,' Southwick growled. 'Dangerous having a fellow walking round the ship imagining things. Remember I once had a drunken sailor sitting out on the bowsprit-end in the dark pretending he was Commodore Nelson in another ship and shouting we'd collide. Gave a damned good imitation of the Commodore's voice, too: fooled me completely —I dam' nearly tacked: quite thought we were in for a collision.'

'Me too,' said Ramage. 'Don't bore me with *that* story, Mr Southwick: you forget I was commanding the ship.'

'And you were, by God!' exclaimed Southwick, and Ramage wasn't too sure whether the Master was saying the first thing that came into his head, to divert the men at the wheel and cover whatever Jackson was doing, or whether he'd genuinely forgotten that the drunken seaman had been Stafford, and it happened in the *Kathleen*.

*

Albert Dyson had been cook's mate in the *Triton* for eleven months and in the Navy three years. The cook's mate was the man who had to light the galley fire, clean out the ashes, polish the big copper kettles in which the food was cooked, and skim off the fat which floated to the surface of the water when salt meat was boiled.

The removal of this fat, known as slush, provided the only call on any skills he had, since he needed no knowledge of cooking. The slush could be sold to various of the ship's company, illicitly and at a profit, because they liked to spread it on the weevily and otherwise tasteless biscuit officially known as 'bread' and which varied between a brick-like

74

hardness or crumbling softness, depending on its age. And he shared his obvious nickname with every other cook's mate in the Service.

'Slushy' Dyson was an angry little man as he swung a leg over the wooden form and stood up. The other men sitting round the table and talking in low voices made him angry. The plan was simple enough and still a complete secret; but now, half an hour before the mutiny was due to start, this blasted argument had started. Although everyone agreed the plan was simple—and sure to succeed—he'd expected objections from some of the men: there was always some awkward bleeder who thought he knew better; but no, there'd been none.

Then at the last minute the trouble had come from his own mess, from the very man who'd been their spokesman. Admittedly Harris had been very quiet since the *Triton* had sailed and hadn't spoken a word. That, Dyson now realized, should have made him suspicious.

More important, though, Dyson's feelings were hurt. He'd always admired Harris—a man whose book learning didn't make him act superior about it; in fact he was always ready to read or write a letter without wanting a tot for his trouble. But now he'd turned nasty.

Dyson objected to being called 'A smelly blob of pig grease'—he'd like to see Harris skimming off all that slush and not get any on his clothes. It's bound to make a chap stink—but everyone was always trying to get a mug of slush free, Harris included. And often he'd given it them—he, Slushy Dyson, who stood to get a crack on the head with the big ladle if the cook ever got to know about it, since the cook took three-quarters of whatever the slush was sold for, be it rum, bacca or credit.

Dyson walked aft to go up on deck: he wanted fresh air and some peace to think things over. They'd wreck everything with their talk. They had their rights—'course they had, otherwise why would the whole Fleet have mutinied? Hundreds of seamen—thousands in fact—knew they had their rights; and that's why the Fleet had rose and why some of the ships had hoisted the red flag, though he didn't agree with that—the so-called 'bloody flag' smelled of revolutionaries.

Sucking in his breath with an angry gesture, he walked round one of the men from the *Lively* stitching a shirt and began climbing the ladder. Two more of them round the coaming: they littered up the ship. All too hoity-toity they were, just because they'd served with the new captain.

He's a bit of a lad though, Dyson admitted as his hands grasped the top rungs: fancy just chopping the anchor cable like that! Well, it didn't make any difference, although Dyson hoped the lad wouldn't get hurt—from what these chaps said he was brave enough, though Dyson admitted he hoped Mr Ramage didn't get any more ideas about putting the ship across the bows of a Spanish sail of the line. Then he laughed to himself—no, tonight's work'd see to that! He stepped on to the deck and turned aft.

Black shapes beside him, a sharp prick on each side of his stomach just below his ribs. Both of his arms seized and twisted, making him arch his back so his stomach stuck out. Knives! Why, its mur——

'Don't make a sound; keep the walking!'

That bloody Italian! Dyson was being forced to walk and he glanced the other way: the West Indian chap.

'All right, all right, take the bloody knives——'

'Shut up!' Maxton hissed, pressing harder with his knife.

The muscles in Dyson's legs began to dissolve; his stomach felt soft and vulnerable, his rib cage hollow except for a heart beating fit to burst. He was going to faint. Oh gawd, if I faint I'll fall, and they'll knife me a'fore they know what's happening, he told himself. He shut his eyes and strained to stay conscious. Ah, that's better. Breathe deeply. Ow! He just stopped himself shouting in pain: the sudden deep breathing made both men wary and both reacted by pressing harder with their knives.

Dyson gulped and began breathing normally and the pressure eased slightly. He kept his eyes shut. They'd stopped walking but he was sure he was going to pass out. Suddenly he felt as though he was falling and thought he was fainting until, in the moment before his head hit the deck, he realized he'd been dropped down a hatch.

Maxton jumped down and landed astride Dyson's sprawling body, which was faintly illuminated by a lantern at the forward end of the wardroom, and Rossi dropped down beside him.

'Out cold as mutton,' Maxton said briefly as he jumped up and began dragging the man forward towards the small hatch in the middle of the wardroom.

It took them less than four minutes to get Dyson down the breadroom scuttle, along a narrow passage and into the breadroom itself. The door was shut but unlocked, the key still in the keyhole.

They bundled the man over and heaved him across the top of some bags of bread, then left, turning the key but leaving it in the lock outside.

'Right, Maxie,' Rossi whispered. 'Back up on deck and report to Jacko.'

Ramage and Southwick, pacing back and forth in front of the wheel, were holding an animated conversation. Ramage had invented a scurrilous story about an unpopular admiral who had died two years earlier—a story he knew the men at the wheel would lap up and repeat, so he could count on their attention being focused on him. Southwick supplemented the story from time to time, and then Ramage saw two shadows gliding forward.

He touched Southwick's arm and they walked a few yards along the weather side.

'Well, I think our first guest is snugged down for the night. Did you recognize him?'

'No—hardly saw him,' Southwick whispered. 'That blasted surgeon—just when you want him to be making a noise he's as silent as the grave.'

'Silent as an empty bottle,' Ramage said. 'Probably passed out. We should have kept him away from it until later. Still, we couldn't be sure when . . . I'd like to know what the hell is going on.'

'Well,' Southwick whispered cheerfully, 'our lads seem to be getting on all right without us. The watch changes in a few minutes.'

*

Harris stood at the main chains staring into the darkness. Usually he liked lookout duty because it gave him time and peace to think over things: to recall the lessons at school and often to wish he'd paid more attention to the teacher. Learning was a wonderful thing: there was so much to learn; so much he wanted to know. So little opportunity to learn. He envied midshipmen and it annoyed him, in the bigger ships, when he saw them sitting round the master skylarking instead of listening to what they were being taught.

The sharp prick of pain beside each kidney, the twist of each arm, the knowledge a man was standing each side of him in the darkness, happened so suddenly in the midst of a mental picture of his childhood schoolroom that it took several moments to sort out memory from reality. Then a voice said with a quietness which only emphasized its viciousness:

'Keep quiet, Harris: not a word, not a movement...'

'What...?'

The points of the knives boring into his back silenced him. The two men seemed to be waiting for something. Then the same man said: 'If you want to live, make the walk with us and don't call for the help; otherwise...' the knife at his right side gave a momentarily harder jab.

Harris nodded agreement and felt himself being turned to face aft. A twist on each arm braced his shoulders back and he was walking. One man was the Italian: he'd recognize that accent and curious grammar anywhere. The other was the West Indian.

And Harris, being an intelligent man, did not try to explain that they'd made a mistake. A minute later he was pitched down the companionway and was still conscious when Maxton landed on his back, winding him.

In a painful haze of gasping for breath he knew he was being dragged feet first through the wardroom. Again he felt himself falling but despite the pain he stayed conscious. Then the stink of mouldy bread, hands gripping his arms and feet, a swift swinging and his body was being heaved up on to something, then a thump. As he groped he felt the rough sacking of bread bags. Distantly, as he finally lost consciousness, he heard a door shut and the metallic scraping of a key turning in a lock.

He had just recovered when the door opened and in the dim lantern light he saw Brookland flung into the cabin, bleeding and whimpering with fear.

The foretopman had, as Rossi and Maxton seized him in the darkness, taken a massive gulp of air to shout. Or so it seemed to Rossi who simultaneously raised the knife a few inches, sticking it expertly into the fleshy part of the man's shoulder, and clapped a hand over his mouth.

Brookland—who had in fact been about to scream with fear, not bellow a warning—felt his shirt warm and wet and sticky and was then nearly responsible for his own death because he fainted. His body suddenly went limp and both men, momentarily thinking he was going to try to break loose, were about to kill him before they realized what had happened.

Unlike Dyson, Brookland regained consciousness as he hit the deck at the foot of the companionway. Muzzily trying to work out what was happening and with his mind so recently full of mutiny, he thought the Marines had gone over to the officers. Then he felt his feet being lifted and he was dragged across the deck. Again a sudden drop and he was lying with his head spinning, a lantern lighting up a strange part of the ship. No—he was by the breadroom door and the bloody Italian was unlocking the door and the West Indian was holding the lantern—and the light glinted on a thin blade of shiny steel.

Being a Catholic, Brookland began muttering aloud a hurried prayer but Maxton, failing to catch the words, suddenly lunged down to warn him to be silent. Mistaking the gesture Brookland, thinking he was within a second of being murdered, shut his eyes and began whimpering like a child, calling to all the saints he could remember.

There was no pain but he felt his body moving through the air and marvelled death was so painless. The marvelling was short-lived: Rossi and Maxton had flung him so far into the breadroom he fell face downwards on to Dyson, whose left foot caught him in the solar plexus so that for several moments he wheezed painfully, fighting to get his breath.

The door shut and it was dark again.

At that moment Dyson recovered consciousness.

'So 'elp me,' he groaned, 'what the 'ell's going on? Who's 'ere?'

Harris answered.

''Arris? You all right?'

'Yes, but I think Brooky's in a bad way.'

'Must be 'im on top o' me an' bleeding like a stuck pig: I can't lift 'im orf.'

'Slide out from under then,' Harris growled unsympathetically, and crawled towards them.

'This you or Brooky?'

'Me—Brooky's just 'ere. 'E's bleeding from the shoulder. Hold 'ard a minute, I've found the wound ... No, it's nothing. Just a shallow dig. 'Ere, Brooky ...'

He shook the man who, having regained his breath, was sobbing again. 'Brooky, pull yourself together. What 'appened?'

'They grabbed me. Stabbed me. Gawd, ten or twenty times from the feel of it. I'm bleeding ter death.'

Two pair of hands felt all over his body.

'No you're not,' Harris said crisply. 'just a cut in the shoulder. Who did it?'

'That dago and the nigger. You?'

'Same. What about you, Slushy?'

'They caught me, too.'

'Where the hell did you get to?' Harris demanded. 'You just left the mess and went forward. We searched everywhere; then the watch changed and we had to get to our stations.'

'I just went up on deck to get a bit o' clean air,' Dyson said sourly. 'You lot were making me sick.'

'Well, what happened?'

'Those two jumped on me as soon as I got on deck.'

'Did you see Mr Ramage or Mr Southwick? They part of it?'

'Not so far as I know,' Dyson said.

'I didn't see them either: just the dago and the West Indian,' Brookland added.

Harris was silent a few moments, then said: 'What the hell can they be up to? Good gawd—you don't reckon the Livelies are mutinying, do you? Why, those sons of bitches might be trying to carry the ship into a French port. Quick, we must warn the captain!'

'Warn him my bare backside,' Dyson said viciously. 'They can kill him for all I care. They've been braggin' about him long enough. I'm sick of the sound of his bleedin' name!'

'Use your brain, you fool,' Harris said urgently. 'If they

carry this ship to a French port it'll mean we'll be prisoners. The Frogs won't encourage mutineers—the idea might spread! Want to rot in a French jail for the rest of your life?'

'Sink me!' Dyson exclaimed. 'Hadn't thought of——'

At that moment they heard the key turn, and as the door opened they saw Rossi holding a lantern and, framed in the doorway, outlined by the light, was Jackson, a belaying pin in one hand and a bottle of rum in the other.

Normally Jackson would never stand out in a crowd. His face was thin, but because Rossi was holding the lantern low the shadows from the jawbone and cheeks made it look cadaverous and menacing. And now, as he stood glaring down at the three men lying on the bags of bread, he seemed to them to be emitting a cold anger, like a full moon glimpsed through lowering black storm clouds.

Harris glanced from the belaying pin to the rum bottle and back again, and was frightened. Then both Dyson and Brookland began whimpering as they thought they'd guessed their fate: that Jackson was going to get drunk, and while he drank, he was going to amuse himself by beating them to death with the belaying pin for trying to spoil his plans.

Jackson, seeing three pairs of terrified eyes glancing from his left hand to his right, suddenly read their thoughts and almost laughed. Instead, to mask any twitch of a mouth hard put to restrain a grin, he motioned Rossi and Maxton into the breadroom and then looked out through the door.

'Staff—come on down and look at our three choirboys!'

A few moments later Stafford stepped into the room and shut the door.

'My, my! Wot *'ave* you been doin', Brooky? You're all covered in blood. Not *yor* blood, I 'ope? And bruvver 'Arris, the edjicated able seaman. Well, and Slushy Dyson! What you all doin' 'ere? Not robbin' the ship's company of their bread, I 'ope?'

He turned to Jackson and said archly: 'Jacko, you know what I suspect?'

The American shook his head.

'I fink they was—oh, dear me, that the wicked word should ever 'ave to pass me lips ... But Jacko, the truth must be told: I fink they was *gambling* ...'

'No!' exclaimed Jackson, falling in with Stafford's serious

manner. 'Not *that*, surely?'

Rossi shook the lantern. 'Not the gambling? *Accidente!* Gambling in one of the King's ships! What would His Royal Majesty say to that!'

'Nah,' Stafford said with a sudden harshness that startled the three men on the bread bags. 'Nah, not gamblin' *in* one of the King's ships, Rossi; gamblin' *wiv* one of the King's ships.'

'That's true,' Jackson said. 'Hold the lantern up a bit, Rossi,' he added, as he was drawling his words. 'Bit more—that's it. Let's have a good last look at them.'

By now Maxton too had caught on to the by-play and was tossing his knife from one hand to the other.

'"Dust to dust and Slushy to slush",' he intoned in his deep, rich voice.

Stafford held up his hands. 'Nah, nah, Maxie, don't be blasphemious, and anyway, Slushy's my bird.'

'Oh no he's not: I want him.'

'Well, yer can't 'ave 'im, so there. Maxie! Take yer pick from the uvvers. What's wrong with Brooky?'

'Somebody's already started on him: he's second-hand. I want a new one.'

''Arris, then. Won't 'e do?'

Stafford's voice was wheedling.

'Oh all right,' Maxton said ungraciously. 'You're picking on me just because I'm not a white gennelman: I'm just a coloured fellah so I have to make do with what's left.'

'Steady men,' Jackson interposed, knowing the three victims believed every word. 'There's plenty more of them; more than a couple of dozen left to share between us.'

Stafford, quick to spot Jackson had accidentally revealed their weakness, said, 'But that's only just one Triton for each ex-Kathleen, Jacko.'

'No,' Jackson said smoothly, 'but some of the lads will swap a Triton for a tot, I'm sure.'

Brookland yelped as Harris suddenly jumped up. He was hardly on his feet before Maxton's knife was an inch from his throat and he found himself looking into a grinning, shiny brown face, the eyes sparkling but bloodshot.

Harris looked desperately at the American.

'Jackson, for God's sake, you've got it all wrong! What

82

you're doing is crazy!'

Jackson managed to hide his surprise. 'Crazy? Maybe it's not in the Articles of War, but it's not crazy!'

'But you'll never get away with mutiny!'

'Sit down or Maxton'll slit your windpipe.'

It gave Jackson a moment to think, but nothing came. Harris sat down, gabbling almost incoherently.

'So help me, Jackson, it's mutiny! Rising against the captain and taking the ship into a French port—what else do you call that? What d'you think the French'll do? They won't give you a big sack of golden *louis* as a reward: they daren't—else every ship in the French Fleet would mutiny! Don't you see that, you crazy oaf?'

For a moment Jackson felt real fear: fear that he had made a complete mistake. Then he thought he began to understand Harris's words. He wasn't sure of the details, but Dyson's expression made him wonder; and Brookland's, too.

Both of them should have been nodding, even shouting, to back up what Harris just said—*if* they agreed with him and were against a mutiny. Instead, they were lying there sullen and silent. Either they disagreed or they didn't care. He decided to back his own guess.

'Maxie,' he said pointing at Harris, 'this man's guilty of disrespect. Just take him outside for a few minutes will you?'

As soon as the door shut behind them, Jackson suddenly stepped over and seized Dyson. Hauling him to his feet, he slapped him hard across the face, jabbing his knee into his groin before letting him collapse to the deck.

The attack was so sudden that Rossi, momentarily thinking Dyson had made the first move, crouched with his knife ready.

Dyson, lying curled up like a whipped dog cowering in a corner, stared up at Jackson.

'Get up!' the American snapped.

'Not bloody likely; I'm staying 'ere. You wouldn't hit a man when he's down.'

'Don't be too sure.'

With that, Jackson kicked him in the ribs. It wasn't a hard kick, but there was very little flesh on Dyson's bones, and he staggered to his feet.

83

'What's it all about?' he gasped. 'Why pick on me?'

'Dyson, you are going to talk to me. A nice friendly little chat. You're going to tell me part of your life story—beginning from the minute I came on board with the rest of the Livelies.'

'Oh no, I'm not!'

Jackson held out first the rum bottle and then the belaying pin.

'Like a drink, Dyson?'

The cook's mate shook his head.

'I should, Dyson. It helps with the pain.'

'Haven't got any pain,' the man said, like a sulky child.

'You haven't—yet.'

Jackson's drawl began to sound like the teeth of a saw dragged across metal.

'Not yet, Dyson. But in the next hour, you greasy little runt, you're going to have so much pain you're going to be begging me to kill you off to put you out of your misery.'

'But why pick on me,' Dyson whined. 'It was Brooky—cut 'im up instead. Brooky started it all. Yes'—he seized at the idea—"'e's your man, not me!'

Jackson paused. Brookland? He was sure Dyson hadn't suddenly named the foretopman to protect Harris: he was so frightened it was much more likely he'd name the real leader to save his own skin. But where did Harris fit in? Why was Harris yapping about the dangers of mutiny—Harris of all people?

Well, if Brookland was the ringleader he wouldn't reveal anything that'd incriminate himself, and anything Harris had to say was likely to confuse the situation even more. No, Dyson was the man to tell the tale.

'Dyson, my greasy little friend, it doesn't matter who we start with because you're all going the same way home. So brace up that tongue of yours and get under way.'

The man wiped his brow. Already white-faced, his skin now seemed sweat-sodden and turning grey. Glancing up, he saw the American's eyes, began to say something and then held his hands out helplessly and looked down again.

Jackson said, 'Rosey, put the lantern over there.'

Dyson watched the Italian take a couple of paces to the corner, put down the lantern, and return to face Jackson, who said in an off-hand tone:

'Rosey, just cut off the top joint of his right index finger.'

Dyson gave a little scream and sat on his hands as Rossi turned towards him. In the moment's silence that followed, Jackson said:

'Wait a second...'

He held out his own left hand and with the right index finger touched each joint.

'...That's fourteen chops for each hand. I say, Rosey, that's twenty-eight and'—he glanced down at his bare feet—'about ten for each foot. Forty-eight: it's going to take time. You'd better give him a drink first. Change your mind, Slushy?'

But the man had fainted. Jackson went to the door and called to Maxton.

'Bring Harris back in here, Maxie, and take out Brookland.'

As he waited, Jackson glanced over at the bloodstained top-man. There was fear in his eyes: bottomless fear, the kind of fear found only in a real coward, for it had paralysed him. He could no longer move a muscle even to save his life.

Maxton had to drag him out of the tiny room and Jackson waved Harris over to where he had originally been sitting on bread bags, and prodded Dyson, who was beginning to stir, with his foot.

As soon as he could see Dyson had recovered sufficiently to know what was happening round him, he said to Harris:

'I've brought you in to watch a cook's mate being butchered. Should be interesting. Think of all the chickens whose necks he's wrung. All those pigs and cows he's slaughtered and cut up...'

Since another of a cook's mate's duties was to act as slaughterer of a ship's livestock, the irony of the remark was not lost on Harris who began to say something, but Jackson held up his hand.

'Your turn for a farewell speech will come, Harris. Until then, one word out of you and I'll let Maxie get to work. Now, Dyson, you feeling better?'

Dyson nodded, then shook his head violently. Too violently, in fact, because he had to close his eyes as the cabin began to spin. Jackson hoisted him to his feet and flung him back so he was sprawled across the bread beside Harris, but with his back to him.

'As you seem to be a bit squeamish, Dyson, I'll give you one more chance to start telling your tale. Otherwise Rosey begins to chop.'

The cook's mate glared at him and muttered a filthy oath. Jackson motioned to Rossi but before the Italian could step forward Dyson held up both hands, as if to ward him off, and whined, 'All right, all right, give me time!'

He took a few deep breaths and, staring down at the deck, said:

'Well, at Spithead we Tritons was just like all the rest of the Fleet. Yes, we'd mutinied because of conditions—and the *Lively* did the same.

'Then half the Tritons get sent to the *Lively* and you lot are transferred. Well, that didn't mean nuthin' to us because the Fleet's working together. Then that Mr Southwick comes out. All right, we let him on board—not many ships would 'ave allowed that, and you know it, but 'e seemed an 'armless old coot.

'That was our mistake, because next day along comes Mr Ramage. Well, we still didn't suspect nothin'. We'd 'eard about him and the *Kathleen* at Cape St Vincent and reckoned the Admirality had given 'im command of the *Triton* as a sort o' reward.

'The next bit you know: 'e tells us to weigh and we won't —none o' the rest of the Fleet would 'ave done, an' you know it. So 'e suddenly cuts the cable and we 'ave to make sail to keep off that shoal. Well, that wasn't fair: 'e 'ad no right to risk drownding the lot of us. When we found out we're supposed to be bound for a long voyage, we decided the best thing to do was to take the ship back to Spit'ead and be along with our mates in the Fleet.'

Jackson nodded, as if waiting for him to continue.

'Well, that's all there is to it.'

'No, it's not—let's have the whole story, Dyson. Did everyone in the ship agree with you?'

'Well, not quite everyone. You, Rossi, Stafford, Evans, Fuller, that West Indian fellow—'course you wouldn't 'ave done: that's why you weren't told about it.'

'And the rest from the *Lively*—were they asked?'

'Not all of 'em, no,' Dyson admitted.

'Any of them? Even one man?'

Dyson shifted uneasily. 'Well, they wouldn't 'ave tried to stop us.'

'How did you word the question?'

'Just asked 'em.'

'You didn't say something like, "If you won't join us, just keep out of the way—or you'll get knifed in your hammocks!"?'

'Well, we 'ad to protect ourselves in case any of them went running to the captain. Stands to reason,' Dyson said defiantly.

'So you threatened to murder your shipmates in their hammocks if they stayed loyal to their captain—a captain who's the finest in the service—and refused to mutiny?'

Dyson said nothing and Jackson suddenly wheeled on Harris.

'You knew better. You're educated, not an ignorant peasant like Dyson. Why did you plan all this?'

The suddenness of the attack had just the effect Jackson hoped.

'I didn't, you damned fool! I was trying to stop them. I . . .'

'Go on, Harris.'

'I've nothing to say. Except you're worse. You shouldn't talk about loyalty—Mr Ramage's a stranger to us. You lot are supposed to be the ones who fought alongside him. But what are you doing now? Mutinying and taking the ship over to the French!'

The man made no attempt to hide his contempt.

'You're worse than mutineers; you're a bunch of traitors —traitors to your country and, what's worse, traitors to the man who trusted you. A good man: a man who can understand another man.'

Although Jackson did not know what Harris meant by the last few words, he'd at last got at the truth of it. Just a few more details to fill in the gaps.

'Dyson, you're a dead fish, but I'll give you a choice. I'll have you killed quickly and painlessly if you answer two questions truthfully. If you don't, or if you lie, you'll start dying in a couple of minutes and Rossi and Maxton'll be finishing you off at sundown tomorrow.'

'What d'you want ter know?' Dyson croaked.

'Who were the real ringleaders of this mutiny?'

'Brookland's the ringleader. He thought of it first. Oh, what's the good, Harris'll split on me, and I might as well get the credit that's due. Brookland thought of it, yes; but I was the brains. I, the one and only Slushy Dyson, who can't read nor write did the planning. Brookland couldn't plan how to divide fifty-eight pieces of salt beef into fifty-eight mess bags.'

Jackson nodded.

'Second question. Are there any others you could call ringleaders? No, put it another way: if you and Brookland are out of the way, will there still be a mutiny in the *Triton*?'

'Not on your life,' Dyson said contemptuously. 'Not a chance. Sheep they are; worse than sheep. You could let Brookland go free, you lot could swim to the shore, and there still wouldn't be a mutiny without me to lead it.'

'You're a clever fellow, Dyson.'

'No, not clever. Just sick of salt beef and salt pork in port when we could 'ave fresh meat and fresh vegetables. Just sick of spending years in a ship and never a day's leave. I ain't seen me wife fer three years. There's four kids I 'aven't seen fer three years—and one kid I ain't never seen. He was born a fortnight after the press gang caught me.

'Four daughters—that's seven years we'd 'oped and prayed for a son. Then I get took up by the press a'fore I even see 'im.

'Listen, you skinny Yankee, you don't know what it's like. In the last two years I've spent five months, two weeks and three days in Portsmouth. Me wife and kids are in Bristol. Did I ever get a week's leave ter go ter Bristol? No—most I've ever 'ad is four hours for a run on shore. And 'ave you ever tried to keep an 'ome and feed six mouths on a cook's mate's pay?

'Afore the press took me up I 'ad a pie shop. I made good pies. I made good money. What my old lady wanted, she 'ad —within reason, anyway.

'But when the price of flour went up, so did the price of my pies. So did the wages of farm workers, builder's men an' the rest. But what about the seamen? Their pay 'asn't gorn up since the days of Charley the Second, and if you don't know the date I'll tell yer—1650. Just short of a hundred an' fifty years ago.

'When did the price of flour last go up? An' bread? Seven weeks ago, and fer the eighth time since the beginning of the war.

'You *really* call it mutiny, Jackson? Honestly? D'you blame the men at Spit'ead? You really blame *me* for wantin' to get the *Triton* back there, so we stand four square with the Fleet and get our rights? You *really* blame me? Anyway, I don't give tuppence worth of cold slush whether you do or you don't: just kill me quick and bolt fer France an' give Boney my compliments an' tell him I 'ope he straps you down on the gilloting as soon as you step on shore.

'An' just one more thing. I expect you'll 'ave ter kill Mr Ramage—in fact yer must 'ave done that already, and Mr Southwick, or they'd 'ave been down 'ere afore now. Well, that's up to the Kathleens but I'll tell you wiv me dying breath that our 'ands wouldn't 'ave been as dirty as yours: we weren't going to 'arm an 'air on their 'eads, and that's God's truth.

'Now'—he tore open his shirt and turned to face Rossi, who was still holding his knife—'Let's get it over with.'

Jackson swung his belaying pin and Dyson collapsed unconscious.

'Fetch Brookland,' he told Stafford.

As soon as the whimpering man was dragged into the breadroom a second blow with the belaying pin left him unconscious beside Dyson.

'Maxie, Rossi—guard 'em. Harris, and you, Staff, come with me.'

He left the breadroom, groped his way along the passage to the ladder leading to the breadroom scuttle, and climbed up to the wardroom.

CHAPTER SIX

Ramage turned the chair round and sat down wearily, an arm resting on the desk. The tan from the days in the Mediterranean had gone; now his face was pale, emphasizing the black smudges under his eyes. The newer scar over his right brow was still a livid mark made worse by his habit of rubbing the older one beside it. Jackson realized he must have been rubbing it a lot tonight as he tried to puzzle out what was happening.

The American, watching him closely for the first time for many weeks, realized he now looked much older. It wasn't a question of age, really. In the Mediterranean he'd still been a lad; now he was a young man. There was a definite change; a maturing, perhaps.

But what now surprised and worried Jackson was that he sensed that somehow the Captain had lost—what was it? Zest? Jackson wasn't sure precisely what 'zest' meant, but further speculation was interrupted by Ramage, who said quietly:

'Well, Jackson, make your report.'

'There's no fear of a mutiny tonight, sir—I'm pretty sure of that much. Nor any other night for that matter.'

'What makes you so sure?'

'We've got the two leaders under guard.'

Ramage felt almost too disheartened to ask their names. He'd been sure he'd persuaded Harris to be sensible, but obviously the man had completely fooled him. Now Ramage felt sick—not over a seaman betraying him, but because he'd been sure the man wouldn't: he'd made an almost fatal mistake in judging a man's character, and good captains couldn't afford such mistakes—unless, he thought mirthlessly, he had a cox'n like Jackson. 'I trust the "guests" are comfortable in the breadroom.'

'Comfortable as we could make them, sir.'

Ramage had to know sooner or later. 'Who are they?'

'The cook's mate, "Slushy" Dyson, and a foretopman called Brookland.'

'Only two? I thought I saw you—er, helping—three down the companionway.'

Jackson grinned. 'One was a mistake, sir.'

'Who was it?'

'Harris, sir. The man you spoke to yesterday morning.'

Was it only yesterday morning? It seemed months ago.

'Why did you suspect him? And why are you now so sure he's innocent?'

Jackson described the events of the past hour in detail. He made no secret of how he'd made a mistake about Harris; nor did he fail to make Ramage laugh with the story of Harris's own mistake in thinking that Jackson was leading a mutiny of the ex-Kathleens. He related almost word for word Harris's savage condemnation of Jackson for betraying not just his lawful captain but a man who'd earned, by his own bravery, the allegiance of the Kathleens.

Ramage nodded, embarrassed but impressed.

'We've got ourselves into a pretty pickle, Jackson.'

'How so, sir?'

Ramage felt too tired to go through everything twice but he wanted to hear Jackson's reactions.

'My compliments to Mr Southwick, Jackson, and if it's convenient to leave Mr Appleby at the conn, tell him I'd like to see him. By the way, where's Harris?'

'Stafford's guarding him, sir. In the wardroom—forward, he can't overhear anything.'

Southwick was soon sitting by the table, blinking in the light of the lantern, and quickly Ramage related the position.

As soon as he'd finished, Southwick looked up at Jackson and said with such sincerity that his massive tactlessness was not noticed. 'You might be a Jonathan, m'lad, but you're a credit to the Service!'

'I agree,' Ramage interposed, 'but for the moment we have problems.'

'Problems maybe,' Southwick said breezily, 'but no mutiny!'

'But problems all the same. Dyson and Brookland are

mutineers pure and simple. Court martial and sentence of death. Jackson, Stafford, Maxton, Rossi and either you or me required as witnesses. It'd have to be at Plymouth and that means a delay of—well, three or four days, and we can't be sure there aren't more mutineers there who'd stop us sailing again. And then there's Harris——'

'But Harris didn't——' Jackson interjected but Ramage raised a hand to silence him.

'Harris knew there was going to be a mutiny; he knew they were planning to take the ship tonight. He didn't come and warn me or Mr Southwick. Remember the wording of that particular Article of War, Jackson?'

The American nodded gloomily.

'And so does Harris, because I reminded him. In fact I repeated the precise wording.'

'Does that mean all three have to swing, sir?'

'Of course, if they were brought to trial.'

'But . . .'

Both Jackson and Southwick said the word together and stopped.

'Go on, Mr Southwick,' Ramage said.

'I was only going to say that although the Articles of War have to be observed, sir, I can't help feeling that Harris is—well, a special case.'

'Any more than Dyson, who has a wife and several children starving on his wretched pay which hasn't been increased for one and a half centuries? And what about Brookland—has he a family? Neither can read or write; but Harris can.'

Ramage's voice was cold and both Jackson and Southwick could not hide their dismay. Finally Jackson said:

'I'm presuming a lot when I shouldn't, sir, and I know that things like being with you when you rescued the Marchesa don't——'

Curious to know what Jackson was going to say, Ramage eased the atmosphere by interjecting, 'When *we* rescued the Marchesa. But spit it out, Jackson, without all this backing and filling!'

'Thank you, sir. Well, sir, I can't help thinking that whatever the legal rights and wrongs of what Harris did, he meant well and the Tritons respect him.'

'What's that got to do with it?'

'Well sir, we've still got a divided ship's company. The Kathleens are sticking together and so are the Tritons. You can tell the Kathleens they're Tritons now and they'll accept it because it comes from you. But without Harris there won't be anyone the Tritons trust that can persuade *them*.'

'Since when do seamen need to be persuaded, Jackson? Discipline, Jackson, backed up by the cat and the Articles of War.'

Southwick looked up as though he was hearing ghostly voices; Jackson looked away as if ashamed to hear Ramage speak so brutally. Then both men looked sheepish as Ramage laughed.

'The trouble is, neither of you listen. You asked me if they'd be hanged and I said—I remember the exact words—"Of course, if they were brought to trial".'

'Ah, "if",' Southwick said, making an attempt to hide his relief: for a few moments he thought the captain had been so frightened of the near-mutiny that he was going to react viciously. He'd seen it in other captains and it was understandable but unforgivable because, Southwick reasoned, you were punishing other men for your own shortcomings. Even a twinge of fear, let alone a touch of cowardice, was a grave shortcoming in Southwick's code.

'Exactly. But, Jackson, as the spokesman for the non-mutinous half of the ship's company, tell me this: are you suggesting that these two men who actually planned to mutiny tonight and take the ship back to Spithead should escape punishment? That Harris, who failed to report it to me, should escape punishment?'

'Oh no, sir!' Jackson exclaimed, realizing there'd be no hanging. 'No sir—that'd wreck discipline. No sir, just that hanging's—well . . .'

'A bit final. But obviously you have another idea.'

Jackson looked startled. 'How did you guess, sir?'

'Because I'm paying for the rum. Two bottles, remember? Plus whatever the surgeon drank.'

Ramage described Jackson's idea and then asked: 'Am I far wrong?'

'No—that's about it, sir,' the American grinned ruefully.

'But afterwards,' Ramage added, 'Dyson and Brookland will be kept under an arrest and put on board the next homeward-bound ship we meet.'

'That's wise, sir,' Southwick said. 'But you'll keep Harris?'

'Yes, I'll keep Harris; but what good he'll be after a flogging I don't know. He's intelligent and sensitive. If I flog him I ruin him. If I don't flog him, I ruin the discipline in the ship and if the Admiralty heard of it, I'd be put on the beach for the rest of my life. I'm damned if I do and twice damned if I don't.'

Jackson began to understand why the Captain appeared to have lost some of his usual zest. It'd be the first flogging he'd ever ordered, and Jackson understood him well enough to know that although it'd scar a seaman's back it'd scar the Captain's soul.

'Sir,' said Jackson cautiously, 'I think if you'd let me talk to Harris before he—well, before he gets his "medicine", I'd make him understand. And perhaps he could be given a dozen or so less?'

'How, without making the rest of the ship's company suspicious—or sympathetic towards Dyson and Brookland?'

'Well, perhaps Dyson and Brookland could sort of aggravate their offences. Like fighting, sir. They're both blacked up a bit.'

' "Blacked up"?'

'Got black eyes—look as though they've been fighting. We could improve that by the morning, too, and clean up Harris a bit.'

'Jackson, obviously you believe in justice, but you like to have a thumb pressed down on one side of the scales.'

★

The three men were standing before him. The corporal of Marines was to his right and six Marines, muskets on their shoulders, stood behind the prisoners, who were frightened, the fear showing through their bleary, drink-filmed eyes.

As the sun broke through a cloud he noticed all three men had to squint: their heads were throbbing from the effect of the rum, and the bright light following much violent movement as they were hustled up on deck from the total darkness of the breadroom must be agonizing.

He looked at them slowly and then, glancing round the ship, noted that most of the seamen on deck were Tritons.

Jackson and his men were out of sight.

Southwick walked from behind him with the cook, who had a plaster covering a cut on his head and stood to the left of the prisoners.

'Well, Mr Southwick, what have you to report?'

'I was going to the breadroom with the cook to survey the bread, sir. I opened the door and when the cook went in he found these three men inside, almost insensible from drink. The whole place stank of rum. Two empty bottles there.'

Ramage suddenly realized he'd made a mistake. The breadroom door had been locked from the *outside*. Had the cook realized the significance or even noticed it? Southwick obviously had from the way he'd phrased his description.

'How did they get the rum?'

'Can't say, sir. They won't say either.'

'Why are those two men'—he pointed at Dyson and Brookland—'so bloodstained? Have they been fighting? And all of them are soaking wet.'

'Yes, sir. From all accounts they had a fight when they got drunk. Then when I called for some seamen to get 'em up on deck to sober 'em up under the wash-deck pump, they started fighting the seamen. Dyson and Brookland, that is.'

Ramage knew too much to ask how and why the fighting started. It wasn't justice; but it wasn't injustice either. Whatever was done to these men wasn't as bad as having them tried by court martial, knowing they'd be hanged.

'Harris, what have you got to say for yourself?'

Ramage sensed a sudden tension round him, then realized every Triton was straining to hear Harris's reply. They must all know he was against the mutiny; they knew he and Dyson and Brookland had been missing for most of the night. And now they must be mightily puzzled to find that Harris and the two men supposed to be leading them to mutiny had spent the night swilling rum in the breadroom.

'Nothing, sir: I'm sorry sir, I was just drinking.'

'Just drinking . . .' Ramage mustered a convincing sneer. 'A dozen lashes for you, my lad: that'll clear the rum out of your system. Take him away!'

The corporal—who acted as the ship's master-at-arms, a title which a century before meant just that but now indicated he was the ship's policeman—barked at two Marines and

Harris was marched below.

Dyson and Brookland remained standing in an ever widening pool of water. Southwick had made a reasonably good job of sobering them up. They weren't still completely drunk, yet they weren't quite sober.

'Brookland, you're the senior man. What were you doing?'

'Just drinking, sir.'

'What happened then, a bottle get up and hit you?'

He heard the Tritons trying to restrain their laughter. It was working . . . so far. There'd been no gasp when he'd sentenced Harris.

'Come on, man, I asked you a question.'

'Don't rightly recall, sir. I was fighting someone.'

'Who?'

'Slushy, I think. But he wasn't in a Marine's uniform. Then there was the cook. And the Master. Lots of Marines.'

'You fought them all?'

'Oh no, sir,' the man exclaimed. 'No, I mean that when I was fighting I . . . I'm sorry, sir, I don't really remember *what* happened, except I was fighting Slushy.'

'Dyson—what have you to say for yourself?'

Dyson shook his head and nearly toppled over. Straightening himself up with an effort he tried to focus his eyes on Ramage.

'Fightin', sir. Brookland and me. My fault, sir. I think I 'ad a fight with a Marine, too. I 'it the cook with an empty bottle.'

'Oh—now why did you do that?'

'Don't get on with him too well,' Dyson said with drunken honesty. 'Wasn't a pre . . . pre-medulitated attackle. I mean I didn't . . .'

'You hit him on the spur of the moment?'

'That's it, sir,' Dyson said gratefully.

'Very well, two dozen lashes for each of you. Now get them below, Corporal; they make the quarterdeck look untidy.'

As the corporal bustled and shouted, the remaining Marines stamping and wheeling amid small clouds of pipeclay, Ramage walked aft to the taffrail and watched the *Triton's* wake.

Guilt, he thought to himself, was a matter of circumstances, necessity and degree. He had just flouted the Admiralty by charging the men with drunkenness instead of conspiracy to

96

mutiny; he'd then flouted the Admiralty again in ordering them to be given what was, in fact, an almost dangerously light sentence. But officially no captain, whether of a tiny brig or a 74-gun ship of the line, could punish a man with more than a dozen lashes. If the crime warranted more than a dozen, then officially the man had to be brought to trial before a court martial, who could order more—as many lashes as they thought fit (there was no limit: 500 was a common sentence for desertion) or even hanging. But it was an order most captains ignored.

Some ignored it for the men's own good—better break a rule and give a man a swift couple of dozen than bring him before a court martial which might take a couple of months to assemble and then decide to make an example of him (or be fed up with a succession of petty cases) and sentence him to a hundred lashes.

But Ramage had no illusions about other captains who broke the rule because they enjoyed seeing men flogged. A few years ago there was the case of Captain Bligh; now there was talk of a captain out in the West Indies, Hugh Pigot, son of old Admiral Pigot, who gloated when he saw the tails of a cat laying open a man's bare back. For a moment Ramage almost envied him: better perhaps to be able to gloat than stand there with your stomach empty because you knew you'd be sick if you ate anything, and breathing deeply and standing on your toes to stop yourself fainting. And hating the circumstances which forced you to have a man flogged.

But Ramage recognized the symptoms of self-pity and told himself: I was given command of a ship knowing what it entails. I have to fill in forms by the dozen for the Admiralty, the Navy Board, the Board of Ordnance, the Sick and Hurt Board . . . I have to take unwilling and often stupid men and train them, and keep them well-fed and as fit as possible despite bad food and often appalling conditions.

I have to lead 'em and punish 'em when necessary. Sometimes when going into action I have to give orders which will certainly kill one, a dozen or all of them. I am—if I do the job properly—their teacher and leader, judge and jury. Yes, and father-confessor and friend as well.

As far as the Admiralty are concerned, whether I succeed or not has little to do with my promotion; where that's concerned it's more important to have influence in Parliament! The surest way to quick promotion is to be closely related to someone worth five votes to the Government in the House of Commons... But whether the system is good or bad, it is the system; neither I nor anyone else can change it, whether——

'Deck there!'

The shout was from the lookout at the foremast and Southwick, snatching up the speaking trumpet, bellowed a reply.

The man shouted back: 'Land, sir. A headland I think, two points on the starboard bow; can just see it in the haze.'

Southwick acknowledged, looked around for Appleby and demanded: 'Would you recognize the Lizard if you saw it?'

'Yes sir, I've seen it several times.'

'Good. Take the "bring 'em near" and get aloft.'

Ramage idly watched him scurry forward and begin the long climb up the ratlines. The Lizard...

*

The blue-grey smudge on the starboard quarter began slowly to fade and drop below the horizon, and Ramage watched the bosun's mate sitting on the coaming of the main hatch. Every movement the man made irritated him; everything about him was irritating.

Evan Evans was a tall and almost painfully thin Welshman who viewed the world, when he was sober, with doleful disapproval. However, his enormous nose—it looked like a purple cucumber stuck on as a joke—had an uncanny instinct for pointing into a tot of rum, and he had been one of the most popular of the *Kathleen*'s petty officers.

But Evans was now making up three cat-o'-nine-tails for the flogging tomorrow morning.

It was a tradition—perhaps there'd been an Admiralty order, though Ramage had never seen it—that a man was never flogged on the day the captain pronounced the sentence: always the next.

No doubt the seamen thought it was to give the sentenced men time to work up a dread of the punishment facing them; but Ramage knew that, by tradition anyway, it was to give the captain time for second thoughts in case he had acted too harshly in the heat of the moment. And, curiously enough, the delay was doubly to the men's advantage. If those to be flogged were popular then many of their shipmates illicitly hoarded their most valued possession, their morning and evening tots of rum, so that (if it could not be smuggled to the prisoners to drink before being marched on deck) they had something to deaden the pain after the punishment. If the punishment was given the same day as the sentence there'd be no time for hoarding.

Evan Evans was working slowly and steadily; there was a dreadful fascination in watching him which, Ramage noticed, everyone else shared: not a seaman walked past without glancing at him. But the man worked methodically, oblivious to stares and, because of his rating, immune from unpleasant comments.

Beside him on the deck were three pieces of thick rope, each a couple of feet long and an inch in diameter. They were for the handles. From a coil of braided line Evans had already cut twenty-seven pieces, each just over two feet long and a quarter of an inch in diameter. They would form the tails.

As Ramage paced miserably up and down the weather side of the quarterdeck, pausing occasionally to glance at the set of the sails and check the course the helmsmen were steering. Evans went on with his work. He picked up one length of thick rope and put it across his knees. From the brim of his tarred hat he took a sailmaker's needle and threaded it with twine.

With a slowness that did not hide his deftness, he made a sailmaker's whipping at one end of the rope, preventing the strands coming undone. After whipping an end of each of the other two thick pieces he put them down on the deck again. Then he patiently whipped one end of each of the twenty-seven tails.

The Lizard was still a smudge on the horizon when he dropped the last one on the deck and stuck the needle back in his hat. He held one of the handles between his knees, the whipped end hanging down, the other end conveniently placed to work on. Unlaying the three strands of the rope for a couple of inches, he took one of the tails and worked the un-whipped end between the unlaid strands of the rope in the fashion of a long splice. Holding it in place with one hand he did the same with another, then a third and fourth until all nine had been spliced into the handle.

Retrieving the needle from his hat and re-threading it, he ran a few stitches through each tail where it was spliced into the rope, which then had one whipping put over the end and another an inch farther down. There'd be no chance of the tails pulling out.

After inspecting it carefully he put the cat down on the deck and took up a roll of red baize material. Measuring the handle against the material, he used an enormous pair of sail-maker's scissors to cut off a strip just long and wide enough to wrap right round it. With all the care of a seamstress making a ball dress for her most important customer, he then wrapped the material round the handle like a stocking, joining it by stitching a seam along the entire length. With the thread cut and the needle stuck back in his hat he held up the finished cat.

Even from five yards away it looked both terrible and grotesque: a vile and deadly tropical plant perhaps, or a deformed octopus—the stiffness of the line made the nine tails stick out like groping tentacles from the red handle.

Ramage was thankful the men had not been guilty of theft because that would have meant the tails of the cat being knotted, three knots in each. Mutiny, desertion, disobedience, drunkenness, bestiality—for all those crimes the cat was not knotted; only for theft.

Yet there was a crude justification for that apparent anomaly—men cheerfully put up with rats on board, and there were weevils in the bread that they shared with the mice and rats, but there was no worse animal in a ship than a thief; a seaman who stole from his shipmates.

As he watched, Evans finished sewing a small bag of red baize with a drawstring round the neck, curled up the cat, put it in the bag and tightened on the drawstring. Then he began making the second cat.

It was a ritual, a tradition, whose origins were probably lost in antiquity, and although he'd witnessed many floggings in ships in which he'd previously served, first as a midshipman and then as a lieutenant, Ramage never realized (perhaps, he thought grimly, because he'd never been responsible for ordering a flogging) just what effect a bosun's mate sitting there making a cat had on the rest of the ship's company. Perhaps even more of an effect—as far as being a deterrent was concerned—than watching an actual flogging.

Always a new cat-o'-nine-tails for each flogging; always the cat was made the day before; nearly always it was given a red baize handle and put in a red baize bag.

Red to hide the bloodstains? Hardly, since the whole ship's company had to watch a flogging and could see the tails becoming soaked in blood and tangled after each stroke, so that the bosun's mate had to straighten them out by running his fingers through them—'combing the cat'. And one look at a man's back after even half a dozen strokes made such niceties as a red handle unnecessary.

No, probably the origin was just that red was a colour of warning; that before the flogging, while the victim was being seized up and a leather apron tied high round the back of his waist to protect his liver, spleen and kidneys from the tails, the ship's company would see the bosun's mates standing there ready, some of them, depending how many men were to be flogged, holding red baize bags.

One victim, one bag. But if he was to get more than a dozen strokes, then more than one bosun's mate, because it was customary to change the bosun's mate after he'd administered a dozen.

Ramage knew of one captain who always made a point of having at least one left-handed bosun's mate on board. If a bosun's mate was right-handed, the tails of the cat fell diagonally downwards from the right shoulder. This captain boasted that his left-handed bosun's mate 'crossed the cuts'.

Shaking his head as if trying to rid himself of the thought of flogging, Ramage turned and looked back at the Lizard. The wind was north, a nice breeze, almost a soldier's wind to give Ushant a wide berth. In fifteen minutes the headland would be out of sight, and he took a bearing, noting it and the time on the slate.

As he put the slate down on the binnacle he reflected how many thousands of times seamen before him had noted the bearing of the Lizard ...

The wretched Duke of Medina Sidonia with the Spanish Armada: the Lizard had been his first sight of the England he was supposed to conquer for his master, Philip II. It was the last sight of England for the Pilgrim Fathers sailing for America; Sir Francis Drake's, too, before he died off Portobello almost exactly two centuries ago. (And how excited he must have felt, before that, as he sailed back to sight it and complete his great Voyage of Circumnavigation—three years in which he encircled the globe.)

Nor did Ramage forget the Lizard was Cornwall. Hidden under its lee was Landewednack, whose parish church was the most southerly in England. There was the fishing village of Coverack whose fishermen often used the stone quay for landing strange cargoes at dead of night, since many of them more often fished for bottles and casks than fish; bottles and casks brimful of smuggled brandy. The French Directory might be at war with Britain, but nothing would interrupt one of Cornwall's profitable industries, smuggling from Brittany.

Ramage already knew from a previous glance at the chart that the *Triton* was steering a course which, if one drew a line on a chart along her wake, would go through the Lizard and diagonally right across Cornwall to touch Tintagel on the west coast, the birthplace—so legend had it—of King Arthur.

For the moment Ramage had little concern for King Arthur: the line, a few miles before reaching Tintagel, passed through St Kew, the home for several centuries of the Ramages.

He imagined a bird crossing the Lizard and flying towards St Kew, mentally ticking off the places it would cross and revelling in their names, delighting in their very Cornishness, their complete difference from other names in the rest of the country. Indeed, the majority of Cornishmen still regarded anyone living outside the county boundary as foreigners.

Over the Lizard, then, passing the little village of Gunwalloe in a small cove among towering cliffs—cliffs at the foot of which was the wreck of a treasure ship belonging to the King of Portugal, the *St Andrew*, driven there to her death by a south-westerly gale more than 250 years earlier. Legend had it that the folk of Gunwalloe saved eighteen great ingots of silver—and four suits of armour, made in Flanders for the King.

On and on: Feock, Old Kea and Malpas, Penkevil, Probus and (too far for the poor bird to see, he admitted, but he delighted in the names) Sticker and Polgooth; and Veryan, near

St Austell, where an ancient king was supposed to be buried in his armour, and beside him a golden boat in which, on the day he rose up again, he would sail away.

Right over Castle an Dinas (a more suitable claimant to being the birthplace of King Arthur than Tintagel, Ramage always thought: any man born at Tintagel, with the sea thundering against the cliffs, would surely have been a great sea king). Then after Talskiddy and Bilberry Bugle the bird would be flying over rugged land laced with sheep tracks, gashed with rocky hills, softened by grassy mounds—Ramage country!

Lying in the cemeteries of the surrounding churches were dozens of long-dead Ramages. Men of honour who'd died in battle, sickness and old age (and some had died dishonourably too: his family had had its share of black sheep). There were Ramages killed fighting the Royalist cause alongside Sir Bevil Grenvile and Sir Ralph Hopton, Sir John Arundel and Sydney Godolphin, Sir Nicholas Slanning and Sir John Trevanion—aye, they and almost every Cornish family, aristocrat or peasant had fought hard against Cromwell's armies.

And there were Ramages whose bodies had been brought back from distant battlefields to rest in the vaults of various branches of the family; and Ramages lost at sea in the King's service whose very existence was recorded now only by memorial tablets inside the churches.

Thinking of his forebears, it seemed the actual moment of death was not important to record: you died when those who lived forgot your existence. Gloomy thoughts . . . and he pictured the bird flying over the River Camel stretching away to the port of Padstow. Once one of Cornwall's great ports, it was now being strangled by a sandbar across its entrance—the work, so the local folk had it, of a jealous mermaid—and well named the Doom Bar, because any ship missing the narrow channel through it on the west side (keeping so close to the rocks her yardarms almost touched them) was indeed doomed.

He recalled the flood stream rushing over Doom Bar and up the Camel to cover the sandy stretches exposed by the low tide, floating the schooner lying aground at Wadebridge itself and delighting the ducks and swirling round the granite buttresses of the old bridge. And a mile or so up the valley, laced with sunken lanes, Egloshayle, where on a moonlit night the villagers gave the church a wide berth for fear of seeing a white rabbit with pink eyes—a rabbit who left the man who went to hunt it dead by the church, his chest full of the shot with which he'd loaded his musket.

And not far away Tregeagle, where one house had regular visits from the ghost of a Cavalier, spurs ringing, curly hair loose over his shoulders.

From Egloshayle the road ran north-eastward to St Kew Highway, with St Kew itself standing back from it. And within a circle of five or ten miles were the villages through which he had been driven as a small child in his father's carriage and later ridden his own horse—Blisand, Penpont, Michaelstow and Camelford, all skirting Bodmin Moor... He remembered rides from Camelford across the Moors to the two great peaks of Roughtor and Brown Willy, towering nearly 1,400 feet over the surrounding countryside as if the guardians of all Cornwall.

And Gianna would be at St Kew within a few days with his father and mother...

Southwick, standing in front of him, had obviously just asked a question, which he repeated as Ramage looked at him blankly.

'Grating or capstan, sir?'

'What?'

The Master had seen the Lizard disappear from view too often not to guess Ramage's thoughts were either on his home beyond the Lizard or of the Marchesa, and he re-phrased the question.

'The floggings tomorrow, sir: shall we use a grating or the capstan?'

'Capstan,' Ramage said automatically, and Southwick thanked him and walked away.

Why choose the capstan? He'd replied without thinking but answered his own question at once. In larger ships it was usual to take one of the gratings covering a hatch and stand it vertically against the bulwark or the fo'c'sle bulkhead. The man to be flogged was made to stand spreadeagled against the grating, and his hands and feet were lashed to it, the gridded wooden bars making it easy to pass the seizings.

Because he was held hard up against the gratings, Ramage had noticed, he could not move an inch to absorb any of the crushing weight of the blows.

But using the capstan, a common practice in smaller ships, was different. The capstan bars, each six feet long, were slotted into the capstan to project horizontally, like the spokes of a wheel lying on its side, at the height of a man's chest—at just the right height to push against.

For flogging, only one bar was shipped and the man stood as though pushing, only his chest was hard up against the bar, his arms stretched along it on either side.

He was then secured to it by seizings round his wrists and just above his elbows; but the rest of his body was free: he could, by arching his back, move an inch or so, just enough to ride the lash. Little enough, but perhaps it helped.

Evan Evans was putting a baize bag down on the deck after completing the second cat and picking up the third handle. And down below, guarded by Marines, Dyson, Brookland and Harris would be ... Ramage began pacing the deck again, wishing for once Southwick was walking with him, prattling away about nothing in particular.

CHAPTER SEVEN

Next morning after the bosun's calls shrilled and the order was passed—and obeyed—for 'All hands aft to witness punishment', Ramage went up on deck in his best uniform, sword at his side, to be greeted by Southwick, similarly dressed.

The capstan was midway between the wheel and the mainmast, instead of right forward, as in larger ships. Being set aft meant it could be used for hoisting the heavy lower yards as well as for weighing anchor.

The Marines were already drawn up in two files, one on each side of the capstan, with the ship's company formed in a three-sided square round it, the fourth side being the quarterdeck.

With Southwick he inspected the ship's company and was surprised to see they were smartly rigged out in clean shirts and trousers, hair newly combed and re-tied in neat queues, and freshly shaven. Then, with their corporal, he inspected the Marines. Their red jackets were spotless, cross-belts stiff with pipeclay, brass buttons and buckles gleamed, their muskets immaculate, the metalwork looking oily but dry to the touch, the woodwork buffed to a high polish.

Ramage then returned to stand just in front of the wheel. A bright sun shone fitfully through broken cloud, the ship was gently rolling and pitching, the tiller ropes creaked as the men turned the wheel a spoke this way and a spoke that to keep the *Triton* on course for the rendezvous with Admiral Curtis's squadron. His clerk handed him a sheet of paper and a copy of the Articles of War, and the Marine corporal —who was not carrying a musket since his main role for the moment was to be master-at-arms—stood beside the prisoners.

Flogging a man was more than a punishment; it was a ritual, a long and complicated rigmarole that Ramage could not alter or shorten, whatever his personal feelings. And as he stood there, his left hand on the scabbard of his sword, holding the Articles of War in his right, the three prisoners standing to attention in front of him, the sails overhead drawing in the north-west wind and knowing that below, locked in his desk, were secret and urgent letters from the First Lord to three of his admirals, he recalled a letter from his father congratulating him on passing his examination for lieutenant. He couldn't remember the exact wording but the gist of it was still fresh in his mind.

If you are to be a true leader—a man others follow because he is a natural leader, not just a legal one who has to bolster his authority with his commission and the Articles of War—you will, apart from obeying, have to *give* orders that make you angry and resentful; make you feel that the Articles or the *Regulations* are too inflexible, forcing you to act unjustly or unreasonably.

Do not forget, however, the Articles and the *Regulations* have evolved since the Navy first began. No set of rules can cover every eventuality—otherwise lawyers would be out of business. There *will* be injustices; but when you command your own ship, the crew will be watching you. They know when a shipmate's punishment is just or unjust. If it is well deserved, neither the man nor the ship's company will complain. If it is not, they will soon let you know in a hundred small ways. But of this you can be sure: if you show any signs of weakness—then they'll treat *you* unjustly, and you'll only have yourself to blame. A weak captain leaves the ship's company at the mercy of harsh officers. A good captain requires the same obedience from his second-in-command as from the youngest boy on board...

And how right the old man was. Yesterday the ship's company were mutinous in everything except actually taking over the ship. Last night (but for Jackson and the rest of the group) they'd have done that too. Yet this morning, for reasons he couldn't explain, there was a completely different atmosphere on board. The men hadn't been singing or laughing before being piped aft to witness punishment; but

—well, he sensed the atmosphere was now fresher, as though some hidden menace and tension had gone.

Perhaps it was more significant that every man had obviously taken particular care with his appearance—they'd all shaved, although it was Tuesday and they were required to shave only twice a week, on Sundays and Thursdays. And there was no order for them to appear in fresh clothes. Certainly they could not wear dirty, but there was a difference between clean and fresh. He was sure it wasn't a bizarre gesture to the men being flogged; a curious defiance of authority. The men weren't subtle enough for that.

Everyone was watching him; he'd been staring at the carved crown on the top of the capstan for several seconds—more likely a couple of minutes. He wondered what they'd think if he told them he'd just recalled his father's advice so that although five minutes ago the prospect of flogging some men nauseated him, he was now going to order the floggings knowing it was both necessary and right.

Suddenly he realized why the atmosphere had changed: the men had known it all the time: three of their number had been caught planning a mutiny and naturally they must be punished.

He felt foolish and inexperienced and hurriedly glanced at the piece of paper, beginning the ritual.

'William Dyson!'

The master-at-arms stepped smartly alongside Dyson as the man took three paces forward.

'Aye aye, sir.'

Ramage had been surprised at the man's appearance—he too was shaved, and dressed in fresh clothes. Now his manner was slightly defiant—no, perhaps not: Ramage admitted he didn't know the man well enough to be sure.

'William Dyson, you were charged by the Master with breaking into the breadroom being drunk and disorderly, fighting and trying to resist arrest.'

To the corporal, Ramage snapped:

'Seize him up!'

Two Marines put their muskets down on the deck. One picked up a capstan bar lying beside the companionway coaming and slotted it into the capstan head; the other led Dyson the few steps to the capstan. His shirt was stripped off, the thick leather apron was produced and tied over the lower part of his back, his arms were stretched out horizontally along the capstan bar, and within two minutes he was ready for the flogging to begin.

But there was still more ritual.

Ramage opened the Articles of War. For once he was thankful for Article Number Thirty-six, nicknamed the 'Captain's Cloak' and so worded that it could be used to cover any villainy that ingenious seamen might devise.

As Ramage removed his hat, Southwick bellowed: 'Off caps!'

'Article number Thirty-six,' Ramage began in a clear voice, as soon as every man was bareheaded. ' "All other crimes not capital, committed by any person or persons in the Fleet, which are not mentioned in this Act, or for which no punishment is hereby directed to be inflicted, shall be punished according to the laws and customs in such cases used at sea." '

Dyson was lucky, since even the drunken night in the breadroom left him open to more serious charges.

'Two dozen lashes—bosun's mate, carry out the punishment!'

After twelve lashes—which Dyson bore without a murmur—Ramage signalled for the flogging to be delayed a minute or two, calling to the surgeon, Bowen, to examine the man. If the *Triton* had carried more than one bosun's mate, another would have taken over from Evans.

The surgeon was obviously at least half drunk and he shambled over. After looking at the cook's mate's face and feeling his pulse he stood back and mumbled,

'Fit for punishment to be continued, sir.'

'Carry on, bosun's mate.'

The tails of the cat were bloody and for the last few strokes the bosun's mate had to run his fingers through them to remove the tangles.

Just before the last stroke was laid on, Ramage said quietly to Southwick: 'Have some men take him down to the sick berth. The surgeon will be down as soon as I can spare him.'

The bosun's mate stood back and the corporal reported:

'Twenty-four, sir.'

'Very well: cut him down and get him below.'

As the Marines released Dyson's arms and unstrapped the apron, Ramage glanced at Brookland and Harris. The former was obviously still feeling the effects of the night's drinking, but Harris, although white-faced, was standing stiffly to attention.

Dyson stood back from the capstan. Suddenly he bent down to pick up his shirt and put it on. Since his back looked like raw liver the movement must have been agonizing, but two Marines, not realizing for a moment what he was doing, stepped forward, the bayonets on their muskets pointing straight at him.

Then, equally unexpectedly, Dyson turned to face Ramage, who groaned inwardly. Oh no, he thought: for God's sake no insults and defiance: you'll have to be given another dozen if—

'Permission to speak, sir?'

Ramage nodded.

'I want to apologize for my behaviour, sir.'

'Very well, I accept it,' he said quietly, knowing that Dyson was referring to the planned mutiny. 'Now get below and clean yourself up.'

Ten minutes later Brookland was walking forward unaided, his punishment administered, and Harris was seized to the capstan bar. For the third time Ramage read out the wording of the 'Captain's Cloak'; once again Evans opened a red baize bag and took out a new cat-o'-nine-tails; once again Ramage said:

'One dozen lashes. Bosun's mate, carry out the punishment!'

Once again the swish of the tails flying through the air; once again that noise like a wet towel hitting a baulk of timber; once again a grunt as the blow knocked the breath from a man's lungs; once again the corporal intoned the number of the stroke.

'One . . .

'Two . . .

'Three . . .'

Then, from aloft, a sudden shout:

'Deck there!'

As Ramage snapped, 'Bosun's mate—wait!' Southwick yelled, 'Deck here—what've you sighted?'

'Sail dead ahead, sir. Can just see her t'gallants.'

Southwick looked round for Appleby, gave him the telescope and pointed up the mainmast.

Ramage said to the master-at-arms, 'Cut him down and get him below, Mr Southwick! Beat to quarters, if you please!'

In time of war, and particularly in this position, every ship was potentially an enemy. For the moment Ramage thought little beyond the fact it meant he was now able to stop, and could later remit, the rest of Harris's punishment.

'Have our pendant and the private signal ready, Mr Southwick,' he said quite unnecessarily.

Southwick was already bellowing orders and the men were already running to their stations. The little drummer began thumping his drum with more eagerness than skill; the corporal hurriedly slashed at the seizings round Harris's arms, eager to resume his other role as a Marine; and the Marines themselves still standing to attention, obviously uncertain whether they should obey the drum or wait for their corporal's orders.

Ramage saw the surgeon lurching towards the companionway and called to him to attend to Dyson, Brookland and Harris. But the man did not pause, leaving Ramage unsure whether he had heard or understood but already decided that the surgeon was his next problem—if the ship ahead was not a French sail of the line.

Whatever she was, she was to leeward and Ramage dare not lose the advantage of being both to windward and being between the ship and the English coast. He ordered Southwick to bear up, and while men ran to the sheets and braces and the Master stood by the helmsmen, Ramage looked up at Appleby perched high in the mast and steadying himself against the roll of the ship, which at that height was exaggerated by the inverted-pendulum swing of the mast. The master's mate hailed that she had three masts, was heading north-east and 'looked large'.

Ramage called to Jackson, pointed aloft and in a moment the American was on his way up the ratlines. Although Appleby's eyesight was good he hadn't Jackson's experience in identifying ships.

Considering it was the first time they had done it since he'd been in command, Ramage noted the ship's company had gone to quarters quickly without the excited nervousness that caused delays: the guns' crews were ready with rammers, waiting only for the powder to be brought up from below; the deck was already running with water and several men were sprinkling sand, so that bare feet would not slip and no stray grains of powder could be ignited by friction.

It was time for Ramage to go down to his cabin and check once again the day's private signals—the secret challenge and reply by which ships of the Royal Navy could distinguish friend from foe.

The signals, kept in a locked drawer in his desk, comprised several pages held together by a heavy slotted lead seal which had been squeezed together so the slot closed tightly along the left-hand edge of the sheets. That alone indicated their importance, and a warning on the first page, twice underlined, said captains were 'strictly commanded to keep them in their own possession, with sufficient weight affixed to them to insure their being sunk if it should be found necessary to throw them overboard'. And, it added, any officer disobeying would be court martialled because 'consequences of the most dangerous nature to His Majesty's Fleet may result from the Enemy's getting possession of these Signals'.

The signals themselves were simple to understand, listing the flags to be flown from the foretopmasthead and the maintopmasthead, and the flags to be flown as a reply by the other ship. Since both signals were given it did not matter which ship challenged first.

The important thing was the date. Only ten challenges and replies were listed, and the final figure in the date was the one that mattered. In the first column headed 'Day of the Month', were, one beneath the other, the figures 1, 11, 21 and 31. Below that was a second group, 2, 12, 22 and followed by 3, 13, 23 and so on until it reached 10, 20, 30. Beside each group were the flags to be flown on those dates —and on this occasion the Navy used civil time, the new day beginning at midnight.

Since it was the 20th day of April Ramage ran his finger along the last set of figures, '10, 20, 30'. Beside them it gave the first signal to be flown and the flags forming the reply.

After locking up the signals Ramage went back on deck, where Southwick was waiting.

'Pendant over red and white at the main; white with blue cross at the fore. The reply is pendant over blue white blue at the main; blue white red at the fore.'

'Very good, sir.'

Within a few moments he had several seamen busy bending the flags on to the appropriate halyards ready for hoisting, and then Jackson called down that he thought the ship was a British frigate.

Swiftly her sails lifted above the horizon as she sailed up over the curvature of the earth towards the *Triton*; soon Ramage could see her hull coming into sight.

'Hoist the challenge, Mr Southwick!'

Suddenly the long, triangular-shaped pendant and the red and white flag soared up the mainmast, and the single white flag with a blue cross was being hoisted at the foremast.

Only a few seconds after the flags streamed out in the wind Jackson called down:

'Deck there! She's breaking out a couple of hoists ... Blue white red at the fore ... Pendant, then blue white blue at the main, sir!'

Southwick acknowledged and motioned to the men at the halyards, and immediately the two hoists were lowered.

'Make our number, Mr Southwick!'

A few moments later the Union Flag with three flags beneath it representing the *Triton*'s number in the List of the Navy was streaming out from the maintopmasthead.

*

The frigate had been the *Rover*, bound for Portsmouth from Lord St Vincent's squadron, and it had taken only fifteen minutes for Ramage to go on board and report to her captain, warning him the Fleet at Spithead was in a state of mutiny, and persuade him to take Dyson and Brookland on board without asking too many questions. Few captains raised objections to getting a couple of extra seamen.

Both men had asked to see him before leaving the *Triton* and, to his surprise, Dyson had requested that he be allowed to stay on board. For a moment Ramage had almost relented; then he thought of the ship's company. He was sure the man would never try any nonsense again; but his mere presence in the *Triton* would be a constant reminder that a mutiny had once been planned. The former Kathleens would certainly never trust him and it might eventually make his life unbearable and in turn lead to more trouble.

But before dismissing both men Ramage reassured them that as far as the captain of the *Rover* knew, they were simply two seamen just flogged for drunkenness. And that was true: for his own sake Ramage didn't want the captain of the *Rover* arriving in Portsmouth with the news that the *Triton* had nearly been taken by a mutinous crew. As it was, the captain had been puzzled at the request and would have refused had he not known of Ramage's part in the Battle of Cape St Vincent.

In the late afternoon the *Rover*'s topgallants disappeared below the horizon to the north-east. In a few hours she'd be off the Lizard and bearing away up Channel. By that time the *Triton* would have met Admiral Curtis's squadron.

CHAPTER EIGHT

The Tropics: to Ramage they were always magic words, but as he stood at the taffrail watching the brig's wake he knew the hot sun, blue sea and sky and the cooling Trade winds had done more than anything to make the *Triton* a happy ship. Now, looking at the men cheerfully going about their work or listening to them dancing to John Smith the Second's fiddle as the sun set, it was impossible to know who was an original Kathleen and who a Triton. Tanned, fit, cheery—and well-trained: all a captain could ask of a ship's company.

After finding Admiral Curtis's squadron off Brest, the *Triton* met Lord St Vincent's squadron twenty miles from Cadiz. After delivering the First Lord's letter, Ramage had answered ten brief questions—brief, but searching—and after a gruff 'Have a good voyage' from the Admiral, made sail bound for the Canary Islands, there to pick up the North-east Trade winds which would carry the brig before them for nearly three thousand miles in a great sweeping curve across the Atlantic to a landfall off Ragged Point, the eastern tip of Barbados.

After leaving Lord St Vincent's squadron, their last sight of land had been Cape Spartel, the north-western corner of the Barbary Coast. From then on a stiff but constant north wind gave them a fast run south towards the Canaries.

Rather than lose the chance the northerly gave them of getting as far as possible to the south with a 'soldier's wind' before meeting the Trades—as well as make an accurate departure—Ramage decided to risk a chance encounter with any Spanish warships patrolling His Most Catholic Majesty's Atlantic islands by passing close to Tenerife, the most imposing of them all.

It had come up over the horizon looking like a series of

sharp-crested storm waves petrified in an instant by a wilful Nature in a petulant mood. And for once the sharp edges, topped by the perfect cone of the volcano Teide, were sharp and clear, instead of being hidden in cloud; through the telescope Ramage could see wide black ribbons down the side of the mountain where streams of lava recently pouring from the crater had solidified.

For a day and a night after that the *Triton* had run south, still holding a soldier's wind; then slowly, almost imperceptibly, the wind had in a few hours eased round to the north-east and the *Triton* had followed, her course curving down to the south-west, out into the open Atlantic and leaving the Cape Verde Islands just out of sight to the south.

Then the wind had picked up its strength and everyone on board knew they were in the Trades. Gradually the following seas increased in size, the Trade wind clouds arrived and settled down into their usual orderly formation.

In an hour or so, Ramage knew he must go down to his cabin and bring his log and journal up to date; but for the moment he stood in the sun, glorying at the way the *Triton* ran before the Trades.

Wave after wave—deep blue laced with white foam, but bright turquoise green when the sun's rays shone through the tumbling crests—swept up astern of the brig, making her yaw like a fat fishwife walking down the street.

A big crest would nudge her on the side of the counter and heave her stern round, and by the time the helmsmen had spun the wheel to bring her back on course another would have arrived to catch the opposite side and give her an unceremonious shove the other way, and the cheerfully cursing helmsmen would begin all over again.

Ramage wished he could be left alone for the whole voyage: he'd be happy enough spending it watching the clouds.

When dawn broke astern each day it usually showed a high bank of cloud to the eastward, although the night sky overhead was normally clear, speckled with so many stars that it seemed to be raining diamonds.

Soon after the sun appeared above the bank and started to get some heat in it, the mass of cloud vanished, as if dried up, and tiny clouds, just balls of white fluff, began to appear, apparently from nowhere. Within half an hour they would grow slightly and, almost imperceptibly, like dancers on an enormous ballroom floor, begin to move into a regular formation, part of a dainty quadrille repeated all over the sky.

By ten o'clock, as the hands were piped to exercise at the guns, the clouds would have formed into a dozen or so regular lines like so many skeins of swans flying one behind the other, converging on a point beyond the western horizon.

Apart from the way they formed into lines, the shape of each cloud fascinated Ramage. Although the base was nearly always flat, the top was an irregular bulge and the front stretched out like a neck. Odd quirks of wind varied the shapes of the tops and fronts so that some clouds looked like a squadron of flying white dragons; others as if all the white marble effigies of recumbent knights had risen into the sky from the tops of their tombs. Still more seemed to be people's faces staring up into the sky—here a jovial and plump Falstaff sleeping off a wild night's drinking, there a lean and hungry-looking Cassius.

But whatever their shape, they always moved westward, as if drawn by some inexorable force; and below them the tumbling seas too moved westward driven, like the *Triton*, before the wind.

Always westward—except for the flying fish leaping up suddenly like tiny silver lances, skimming a few yards or a hundred, rising up the forward face of a wave and swooping over the crest and down again, miraculously staying a few inches above the sea until, leaving only a tiny ripple, they vanished as swiftly as they appeared. One, six, a dozen and even fifty at a time.

Then one of the crew would shout and everyone would crowd the ship's side to watch dolphins racing past, crossing close under the plunging bow, twisting swiftly in the water in a swirl of white and steely blue to pass so close across the bow again it seemed impossible the stem would not hit them.

Then, a few minutes before noon each day, he and Southwick would be standing amidships, where the effect of the brig's pitching and rolling was less, quadrants in hand, taking one sight after another, a man calling the time. Minute by minute the sun's image in the quadrant's shaded mirrors —reflected down until it appeared to rest on the horizon, allowing the angle to be measured—continued rising slowly. Then it slowed and gradually came to a stop as the man called noon, and hung there a few moments, apparently motionless. Ramage and the Master would read off the highest angles shown on the quadrant and resume watching the sun until certain the altitude was beginning to drop. The ritual of the noon sight, and a few minutes of addition and subtraction soon gave them the *Triton*'s latitude.

And then it was afternoon, with the sun—high now they were so far south and hot enough for an awning to be rigged over the quarterdeck—gradually dipping until it was dead ahead. The sunsets, different each evening, were always fantastic. The clouds would have fattened or lost formation and the setting sun, like an angry artist daubing paint, changed them into strange masses of garish yellow with red edges, or pink with a scarlet fringe, but above them and beyond them the sky too would be changing from the deep blue overhead to the palest blue on the horizon, cloud and sky contrasting raw colours and delicate tints.

Quickly the colours would go, leaving the clouds dull grey and, by comparison, menacing; then, with a suddenness surprising to anyone used to the long evenings of the northern latitudes, it would be dark. Later the clouds would vanish to leave the stars brighter than one could ever imagine. And right astern the moon slowly rose, turning the *Triton*'s wake into a bubbling trail of silver.

And later, lying comfortably in his cot as it swung with the brig's roll, Ramage would hear the water rushing past the hull, roaring, bubbling, gurgling as the brig slowed momentarily in the trough of one wave, surged along on the forward face of the next, and then see-sawed as the crest passed beneath her and she slid into the trough.

Every glass, every bottle, every knife, fork and spoon in the sideboard rattled and clinked; everything that could move even an eighth of an inch in the cabin did so with all the noise it could muster. And the ship's hull groaned as the crests and troughs constantly stressed and supported, lifted and dropped. Stringers and futtocks, beams and knees creaked in protest. To a landman it would seem the ship was breaking up; to a seaman it meant the ship was showing its strength, bending like a flexing cane instead of remaining rigid and brittle.

But Ramage admitted there were bad days: days when the Trades suddenly stopped, leaving the *Triton* wallowing in a heavy sea without the press of wind in her sails to stop her rolling. the atmosphere humid and oppressive. The seas would flatten quickly, but for an hour or two it always seemed she would roll her masts out. The white puff-ball clouds disappeared and in their place grey-blue patches on the horizon would quickly spread into near black squalls rushing silently down on the ship, like a hawk dropping on its prey.

One moment she would be pitching and rolling with not enough wind to blow out a candle; then, its edge marked only by a white line of tiny crests, the squall would strike and in a matter of seconds the helmsman would be fighting the wheel to force the *Triton* to bear away under a reefed foretopsail.

Blinding rain, howling wind, the knowledge both you and the ship were fighting for your lives, the deck running with water from rain and driven spray, always the fear one of the masts would go by the board—and then suddenly sunshine, the wind and black clouds gone as quickly as they came and even before you could pick up the speaking trumpet to give orders, the deck steaming as the sun's heat began drying out the planking. Seamen would strip off shirts, wring out the water and put them on again. (A fortunate few would have collected some of the rainwater to use for washing clothes.)

The nights were dangerous when the Trades decided to be wilful. The *Triton* would be running in a steady wind, the stars bright, and suddenly a lookout would call a warning, or he or Southwick would spot it: a patch of sky astern with no stars. No hint of cloud, just that the stars had vanished. A minute or so to see which stars round the patch were being obscured—to determine the course of the squall—and then all too often, a hurried call for all hands to furl everything but the foretopsail which would be double reefed . . .

*

Ramage was just thinking of going below when Southwick, who was officer of the watch and had been tactfully keeping to the other side of the quarterdeck, leaving him to his thoughts, came over and said casually, 'Sawbones had a bad night, sir ...'

The old Master said it sympathetically but firmly. Ramage knew he was being told that the problem of the drunken surgeon, Bowen, must be tackled very soon; and in his clumsy way Southwick was trying to prod him into doing it now, realizing how repugnant the task but knowing, with all his years at sea, that it would get worse the longer it was left.

Ramage nodded. 'I heard him, If he yelled to his steward for one new bottle he must have yelled for half a dozen.'

'Four times,' Southwick said grimly, 'I counted. How do you stand under the *Regulations*, sir; can you forbid him any liquor?'

Ramage appreciated the 'you': Southwick was well past fifty, Ramage just past twenty-one. If Southwick was anything but a good man, he'd use 'we' as much as possible, just to let the captain know how much he depended on the Master. But not Southwick: he was content and accepted the situation—and perhaps knew Ramage appreciated it. Indeed he must know, since there were three or four score unemployed masters at the moment, probably even more, and Southwick knew that Ramage had asked the First Lord for him in the *Triton*.

None of which had much relevance to Bowen's drinking.

Ramage shook his head. 'I don't think the *Regulations* cover it. I can suspend him from duty pending an inquiry, that I do know. But it doesn't solve the problem.'

'I agree,' Southwick nodded and Ramage, realizing the old man wanted to say more, prompted him by adding:

'We can get rid of him as soon as we get to Barbados—though how we'd find another one I don't know. But he's probably a very good doctor when he's sober and we're going to need one in the West Indies.'

'That's what I was thinking, sir. Yellow fever, blackwater ... doesn't do to think about all the diseases, even with a good "sawbones". In fact it's got a lot worse in the last year or so, from what I heard in a letter I had in England. A lot worse.'

'In what way?'

'Just the sheer number o' men dying, sir. I kept the letter. It's from the Master of the *Hannibal*'—he rummaged in a pocket and brought it out. 'These are the figures he gives.

I hope they won't worry you too much, sir?'

'No,' Ramage said dryly. 'I've been to the West Indies before . . .'

'Well, the soldiers to start with. Out of nearly 16,000 white soldiers stationed there at the time, 6,480 died from fevers in the year ending last April—that's forty per cent. In the Santo Domingo campaign of '94, forty-six masters of transport ships and 11,000 men died. The *Hannibal* buried 170 of her crew in a month and lost two hundred in six months. Jamaica to Port au Prince is less than 300 miles, but the *Raisonable* frigate had yellow jack on board and buried thirty-six of her crew on the way. That's one man in three . . .'

Ramage held up a hand to stop the recital. If 16,000 troops were sent into battle and lost 6,500 killed, it would mean they'd suffered a disastrous defeat. A sail of the line going into action and losing two hundred men out of about seven hundred would mean she'd been battered and probably sinking . . .

'Send Bowen to the cabin.'

'He mayn't be sober, sir . . .'

'Probably not; but I'll see him in fifteen minutes. As sober as you can make him . . .'

'I understand, sir. Five minutes under the wash-deck pump, if need be!'

CHAPTER NINE

Ramage looked up from the desk as the door opened. From outside a man said: 'You thent for me, thir?'

The blasted fellow had forgotten his false teeth.

'Come in, Bowen.'

The surgeon shuffled in like a sleepwalker, walking in a reasonably straight line but only because what would have been staggers to left and right were being counteracted by the *Triton*'s rhythmic rolling.

Bowen had once been tall, and, despite a weak mouth, handsome. And from what Southwick said, once an excellent surgeon in London with a long list of fashionable patients. Then, for reasons no one knew, Bowen found his hand preferred reaching for a glass of gin rather than a scalpel.

Ramage looked up at the man again, hating what he had to do. Bowen's carriage had obviously once been proud and erect; but now—even allowing for the low headroom in the cabin—the shoulders were hunched and his head rested athwart them as though the neck had all but given up trying to do its job. Both arms hung loosely, the muscles slack, and being long they gave him an ape-like appearance.

But the clothing and the face revealed the full story. His shirt, greasy with dirt, obviously hadn't been off his back for a fortnight; the coat and breeches were stained by liquor slopping from glasses held by a shaking hand, and the humidity was producing a crop of mildew.

The face was grey; not the greyness of someone rarely in the sun, but the greyness of a very sick man. The cheeks sagged and the mouth hung open, lips slack, as if the muscles were too gin-sodden to hold the flesh in place. There was a slight hint the muscles on the left side were still trying because the right side of the mouth hung lower, the lop-sided effect increased by a habit of permanently tilting his head to the right. His grey hair, just pushed clear of the brow, was greasy and unkempt, matted together like a wet deck mop.

Ramage thought sourly he could well be one of the wretched, liquor-sodden creatures loitering outside some sordid gin palace, pleading with the potman for a glass of swipes or begging a penny from a customer for a drop of gin. Yet almost unbelievably those long and still delicate fingers, now trembling and spasmodically clenching, had been capable of fine and delicate surgery; that brain, now lost in the befuddling fog of gin fumes, could diagnose and treat complex illnesses. Although any man's death was a tragedy, sometimes the way a man lived was worse.

'Sit down, Bowen.'

The man nodded gratefully and stupidly, groping for the chair and lowering himself into it. Then slowly he raised his head and tried to focus his eyes on his captain.

At that point Ramage realized that in all the past days and hours of thinking about the man, he had not only failed to think of a solution, but now couldn't think what to say.

Yet ironically his position was the reverse of that of a doctor. He knew what the illness was, but until he knew what caused it neither he nor the medical world could cure it. What made a man crave liquor to the exclusion of everything? Perhaps Bowen——

'I'm afraid I haven't had much chance to get to know you, Bowen.'

'Thmy fault, thir—I've been too beathly drunk to be fit company for anyone.'

The answer was so honest Ramage began to feel sympathetic.

'Perhaps. Tell me, how old are you?'

'Fifty, thir; old enough to know better and too old to do anything about it.'

He had obviously long since given up the struggle: Ramage sensed the man now had no desire to change.

'And how long in the Service?'

Bowen was obviously thinking hard, groping in his memory as if in a dark room scrabbling for something in a drawer.

'Two yearth, thir.'

Ramage, who constantly fought an inability to pronounce the letter 'r' when he was excited, knew he couldn't stand a

123

long conversation with a man who lisped and hissed.

'Sentry! Pass the word for my steward! Now, Bowen, where the devil have you left your teeth?'

'I ... I ... I can't remember, thir.'

'Think, man! You had them for breakfast, didn't you?'

'No ... didn't eat breakfatht.'

'Supper, then.'

'Nor thupper; at leatht, I don't think tho.'

Douglas, the steward, appeared as Ramage realized the man probably hadn't eaten a proper meal for days, if not weeks.

'Douglas, Mr Bowen has mislaid his teeth. They're in his cabin somewhere—fetch them, please.'

As Douglas left, Ramage turned back to the surgeon.

'How long have you been drinking like this?'

'Like what, thir?'

The voice revealed he was—well, not exactly cringing, nor trying to seem innocent. Ashamed? Yes! So perhaps there was the remnant of pride there, and he prayed it had not sunk too deep.

'Don't play the fool,' Ramage said harshly, hoping the man would soon be completely sober, and that a few hard words would speed up the process. 'You're a gin-sodden wreck; just a pig swilling from a trough. Now, how long have you been drinking like this?'

Pressing his hands to his temples, Bowen seemed to be trying to stop his head spinning. He stared at the deck a few inches in front of Ramage's feet and said in a near whisper:

'Three yearth, thir.'

'For a year before you joined the Service?'

'Yeth ...'

'In other words, your first year's drinking wrecked your life. Eventually only the Navy would employ you as a doctor?'

'I thuppothe thath true, thir: I hadn't thought of it.'

Douglas knocked at the door, came in and discreetly handed the surgeon his teeth as though they were a pair of spectacles.

He left the cabin and Ramage busied himself with some papers while Bowen fitted them, fumbling with shaking hands.

'Thank you, sir.'

Ramage nodded and turned back to face him.

'Tell me, Bowen, he said conversationally, 'when you were a doctor in London, I imagine you often had patients who drank too much and came to you for treatment?'

'I'm afraid so, sir. Drink's a curse which afflicts the rich and poor alike. Cheap gin or expensive brandy—the effect, medically speaking, is just the same.'

'If it isn't cured, I suppose the patient dies?'

'Invariably. The liver, you see: it can't stand the damaging effect of all that liquor.'

Ramage realized Bowen was now talking in a completely detached manner; once again a doctor discussing a medical problem. Well, he thought grimly, maybe 'physician, heal thyself' might work.

'What do doctors consider the chances of effecting a cure? How many, say in a hundred cases?'

'Depends entirely on the patient, sir. And on his family and friends. No nostrums can cure. Fashionable quacks prescribe expensive medicines and treatments, but the patients die or go mad and the quacks get rich ...'

'But what starts a man drinking so excessively? I mean, not every hard drinker gets like—well permanently besotted.'

'Well, that's hard to say. Most people drink a normal amount—a glass of claret, a sherry, port, a good brandy after dinner. Hot toddy on a cold night. They have a drink because it tastes well, it livens the spirit ...'

'But that's far removed from being drunk all the time.'

'Yes, that's the puzzling part. It's not a fashionable view among medical men, but I think it is an illness, like a fever. It affects some and not others. Like yellow jack. It strikes down one man and leaves another.'

Ramage was interested now, conscious that something quite different was emerging from the drunken man seated in front of him. Bowen's voice was becoming brisk and assured. Although the words were slightly blurred, for he was not yet fully sober, here was the man of medicine talking to the brother of a patient.

'You see, sir, the strange thing is you can take two men and each can drink the same amount. Wine with the mid-day meal, wine and brandy at supper. Perhaps several brandies. Now one of those men will, all his life, drink the same amount with no difficulty. He'll never feel the need to drink more.

'But the other man,' Bowen continued, his eyes brighter now and emphasizing his words with a wagging finger, 'will find he starts having just one more drink on each occasion. Particularly in the evening. One more, then another. He doesn't get particularly drunk—until perhaps one evening he's enjoying an argument, or quarrels with his wife, or something is worrying him. Then he gets very drunk. The next morning...'

Ramage nodded. He knew the feeling, though in his case because he'd drunk more in one evening than he had the previous month.

'Yes,' Bowen said sharply. 'Next morning he feels terrible. But by midday he has got over it. But it happens a few days later. And again and again. Then some friend offers him a drink before breakfast one morning when he feels dreadful. The friend assures him one drink will make him feel better. The thought is revolting because his head is throbbing, mouth dry, stomach upset... But he takes the drink... And almost immediately he *does* feel better.

'That,' he almost shouted, pounding his knee with his fist, 'that's the moment the illness starts. I am certain that's the point when the liquor has so penetrated the man's essential parts that he's lost.

'But of course he doesn't know it. On the contrary, he thinks he has made a discovery more important than finding a way of changing base metals into gold: he's learned he can get vilely drunk but next morning feel no after-effects—as long as he can have just one drink.'

'Just one?' Ramage's eyebrows lifted in disbelief.

'Ah!' Bowen said knowingly. 'He thinks it's only one, and one's enough for a while. Then comes the day—the second stage of the fever, in fact—when one isn't enough. He needs two to stop the headache, settle the bile, focus the eyes, stop the slight tremble which has begun to affect his hands. Then as the weeks go by it's three, four, five—and he's drunk by noon.'

'By this time he's past curing?'

Bowen shrugged his shoulders. 'By this time his life is

collapsing, unless he is a man of leisure. If he's a professional man—a man of medicine, for instance—he finds his patients complaining he's drunk when he examines them at ten o'clock in the morning, so he sucks cashews to disguise the smell on his breath. His wife begins to complain, and he gets angry with her. A friend might drop hints. Then he suddenly finds many of his patients are calling in other doctors.'

'But are his actual abilities affected by then?'

'I don't know,' Bowen admitted. 'Probably, because he's not so alert, and he'll be getting worried. Fewer patients means having fewer bills . . .

'Anyway,' he continued, 'the man has already begun to feel ashamed. He's already keeping a bottle hidden away, so he can have his first drinks of the day in secret. At first he thought it *was* secret; then he discovers everyone knows. That makes him more ashamed. Then he swears he won't have a drink before noon—but noon gets earlier every day, and so does the evening for his evening drinks. And he finds he can't stop. Drink, drink, drink . . . In secret, or openly and defiantly. He's possessed by a devil. In lucid moments he knows his family, his career, his very life is ruined; and a drink—he thinks one drink—is enough to drown the thought for a while. It isn't of course; it never is. Since he's sick, the very nature of the sickness means one drink is too many—and a thousand not enough. Well-meaning friends, parsons, priests—even doctors—bid him have courage, have strength, leave the bottle alone! They extract promises—and he gladly gives them: anything for peace, anything to make them go away—so that he can get at the bottle he's hidden somewhere.'

'But the promises?' Ramage asked.

'Oh yes, they're meant at the moment he makes them. That's what's so degrading because a moment later the fever drowns them. The man knows nothing can save him: he's doomed to drink and drink until he dies or kills himself.'

'Why don't more of them kill themselves?' Ramage asked brutally.

'Pride,' Bowen answered simply. 'Just the dregs of pride. No man wants to leave behind as his epitaph that he killed himself while blind drunk.'

A pencil on the desk rolled back and forth in time with the *Triton*'s roll; glasses and decanters clinked in the racks; the bright light coming through the skylight made strange shadows dance from side to side across the cabin. And Ramage knew Bowen had given him some clues to the problem, but not enough to provide the answer. And in fifteen minutes he had to take over the watch on deck from Southwick.

'Well, Bowen, this imaginary man we are talking about is, of course, you; but I am not a well-meaning friend, a parson, priest or doctor. I'm commanding the *Triton* and responsible to God and the Admiralty for the lives of the sixty or more men in her and for every sliver of wood and ounce of iron of which she's made.

'In a week or so we'll be in the West Indies,' he continued.

'The *Hannibal* recently lost 200 men from yellow jack. In the *Raisonable* frigate, thirty-six of her crew—one man in three—went over the standing part of the foresheet on a voyage of 300 miles. Yellow jack, a couple of broadsides from a French frigate, a mast going by the board in a squall—this could happen to us, and you'd have thirty men to attend to. And you'd be drunk. One more drink would be too much to pull you round,' he said angrily, throwing Bowen's phrase back at him, 'and a thousand wouldn't be enough.'

Once more Bowen's hands were pressing his temples. The authoritative air of the man of medicine had vanished; he was staring at the deck, a crumpled, liquor-stained and liquor-sodden apology for what had once been a man.

And, facing him, Ramage felt a desperate helplessness. Did the man need sympathy? No—he had that from the 'well-meaning friends'. Harshness? Presumably he'd had that from his wife. Discipline? There'd be no one to enforce it.

Yet there'd been the clues. The drinks in the morning and the secrecy. Bowen admitted he thought that was when the illness started. The secrecy, the shame, and yet underlying it all Ramage sensed there would still be a remnant of pride.

But where to begin? Damn the man; he had enough to think about without doctoring a doctor. Well, what set a man off drinking to excess? In a social sense—let's start there. Two types of drinkers—those who get drunk during the course of an enjoyable evening; those who arrived at a reception already half-drunk. Why? Because they were too shy to arrive sober: they needed a drink or two to give them courage to meet strangers. Was that a clue? Professional men—was the pattern the same?

'Bowen,' he said, 'give me an honest answer. Did you begin drinking heavily because you imagined you were losing some of your skill?'

Bowen nodded. 'A run of unsuccessful operations. Several patients died. Two were friends. I lost confidence; I needed a drink each time.'

'Think now; is that really how the drinking began? Because you lost confidence in yourself?'

The man refused to look up.

'Yes, that's how it began,' he said softly. 'To begin with, one drink was enough to restore the confidence. Then it needed two. Then three. But between each bout more of my confidence was gone—I think that was the trouble.'

'Right,' Ramage snapped. 'Now we know the cause: you lost your confidence. Why? *Were* you making mistakes?'

'I don't think so.'

'Don't *think*. You must know by now.'

'No, I wasn't making mistakes. I was trying too hard. I was expecting myself to perform miracles. I tried to cure people other doctors had given up.'

'So you know now you were deluding yourself; it wasn't that you'd lost your skill.'

'Yes,' the surgeon said miserably. 'I know *now*, today, but it's too late.'

'Oh no it's not!' Ramage exclaimed. 'For your sake, it'd better not be.'

But what to do now? Yes, the man still had some pride left. And common sense told Ramage that pride was the most important clue.

That was why he hated ordering the flogging—it gave a proud man an overpowering sense of disgrace and merely made a bad man worse. Pride made a good seaman—pride at being the first to reach a yard up the ratlines, at turning in a neater splice, making a better shirt than the purser sold.

'Bowen,' he said quietly, 'I believe that four years ago you were among the best of the doctors in London.'

The man nodded but still looked at the deck.

'For that reason I'm glad to have you as the surgeon in the *Triton*. My life might well depend on your skill, just as much as the life of any—and every—man in the ship's company. But we aren't in the Channel now, where constipation and rheumatics or "shamming Abraham" are all you have to prescribe for. We'll soon be in one of the unhealthiest spots in the world.

'This ship will arrive there with a greater advantage, medically speaking, than the present flagship: a fine surgeon.

'But before you are a damned bit of good to me and to the ship'—he spoke more sharply now—'*we* have to cure *you*. Or maybe you have to cure yourself. You're popular with the men; Southwick and I know your professional record. You've nothing to be ashamed of—providing you keep off the drink.'

'But I can't,' Bowen said with a shattering simplicity. 'It's no good me making any promises—I'd only break 'em. I promised my wife a thousand times, and since I've broken every promise to her, obviously I'd break one to you.'

Had Bowen unwittingly just prescribed his cure? Ramage said quickly:

'There'll be no promises, Bowen; simply an order. It may sound harsh, but remember this: I'm responsible for the well-being and efficiency of sixty men, apart from the safety of the ship and carrying out the orders I've received. If one man in this ship's company suffers through your drunkenness . . .' he left the threat unspoken.

'The order is this, Bowen: during the next four days you'll be rationed to a gill of rum a day, half at eleven o'clock, and half at supper-time. Southwick will issue it to you. For the four days after that you'll have half a gill, issued in the same way by Southwick. Then no more: not one drop.'

'Oh God,' Bowen groaned, 'you've no idea what you're doing . . .'

Perspiration soaked the man's clothes; it was dripping from his face. His hands trembled as they pressed against his temples; his eyes seemed glazed.

'I've no idea what private hell you'll be living in, I admit. But I know to what private hell you can send one of my seamen if you butcher him with an unnecessary or badly done amputation. Or kill him because you're too drunk to give him the right treatment for yellow jack or scurvy or whatever it happens to be.'

Bowen's whole body was shaking now and his eyes were focused on the cut-glass decanters in the rack behind Ramage.

'My orders will be given to Mr Southwick in a few minutes. There'll be a Marine sentry outside your door and you'll not leave your cabin without getting my permission. On the other hand you won't spend much time in your cabin: you're to stand watch with Mr Southwick. In other words, you'll only be in your cabin while I or Appleby are on watch.'

'Very well, sir.'

Bowen stood up and Ramage saw a cunning look in his eye.

'By the way,' Ramage added quietly, 'your cabin will be searched before you return to it. And my orders are that if you so much as sniff at the cork from a bottle of liquor, apart from your ration, you'll be placed under arrest; put in irons, if necessary.'

'But I'm the surgeon,' Bowen protested weakly. 'You can't put me in irons like a common seaman. I'll protest to the Admiral. I'll demand that you be brought to trial ... for oppression, for defiance of the *Regulations*, for——'

'I can have you put in irons, Bowen: one Marine can carry out *that* order, and the devil take any *Regulations*. As for protesting to the Admiral—well, you'll have been in irons for days before you get within a mile of the flagship. And even from a hundred yards away, you'll find it hard to deliver your protest if you're in irons. Now, get up on deck while someone clears the drink from your cabin!'

Bowen shambled out and Ramage, feeling like a man who'd been flogging a stray dog with a horse-whip, passed the word for Southwick, who came down with such alacrity he'd obviously been waiting anxiously to hear what had happened.

Nodding his head as Ramage related what had passed, he looked doubtful when he heard of the order, then nodded again when Ramage said the surgeon would be sharing his watch.

'Aye,' he said, 'it may work the cure. If it does, you'll have saved his life the same as fishing him out of the sea. It's the loneliness that'll be hard to bear. I think you've hit on it, sir: we've got to keep him occupied every moment he's awake. I've been told he's a great chess player.'

That remark seemed so irrelevant that Ramage snapped:

'That's a great help. Rum and checkmate in two moves.'

The Master grinned. 'No sir, I meant that perhaps a few games of chess would help. D'you play?'

'Badly. I just about know the moves.'

'I'm not much good either; but maybe it'd do his self-respect a bit o' good to beat the pair of us, because his self-respect's all he's got to save him.'

'Is there a set of chessmen on board?'

'Yes—I've a nice set I bought in the Levant years ago. Used to play a lot in my last ship—sorry, not the *Kathleen*, the one before that.'

'Very well, Mr Southwick. By the way, see that Bowen eats regular meals, even if they choke him. And we'll make it part of the treatment—or punishment—that he has to play a couple of games of chess with you every forenoon, and with me every evening. It may bore him; but who knows, it may make us chess champions of the Caribbean!'

*

Late in the afternoon four days later Southwick came up to Ramage on the quarterdeck and, indicating the men at the wheel within earshot, said, 'I'd like to have a word with you, sir.'

The Master looked worried: his usual cheerful face was—well, Ramage couldn't be sure. Not angry, not depressed—puzzled, perhaps. The two men walked aft to the taffrail and Ramage raised his eyebrows.

'It's Bowen, sir.'

'It's always Bowen,' Ramage said irritably, 'but I thought he was looking a lot better this morning.'

Southwick brightened up. 'That's just it, sir! He didn't come to me for his tot this morning, nor at four o'clock. I've just luffed up to leeward of him and his breath doesn't smell of drink. I think,' he said with something approaching awe in his voice, and pronouncing each word carefully in case Ramage missed the significance, 'I think he hasn't had a drink all day.'

Ramage stared at him; Southwick stared back. Both men seemed to be looking at some sea monster or ghost; at something they could hardly let themselves believe.

For a few moments Ramage wondered if this was the end of a nightmare which had begun three days ago. The day after

132

his order to the surgeon, he, Southwick and the Marine sentry had ended up wrestling with a violent and screaming Bowen: a man temporarily insane. Even as they held him pinned to the deck in the wardroom he'd been screaming things which made Ramage's blood run cold: a telescope in a rack over the doorway to Southwick's cabin had become, in Bowen's frenzied mind, a Barbary pirate's sword which was whirling and twisting in the air without a hand to guide it but intent on disembowelling him. Then the moon-faced Marine had become a roaring lion and the wardroom a jungle in which Bowen was lost and about to be savaged. The deckhead and beams above had then suddenly become the upper part of a giant press that was slowly descending to crush him. The Marine's red jacket became tongues of flame setting the ship on fire. And so it had gone on.

By the time they managed to calm the man down they were all shaking, not only from the effort of holding him but because they were completely unnerved: Bowen's fears had been real enough to his tortured mind and his screams and frenzied yells of warning gave a terrible reality to his delusions. His shouts as the pirate's sword swooped and twisted, missing him each time by only an inch or so, almost made it visible in their own imaginations as well as his. As they glanced up at the deckhead on which Bowen's eyes had been focused, wide and staring, his hands fighting to get free to try to push it back up and prevent the press crushing him, to Ramage at least it seemed for a moment the deckhead was actually moving down.

That night two Marines had guarded Bowen in his cabin and for his own sake Ramage had him secured in a hurriedly-made strait-jacket. Next morning the delusions had gone and he remembered Southwick was to issue his drink and the Marines had to restrain him until the proper time.

After he'd had the drink he'd been all right for most of the afternoon, only becoming wild an hour before his evening tot was due. Later Southwick had made him march up and down the quarterdeck for the first part of the night and Ramage had kept him up for most of the rest, until the man was so physically exhausted he'd begged to be allowed to go down to his cabin to sleep.

Next morning he'd been ordered up on deck again and Southwick, with a dogged relentlessness, had made him talk.

Finally he'd brought the subject round to chess and, after provoking an argument about it, had made a contemptuous challenge that he'd beat Bowen at a game even giving him an advantage of a rook and a bishop.

That had made Bowen so angry he'd accepted the challenge —but only on condition Southwick gave him no advantage. At the change of watch both men had gone down to the wardroom for a meal without Bowen remembering his tot was due.

As Southwick related it to Ramage afterwards, the game had been vicious: the Master had found himself in difficulty within five moves. Faced with a disastrous defeat inside ten minutes, instead of the game lasting the intended hour or so, Southwick had used a trifling excuse to get up from the table, knocking over the chessmen as he did so. Bowen had been unruffled, started a new game, and within ten minutes Southwick was again facing checkmate.

Arguments, moves and counter-moves, mate and checkmates; games lost by Southwick with Bowen playing a rook and bishop short; successive games lost with Bowen not having a queen on the board either, had taken them up to suppertime. Then Bowen had demanded both his noon and evening tots together but received without argument only one.

That night Ramage sensed the chess victories had done something to Bowen and later heard him good-naturedly baiting Southwick, offering to play him with the Master using bishops as extra queens.

And now here Southwick was reporting—on a day when a succession of squalls had kept the watch on deck so busy furling and setting sail that there had been no time for chess— that not only had Bowen failed to demand his tots but apparently was not broaching a secret supply either ...

'I'd be glad of your company at supper, Mr Southwick, and Bowen, too. Perhaps you'd pass the invitation to him. Put your chess set in my cabin, and warn Appleby he might be relieved late tonight.'

Southwick grinned and walked forward to find Bowen, leaving a puzzled Ramage pacing the deck. It was too quick for a cure; but instinctively he felt that at least Bowen was getting the right treatment.

That night, as the steward Douglas took away the plates and removed the cloth he did not, as he would have otherwise done, put down fresh glasses and a decanter. Instead, Ramage glanced up at Bowen and said innocently, 'I hear you have been giving Southwick a thrashing at chess.'

Bowen laughed and looked slightly embarrassed.

'Southwick hasn't had the practice I have.'

'Is it simply practice?'

The surgeon was obviously torn between honesty and a wish to avoid hurting Southwick's feelings.

'Mostly, sir. There are certain basic situations you learn about and try to avoid—or create.'

'Trouble is, I haven't a good memory,' Southwick growled.

'Memory hasn't a lot to do with it, unless you want to use some of the stylized opening gambits. That makes for a dull game anyway.'

Ramage was interested now, having always complacently blamed his poor play on a notoriously bad memory.

'Come, Bowen! Surely a good memory is important.'

'No, sir,' the surgeon protested, 'That's a commonly held view but a wrong one, I'm afraid. I'd say the two most important factors are an eye to spot a trap, and the will to keep attacking.'

Southwick eyed Ramage. 'You should be a champion, sir.'

'Yes,' Bowen said eagerly before an embarrassed Ramage could interrupt. 'From what I've heard you should be a first-class player and I'm surprised you're not.'

'There's not much time to play chess at sea . . .'

'No,' the surgeon admitted, 'but——'

'Yes, we've got time for a couple of games now. But I warn you, I'm hopeless. Southwick, you can act as a frigate—keep a weather eye open for enemy traps. You agree, Bowen?'

'Certainly, but I'm sure it won't be necessary.'

'I haven't played for a couple of years: I can barely remember the moves.'

Douglas, previously primed, moved forward with the chess board and an inlaid box containing the chessmen. Bowen opened the box, took out two pieces, juggled them in his hands beneath the table, then held them both up for Ramage to choose.

It was white, and they set up the board. Ramage remembered vaguely that advancing a king pawn two places was regarded as a good safe opening move and made it. After that, it was like trying to repel dozens of boarders single-handed in thick smoke. Despite Southwick watching every move, pointing out possible threats, Bowen's bishops, knights and rooks were everywhere and apparently doubled in numbers. Three of Ramage's pawns, a bishop, then a rook were dropped in the box as they were taken. A knight and the other bishop followed; Bowen had lifted the queen off the board and dropped it in the box and it was only when he moved his knight into her place that Ramage saw what had happened. Bowen had merely said 'Check' and, as Ramage went to move the king out of danger, added politely, 'I really do think it's checkmate, sir.'

'And it is, by God!' exclaimed Southwick. 'Well I . . .'

'Me too,' Ramage said ruefully. 'I'm glad we didn't have a guinea on that game.'

'I prefer not to play cards or chess for money, sir,' Bowen said. 'Makes for bad feeling if someone gets excited and turns what's supposed to be a game into something approaching a duel, with cash if not honour at stake. It doesn't improve the game, either.'

'Quite right,' Southwick rumbled. 'Quite right—hate to see it myself. What about another game—and you leave the queen and both bishops in the box.

Bowen hesitated and looked up at Ramage, who guessed he was thinking it was perhaps unwise to beat his captain too often.

'And a knight and a rook too!'

'I'm sure that won't be necessary,' the surgeon said, reassured. 'After all, I've been playing the game for . . .'

He broke off, embarrassed, but Southwick grinned, '. . . more years than the Captain's been born . . .'

'Well, yes, but I didn't——'

Ramage said, 'That gives me an excellent excuse for losing every game. Your first move, Bowen. Now, Southwick, keep a sharp lookout! If I ever become an admiral and command my own squadron, I'm getting more and more doubtful about letting you command a frigate!'

In nine moves Bowen looked up at Ramage, who said, ruefully, 'Don't bother to say it—checkmate!'

The third game lasted several more moves and Ramage was able to watch the surgeon. The hands still trembled but the eyes were clearer. The greyness of the skin had not quite gone but the face muscles had tightened up and the mouth did not hang open slackly. Clean linen, stock neatly tied . . . And Bowen was alert; in fact a new man. It sounded a cliché but Ramage could think of no other description. Alert, decisive, and completely in control of both himself and the situation. His eyes would move across the board three or four times, then his hand would reach out and without a moment's hesitation move a piece with thumb and index finger (all too often lifting off one of Ramage's pieces with the ring and little finger at the same time) and he'd wait without fidgeting while Ramage tried to think up a counter-move, often aided by Southwick. When the game ended, Bowen, at Ramage's request, explained some of their worst mistakes. They seemed obvious enough—afterwards.

Finally the Master said: 'I'd better go and relieve the master's mate—he's had his watch stretched out. If you'll excuse me . . .'

Ramage nodded, but the surgeon made no move to leave.

Instead he put the chessmen back in the box and folded the board. For a moment Ramage wondered if he should make some remark, but Bowen, looking at the table top, said:

'This is the first day for more than three years . . .'

Ramage still said nothing, deciding it was best for Bowen to unburden himself if he wished, or keep silent.

'. . . I've wanted it, God knows—but perhaps God has also given me the strength not to go to Southwick's cabin and beg . . .'

It took Ramage several moments to realize the significance of that single word 'beg'. Bowen had at last fully recovered his pride: to him, getting a drink now meant 'begging' one from the Master, whom he'd roundly beaten at chess and who——

'. . . Not just God, though . . . I think the last few days must have been just as bad for you and Southwick as for me . . .'

He was silent for a minute or two and Ramage said:

'Perhaps not in the way you are thinking. We were only afraid we'd fail.'

'You mean that *I* would fail,' Bowen corrected gently.

'No, I think the first three days were up to us. After that it was up to you.'

'I only pray I can keep it up. But I'm not going to make you any promises, sir, and I hope you won't ask for them.'

Ramage shook his head.

CHAPTER TEN

Southwick's last sight put the *Triton* roughly three hundred miles north-north-east of Barbados and he was reporting the fact to Ramage when the lookout in the foremast hailed the quarter-deck to report a sail lifting up over the horizon fine on the starboard bow.

The young master's mate, sent aloft with a telescope, was soon shouting excitedly that the ship had a strange rig and seemed to be steering to the north-west. Southwick growled his doubt—that would be the course of a ship bound from West Africa to round the northern Leeward Islands and then square away for America.

Then Appleby reported hesitantly, his voice revealing doubt, that she'd lost her mainmast, and a few moments later, this time with more certainty, that she was fore-and-aft rigged; probably a schooner which had lost her mainmast, because the only mast standing was too far forward for her to be a cutter.

Ramage had already ordered the quartermaster to steer a converging course, and as Southwick sent hands to sheets and braces, he called Jackson, ordering him aloft. Handing the American his telescope, he said: 'She might be a "black-birder".'

'Was thinking that m'self, sir: position's about right if she's staying outside the islands and bound for America.'

With that he ran forward and climbed the shrouds.

Southwick bent over the compass for the third time, grunting as he stood up.

'If she's making more than a couple of knots I'd be very surprised; her bearing's hardly changed.'

Bowen, who was standing near Southwick, said almost to himself, 'If she lost her mast some days ago she'll be in trouble.'

'Aye,' Southwick said heavily. 'Losing a mast is always trouble. Especially in these seas. She'll be rolling like a barrel—wind on the beam.'

'No, I meant provisions,' Bowen said. 'A few hundred slaves . . . I don't imagine they carry more than the bare minimum of provisions based on a fast passage.'

And Ramage found himself nodding as he listened: he'd been thinking that as he warned Jackson. The schooners in the West African slave trade usually made a fast passage from the Gulf of Guinea across the Atlantic to the West Indies and America. An extra week meant tons of extra food and water.

'Deck there!'

'Well, Jackson?'

'She's a "blackbirder" all right, sir. Lost her mainmast all right, but the foremast's standing and she's carrying a foresail, topsail and headsails.'

Bowen was enjoying himself for the first time in his two years at sea: previously he'd been too besotted to care that each successive ship to which he'd been transferred had been smaller; to him the *Triton* had been just another small cabin in which he could stretch himself out with a bottle and glass. Rarely in those two years had he ever gone on deck, and then only if he had to make a report to the captain.

Now, beginning with the enforced walks on deck with Southwick, he was taking an interest in the handling of a ship. Most of it was still strange—such a mass of ropes, and he didn't understand many of the shouted orders or the reasons for them. But he saw now that what always seemed confusion was in fact highly organized movement by the men.

And with his mind now clear for the first time in years— he'd been four days without touching liquor—Bowen tried to analyse why the *Triton*'s captain was such a remarkable young man.

Watching him talking to Southwick, Bowen realized for the first time that they were an oddly assorted pair. Apart from anything else the Master was more than old enough to be his captain's father yet was clearly devoted to him. And Bowen saw that such devotion came as much from a professional respect as a personal regard.

The lieutenant wasn't as tall as he looked—it was the wide shoulders set on a slim body, and the narrow face, that gave the impression of height. Yet there was something more—was it poise? Bowen knew it was an odd word to use about a naval officer standing on the quarterdeck of one of the King's ships rolling along in the Trades, but it was the right one, because he both belonged there and commanded it. Uniforms apart, anyone suddenly arriving on board would never have to ask who was the captain.

Nor was it just his physical appearance. No, more that one sensed his power rather than saw it. Like a clock! Bowen grinned happily at the aptness of the simile. Yes, a clock in an elegant case. It looked well whether in a drawing-room or the cabin of a ship; and it regulated all their lives without fuss and without them realizing it. And since the clock kept accurate time and was so perfectly controlled one forgot there was more to it than the face and the case; forgot that inside was a powerful mainspring controlling a complicated mechanism, and from that mainspring everything else about it derived. True, there were escapements and other pieces of finely-engineered machinery to control the mainspring, but without it all the rest was useless.

And so many men, Bowen reflected, were born without the equivalent of that mainspring. Perhaps only one in a thousand had it; less than one in ten thousand had one that never faltered.

Curious the way he occasionally rubs the older scar over his right brow—never the newer one. Even more curious how he snatches away his hand the moment he realizes he's doing it, as though ashamed of the habit. There, he did it again—and Bowen saw it was instinctive: he rubbed it when he was thinking hard, and probably when nervous, though the youngster seemed to have nerves of steel. And now he's snatched the hand away again and clasped both hands behind his back.

A fine profile. Face on the thin side, half-starved aristocratic, and it made the jawline seem harder than it was. But the eyes—Bowen almost shivered. Dark brown, deep-set beneath thick black eyebrows, they mirrored his moods. They'd laughed when he'd checkmated him for the fifth time, Bowen recalled, but by God a few days earlier they'd bored into him like a pair of augers when Ramage tried to discover what had started the drinking. And they'd been cold and hard when giving the order to stop the drink.

And Bowen realized that until this moment he'd never fully accepted that the captain was barely twenty-one. Yes, he'd hated the probing questions; he'd hated the order depriving him of his liquor. He'd hated Ramage, too, but the hatred had been aimed against his authority, against a person with the power to stop the liquor. Never for a moment had he even resented that the man giving the orders was only a youth.

Bowen then thought carefully *why* he'd just accepted it. Well, it seemed appropriate: the man had a natural air of authority—and it *was* natural, not just because Ramage had a legal authority backed up by the Articles of War. This much Bowen had learned only in the last few days, because for the first weeks after Ramage had taken over command Bowen had been too drunk to realize there was even a risk of mutiny, let alone that the ship's company had refused to weigh anchor at Spithead.

In fact, Bowen admitted, he was now both resentful and ashamed that drink had made him miss the battle of wills: it would have been fascinating to see how one man could by sheer strength of character—since the Articles of War were useless in such circumstances—force sixty men to carry out his orders, sail the ship clear of the Channel, and by the time she was off Cadiz have spliced the two separate sections of the crew, the original Tritons and the twenty-five men from the *Lively*, into one and have them working cheerfully together, proud of their ship and proud of their captain. It was a feat of leadership that interested him both as a man and a doctor.

Southwick had clearly been a great help. Watching the stockily-built Master, his white hair flowing out from under his hat, his face as chubby and red as a farmer's, it was obvious he and the Captain formed a remarkable partnership.

Although Southwick obviously wasn't overburdened with brains he had a generous nature, was a fine seaman, and from all accounts was a demon for battle and quite fearless. Bowen had yet to see him lose his temper: if a seaman was hesitant about the way something should be done, Southwick made sure the proper way was explained to him. That, too, was true leadership and rare since in most ships a hesitant seaman caught a bosun's mate's 'starter' across his shoulders.

And he knew enough of the Service to realize that years ago Southwick had failed to get that essential 'interest' on the part of a captain or admiral to become the master of a ship of the line. Instead, he had always remained in fourth- and fifth-rate ships—cutters, brigs and suchlike.

Yet in one way this was probably a good thing—in the *Triton*, with a ship's company of sixty or so, Southwick's cheerful personality and superb seamanship was a powerful influence: probably the most powerful single influence in the hour-to-hour running of the brig. He'd be wasted in a ship of the line, where three or four lieutenants between him and the captain would swamp his merits.

Anyway, the important thing was that Southwick was happy to serve under a captain who must be a third of his age. An elderly master with a young captain could, through jealousy (or more likely, a justifiable contempt for the young captain's abilities) make everyone's life a misery by just carrying out his duties to the letter—but no more—and tripping up the captain.

It was easy enough with an inexperienced young captain who owed rapid promotion to his father's influence with an admiral or in politics.

Here, then, was a remarkable combination: an old master wise enough to know when to give advice; and a young captain with enough confidence in himself to listen to it.

Yet Bowen also saw how lonely was the Captain's life. By tradition he lived on board in isolation; he had all his meals alone—unless he invited one of the officers, which in the *Triton* meant Southwick or himself; and on his shoulders rested the safety of the ship and the safety and welfare of the crew.

Whether the ship was in storm or sunshine, the crew sick, healthy, happy or mutinous, if she was well sailed or badly navigated ... all was the Captain's responsibility. One mistake on his part could sink the ship, kill a man—or kill the whole ship's company. Bowen shivered at the thought and was thankful the responsibility for the men's medical welfare was the only one that sat on his own shoulders—and one, come to think of it, which also ultimately rested on the Captain's.

Bowen had been so absorbed that he was surprised to see

how close the *Triton* now was to the other ship. She looked deuced odd with just the one mast instead of two, but her hull was shapely: none of the boxiness of a ship o' war. Seeing Jackson swinging off the lower ratlines to the deck and walking aft to report, Bowen edged over to listen.

'She's not American, sir: I'll take an oath on that.'

'But she's hoisted the American flag,' Ramage said mildly.

'Aye, sir, and she's not Spanish even though she hoisted the Spanish flag for a couple of minutes before she ran up the American. She's just not built right, sir.'

Bowen listened more attentively, realizing he'd not heard hails about the flags.

Southwick said: 'From the course she's steering I think she's bound for one of the Carolina ports: she's staying so far to seaward. I'll take a bet she plans to round Antigua and Barbuda and then square away for somewhere like Charleston.'

'She may be bound there, sir,' Jackson said respectfully, 'but she's not American built.'

Ramage was puzzled, because she looked American to him: beamy, low freeboard, a sweeping sheer—really a beautiful sheer—and schooner-rigged. Obviously very fast, and specially built for the slave trade.

'What makes you so certain, Jackson?'

'Hard to say, sir. Nothing particular, just that she doesn't look right for an American-built ship.'

'Not having a mainmast alters her appearance,' Southwick pointed out. 'And her bulwarks are all smashed up amidships. That gives her an odd look.'

Over the past few months he'd grown to like the American and respected him; otherwise the idea of actually discussing such a thing with a seaman would have been unthinkable.

'Well, we'll soon know,' Ramage said. 'Juggling with flags makes me wonder.'

'Could have been a mistake,' Southwick said. 'The Spanish flag wasn't up long.'

Ramage nodded, rubbing his brow.

'That's true, and they've obviously had to rig signal halyards. Nevertheless, Mr Southwick, give the gunner's mate the key to the magazine and beat to quarters if you please. Some of her bulwark may be stove in, but she carries five guns a side, and that's all we have.'

With only the foremast standing the ship certainly looked odd, but to Bowen's eyes there was something else: the way she was painted. Although the lower part of the hull was black, the upper part, including her bulwarks, was green. But the foremast was white and by contrast almost invisible against the glaring blue of the sky.

The green strake on her hull was dark: not the green of the sea in northern waters, more the green of Tropical vegetation. And with most ships' masts painted black or a buff colour, one's eye was always surprised at seeing any variation.

He commented on it to Ramage, who nodded.

'The hallmark of a "blackbirder",' he explained. 'Like the rest of them she has to go up the big rivers in the Gulf of Guinea to load the slaves, and our ships are watching for her. But it's almost impossible to spot a black hull with that wide strake of dark green hiding in a river close up against the mangroves. Because they're painted white the masts don't show against the sky-line. You'd expect light blue to be more effective, but somehow it isn't.

Vaguely Bowen remembered the violent Abolitionist rows there'd been in London a year or so ago, but he'd been drinking too heavily at the time to be able to recall the details.

'Where do we stand on slavery now?'

Ramage laughed bitterly.

'Somewhere in the middle. The House of Commons agreed to Wilberforce's bill for Abolition in '91—that's six years ago. That said the slave trade would gradually slow down and then stop altogether in January last year.'

'So we've forbidden it?'

'No—when the bill went to the House of Lords they sat on it. Wilberforce has tried to push it through, but the Revolution in France frightened a lot of his supporters. Then when Wilberforce reminded the Commons in January last year that the date on which they'd already agreed slavery should stop had just passed and the House of Lords still hadn't moved on the Bill, you can guess what happened: being politicians they voted to postpone consideration for six months, since it was highly controversial. That's the last I heard of it. But of course there's the Act of 1788.'

Bowen, who'd taken little interest in either politics or

Abolition, shook his head.

'I don't recall the details. What did that do?'

'Not much—it set out minimum standards for British slavers. Not less than five feet headroom between decks for example, and a slaver of less than 160 tons burthen can carry only five slaves for every three tons; and three for every two tons if she's less than 150 tons . . .'

'How strictly does the Navy enforce the law?'

'Oh, very strictly—when a ship's found breaking it. That's not very often and they pay a small fine. Means nothing to these fellows.'

Just as Bowen was about to ask another question, Ramage ordered Southwick to get a boat ready for hoisting out, with an armed boarding party.

Bowen then saw a skilful display of near insubordination by Southwick, realizing half-way through that there must have been many similar arguments in the past on the same subject.

After Southwick had given the order which set men preparing the boat and sent boarders to collect cutlasses and pistols, he said casually to Ramage that he was going below to change his uniform.

When the Captain raised his eyebrows questioningly, Southwick explained, as though stating the obvious, that the uniform he was wearing was shabby. The Captain, equally innocently, replied that since he'd worn it on board for several weeks, it hardly mattered now since no one would be seeing him, but would Mr Southwick please take the conn for a few minutes while he himself went down to change.

It had been Southwick's turn to raise his eyebrows, and Bowen was quite surprised how high they went: they seemed to slide half-way up his forehead.

'But surely, sir, you'd prefer me to board her.'

Bowen knew he'd burst out laughing if he continued watching the exchange and turned away. If the pair of them played chess as skilfully as they politely battled with words . . . Southwick was patient and polite; so was the Captain. Finally Ramage said flatly he was going and that was that. Southwick merely replied, 'Aye aye, sir,' and turned away with a sigh.

By now the brig's carronades were loaded and run out; the decks were wetted and sand spread—though just as Bowen noticed the water was drying quickly on the hot planks,

Southwick called for the men to carry on wetting, so they continued walking back and forth, splashing liberally from leather buckets.

And Bowen was thoroughly enjoying himself. The sky more blue than ever he remembered it; the sea more vivid and sparkling. The squat carronades now became menacing weapons of war; boys, hitherto noisy wretches always up to mischief, now sat on their cartridge boxes along the centre-line, one between each gun on either side, and their nickname, 'powder monkeys', for once was appropriate.

Then behind him he heard Ramage talking to Southwick.

'Looks as though she's going to need a shot across her bow.'

'No, sir,' Southwick grunted and Bowen turned to see him watching the schooner through the telescope. 'No, there's a group of men round the mast—reckon the halyards are in a fair tangle with all the jury rigging they've had to set up to hold the mast.'

Even as he spoke the flying jib began to drop and flap, men out on the bowsprit stifling it as it came down. The peak of the foresail gaff dipped slightly, then dropped a few more feet. Suddenly the schooner turned to starboard, heading up into the wind, and the gaff dropped quickly, the big sail bellying before being swiftly sheeted in. Within a couple of minutes the schooner was wallowing in the swell waves, every sail furled.

'He wants some help from us all right,' Southwick commented.

Bowen saw his chance and seized it.

'That falling mast must have injured a lot of men, sir,' he said to Ramage, who eyed him thoughtfully, then smiled and nodded.

'Yes—I'll take your mate with me.'

Bowen's disappointment showed in his face and Ramage laughed.

'All right, Bowen: stow your butcher's tools in a bag!'

*

Five minutes after the *Triton* had hove-to four hundred yards to windward of the schooner, the jolly boat, with Jackson at the tiller and Bowen and Ramage sitting in the sternsheets, was pulling down towards her. With her sails furled and so much windage on the foremast and bowsprit, she had paid off to lie with her starboard quarter towards the approaching boat.

Bowen was surprised how high the seas were. From the deck of the *Triton* he had, for many days, seen them roll up astern, sweep under her and go on ahead; but against an empty horizon there was nothing to measure them. The *Triton* had hove-to only a couple of cables to windward but the jolly boat was barely half-way between before both were hidden from view each time it dropped into the troughs.

Jackson eased over the tiller so the boat passed across the schooner's stern, and as Ramage turned slightly to look at her he grunted. Bowen looked questioningly.

'Don't point and don't stare at it as we get closer; but her name's been changed recently.'

'How do you know, sir?'

'Just look at the reflection from the paint on the transom.'

Bowen read the schooner's name—*The Two Brothers*—painted on a strip of paint that was not only fresher than the rest but a couple of feet wider than the name: there was a good foot to spare before 'The' and after 'Brothers'.

'You mean the new paint's covering another name!' he exclaimed excitedly. 'Why, yes! The original letters—oh, blast it, I can't see them now—but they're raised up a bit and I spotted them in the reflection.'

Ramage nodded. 'But her captain will tell us she's *The Two Brothers* of Charleston . . . and have papers to prove it.'

His voice was flat and Bowen wasn't sure he'd understood; but he saw Ramage had again turned slightly to keep the schooner in view without being too obvious about it. They were close now—forty or fifty feet. Bowen could hear the heavy splash as the schooner's counter plunged down each time she pitched.

Ramage, his lips hardly moving, was saying something to Jackson.

'In addition to the broadside guns she has ten one-pounder swivels on the bulwarks, set well inboard. Easy to squat on the bulwarks and fire them across the decks. Useful if the slaves make trouble, and notice each of 'em has a couple of men lounging near-by . . . Barking dogs—they'll be big, savage brutes, trained to attack anyone with a dark skin . . . There! Through the entry port, did you see that flash of brass? A nasty big brass blunderbuss. There'll be plenty of those on board . . . Phew!'

As he spoke the rest of the men in the boat, both oarsmen and boarders, groaned in protest and Bowen felt sick. They were now just to the leeward of the schooner and thirty feet off, and the wind brought down a stink which made the Fleet Ditch smell as fresh as a pomander full of new lavender.

The surgeon realized the men were not just groaning; they were protesting. And well they might. The schooner smelled like a gigantic midden, and though accustomed to the stench of hospitals and narrow streets piled with muck which was cleared away only by the rains and scavenging dogs and rats, he found this was worse because it was caused by two or three hundred human beings chained below in the schooner.

No seaman could bear the sight of a 'blackbirder'—he'd just realized that. And it was a curious thing, Bowen reflected, since a seaman's life on board a ship o' war of any nation seemed, to a landman, little removed from slavery.

Suddenly Jackson was singing out a string of orders, oars were being tossed, the boat was alongside and the bowman hooked on. Ramage, already standing, waited as the boat rose on a crest and jumped for the wooden rungs of the rope ladder hanging over the bulwark. A moment later he was climbing up it and Bowen was praying he'd even be able to grab the ladder, let alone do it as lightly and easily. The boat dropped in the crest and Jackson said quietly, 'If you'll excuse me, sir—just in case there's any trouble up there . . .'

With that he squeezed in front of Bowen, jumped and in a moment or two was out of sight over the bulwark. Feeling particularly clumsy, Bowen waited as the boat rose on the next crest, jumped and clung desperately to the ladder. As he climbed laboriously he remembered his bag of instruments and turned to see a seaman holding it and waving him on. He just had time to note ruefully that being a seaman involved having a mind that grasped everything like a fifty-tentacled octopus before he reached the deck.

As he looked round he was immediately reminded of standing back-stage at a theatre watching a dress rehearsal before the opening night, when everyone was in the right costume and speaking the right words, but the stage was littered with carpenters finishing off the scenery. The remains of the main-mast were lying along the deck surrounded by wood shavings and carpenters' tools: the bulwark opposite was broken down; the deck gouged and dirty.

Ramage was standing stiffly in front of a very tall, very thin man, who was completely bald, and Bowen realized his captain had just ignored the hand proffered to be shaken.

The tall man, wearing a faded red woollen shirt, grubby, once-white cotton trousers, and a red band round his forehead to stop perspiration running into his eyes, let his hand drop to his side again. He spoke with an American accent.

Ramage had already introduced himself and now asked: 'What ship is this?'

'Well, now 'tenant, you saw the name clear enough didn't you?'

'That doesn't answer my question.'

'I guess it'll have to, 'tenant, because that's us—*The Two Brothers*.'

'It won't, though,' Ramage said flatly. 'I'd like to see the ship's papers.'

'Gladly, 'tenant, gladly. Perhaps you'd step below.'

'Are you the captain?'

'Yes, the master under God, as they say: Ebenezer Wheeler, 'tenant, at your service.'

He gave a mocking bow and as his shirt front fell open Bowen realized he was not just bald but completely hairless. Common enough after some of these jungle fevers . . .

'Perhaps you'd introduce your officers.'

Wheeler refused the bait.

'That won't be necessary, 'tenant. Now you just come below and inspect my papers. I've a favour to ask, too.'

He pointed aft and Bowen saw that as Ramage turned he glanced at Jackson. To the American captain it would have been imperceptible; but Bowen knew some order or idea had been passed. As Ramage walked to the companionway, followed by the American captain, Bowen noticed that Jackson stood so that as the *Triton*'s boarders came up over the bulwark they'd be bunched up. A whispered instruction could be heard by all of them.

As Ramage strode towards the companionway he hurriedly summed up what he had seen—his eyes had been noting facts which his brain could not attend to while he talked with the captain. The mainmast was broken off eight or ten feet above

150

the deck and they'd managed to get it back on board, where it was now lying diagonally across the deck. The topmast wasn't in sight: that must have been lost, along with the gaff.

Enough wood chips and shavings to fill a dozen sacks were scattered around the deck where men had chopped off the jagged splinters and begun to shape the stump and the upper part ready to scarph the two pieces together. But the carpenters' tools were lying around as if no one had done any work for a day or so. The only adze in sight had bright red rust marks on the blade, and there were flecks of new rust on three saws. Why had work stopped? Scarphing was no problem.

It wouldn't be easy to get the mast up even though the foremast was standing. Not easy, but not impossible since they could rig shearlegs. They'd need to use a dozen or so pieces of two-by-four-inch planks to make the splints at the join—'making a fish' as the carpenters called it. But he hadn't noticed a single plank on deck...

What else?

Four huge brindle-coloured hounds held by seamen on rope leashes; men standing around, apparently idling, but each with a brass musketoon by his side. And another smell—a curious, familiar odour which wasn't part of the stench of a slave ship, but which for the moment he couldn't recognize.

And from below the rhythmic moaning—like monks chanting in a distant hilltop monastery—of the slaves lamenting. A small pile of whips at the foot of the foremast—brutal affairs, handles eight feet long and tails as much again, knotted every few inches.

As he turned to go down the companionway Ramage was able to see Jackson had understood, and the ten men forming the boarding party also appeared to be standing about idly—but they were between the slave ship's crew and the ladder to the captain's cabin.

The cabin was the full width of the ship and surprisingly large, but the headroom was surprisingly low. Well furnished, too—a silver teapot and some good china in a rack at the end of a table made of fine-grained, highly-polished mahogany. A cavalry sword with a curious silver-thread pattern on the scabbard rested in a rack on the starboard side. Four or five cut-glass decanters, the many faceted stoppers winking as they reflected the light, sat elegantly in fitted racks on the sideboard. And a long bookcase with several books in it. Leather bindings worn and mottled in dark stains where the mildew had attacked. A cloth flung over the books hung down just enough to hide the titles. Curious, for otherwise the cabin was very tidy. Ramage found it hard to think of the captain reading books. Again the curious odour.

The American followed him in and pointed to a chair as he went to a small desk beneath the large skylight. His head was small, the nose narrow but prominent, the ears large with pendulous lobes. Chin narrow and long. The baldness made the man's head in profile look like a vulture's.

He took a folder from a drawer in the desk and as he put it down he grinned, exposing teeth yellowed with decay and tobacco juice.

'First, 'tenant, what'll you drink?'

Ramage shook his head.

'Now, now,' the American chided, 'can't have the Royal Navy accusing us Jonathan of being inhospitable.'

'You've offered hospitality,' Ramage smiled frostily, 'but the sun's not over the foreyardarm yet.'

'True, true. Now, look'ee here'—he opened the folder and took out papers—'Certificate of registry, duly signed and sealed in Charleston . . . Bills of lading . . . Charter agreement with Benson and Company of Charleston, signatures duly witnessed . . . Everything's here and in regular form.'

Ramage took the certificate of registry and unfolded it. Glancing at Wheeler's hands he saw they were filthy and obviously always were, but the certificate was clean. The paper was thick and had been folded twice. Ramage inspected the document and then folded it once and put it back on the desk. The upper side lifted slightly. The certificate said the ship had been built at Charleston five years earlier, but the certificate—and the paper on which it was written—was at most a few months old.

'The muster book?'

Ramage watched Wheeler closely and the American's eyes glanced for a moment not at the desk but at the sideboard and then focused on the folder.

'Well, 'tenant, to be truthful I don't know where it is right now, and anyway I can't see it's any interest to the British Navy.'

'On the contrary, it's of great interest. If you've any British seamen on board, I can press them——'

'Well, we don't have, so you can rest assured on that point.'

'I'd still like to see it. Perhaps you'd get it from the sideboard.'

Wheeler looked up, startled for a moment; then his eyes narrowed. His cranium had a ridge across the top that came down the brow to his nose.

'Now see here, 'tenant, I'm not used to being dictated to on board m' own ship. You go back and tell your captain that.'

'I am the captain,' Ramage said shortly. 'You had a favour to ask, I believe.'

'Oh yes,' Wheeler said with an easy grin. 'You've seen the mainmast, or what's left of it. We lost it eight days ago—after being becalmed in the Middle Passage for thirteen days— thirteen days! Never been becalmed there for more than three. Then this squall caught us in the dark. Took us three days to get the mast back on board and the foremast jury rigged so we could set a stitch of canvas.'

'So you've used up more than three weeks' extra provisions. You're three weeks' short in other words.'

'That's about the size of it. Still several bags of yams and coconuts left. Short of rice and beans. Plenty of palm oil. And we catch fish—they love it, heads and all. Lucky we've plenty of brandy: they get two tots a day—keeps 'em happy so they don't notice they're hungry. But all that's not so important: we haven't the lumber to fish the mainmast—without tearing the ship apart—and make up a gaff. I need six ten-foot lengths of two by four and a spar for the gaff. I'll pay well for it—can you help?'

Suddenly Ramage recognized the odour. Garlic. The whole ship reeked of it. This cabin reeked of it. But there was none of it on Wheeler's breath.

'Six ten-foot pieces of two by four, you said?'

'That's right, 'tenant—Capting, rather—and then there's the gaff.'

'And an extra squaresail yard to make shearlegs?'

Wheeler looked embarrassed. 'Yes, I was just coming to that. We've got the foretopsail yard, but like the foresail gaff, it's got a patch of rot in it. I doubt if either of 'em will see us into Charleston.'

'Spare yards are expensive—and difficult to come by in the Caribbean.'

Wheeler mustered a grin. 'Especially a few score miles east of Barbados.'

Ramage wanted a few more minutes before he fired his broadside; he wanted to be sure of the target, so there'd be no bloodshed.

'Well, is that all you want?'

'Water, Capting, if you've any to spare. An' bread—I'd be glad to buy a few sacks. We have a hungry cargo.'

'How hungry?'

'Pretty. We're so short of victuals they've been on quarter allowance for two weeks.'

Ramage nodded in feigned sympathy and Wheeler grumbled:

'This'll knock every bit o' profit out o' this voyage—an' more. Now's the time we usually double the rations—fattens 'em up just right for when we get into port and they're put to auction.'

'Like cattle,' Ramage commented understandingly.

'That's right, Capting, just like cattle. No farmer likes to drive his herd to market and sell the same day: he wants them to spend a day or two on grass or hay to put the shine back on their coats. Same with slaves.'

'I imagine so.'

'Exactly the same. If they get sick or starved it shows on their skin, y'know. It goes dull; no gloss to it. Give 'em a few days on bread sopping with palm oil and they soon shine up.'

Suddenly Ramage snapped: 'Fetch *m'sieur capitain*.'

Wheeler gave a start and automatically put his hands on the desk to stand up, before recovering and sitting back in the chair. There was a pallor now under the brown, leathery skin of his face; the eyes were shifty; the skin over the skull taut and bloodless under the tan.

'Sorry, Capting, I don't speak Spanish. Or was it French?'

The smell, the crude deception, the horror of what he knew was below deck, finally sickened Ramage: rubbing the scar over his brow, he could see Wheeler only in a red fog of anger. He knew he could shoot the man with no compunction and was glad he wore only a sword.

'This ship is a prize to His Majesty's brig *Triton*, Wheeler.

She's French. You're probably the mate, or possibly the bo'sun. As far as I'm concerned you're French too, though for all that Yankee accent I suspect you're English, which would make you a traitor instead. Anyway, you haven't missed my point, I trust——'

'Don't move, your life ain't worth a candle!' Wheeler snarled, and his right hand came up with a pistol. The thumb moved forward and as it went back there was a click as he cocked the pistol. 'Nor the puff to blow it out.'

Ramage shook his head. 'I'm sorry. Wheeler, it won't do. Don't be a fool——'

'I've nuthin' to lose,' Wheeler almost shouted, revealing an accent Ramage couldn't place more specifically than Midland, 'the Royal Navy's been looking for me for years!'

Ramage spoke loudly and deliberately.

'You won't gain anything by threatening me with a pistol.'

'No?' jeered Wheeler. 'Well, I ain't threatening, I'm promising! Correct Mr Lieutenant, I'm not the Captain of this ship; I'm the mate, but I have a share in her. Correct, she's really French; those papers are forged. Correct she's now a prize to His Royal Majesty King George the Second——'

' "The Third",' Ramage corrected mildly, glancing up at the skylight, trying to gain time.

' "The Third", then, not that it's going to make any difference to you. Correct, I'm as good as your prisoner. And I'll go further—if I was ever brought to trial I'd swing from the foreyardarm, so I've nothing to lose; but so help me God, I'm not going to quit this world alone, Mr Lieutenant. I'm taking you with me.

'If it hadn't been for you I'd have retired rich in my old age. I've a house in Charleston—and every brick of it paid for. Not bad for a man who had "Run" put against his name in the muster book of a British ship o' war only six years ago, eh?

'So say your prayers, Mr Ramage. Your old father's going to mourn you. Yes, I remember him; even served in his ship once. Five, Mr Ramage, start saying your prayers, Mr Ramage, 'cos when I've counted five you're going to be dead, and it's only fitting to give a man time to make his peace.'

He raised the pistol and Ramage was looking straight into the muzzle, which seemed to grow in size as he watched. Wheeler was holding it canted slightly to his left, to be certain the priming powder in the pan covered the touch-hole and there'd be no chance of a miss-fire.

'One, Mr Ramage,' he said, and the first joint of his index finger whitened as it tightened slightly round the trigger. 'Two . . . I don't see those eyes closed in prayer . . .'

And suddenly Ramage was very frightened and oddly resentful: it was a waste—he was going to die, and so stupidly, at the hands of a trapped deserter.

'Three . . .'

After all that . . . rescuing Gianna, the *Belette* affair, capturing the Spanish frigate, ramming the enormous *San Nicolas* at Cape St Vincent——

'Four . . .'

Only a few seconds. Gianna would——

A sharp, ear-shattering explosion, a faint crash of broken glass, but mercifully no pain.

Wheeler's hand fell to the table still clutching the pistol and he leaned forward, his head dropping on to his arms as though he was tired.

Ramage, suddenly realizing the pistol had not fired, saw half the man's face was torn away. A moment later more glass fell from the skylight overhead; two feet and then the legs came into sight through the hole, and Jackson dropped on to the desk.

'You all right, sir?'

Ramage swore violently.

'You left that damned late, Jackson!'

The American looked crestfallen. 'Didn't think he'd go through with it, sir. I reckoned he'd stop at three and try to strike a bargain. I had to back and fill round the skylight so my shadow didn't show.'

'Bargain! Bargain—what, with his pistol aimed——' Ramage shouted, breaking off as he realized the shock was making him lose control of himself.

'Had a bit of trouble on deck, too, sir,' Jackson said laconically, jumping off the desk. 'As soon as I heard him say who he was I had to signal the Tritons to cover the Frenchies —and I was scared stiff there'd be a shot fired. If there had been . . .'

Wheeler would have shot him straight away, Ramage realized.

'Very well, Jackson, let's get on with it. I want those papers collected and taken over to the *Triton*—don't let the blood soak them. The real ones are in the sideboard, but clear the desk as well.'

CHAPTER ELEVEN

Sitting in his cabin on board the *Triton* and reviewing the last couple of hours as he filled in the log, Ramage realized how little his brief written report to Admiral Robinson would tell of the story, because it was impossible to visualize unless you had been on board a slaver.

She was *La Merlette* of Rouen. Her owners had a cynical sense of humour: '*La merlette*'—a hen blackbird. Built ten years ago, 260 tons burthen and ninety feet long on deck, she carried 375 slaves...The captain was a happy and portly little Rouenais who'd immediately stepped forward and revealed his identity when he realized Wheeler had been shot dead.

He was proud of his ship, rueful that his subterfuge had failed, and as he took Ramage round on a tour of inspection was equally proud of the way the slaves were cared for. He could, Ramage thought, have been a vintner proudly displaying his cellar of wines.

And that wasn't a bad simile either, for below deck *La Merlette* was like a long, narrow and low cellar. The ship was divided into five sections. Forward, the seamen lived in the fo'c'sle and each had a bunk, but since there was less than four feet of headroom, the captain explained, they usually slept on deck at sea in the tropics.

Abaft the seamen's accommodation was the space for the male slaves: a forty-feet-long compartment the width of the ship. Even staring at the slaves, lying, squatting and sitting, Ramage could hardly believe it. There was less than five feet headroom, so he had to crouch as he walked. Running the full length of the compartment on each side were two shelves, the lower about a foot from the deck, the second two and a half feet above the first, and each a few inches wider than the length of the slaves lying on their backs side by side, feet outboard, heads towards the centre-line.

Ramage looked closely at the first few slaves—the only ones he could see clearly since the light from the hatch hardly penetrated more than a dozen feet. They were all secured by hinged metal collars round their necks. Each end of the collar was bent out at right angles to form a flange and had a hole in it. In the shelf beneath each slave's head a slot was cut in the wood so that both flanges when pressed together went through it and a padlock was slipped through the holes from the underside.

Each slave could move his arms and legs—though little good it did, since the collar held his head and he was close between fellow-slaves. A canvas scoop—a windsail—was fitted at the after-hatch to catch the following winds, and the forward hatch was open, forcing a draught through the length of the compartment.

Along the centre-line, between the shelves on either side, there was a low, wide bench on which sat three rows of slaves, facing the starboard side. All of them had their knees drawn up and Ramage soon saw why: each was in leg irons. A man on the starboard side could not push back to straighten his legs because of the man behind him in the middle row. The third slave, his back to the larboard side, would slide off the edge of the bench if he straightened up . . .

The leg-irons were simply U-shaped metal straps fitting over the ankles. A metal rod with a knob at one end went through holes on each side of the iron and also through an eyebolt fitted into the bench. The knob prevented the rod being pulled out one way, a padlock through a hole at the opposite end stopped it being pulled out the other, and the eyebolt held it to the bench.

The slaves watched warily as Ramage, the French captain and a couple of the *Triton*'s boarding party walked through. The stench was appalling—bilgewater, sweat, urine . . . Yet the slaves' quarters were clean—scrubbed out every day, the French captain explained, while the slaves exercised on deck. But, he added, all their lives the slaves had relieved themselves wherever they happened to be in the jungle and it was impossible in such a short voyage to train them to wait until they were led up on deck.

Although the slaves—all of them young men or boys—

were silent they were not sullen. Fearful, certainly, since the mere noise of the sea against the hull of a ship running in the Trades was frightening, and a thousand times worse if you were shackled down.

The crash of the mast going by the board, Ramage realized, must have sounded like the end of the world.

All the men had deep scars on their cheeks: the different tribal marks deliberately cut by the witch doctors during strange initiation rites. Some had two, three or even four vertical scars an inch long on either cheek; others ran horizontally. And many of the men sitting on the bench had the even more horrifying tribal marks running down their backs. These looked, in the half-light, like pieces of thin rope a couple of feet long stuck on the skin parallel to the spine.

The moment he saw these scars Ramage recalled his first trip to the West Indies, when the overseer at a plantation had explained what they were. The process began at puberty —one or more long cuts was made down the back and mud rubbed in so the flesh healed leaving a raised scar. This was cut again, and more mud rubbed in, Gradually the ridge grew higher, fattened along the centre because of the mud but contracted beneath by the original scar, until it was almost as fat as the top joint of a man's little finger: a long, thin brown sausage glued lengthwise to the skin. Adornment, tribal customs, a sign of manhood—whatever it was it looked worse than any seaman's back scarred by a cat-o'-nine-tails.

Most of the slaves would be under twenty-four years old— the demand was for youngsters. In Jamaica, he recalled, there was a £10 duty on every one landed who was over twenty-four.

Ramage had then gone on to inspect the women's compartment, which was the next aft. Fifteen feet long and also the full width of the ship, it was laid out like the men's. But it was too much and he hurried through and up the hatch, unable to face the terrified, appealing eyes that watched him. Women—they were young girls for the most part, few over eighteen.

The women's compartment was separated from the captain's cabin aft by two bulkheads which also formed cupboards. Ramage was surprised to find that abaft the captain's cabin there was another cabin fitted with more berths. When asked whose they were the Frenchman shrugged, saying he disliked being on his own, with the slaves between him and the crew, and the petty officers used it.

Shutting out the memory of what he had seen, Ramage filled in the log, noting the time and position the schooner had been sighted, weather conditions, and describing briefly how the man claiming to be the schooner's American captain had been shot. Then details of the prize's tonnage and cargo.

He did a sum on a scrap of paper. Slaves were fetching a high price in Jamaica and *La Merlette* carried 375. Or rather, had shipped that number, but eleven had died. An average of, say, seventy-five guineas a head meant that her present cargo was worth more than 27,000 guineas. Add in the value of a well-built, fast ship . . .

Which brought him back to the next decision facing him. Southwick and the carpenter's mate had been over to inspect *La Merlette* and both now reckoned the chances of repairing the mainmast were almost nil because, unless there was an almost flat calm, it would be impossible to raise the mast into position. Plus three days' work actually fishing the mast, replacing the rigging and setting it up. How long would they have to wait for a calm day? It could be two days—or two weeks.

Another factor was that the schooner carried a large crew, and a cut-throat mob they were. They needed to be, with the constant threat of the slaves rising against them, and they shipped in slaves only because of the pay, which was very high since sickness was the worst enemy—Ramage recalled:

> *Beware and take care of the Bight of Benin,*
> *There's one comes out for forty go in . . .*

It was an old song and probably true. Anyway, the schooner would need a prize crew of twenty since her penny-pinching owners were forced to give her a crew of twenty, and there were the slaves to guard. And the First Lord's orders precluded him from delaying the *Triton* by escorting the schooner into Barbados.

Well, there was no choice: he could—indeed he'd have to —keep the French prisoners on board the *Triton* and let Appleby and twenty Tritons take in *La Merlette*. That meant there'd be forty men left to work the *Triton* and guard twenty very tough prisoners. He could only pray that neither ship met a French privateer. Still the French captain was cheerfully reaching along to windward of the islands with only the foremost standing. Barbados was at most a couple of days sailing for *La Merlette* and dead to leeward. Young Appleby would have no difficulty getting there even if he jogged along under headsails alone.

Yet it'd be easier to leave *La Merlette* to her French crew: her captain could make Guadeloupe, where he'd already said she was due to call anyway before going on to Haiti. But Ramage dismissed the idea: Admiral Robinson would be extremely angry at letting such a prize slip through his hands.

Ramage glanced up at the skylight and at his watch. Just under a couple of hours of daylight left. Now he'd made up his mind, it was time to transfer the French prisoners to the *Triton* and send over spare provisions and water to the schooner. Appleby would be delighted at the honour of sailing the schooner into Barbados with only the foremast standing. Bringing in a prize with a 27,000-guinea cargo on board would go a long way towards ensuring Admiral Robinson's interest in helping him pass for lieutenant. As far as Ramage could see, that was the only way the master's mate would ever make it, since he had the brain of an ox.

With Wheeler dead, there was only the French captain and one other officer. They could have Appleby's berth—easier to guard them there, too. He called to the Marine sentry to pass the word for Southwick so he could give the necessary orders.

*

The French prisoners had been herded below under a Marine guard; food and water transferred to *La Merlette*; the prize crew were on board. Ramage was pleased he'd remembered to include Harris among the crew because he would be one of the senior ratings; and Appleby also had Stafford and Fuller with him. Since the *Triton* had been stripped of her best men, Appleby would have only himself to blame if things went wrong.

Ramage stood at the break in the gangway as Appleby came up from below, a chart rolled under his arm.

'Have you forgotten anything?'

'Don't think so, sir,' he said cheerfully, forgetting his Captain's dislike of vague answers.

'Either you have or you haven't. Chart, sextant, tables, almanack?'

'Got them all, sir.'

'Latest position from Mr Southwick, course to steer, chronometer checked with *La Merlette*'s?'

'All done, sir.'

'Ensign, set of flags, rockets, false fires . . .?'

'All on board, sir.'

'Very well. We'll be in sight for much of the night, so don't be afraid to send up a rocket if you've forgotten anything or find you can't manage.'

'Aye aye, sir,' Appleby answered patiently, and Ramage realized he sounded like a mother fussing the first time her son left home for school.

'Good luck, then, and don't forget to salute the Admiral if you find him in Barbados!'

Half an hour later the *Triton*'s boat was back and it was being hoisted on board, *La Merlette* began setting sail and getting under way. As Ramage watched, the surgeon came up and commented:

'Appleby's first command! He must be excited!'

'I suppose so,' Ramage grunted. 'He's the dullest dog I've ever met. Has no—no push, if you know what I mean.'

The surgeon nodded. 'Still, he tries—and he's very young.'

'Yes, about fourteen months younger than I.'

'I beg your pardon, sir, I didn't——'

Ramage laughed. 'It's a compliment, Bowen.'

'This French captain,' Bowen said, hastily changing the subject. 'What sort of man is he? I mean, how can someone trade in human lives? It seems—well, against everything their Revolution was supposed to stand for.'

'I've been wondering the same thing. He reminds me of a typical French grocer: cheerful, fat and sharp as a needle.'

Bowen said, 'I must admit I'm an Abolitionist, sir. I've never done anything about supporting Wilberforce, but I admire his work.'

'So do I. At this very moment I feel like resigning my commission and offering him my services.'

'A laudable spirit, if I may say so, sir,' Bowen said seriously. 'But at the moment the country faces worse enemies than slavers. While we condemn a cruel slaver we mustn't forget the first three years of the French Revolution saw more cruelty performed by Frenchmen against Frenchmen in the streets of Paris alone than there's been in the Bight of Benin in the last fifty years.'

Ramage nodded, thinking of the thousands who'd been led to the guillotine merely because they had been born in the upper or middle classes, not because they opposed the Revolution. And they'd been followed by hundreds of people falsely denounced to the Directory by their enemies to pay off old scores.

'Well, one way we can find out what the Frenchman thinks is for me to invite him to dine with me tonight. The idea isn't very appealing—I'd sooner heave him over the side. But it's customary for the Captain to make such an invitation—though hardly to a slaver.'

The Surgeon did not try to hide his interest.

'Perhaps you would join me, Bowen. I can't ask Southwick as he'll be on watch.'

★

The French captain, Jean-Louis Marais, spoke good English, ate heartily (though hinting that a clove of garlic would have improved the meat) and sniffed delicately at the brandy. His chubby face was non-committal; then he glanced over the top of the glass and said:

'Good—yes. But M'sieur Ramage, I hope you won't think me impolite if I regret that I forgot to make you a present of my spirit locker before we parted company with *La Merlette*?'

Ramage, who found himself liking the Frenchman's irrepressible cheerfulness—he could keep grinning within a few hours of finding his ship captured and himself a prisoner of war—couldn't resist saying: 'I hope you won't think *me* impolite, M'sieur Marais, but by that time it was hardly yours to give ...'

'*Touché!* But your King wouldn't have begrudged it'

'I fear he would; in fact his regulations particularly forbid taking anything out of a captured ship until she has been "adjudged lawful prize" in some Admiralty court——'

'A barbarous regulation!' Marais exclaimed. 'Why——'

'Another says that "None of the officers, mariners or other persons on board her shall be stripped of their clothes, or in any sort pillaged..."' Ramage added dryly. 'Now *that* is barbarous.'

'My shirt is of little value, but my heart is of pure gold.'

'We'll have that, then—don't you agree, Bowen?'

The surgeon nodded. 'Yes—I can remove it without spoiling the shirt.'

'Ah, what an evening,' Marais said, still sniffing the brandy between sentences. 'A good dinner, good company— and a good surgeon to do whatever the host requires, quickly and painlessly!'

Bowen said evenly, 'Since you owned a slaver, I imagine not only your heart is made of gold.'

'You overestimate the profit,' Marais said blandly, 'and you flatter me. I regret I am not the owner—was not the owner,' he corrected himself. 'Merely the captain.'

'But surely it's a profitable trade,' Ramage said.

'It's a gamble. When you win, you make a lot of money. When you lose, you lose heavily. There's no—how do you say? No "happy medium".'

'But on a round voyage surely you can hedge your bet?' Ramage asked. 'There's profit on the goods you carry from France to the Cape Coast, and profit in carrying sugar, spice and rum from the West Indies to France. Surely your gamble is only from the Cape Coast to the West Indies with the slaves?'

'True,' said Marais. 'But that's also where the major profit is. Don't forget these are fast ships, well-equipped and splendidly built. You saw there's little cargo space—no depth in the holds. And the crews have to be large and need to be paid very well—twice as much as in merchantmen. So for two thirds of a round voyage—from France to the Cape Coast, then from the West Indies back to France —they are expensive and half of them unnecessary.'

'What's the usual profit on a slave?' Bowen asked bluntly.

Marais shrugged his shoulders. 'M'sieur Bowen, be thankful that in the world of medicine you are never concerned with the words "net" and "gross". But a fair question deserves a fair answer. We don't buy the slaves with cash—

it's all bartering with the goods we carry out from France. But it works out at—forgive me, I must change the coinage— yes, about twenty-five guineas a slave: that's what we pay the chiefs and traders for a male. About fifteen guineas for a female. And we sell males at'—he paused, changing French *louis* into English money—'between fifty and sixty guineas each, providing we are among the first slavers in after the hurricane season ends or the last in before it starts. So our gross profit is between twenty-five and thirty-five guineas for each slave. But ten per cent might die on the voyage— it's rarely as high as that, incidentally—or we might arrive within a week of another slaver, in which case naturally the market price is lower.'

Bowen was obviously both horrified and fascinated by the way Marais discussed the slaves as if they were sacks of sugar or puncheons of rum.

'I don't see how you can make a loss?'

Marais' eyes looked up at the deckhead, shrugging his shoulders and holding out his hands, palms uppermost.

'M'sieur Bowen, I would like you as a backer. If I had a ship but no money to finance a voyage, I wish I could meet you and persuade you to take shares!'

'Why?' Bowen asked innocently.

Marais was serious now: the sharp little eyes focused on the surgeon, the palms of his hands were flat on the table, shoulders hunched forward. The lamp swinging in its gimbals on the bulkhead threw shadows which changed his face from that of a jolly grocer to the captain of a slaver used to dealing with desperate situations which needed desperate measures.

'Take your field, M'sieur Bowen, medicine. The Cape Coast is the unhealthiest place in the world. I often have to take my ship thirty miles up rivers to collect my cargo—in itself a great risk to the ship. I've read the burial service over more bodies consigned to those rivers than ever at sea. I sail from France with a crew of thirty-five—because I need twenty left alive for the passage from the Cape Coast to the West Indies. Many times I've made a passage with only a dozen . . . The rest have died of sicknesses for which there is no cure, only a death of the most painful kind. When you came in sight,' he said to Ramage, 'only twenty of the thirty-five who left France had survived: fifteen died in the Bight of Benin—one stabbed by a treacherous slave-trader, the rest from sickness.'

'But losing crew from sickness is hardly a financial loss,' Ramage objected pointedly.

Marais gave a sly grin. 'I understand the implication; but there is a loss because men who ship in slavers are not gamblers. They won't sign on and agree to collect their pay at the end of the round voyage, so if they died the owner doesn't have to pay, which is what you are thinking. Oh no! They want a large advance before they leave France. Why, I——'

'Come, come,' Ramage interrupted. 'If you paid such large advances they'd desert on the eve of sailing.'

Without saying it, Marais' hands and a twitch of his head indicated this was proof enough of the crude way of British sailors but that French sailors were cleverer.

'The advance, usually four months' pay, is delivered by my agent to whoever the seaman nominates—a week after we have sailed.'

'What do you barter for the slaves?' Bowen asked.

'All sorts of manufactured goods. Cloth and clothing— the brighter the better—brass and iron cooking pots, beads, knives, looking-glasses—they're very popular—liquor, muskets, shot, powder, cutlasses——'

'Muskets and shot?' exclaimed Bowen.

'Of course—the chiefs pay well for them. They're cheap affairs, naturally; more danger to the men that fire them than their targets!'

'And how—well, what happens when you first arrive on the Coast?'

Marais grinned at Ramage. 'First we discover whether there are any British ships of war in the area. Then—well, let's describe it as it was before the war, then I shan't give away any secrets.

'First, M'sieur Bowen, there's a slaving season—that's obvious, because we don't want to arrive in the Caribbean during the hurricane season. So on the Coast the trading settlements and local native chiefs have been preparing for us by collecting slaves. When enough slave ships arrive, the slaves are taken to the market and each captain inspects them.

As he chooses one, so he bargains with the owner—usually a slave-trader or the agent of the particular chief—and agrees on the price.'

Bowen asked: 'These chiefs—where do they get the slaves?'

'You might well ask! From many places. To start with a chief takes up any young men or boys in his own tribe who have misbehaved. Not criminals necessarily, you understand? Then, if it's a large tribe and the chief wants a lot of muskets, or a lot of bright clothes for his wives—well, he's likely to march some of his own people to the settlement.

'Of course, the tribes often raid each other's villages to capture men to sell as slaves. That's quite usual—you can always tell by the tribal marks on the faces. If you see a chief's agent at the market has, say, two vertical scars on his cheek and the slaves he's offering have one horizontal scar, you know they're prisoners of war from another tribe. If they are the same scars—well, the chief is either selling those who've misbehaved, or he's getting greedy.'

'But surely you don't get all your slaves at the settlements?' asked Ramage, remembering Marais' reference to rivers. 'Most of the settlements are on the coast, aren't they?'

'We get perhaps half from the settlements: the best—and the most expensive. The rest we find up the rivers, visiting small villages.'

'You capture them,' Bowen said bluntly.

'Oh no!' Marais exclaimed. 'For a start it'd be too dangerous to send a party of seamen on shore; in fact we usually have a guard boat rowing round the ship day and night. No, a hundred seamen wouldn't last an hour in that jungle—they'd be riddled with spears and arrows from three yards away by natives they couldn't even see, or else they'd come back riddled with sickness.

'Oh no, M'sieur Bowen, we arrive at a village and wait. First a representative of the chief—perhaps even the chief himself—comes out in a canoe for a palaver. He tells us how many slaves he has and the price he wants. One of my men—usually the mate—goes back with him and inspects them. When they return, we agree on the price. And usually, after dark, more canoes arrive with slaves from villages near-by.'

'Where do the other slaves come from then?'

'I never ask, but it's obvious.' Marais shrugged his shoulders. 'You must understand that a man with two sons and six daughters considers he has six useless mouths to feed: he values only his sons. So he's likely to sell some of his daughters. If he has little land and many sons—well, the extra sons too. Particularly if he dislikes any of them.'

Bowen groaned.

'My friend,' said Marais, 'don't be shocked; don't judge them by *your* standards. These people live different lives and have different codes. They're happy and they work just enough to avoid starving. And it's difficult to starve because fruit and many vegetables grow wild in the jungle, and they catch fish in the rivers.

'And you must remember the family is not the family as we Europeans understand the word. Before I went to the Coast I'd have been shocked if I'd known what I'm telling you now. After twenty years, I understand.

'Incidentally, things *we* do shock *them*. The idea of spending sums of money in building enormous ships solely for fighting—that shocks them. They have large canoes—but when they're not fighting another tribe they're used for fishing or trade.

'You consider government. When a chief dies, all the elders elect a new chief—the man they think is best qualified to lead them in battle, administer justice and so on. The European system makes them laugh—a hereditary king whose son'—he glanced significantly at Ramage—'might be stupid or insane or otherwise totally unfit for the crown; then three or four hundred "minor chiefs" elected without qualifications by fools who were probably bribed with pints of ale ... You'll admit the results in Europe are a series of situations where nothing gets done and the minor chiefs—your Members of Parliament, the French senators—simply make speech after speech. Who's to say which system is best? In my opinion one system suits the Cape Coast, another suits Europe.'

'When you have the slaves on board,' Bowen asked, 'how are they fed, exercised, cared for?'

Marais looked at him squarely. 'M'sieur, I think you are a supporter of that M'sieur Wilberforce. But always remember this—it would be madness for a slaver captain not to care for the slaves. For every slave that dies—pouf, there's a twenty-five guinea investment and another twenty-five guinea profit thrown over the side. If you had hundreds of guineas invested in a company, I think you'd make quite sure the company's goods were well cared for.

'However, to answer your question. The slaves—in *La Merlette*, anyway, and she is typical—get three meals a day, and the food is what they're used to. Once we're at sea they spend at least five hours a day on deck. True, each pair of men is shackled together with leg irons, but they get plenty of exercise—they even manage to dance. Their accommodation is cleaned out while they're on deck, and we give them brandy each day.'

Ramage grunted. For all the talk—and Marais was sincere and the logic of some of his arguments was inescapable even if you disagreed with him—it didn't change Ramage's views on slavery. That chiefs of tribes would sell their own youth into slavery didn't justify slavers buying them. Nor did it justify plantation owners buying them from the slavers.

Marais obviously guessed his thoughts.

'What's the Royal Navy's bounty for seamen now, M'sieur Ramage?'

'That's hardly relevant.'

'No? Your country's Navy and mine are manned in the same way. Prisons are emptied and men herded on board ships of war in which they stay for years, usually without shore leave and for wages hardly worthy of the name. Or a starving man is offered a pitifully small crust of bread—a bounty—to join. To stay alive he accepts—and at once becomes a slave of your King or, in the French ships, the Directory.

'Perhaps not even a starving man. A farm labourer gets drunk—and wakes up to find himself in a boat on his way to a ship of war, having been knocked on the head by a press gang. He's left a wife and children at home to starve,' Marais continued.

'In France and in Britain the price of bread and potatoes goes up every few weeks. Staple foods, M'sieur Ramage: foods that town-dwellers cannot grow, nor can many of the country folk. So, the poor are almost starving. Can you imagine a plantation-owner who's paid more than fifty guineas for a slave letting him starve?'

'Slavery is for life,' Bowen pointed out. 'A seaman serves only for the war.'

'And when the war ends? Why, he's thrown out—along with thousands of other seamen, and soldiers too—and can't find work. All he knows is seamanship. He doesn't know where his next meal will come from; he may have lost a limb; his constitution is probably ruined through hard service in bad climates. Scurvy will have lost him his teeth; malignant fevers will plague him always. Yes, a slave's a slave all his life—and that means regular meals all his life, too.

'Your M'sieur Wilberforce means well, and so do you gentlemen. But shouldn't we look at the starving people living lives little removed from slavery in the narrow streets of our towns, or in hovels in our villages, before we condemn slavery? Only cheap gin or wine to keep them warm in winter: no fires, no fuel, very little food?'

'I'm sorry, M'sieur Marais,' Ramage said abruptly, 'nothing can be achieved by talking about it. Are you by any chance a chess player?'

Marais' eyes lit up. 'Ah—chess! How I wish for a good game. When I choose my officers, always I ask if they play chess. But never...'

Ramage glanced at Bowen. 'I think you'll have time for a few games before we reach Barbados. I'll have the steward take the chess set to your cabin, Bowen. Oh, by the way, M'sieur Marais, to save you the embarrassment of playing chess with a sentry standing behind you, if you gave your parole...'

'Gladly,' said Marais, 'If I escape I have to swim to Guadeloupe. If I give my parole I can play chess in comfort. Thank you for a pleasant evening.'

Bowen led the way out of the cabin and Ramage looked round for his hat to go up on deck. Two more nights in the Trades, and then Barbados, and under the orders of the Admiral... He realized he'd be more than happy if the Atlantic crossing lasted another couple of months. He was happy with his own little floating world. It had been a challenge to change a mutinous crew into a loyal one, and he wasn't the slightest bit ashamed of his pride in having achieved it.

CHAPTER TWELVE

With Barbados only a few score miles to the westward, Ramage sat on the aftermost starboard carronade—his favourite spot since it was sheltered from the scorching sun by a small awning—and reflected how few days had passed since Southwick had persuaded him to deal with the problem of Bowen.

The voyage was nearly over; Bowen may or may not be cured permanently but certainly had not touched a drink for more than a week. He could now watch others drinking without becoming soaked with perspiration as he silently fought himself to avoid reaching for a glass.

The tropics—still the words gave Ramage pleasure. But now, approaching the islands which stretched in a chain shaped like a new moon from the South American coast at the east end of the Spanish Main to Florida, he knew the lives of the men in the *Triton* would probably depend more on Bowen's skill than his own.

Dozens of islands ranging from Cuba in the north, six hundred miles long, to barren rocks barely a mile wide. But all of them islands containing great extremes: great beauty and great ugliness; much peace and much violence; much pleasure and much pestilence.

One week the heat and humidity would be tempered by the fresh Trade winds into a blissful climate; another, when the wind dropped, would be damp and unbearably hot, draining every man's energy, mildewing his clothes, sapping his spirit.

A perfectly fit and strong man could admire the frangipani, its delicate white blossom with gold centres flowering on leafless trees clinging precariously to a cliff face; he could stare at the almost unbelievably beautiful flamboyant tree covered in brilliant scarlet blossom, an enormous ball of flame. And that night the man could be struck down with some disease like the black vomit, which within twenty-four hours, would leave him dying with insects crawling wherever life oozed from his body.

Islands where moderation did not exist.

The first day of the rainy season came—and almost overnight the sun-scorched brown hills turned green with tiny shoots sprouting like down on a boy's face. The sun nourished the plants so they grew fast and then, as they flowered, scorched them to death, and while the sun and rain rotted the remains the ants, scorpions, lizards and great buzzing swarms of flies hunted and feasted...

The trunk of a fallen tree apparently solid—until you touch it and it crumbled to powder, riddled with termites...

And beside the rotting piles there'd be scatterings of poinsettia—the Spanish *Flor de Pascuas*, the Italian *Stella di Natale*, the Flower of Christmas—growing wild and profuse, each slender stem topped by petals hanging down like leaves in a brilliant red star.

The dull green of the *lignum vitae* tree, the wood of which was so heavy it sank in water but whose tiny, gentle blue blossoms, no bigger than a small button, gave no hint of its enormous strength. And the chenille plant whose native name, Red Hot Cat Tail, aptly described its flower.

He remembered the pelicans, broad-winged and cumbersome, with long beaks and pendulous sacks beneath, standing on a coral reef like a group of wizened sagging-jowled old men gossiping of politics and bygone days. It was such an effort for them to get into the air but, once flying they did it lazily, almost without effort. Yet when their little button eyes spotted a fish they flopped down to catch it in such a clumsy dive it seemed that flying had suddenly exhausted all their strength.

And, for comparison, the little white egret, smaller, more graceful than the European heron, high-stepping on deep, stinking mud at the edge of a mangrove swamp with all the delicacy of a little princess entering a ballroom knowing she was watched by ten score guests.

The osprey hovering on an air current in the lee of a hill and swooping on to some unwary fish in a lagoon below almost faster than the eye could follow—and gaudy parrots squawking raucously in the jungle. Tiny humming birds, like large bees; mocking birds whose shrill whistles were like human beings signalling to each other.

Memories tumbled over each other, none blurred by time. Amaryllis with its trumpet-shaped flowers; the long, silver barracuda streaking through the sea, face as ugly as a pike's, teeth sharper than razors; sharks with blue-grey backs and white bellies, scavenging, the vultures of the sea. Papaya trees with their delicious soft orange-centred fruit growing in clusters at the top of the trunks. Tamarind with hard, coloured seeds which the natives strung together into bead necklaces. The aptly and tragically-named Belle of the Night, whose buds opened as night fell to reveal white petals and a golden centre (to those with lanterns who cared to look, or who admired in the moonlight) and which closed as the sun rose, never to open again.

The coral reefs waiting to rip out a ship's bottom, but swarming with fish so gaily coloured in such strange patterns they might have been created by an inspired artist in the last stages of a drunken frenzy. Long sandy beaches backed by many types of palm trees.

And at the back of the beaches, neat holes, the homes of land crabs which the natives caught at night, luring them with flaming torches.

Everywhere among the islands mosquitoes, whining and biting, leaving smudges of blood when you slapped them on your flesh. In the rainy season they were reinforced by sand-flies, almost too small to see but which waited for the sun to dip towards the horizon before emerging to bite with the sharpness of needles, leaving angry, itching weals.

Shiny black scorpions, smaller than one had expected. Centipedes, lurking under stones and twigs, or hiding in the beams of a roof or ceiling and dropping on your arm to give you a bite which swelled like a Scotsman's haggis.

Long-tailed, impertinent blackbirds, bigger than those in Europe, strutting around like young midshipmen on a flag-ship's quarterdeck, lacking only a telescope tucked under a wing.

Clothing mildewed, rotted and decayed; iron rusted and flaked until nothing was left but a dull red stain. Nothing moved, yet nothing stood still. Like jagged rocks in a pool, the Windward Islands stood four-square at the southern end of the Caribbean. On them men built houses and hurricanes blew them down. Coral reefs grew, then the coral died and the seas smashed it, hurling the pieces upon the beach where, along with sea shells, the waves pounded and ground it into gleaming sand.

In the jungles trees died and fell to give life to termites; animals died, but their bodies gave life to beetles and maggots; sailors died—and, Ramage thought bitterly, gave life to clerks filling in forms at the Navy Board.

Southwick came up from below, where he had been working out his noon sight and, squinting in the bright sunlight, reported: 'We should sight Ragged Point before noon tomorrow, if this wind holds.'

'How much before noon?'

'Between ten and noon.'

'Hmm . . .'

Knowing the captain was thinking of the risk of running on to the island in the darkness, Southwick said: 'I don't think we need heave-to tonight, sir. I'm reasonably certain, and there's been no north-going current for the past five days.'

Every captain—and master too—making the Atlantic crossing had one fear about making his landfall: that he'd be a few miles ahead of his reckoning so that in the darkness the ship would run up on the low-lying, rocky and wave-beaten east coast of Barbados. If you were too far north or south you could pass it in the night and, if to the south, run on to the rocks (some forty feet high and barely twenty wide) and tiny islands of the Grenadines beyond.

Well, Ramage knew Southwick was a good navigator but at this stage in the voyage all captains and all masters tried to outdo each other in showing confidence, yet most of them —the conscientious ones, anyway—always had a nagging doubt.

An error in the quadrant, in the chronometer, an unexpected current during the night between sights . . . All could land you on the beach at Barbados, where even in a calm day the swell waves thundered their way through outlying reefs and sent a fine spray drifting inland for several hundred yards, an almost invisible mist.

The lighthouse—one could never trust that a light had been lit; and even then couldn't be sure it wasn't put up by a wrecker in a position where it'd lead you on to rocks. More fortunes than anyone liked to admit had been made by wreckers in these islands; in Barbados alone two or three of the leading families were reputed to have a hand in it.

*

Soon after dawn next morning it seemed to Ramage every man in the ship was rubbing, scrubbing, polishing or painting. His own steward could hardly wait to get him out of the cabin to start pressing clothes which, for the previous three or four days had been hung up to air.

Seamen were busy with cloths and brickdust, rubbing vigorously to give all the brasswork an extra shine. The decks had already been holystoned and washed down.

The gunner's mate and a couple of men were methodically wiping over each carronade with oily cloths. Two days ago they'd gone round with a bucket of blacking—a mysterious mixture of vinegar and lamp black—painting it on spots where rust marks had been removed, and repainting all the shot in the racks.

There was still a strong smell about the ship: for the past two days the men had been painting the standing rigging with a mixture of Stockholm tar, coal tar and salt water which had been heated up in a fish kettle (and as they wielded their brushes Southwick danced around below, cursing them for spilling drops, despite the old awnings spread over the deck which had been liberally sprinkled with sand as an added precaution).

At the bow three men were putting the finishing touches to the *Triton*'s figurehead. The wooden replica of the son of Poseidon and Amphitrite was small and well-carved and his head was bent forward slightly, as if supporting the bowsprit. His fish's tail twisted down the stem and the outline of each scale was picked out in gold leaf. The face was—as Southwick commented many weeks ago—'friendly enough for one o' those Greek chaps' but the triton shell which by tradition he held in his hand had been broken off at some time and replaced with one carved from green wood which the hot sun had now split.

And it was going to cost Ramage a guinea before long (in addition to the price of the gold leaf, which had to come out of his own pocket since the Admiralty issued only small quantities of yellow paint for ornamental work). Ramage had idly commented to Southwick that the spiral-shaped triton shell actually existed in the West Indies and to Ramage's surprise the old Master had become quite interested, having previously thought that, like Triton himself, it was a stylized object.

Anyway, it seemed that Southwick had told the master's mate, who'd told a quartermaster. Soon a request had come back from the ship's company: if they found a real triton shell could they use it to replace the wooden one?

This, Ramage realized in retrospect, was one of the first solid indications that not only had the original ship's company and the former Kathleens become firmly knitted together, but they'd developed a pride in their ship. And pride in a ship, he knew only too well from past experience, meant a happy ship. So he'd agreed, offering a guinea to the man who found a shell of the right size to fit into Triton's hand.

The men had been delighted—a guinea was within a shilling or two of a month's pay for most of them; but Ramage knew whoever found such a shell would have earned it—the wooden one was a foot long, and the shells were rarely more than eight or nine inches. He also knew that the man who found it would be the proudest in the ship . . .

Occasionally Southwick, his white hair flying in the wind, stumped up to the bow to watch the gilders at work. It was a fiddling but fascinating job, and Ramage too had watched them begin. After cleaning up the whole carving and scrubbing it with fresh water and soap to remove salt and dirt, they'd let it dry, one of them watching in case spray deposited more salt on it. They'd then carefully covered it with canvas for the night and next morning were badgering the bosun's mate for a tin of yellow paint, wanting to pour off some of the thick oil on top to use as size.

Leaving the oil to stand in a pot, they'd painted the figurehead with the appropriate colours, and when they were dry, brushed on the size where the gold leaf was to be applied, and left it until it was almost dry.

By that time they'd managed to wheedle a chamois leather from Southwick and sewn it into a small, flat pad. Once again, with all the enthusiasm of schoolboys, they'd gone back to the bow, secured ropes round their waists in case they fell, and despite the pitching and rolling, with the sea bubbling and spouting only a few feet below them, managed to transfer the gold leaf piece by piece from the book in which it was kept to the chamois leather pad.

One man had obviously worked as a gilder because each time he had, with a quick twist of the wrist, pressed the pad precisely against the place where the leaf was to be applied, so the leaf stuck to the size. Since each leaf was about two inches long and one inch wide, and so light that a gentle puff was enough to blow it three or four feet, Ramage was glad to hear they'd lost only three leaves in sudden gusts of wind.

★

Just after nine o'clock the foremast lookout's hail of 'Deck there!' stopped every man within hearing, and was followed by 'Land ho! From two points on the starboard bow to one point to larboard, sir!'

'You wall-eyed monkey,' Southwick shouted, 'why didn't you sight it sooner? And how far?'

' 'Bout seven miles, Lot o' haze ahead, sir,' came the cheerful reply. 'Must have lifted suddenly.'

Southwick glanced at Ramage. It was a good enough reason: the sun had heat in it now and haze over land in the early morning was not unusual, lifting as soon as the land heated up.

Ramage couldn't resist saying, 'Bit ahead of your reckoning, eh Mr Southwick? Between ten and noon I thought you said. Or was it nine and noon?'

'Ten, sir,' Southwick said ruefully. 'Still, that's——'

Seeing the Master was taking him seriously, Ramage interrupted: 'But for the haze, it'd have been seven-thirty.'

'But sir, after logging more than 2,900 miles . . .'

Ramage laughed. 'Well, it's a long way from Spithead, anyway!'

★

From being a long purplish bruise low on the horizon the east side of the island gradually took on a definite shape and slowly changed colour as the *Triton* closed the distance, turning a few degrees to larboard to head for South Point with a stiff breeze hustling her along at better than eight knots.

The purple gave way to a light brown as the contours of the hills slowly emerged, showing shallow valleys between them; then with the brig drawing nearer and the sun rising h'gher the brown became green; the rich and fertile green of land well-farmed, the large fields of different crops showing like a chess board.

The land was lower than Bowen had expected: instead of a high rocky island capped with tall palm trees and standing four-square against the full force of the Atlantic swell with high overhanging cliffs—for there was nothing between it and Africa more than 3,000 miles to the east—it was low with rolling land behind it; more like the Sussex coast.

As he commented on it to Southwick, the Master grunted.

'Barbados always disappoints people new to the Tropics: I always say that from seaward it looks like the east end of the Isle of Wight. But wait until you see the rest of the islands: Grenada, St Lucia, Martinique—they're just what you expect: mountainous thick jungle ... deep bays and beaches and thousands of palm trees ... But for all that, give me Barbados: most civilized of 'em all, except for Jamaica.'

Nevertheless, as the *Triton* approached, Bowen admitted the island was a beautiful sight: the deep blue of the sea stretched to within a hundred yards of the shore and then, merging into pale, sparkling green as it swept over coral reefs and outlying shoals, it broke in a narrow ribbon of white foam on a strip of silver sand. Beyond were green, gently-sloping fields but very few trees, all of which seemed to be small pines, leaning over at an angle to the left.

'The wind,' Southwick explained laconically. 'Always blowing from the eastwards—makes 'em grow like that. Ah—there are some palms for you.'

Bowen took the proffered telescope and low down, just at the back of the beach, were a few clumps of palm trees, the only ones for a couple of miles either way. He gave the telescope back to Southwick, who sensed his disappointment.

'Plenty more in the lee of South Point—the headland over there. We round it and the next one and anchor beyond in Carlisle Bay. The windward sides of all these islands are barren. Nothing between them and Africa. The lee sides usually have plenty of jungle—completely sheltered, and of course there's a lot of rain.'

'What are those brown patches scattered where the water's bright green?'

'Coral heads. Living coral. Usually only a few feet of water over them. They'd rip the bottom out of a ship. The pale green water usually shows there's a sandy bottom.'

Bowen remarked on several windmills along the coast, identical in shape to those in England.

'Use 'em for the sugar cane,' Southwick explained. 'Instead of having circular grindstones like you use for grain, they use rollers. The sugar cane—it looks like great stalks of wheat, eight feet high and more, and nearly as thick as your wrist— is run between the rollers which squeeze out the juice. It runs off into a lead-lined sink and into vats, where it's boiled.'

'Then what happens to it?'

'Shipped to England in casks. The most stinking cargo there is, too: never go passenger in a ship carrying molasses . . .'

The *Triton* passed South Point and soon the crescent-shaped Carlisle Bay came into sight, with Bridgetown sprawled comfortably along the western side. Ramage saw at anchor the Admiral's flagship, the 98-gun *Prince of Wales*. The *Triton*'s pendant numbers were already hoisted and men were standing by at all her carronades, which were loaded with blank charges ready to fire a seventeen-gun salute.

The gunner's mate was by the foremast ready for Ramage's signal to begin firing while powder boys stood by with extra charges ready to re-load seven of the guns to complete the salute.

There were only two frigates and some squat, ugly transports at anchor near the flagship while a small schooner approached from the west, still hull down over the horizon, her sails showing like tiny visiting cards.

The news of the *Triton*'s arrival must have reached the flagship an hour or so earlier, signalled along the coast, and everyone on board—as well as dozens of people living on shore—would be waiting anxiously for any mail and newspapers she might have brought out.

Ramage signalled to the gunner's mate who bellowed:

'Number one gun—fire!'

Even as the gun leapt back in recoil on the starboard side, the explosion echoing across the bay and the smoke blowing forward, the gunner's mate had begun the chant which ensured each gun fired at the right interval, muttering all but the last four words to himself:

'*If I wasn't a gunner I wouldn't be here*—Number two gun fire!'

The first gun on the larboard side leapt back in recoil, the crew at once beginning the routine of re-loading.

'*If I wasn't a gunner I wouldn't be here*—Number three gun fire!'

As the guns fired one after the other Ramage realized Southwick was also totting up the number of rounds—it wasn't unknown for a gunner or his mate to miscount.

Fifteen ... sixteen ... the smoke was drifting back to the quarterdeck, catching in everyone's throat ... seventeen. The gunner's mate was moving aft, the men began sponging the guns before securing them.

Even as the first boom of the flagship's reply echoed across the water she hoisted several signals. Southwick glanced at the first with his telescope, groaned and said contemptuously:

'He's one of those ... I was afraid o' that.'

Even before Jackson started reading out the signals Ramage guessed the first one would say where the brig was to anchor, but if the Admiral was a fussy man ...

'Captain to come to the Admiral, sir.'

'Sick to be sent to the hospital ship, sir ...'

'Damn and blast it, make a note of them!' Ramage snapped at the American. 'Just tell me any more that affect us anchoring.'

He bent over the binnacle, watching the bearing of the flagship. Men were standing by at sheets and braces; topmen were at the foot of the shrouds ready to swarm up and out on the yards to furl the sails. The fo'c'slemen were awaiting the orders that would let the anchor splash into the sea and send the cable racing out through the hawse so fast the smell of scorching would come aft to the quarterdeck.

In his cabin two leather pouches and his newest uniform awaited Ramage. The smaller pouch, which had a lead weight in it so if thrown overboard it would sink immediately (a reminder they might have been captured on the voyage from England), contained the secret letter from the First Lord to Admiral Robinson. The larger one held all the prosaic paperwork the Admiral would require—the *Triton*'s log; 'weekly accounts' describing her condition; Sick Book, listing all the men who had been ill during the voyage and the treatment given; returns from the bosun's, gunner's and carpenter's mates; a list of remaining provisions; several reports of surveys signed by himself and Southwick—on a leakage of beer from several badly-made barrels, on various casks of salt beef and pork, each of which contained fewer pieces of meat than was painted on the outside, and on a sail too ripe for further repairs. And, most important of all, there was Ramage's report on the capture of *La Merlette*, together with all the relevant documents—and they were many.

Yet, Ramage thought sourly, within ten minutes of being on board the *Prince of Wales* the Admiral's wretched secretary would triumphantly announce that Ramage, his clerk and Southwick had forgotten some tedious and unimportant form . . .

The brig was within a hundred yards of where she was to anchor. Ramage only hoped the men remembered his signals and was pleased the Admiral had chosen a spot so near the flagship. The *Triton* was—if all went according to plan!—about to furl all sail, anchor and hoist out a boat without one word being spoken: everything would be done by signals from Ramage.

He made the first signals with his right arm. In a few moments it seemed that every man in the ship was either hauling a rope or climbing the rigging. The yards were hauled round, the bellying sails flattened and then fluttered; men swarmed out on the yards to furl the sails neatly, securing them with gaskets.

Even as that was happening Ramage was signalling to the quartermaster and the brig turned to head right into the wind's eye, gradually slowing as she did so. The sound of water sluicing away from the stem, rushing along her sides and gurgling under the counter, which had been part of their lives for so many weeks, died away, leaving a silence which was unsettling.

Slowly the *Triton* lost way. Southwick, watching over the taffrail, lifted his hand as she began to drift astern and Ramage signalled to the men on the fo'c'sle. A moment later a splash told him the anchor had been let go; then he saw the cable snaking out through the hawse, tell-tale whisps of blue smoke vanishing in the wind.

From where he was standing Ramage could see the compass without moving. He checked the bearing from the flagship: by the time the *Triton* drifted astern to the full scope of her cable she'd be in the correct position. And Southwick was already signalling to more men, making sure that all the yards were square—not an inch lower either end, precisely horizontal, all at right angles to the masts. The boat would be hoisted out within a couple of minutes. Ramage looked at Southwick and pointed below, indicating he was going to change. A man may have sworn under his breath, he thought, otherwise not a word had been spoken. But probably the Admiral had been asleep . . .

*

But the Admiral had not been asleep: as Ramage, hot and sticky in full uniform, reported to him in the great cabin of the *Prince of Wales*, he was greeted with a breezy, 'Like to see a ship well handled, m'lad!' and an outstretched hand which shook his with a firm grasp.

Admiral Robinson's appearance and manner belied the impression given by the string of signals which greeted the *Triton*. Tall, almost plump (he had the figure of a man who once had been a great athlete but now the muscle had turned to fat) he would have passed for Southwick's younger brother —his face was round, almost cherubic, pleasant and open. His nose was larger, and its redness owed more to claret than the hot sun; the eyes were alert and clear blue; his blond hair was bleached by the sun into a pale yellow which blended with the streaks of white.

After asking what sort of voyage Ramage had had, nodding approvingly when told about the capture of *La Merlette*, and inquiring after the health of Ramage's parents (hinting, Ramage wondered, that he had no animosity towards the Earl?), he said: 'I wasn't expecting you, m'lad: I asked the Admiralty for five more frigates!'

'I don't know about the frigates, sir; I've brought letters from Lord Spencer.'

He fished in his pocket for the key, which was completely embedded in a large piece of red wax, with the Admiralty seal on both sides. He gave both key and the small locked pouch to the Admiral, who called for his secretary, handed him the lump of wax and said curtly: 'Break out the key—not in here, I don't want chips of wax over everything.'

'You were lucky with *La Merlette*,' he commented as the secretary left the cabin and, to Ramage's surprise because he'd forgotten the point, continued: 'You were sailing under Admiralty orders, so naturally I don't qualify for a share in the prize money. The thieving old Commander-in-Chief doesn't take his eighth—more's the pity as far as I'm concerned. But if she's as sound as you say I'll buy her in—I need all the small vessels I can get my hands on.

'Being Commander-in-Chief on this station's like trying to run a post-chaise service—never enough coaches or horses and too many passengers all wanting to go in different directions at the same moment. Ah, Fanshaw, the magic key—thank you.'

As he unlocked the pouch Ramage rose to leave him alone to read the letters, but the Admiral glanced up and shook his head.

'Make yourself comfortable, m'dear fellah. A drink? Tell Fanshaw what you want—just excuse me a moment.'

Lifting his spectacles, which had been hanging round his neck on a piece of ribbon, he adjusted them and broke the seal on the first of the letters.

Ramage shook his head at Fanshaw, declining a drink, and watched the Admiral's face. Not a muscle moved as he turned the page and read on, then read the whole letter a second time. But there was no doubt that the first letter was the vital one.

'Bad business, Ramage. You know what this is all about'—he waved the letter—'and his Lordship says you can answer any questions. Tell me, are the Jacobins at the back of it? The Irish? Those damned corresponding societies? Or all three?'

'None, sir, as far as I could see. I think the men simply feel mutiny is the only way to get what they want. At least that was certainly the case in the *Triton*.'

'What, they mutinied as well? His Lordship says'—he waved the letter again—'there's no sign of the mutiny ending. It hasn't ended has it?'

'It hadn't when we sailed. Yes, the Tritons had mutinied.'

'How did you get under way from Spithead, then?'

The Admiral asked the questions swiftly: he was obviously a man who thought, spoke and acted quickly: his voice had a decisiveness about it that Ramage liked. Although his eyes rarely moved, they were sharp. Ramage realized he was a man who did not make any unnecessary movement—apart from waving the letter.

'We were anchored in a strong wind with a shoal to leeward and it was high water, sir. When they refused to weigh I—well, I cut the cable with an axe and ordered 'em to make sail. They didn't have much choice: we'd have gone up on the shoal in three or four minutes ...'

The Admiral's expression did not change but his eyes narrowed. 'That's all there was to it?'

'In getting under way, yes. But luckily some men just transferred to the *Triton* and who'd served with me before discovered——' He stopped just in time: in another moment he'd have revealed the whole plot: a plot not mentioned in the log, nor in his journal ...

'Discovered what?'

'Discovered that mutiny was pointless,' Ramage said lamely.

The Admiral smiled. 'It all sounds an interesting yarn: you'd better come to dinner and tell me more about it. I have a house just by the jetty. We dine early—four o'clock, in an hour's time. As you're now to serve on this station I'll give you your orders at the same time because you'll be under way again as soon as *La Merlette* comes in with the rest of your men.'

'Aye aye, sir.'

'You don't seem very disappointed, Ramage. Most officers just arrived from England could find fifty reasons why they wouldn't be able to sail again inside of three weeks.'

'Social——' he just managed to stop a tactless remark, but the Admiral completed the sentence.

'Social life on shore doesn't interest you?'

Ramage reddened. 'In one sense, no sir.'

The Admiral laughed. 'But you're prepared to put up with the invitations of flag officers and commanders-in-chief, eh?'

There was no point in wriggling and the Admiral was taking it in good part, so Ramage laughed.

'Yes, sir. But I've also a good ship and a good crew, and now I know what they're like on a long passage I'd like to try 'em on different fare.'

'Different fare it'll be, I promise you that,' the Admiral

said and his tone was suddenly serious. 'But hurry along now or you'll be late for dinner. If you've mail on board, tell my secretary and he'll send a boat over to collect it. You've no need to water and provision: you won't be going far. And try to remember everything about London fashions—the women'll be all agog!'

★

As soon as the three wives had withdrawn, the Admiral looked up at Ramage and said: 'Your written orders will be prepared in the morning, but I want to run over the gist of them now so you can ask questions. Both Captain Chubb and Captain Dace had precisely the same orders very recently, so you can have the benefit of their experience.'

Both Captains looked embarrassed, but since the tone of the Admiral's voice had not changed, Ramage thought for a moment it was a natural modesty, then realized they must have failed to carry out the orders.

'Grenada had a violent insurrection a couple of years or so ago—do you know much about it?'

Ramage shook his head: he remembered some references in a newspaper but that was all.

'Well, you'll find out all about it when you get there, but briefly a man called Fédon led a revolt that all but threw us out of the island. Backed by the French, of course, and dozens of innocent people—planters and the like—were murdered. We landed more troops and the revolt was put down. Now the island is quiet again and trying to recover. Any questions so far?'

'Is there a chance of another revolt, sir?'

'No. But that's not to say there aren't people in the island who'd like to see the French take over; just that they don't amount to anything.

'Very well, Ramage, now for your part. Grenada is a rich island—mostly from sugar, molasses, rum, cotton, cocoa, and some coffee—but not very big. They don't import much, which means of course that merchantmen from England don't call there very often. Instead, the island schooners carry the produce up to Martinique, where it's transhipped.'

Ramage nodded, but so far he couldn't see where the *Triton* came into it.

'About four schooners a week sail from Grenada for islands

to the north and at least two are bound for Martinique with cargoes for transhipment to England. The rest are carrying out local trade and don't go farther than St Vincent. Can you guess your orders yet?'

Managing to hide his surprise at the sudden question, Ramage thought quickly. Had there been a slight emphasis on the word *sail* in the phrase 'sail from Grenada'? And the Admiral was obviously concerned with those bound for Martinique. It was worth a try.

'The schooners for Martinique sail, but they don't always arrive, sir?'

The Admiral glanced at Chubb and Dace, then looked straight at Ramage. 'Was that a guess, reasoning, or do you already know something about this?'

'Half-way between a guess and reasoning, sir.'

'Well, that's what happens. They sail from Grenada and some never arrive at Martinique, which is only about 160 miles away. And all the islands they pass are held by us. The Grenadines—lumps of rock: not even a rowing boat could hide among them. Then Bequia—the Army has a small garrison there. St Vincent and St Lucia both with plenty of troops. The longest stretch of open water is from St Lucia to Martinique, and that's only twenty miles or so. But for all that, some of the schooners just vanish.'

'Could it be treachery by the skippers, sir?'

'No, we thought of that. The skippers are local men; they've everything to lose. They and the schooners really do vanish; we've never found a trace of man or vessel that's failed to reach Martinique. Nor do the schooners ever turn up later flying the Tricolour. Very well, that's about all we know. Your job is to go to Grenada, find out what happens and put an end to it.'

'May I ask what measures have been used up to now, sir?'

'Tell him,' the Admiral instructed the two captains.

Both glanced at each other. Dace cleared his throat and, without looking at Ramage, said in a monotone:

'There aren't enough escorts—none in fact—so convoys can't be sailed, and anyway even if they could the freight rate's so high now the schooners prefer to make a dash for it. They reckon they can make three round voyages—if they don't get caught—in the time it'd take a convoy to get there and back;

particularly since it takes twice as long to unload ten ships arriving all at once in a convey than it does ten ships arriving singly at regular intervals——'

'He knows that!' the Admiral interrupted impatiently.

'—well, Captain Chubb and myself started patrols between Martinique and Grenada. He took the windward side of the islands and I the leeward side. We did that for two months. We saw nothing.'

'The schooners were still captured?'

'Yes,' Dace said uncomfortably, glancing at the Admiral.

'Did any of them take the windward side or all of them keep to the leeward, sir?'

Dace again looked embarrassed and from the way the Admiral glanced up Ramage guessed the idea hadn't occurred to any of them. What he intended as an innocent question now left an admiral and two captains looking foolish.

'Would it have made any difference do you think?' the Admiral demanded.

Dace shook his head. 'And I doubt if they'd try: they'd have a long beat to the eastward to clear St Vincent and St Lucia. They're an independent crowd, the schooner-owners.'

Ramage asked: 'Is there any point on the route which it's known the schooners always pass safely?'

Chubb nodded. 'They pass Bequia. Beyond that we're not sure. Perhaps St Vincent, but it's usually dark by then.'

'But the local traders to St Vincent—are they ever captured?'

'No.'

'What was the result of sailing them from St George at different times?'

Dace answered. 'None, because they have to spend a night at sea whatever time they leave St George's——'

'Damn it man!' the Admiral exclaimed. 'How many times do I have to say it. The capital of Grenada is St George. It's clear enough on the chart. Why do you people insist on calling it St George's. St George's *what*? It's named *after* the saint, it doesn't *belong* to him!'

'I beg your pardon, sir. Well, we've tried sailing them at dawn, noon, dusk and the middle of the night. Didn't make any difference.'

Ramage decided he'd find out more when he reached St

George: neither captain could tell him much and he was merely stirring up a lot of resentment by asking questions the answers of which could only emphasize that a lieutenant with a brig was now being given orders for an operation which two post captains commanding frigates had failed to carry out.

'Well, there you are Ramage,' the Admiral said, and Ramage had an uneasy feeling he had read his thoughts. 'We'll join the ladies: they'll want to hear news of the latest fashions in London—and the gossip.'

CHAPTER THIRTEEN

Southwick listened gloomily as Ramage finally told him about the Admiral's orders and then exclaimed indignantly: 'A needle in a haystack sort of job! How does he expect us to do it when a couple of frigates failed?'

Ramage shrugged his shoulders and said without conviction, 'We draw less—we can get into places a frigate can't.'

Southwick shook his head. 'No, sir: I know these islands pretty well and there's deep enough water wherever they'd need to go. Leastways, they can get in close enough to see. No, I reckon I know what's happened.'

Ramage, idly watching Grenada looming up in the distance, said: 'Out with it, then!'

'Well, with all these schooners vanishing, the planters must be screaming over produce rotting on the quayside and freight rates rocketing, and the owners because insurance rates will be astronomical. And you can almost hear the underwriters in London yelping out as they pay for claim after claim. Wouldn't surprise me if they're refusing to write any more policies. Don't blame 'em either. If neither schooner-owners nor planters get insurance...'

And Southwick was right: the planters had enormous influence in Parliament, and so had the underwriters. Long ago Admiral Robinson would have had peremptory orders from the Admiralty to dispose of the privateers. Now——

'You know what I think, sir?'

And Ramage was sure he did—that was why he'd kept the orders to himself for two days—but there was no harm in hearing Southwick's conclusions now.

'I reckon it's happened like this, sir. As soon as the Admiralty started chasing the Commander-in-Chief, he sent off a couple of frigates, but in two months they haven't caught a single privateer. Now, the Admiral knows he's going to get a real rubbing down as soon as word goes back to London that three months or more later the situation's as bad as ever, and he wants to protect himself and his two captains . . .'

Ramage nodded—he'd thought that, realizing the Admiral was not only shrewder than he'd given him credit for but considerably more ruthless.

'. . . And he knows your stock's pretty high after the Cape St Vincent action, sir. So just as he's wondering how to tell the Admiralty he can't smoke out the privateers but at the same time shield himself and two of his captains, along comes the *Triton* to join his command.

'So you get the job. If you fail—too bad. If you succeed—well, as far as he's concerned you're welcome to what little credit there is. And it won't be much—why, the Jamaica frigates are doing this sort of thing every day along the coast of Hispaniola.'

Ramage nodded, reflecting how Chubb and Dace must be laughing. Ten minutes' embarrassment while a lieutenant asked them questions was a small price to pay to get rid of any responsibility.

Two hours later the *Triton* was running fast along the south coast of Grenada, helped by a couple of knots of current streaming into the southern end of the Caribbean from the Atlantic.

The island was a pyramid, the high mountains in the centre surrounded by concentric rings of ever-lower hills until, at the coast, they ended in cliffs rarely more than fifty feet high.

Like great black fingers, many peninsulas stuck out along the south coast, the trade winds raising a heavy swell which battered the headlands incessantly, undercutting the rock until great pieces toppled into the sea. Between each headland was a long narrow stretch of calm water, often extending inland for a mile or more, and ending in mangrove swamps.

Pointing out two of them to Southwick, Ramage said:

'Look—that's Chemin Bay, between Westerhall Point and Point of Fort Jeudy. You'd never believe there's a lagoon leading off to one side at the far end big enough to take three frigates at anchor. And just to the west is Egmont, with another one.'

'Just the place for privateers!'

Ramage nodded. 'Fortunately the other islands aren't made

the same way!'

'Just as well . . . A few guns up on those headlands and you'd never get in.'

The island, roughly rectangular and lying lengthways north and south, had a great bight extending up from its southwest corner and at the head of it was the harbour and capital, St George. The *Triton* was steering to pass Point Saline, the south-west corner of the island—and the last sight of land for ships bound south to Trinidad and the coast of South America —before hauling her wind and beating up to St George.

Southwick commented, 'The stretch of the coast puts me in mind o' Cornwall—sheer cliffs and rocks and too much wind for trees to grow properly. Just look at those small ones— some kind of fir, are they?—all leaning over to leeward!'

But Ramage did not want to be reminded of Cornwall: already the long Tropical nights were bedevilled by memories of Gianna: lying in his cot his imagination nearly drove him mad when he thought of the long months there'd be before his fantasies gave place to reality and he'd see her again.

Looking down at the small sketch he was holding showing the harbour and lagoon of St George and then across at Point Saline, he nodded significantly at Southwick, who started bellowing orders which sent men running to the sheets, braces and bowlines, ready for the turn which would take the brig round the Point and bring St George into sight.

*

St George was built on several hills, with steep cliffs on the seaward side. The entrance to the harbour, little more than a slot cut in the cliffs, led straight to the quays built round three sides of a rectangle, the town ranging over the hills on the west and north sides. To the east, hidden from seaward, was a huge, almost circular lagoon, the sea-filled crater of an extinct volcano and surrounded by steep hills to form a natural amphitheatre.

But at the point where the rim of the lagoon joined the east side of the harbour a coral reef had grown, closing the channel to everything but open boats.

'A damn shame,' Southwick had grumbled. 'That could be one of the finest hurricane anchorages in the Windwards! Worth using a few tons of powder to blast a channel through.'

The town and harbour were well protected against attacks from seaward by Fort George, built high on the hills at the west side of the entrance and covering the whole bight.

The Fort, massively built of stone, was also the head-quarters of Colonel Humphrey Wilson, the military commander of His Majesty's land forces in Grenada, and the man on whom Ramage was about to pay his first official visit.

But for a few minutes Ramage stood beside one of the eighteen-pounder guns poking its muzzle through an embrasure in the massive walls round the top of the Fort, refreshing himself in the brisk wind after the heat of the quays in the harbour below.

Facing eastwards, he had the open sea on his right—with the *Triton* anchored a quarter of a mile out—the lagoon facing him, and the open-ended rectangle of the harbour to his left.

Several small rowing boats were scattered across the lagoon, but most were close by the coral reef, each with two or three men fishing with tropical lethargy, hidden from the heat of the sun by wide-brimmed straw hats or pieces of sacking propped up with sticks to make a little shadow. Occasional movements by one of the men and glints of silver as the fish jumped clear of the water, showed there was plenty to be caught.

Ramage watched two of the *Triton*'s boats laden with casks pulling for the reef: Southwick was taking the opportunity of getting fresh water from the big cistern on the far side of the lagoon.

On the shore just short of the reef two island schooners were lying over on their sides like stranded whales, hove down at the careenage by tackles to their masts so their bottoms could be cleaned. Smoke from the nearer one showed she was being cleaned by the old-fashioned method of breaming, men running flaming torches made of reeds along the planks, melting the old coating of pitch and burning off the weed and barnacles. The other one was already cleaned off, and Ramage could visualize her crew smearing on a thin layer of new pitch before coating it with a mixture of sulphur and tallow, in the age-old battle to kill the teredo and gribble worms who used the planking as both a home and a life-long meal.

Two small cutters were unloading a cargo at the quays; a

third was alongside a schooner to which it was transferring its cargo. Obviously the cutters collected freight from the smaller bays and harbours round the island and brought it to St George, where it was transhipped to the larger schooners plying between the islands.

A second schooner farther along the quay was being loaded from carts, the crew hoisting up sacks with a tackle from the mast. A third, beyond it, was almost fully laden. Even from five hundred yards away Ramage could hear the shouting and yelling of a couple of dozen men heaving at the tackles, and pulling and pushing the sacks as they swung on board in a welter of good-natured confusion. To a prying eye, he noted as he turned away, it was obvious all three schooners would be ready to sail in a few hours.

The sun's glare forced him almost to close his eyes as he took off his hat to wipe away the perspiration; then he hitched at his sword belt, straightened his stock and walked towards the military commander's office in the fortress.

The sentry detailed to escort him from the guardroom at the entrance gave an audible sigh of relief, obviously impatient with young naval officers stupid enough not to stand in the shade.

*

Colonel Wilson, upon whom the Governor leaned heavily for advice, was a man who loathed the tropics, loathed his office in Fort George, loathed Grenada, and was within a few paces of loathing all naval officers solely because, unlike his, their stay in the island was always brief.

All this Ramage had already heard in Barbados, but most of it was obvious within a few moments of entering his office after being announced by the sentry—a crudely-contrived insult, Ramage noted, since it was a matter of courtesy that an A.D.C. should have been available the moment the *Triton* anchored after firing her salute.

'What's your name?' the Colonel barked by way of a greeting. 'What's your business?'

Obviously the Army was no different from the Navy in the low proportion of officers who were also gentlemen.

'Ramage, sir; Lieutenant, commanding His Majesty's brig *Triton*. You'll have heard your guns replying to our salute as we arrived.'

'Your business?'

A round, red face mottled with purple; two bloodshot, watery eyes astride the bridge of a bulbous nose; enormous ears like handles on a jug; nominally clean-shaven though obviously his razor had been resting for a couple of days; a mouth once firm but the lips now slack and petulant; hands large, flat down on the desk and displaying filthy nails; the cuffs of his shirt dirty and those of his uniform frayed ... Snuff had been spilling down the front of his coat for weeks.

Although a half-empty bottle of rum, a glass up-ended over the top, was clearly the most important item on his desk, Ramage realized that the man's shoulders were the most significant part of him. Obviously they had once been braced back with a military erectness; but now they were permanently hunched forward and sagging. He was a symbol of tropical boredom and ill-health. He'd probably seen three-quarters of his regiment dying from sickness and drowned in rum his disappointment at not getting promotion.

Yet the dark rings under the eyes and deep vertical wrinkles each side of his mouth were not entirely due to drink. Probably there was a nagging wife in the background, a woman whose social aspiration had overtaken her husband's ability to buy or obtain promotion. All these things had charged a high price against the Colonel's physique ...

But Ramage knew he had to work with the man: his orders were so worded by Admiral Robinson (purposely? he wondered) that although he had to protect the schooners and deal with the privateers, the military commander was responsible for what went on inside the harbour. Which, Ramage suddenly realized, meant that the Colonel could interpret them to say he decided when the schooners sailed.

'From Admiral Robinson, sir,' Ramage said quietly, placing a sealed envelope on the desk.

'Wait outside while I read it.'

Ramage flushed, paused a moment and then turned on his heel, closing the door quietly behind him, and determined to make all allowances for the man's three years' service in Grenada. Three or four minutes later Wilson bellowed for him to return.

'Don't know what the Admiral's doing, sending me a youngster and a brig,' he snapped. As he folded the letter he added sourly. 'Can't show you these orders, they're secret, but——'

'I've already seen them,' Ramage couldn't help interjecting. 'The Admiral showed them to me before they were sealed.'

'Most irregul——' The Colonel broke off, obviously realizing it was unwise to criticize the naval Commander-in-Chief. 'Very well then, you'll sail at once and begin your patrols. Don't want your damned sailors roistering round the town——'

'I think, sir——'

'Don't interrupt—and don't think. I do the thinking. I give the orders.'

The insult was crude, but more important was that the Colonel obviously knew he was overstepping his authority and was testing how far he could go. Ramage sensed that if he was to achieve anything in the next few weeks, now was the time to regain some of the initiative.

'I have my orders from the Admiral, sir. Part of them is referred to in his letter to you, which I've just delivered.'

He paused to let Wilson absorb the point and then added quietly: 'The rest, which aren't referred to, concern the way in which I deal with the privateers, so if you'll forgive me I'll take my leave and——'

'Now Lieutenant, don't rush things: far too hot for that!'

Wilson lifted the glass off the bottle, took another from his drawer and began pouring.

'A drink, perhaps? I want to hear the news from home. Did you bring any mail or newspapers? All the ladies'll want to hear of the latest fashions.'

The change of face was too much for Ramage.

'No mail or newspapers, sir. And it's a little early for me to have a drink, so if you'll——'

'I won't, so sit down again. Sorry for my temper: never good at the best of times and this schooner business is wearing me down. Dam' Governor sends me notes daily; a deputation of ship-owners is due here this afternoon—the fifth in five weeks. Plantation-owners trot up to Government House every day and since I'm only a soldier I can't do a dam' thing about it except listen to the same old story and make the same old excuses.

'Two bloody frigates patrolling up and down the islands for a couple of months and never sight or sound of free-booters. In fact they more than hinted there weren't any—that the schooners were sailing off and handing themselves over to the French or Spanish. So just when I'm expecting the Admiral himself with a squadron, you arrive! Not your fault; not blaming you, m'lad.'

He paused for a breath, took an enormous gulp of rum, and Ramage noticed the dark patches on his coat showing how much the Colonel was now perspiring: it was running in streams down his forehead, being diverted along his eye-brows, then trickling down his cheeks. Yet the room in the Fort was cool from the breeze. Unwillingly, Ramage began to feel sympathetic: the Colonel was a convenient whipping boy for everyone.

'The Admiral doesn't mention any plan, Ramage.'

'No, sir.'

'Leaves it all to you?'

'So I believe, sir.'

'Well, you have your orders, surely?'

'They're secret, sir.'

It was unfair but Ramage could not resist it.

'Quite so, quite so. Now is there any way I can help ...'

'I'd like some facts and dates, sir, about the schooners already lost.'

'Well, I'm afraid I haven't got 'em. I don't——'

'You mentioned the deputation of ship-owners. Is there a particular one who acts as spokesman?'

Wilson's watery eyes lit up.

'By jove, yes: Rondin! Owns half the schooners. He's a cold fish—has the Governor's ear, too! He's your man!'

'If I could see him ...'

'Of course—look'ee, Ramage, I'll arrange it for this after-noon. That'll head off the deputation, too. I'll send word—maybe you'd like to go up to see him—lovely house on the other side of the lagoon?'

'At four o'clock then, sir? And transport?'

'Of course, of course ...'

*

The house of Mr Rondin was large and spacious as became

a leading businessman of Grenada and cool with high ceilings. But there was too much silver, too much ornate chinaware, too many cut-glass decanters on display to indicate anything but that the Rondin's were *nouveaux riches*.

And Rondin greeted Ramage with a curious obsequiousness in a large, octagonal drawing-room which had windows on five sides. A tall, angular man with white hair smoothed unfashionably flat on his scalp, his face equally unfashionably tanned by the sun, he bowed a greeting:

'My Lord, I am John Rondin.'

Since he never used his title in the Service, for a moment Ramage was startled: then he realized Colonel Wilson must have emphasized it, probably making the most of what the Admiral had sent him. A lieutenant and a small brig was not much of a hand to deal; but shuffling in that the lieutenant was a lord and heir to one of the country's oldest earldoms —well, it might take one trick, or at least divert some attention from the smallness of his ship.

As he shook hands, Ramage sensed Rondin's grey eyes were missing nothing—yet there was no impression of prying. As soon as they were seated in comfortable cane armchairs and the coloured butler was pouring them drinks, Rondin said:

'Does the Admiral intend sending more ships to reinforce you, my Lord?'

Ramage inclined his head towards the butler. Rondin nodded almost imperceptibly and promptly changed the subject: 'You had a pleasant voyage from England?'

'Yes—good weather most of the time, apart from the usual blows in the Bay of Biscay.'

'Ah—the underwriters' nightmare! I wonder how much that Bay's cost them in claims for total losses...'

Ramage laughed. 'Not enough to make them refuse to cover that part of the voyage.'

'True—they grumble, they increase premiums, but they rarely go bankrupt.'

'The essence of underwriting. Rather like being a bookmaker—always hedge your bets.'

'And that's just what it is,' Rondin said, motioning the butler to leave.

As soon as the door was closed he continued: 'You were

quite right, my Lord: that man has been with me twenty years, but walls can have ears.'

Realizing his caution had reflected on Rondin's employees, Ramage began to apologize but Rondin waved his hand.

'You were quite right. I think I can guess what's in your mind, but I'll know in good time. Now tell me, do you expect reinforcements?'

'No.' Ramage said bluntly. 'That doesn't mean the Admiral isn't very worried, but he hasn't any other ships to spare.' Ramage considered the lie was justifiable. 'Yet I begin to wonder if a dozen frigates would help. However,' he added warily, 'I'd be glad of your views.'

Rondin lifted his glass and held it against the light, looking questioningly at the rich brown liquid. 'I should have thought a dozen frigates would be just about enough—but forgive me, I'm not a naval man, merely a poor ship-owner becoming even poorer as the weeks go by ...'

'Perhaps I've misunderstood the situation, sir,' Ramage said innocently. 'Surely the schooners are being lost between here and Martinique?'

The ship-owner nodded.

'And to privateers which—as far as anyone knows—materialize out of thin air, make their capture, and vanish with the schooner?'

Again Rondin nodded, and Ramage searched for a simile. 'Then surely, it's rather like a farmer losing cattle between the farmyard and the meadow. He sees them leave the farmyard, watches them part of the way to the meadow—and they don't come back at milking time.'

Rondin said: 'Yes—somewhat simplified, that's the position.'

'Yet with only 160 miles to sail to Martinique and two frigates patrolling the route, the schooners were still captured, even though they were almost in sight of a frigate most of the time.'

'Yes—in daylight, anyway, but don't forget they make part of the passage at night.'

'No, I wasn't forgetting; that's why a dozen frigates are either not enough or too many. On a moonless night, visibility is about half a mile, so to cover the night passage you'd need a frigate at least every mile. Ten hours of darkness at say five knots—fifty frigates . . .'

Rondin twiddled his glass and said nothing for a full two minutes, his eyes focused on the tip of Ramage's sword scabbard. Ramage waited, wondering if the idea would come to Rondin: it would be easier if the ship-owner thought of it: there'd be a lot more collaboration if Rondin thought he was nourishing his own plan.

Finally the man began talking, as if to himself.

'The wolf is hiding in a wood very near to the farmhouse . . . Perhaps somewhere so near that no one thinks of looking there . . . He has powerful ears, eyes, nose . . . Or maybe his mate is even nearer and warns him . . .'

Ramage was thankful that Rondin was shrewd; but how near the farmyard would he accept as feasible? It was worth letting the idea mature a while before going into detail. So Ramage asked

'Can I have some facts now, Mr Rondin; details of how many ships have been lost, dates, cargoes, nationalities of their masters, where bound—that kind of thing?'

Rondin walked over to a desk. 'I have most of the answers here: I recently wrote a report to the Governor listing the schooners lost and the dates they sailed.'

Taking out four or five sheets of paper, he glanced at them and gave them to Ramage, who asked:

'Are schooners bound for Martinique the only ones lost?'

'Yes.'

'Never those for St Lucia or St Vincent?'

'Few go to either island. Cargoes are transhipped at Martinique: that's where the home trade assembles to wait for a convoy.'

'Is there any pattern to the losses? Any particular cargoes or particular owners?'

'No—I've looked already.'

'And the sequence of losses—three schooners lost one after the other, say, then two get through safely?'

Rondin shook his head.

'What about those that get through to Martinique—have any been captured on the return voyage?'

Rondin's face suddenly became animated.

'That's strange—and I hadn't thought about it! No, not one that reached Martinique has ever been captured on the way back—when it was sailing empty in other words. Surely that's very significant?'

Ramage shook his head. 'Only in showing a laden schooner is valuable and one in ballast isn't. Privateersmen are interested in cargoes, not hulls. No profit in a hull—they can't sell a schooner as a prize.'

'What do you think they do with them?'

'I don't know—perhaps sink them or sail them down to the Spanish Main. That's a possibility, but it means using a lot of men as prize crews—and getting them back again.'

'And you don't think it's likely?'

'For the moment, no,' Ramage said. 'But before I ask my next question, let's go over again the facts we know. Although some schooners leaving here bound for Martinique never arrive at Fort Royal, there's no indication they pass it. Therefore they're captured between here and somewhere south of Martinique. Yet all the islands between Grenada and Martinique are British owned, and only St Vincent and St Lucia are of any size. No French or Spanish islands to leeward—unless you count the Spanish Main. And the privateersmen want the cargoes, not the hulls . . .'

Rondin said quietly, 'I think I can guess that next question of yours. If I'd thought of it earlier, we might have solved all this business long ago, Instead it takes a young naval lieutenant who hasn't been in Grenada for more than a few hours!'

Ramage smiled. 'I think you'd better hear the question first and make sure it's the same.'

'It is; I'm certain of that. It's the key to the whole thing. But you ask it!'

'Very well. Where do the privateersmen dispose of the cargoes since these are all British islands?'

The ship-owner nodded. 'And all the time we could only think of our ships being lost! We went to see the Governor; the Governor wrote to Admiral Robinson, and he sent frigates which searched . . . If only I'd sat down and thought!'

'The trade returns for each of the islands,' Ramage said. 'How often are they produced? I mean, can we compare each island's exports *to England* for say, each of the last six months and see which one's suddenly increased?'

Rondin stood up and began walking back and forth across

the room, staring out over the lagoon and towards the setting sun. Then he began talking angrily.

'We can't get those figures for months but, by God, they'll not only give the answer but they'll show what's happening. What a fool I am! Hundreds of tons of produce leaving Grenada and then vanishing—yet it can't vanish! But I of all men should have known: nothing has a commercial value unless there's a market for it. Somewhere, somehow, those hundreds of tons of stolen produce are being sold and shipped to England. But sold by whom—and to whom?'

He turned to Ramage, arms outstretched. 'Give me a frank answer. Do you think that's the only possibility? That after the cargoes are stolen, they're shipped out of some other island in the normal way of trade—legally as it were? That these thieves have a way of channelling their booty through plantation-owners?'

Ramage nodded. 'It's my guess; as you've just said, nothing has a value unless there's a market for it. At least, not in this sense. Who would systematically steal something if he couldn't dispose of it?'

Rondin flopped down in his chair and drained his glass with a gesture that seemed to Ramage approaching despair. Bellowing for the butler to refill it, he muttered: 'It means our own people are betraying us: other plantation-owners in some other island.'

'Only one or two, perhaps,' Ramage pointed out, pausing as the butler came in, refilled Rondin's glass, noted Ramage's was still untouched, and left the room again.

'But since the trade returns can't help us,' he continued, 'we're almost back where we started—watching the schooners sailing out of the harbour entrance and vanishing.'

'Yes—forgive me young man: this is a hard blow for a man in my position. Competition in business, yes that's fair and one expects it; but treachery . . .'

*

Back on board the *Triton* Ramage read through the papers given him by Rondin, thought briefly of the captured schooners' cargoes, and decided to read the papers yet again, despite the fact the heat made him feel sleepy.

The figures of the losses were detailed. In the past four

months, thirty-one schooners had sailed from Grenada for Martinique and twenty-one had been captured. As he read the names and the dates they sailed the drowsiness vanished: there was a pattern!

If a schooner sailed several days after another, it was captured. If a third sailed within two days it invariably arrived safely in Martinique but a fourth leaving a couple of days later would be captured. When the fifth and sixth sailed almost immediately, they'd get through. But not the seventh if it waited two or three days.

He rubbed his forehead, excited but puzzled. A pattern, yes, but what was its significance? Then in a few moments it dawned on him that the pattern was set by the time it took to unload one schooner. Unload and get rid of the cargo, to be more precise.

Again he checked through the list of ships and dates. No, although there was not one instance where the privateers had taken a schooner less than four days after capturing another, there were many cases where schooners had arrived safely in Martinique having sailed less than four days after one which *had* been captured.

Four days . . . yet Rondin had assured him it was not difficult to unload a schooner in one day, though more usually it took two.

Why four days, then? Surely the privateersmen weren't short of men? Ramage pictured them swinging the sacks of cocoa beans and barrels of molasses up and out of the holds and over the side on to the jetty then—*jetty*! Did they have a jetty? A jetty with a road which carts could use to carry away sacks and barrels?

Perhaps not, he thought excitedly; supposing they had to unload in some isolated spot which could be reached only along tracks suitable for pack animals?

One or two sacks for each animal . . . Sacks which if left piled up on the ground would spoil in the heavy tropical showers: molasses barrels which would split and leak in the heat of the sun . . . That could reduce the unloading time to four days: four days in which they dare not bring in another prize.

Dare not? The cargo would be safe enough if left in the schooner's hold. Well, that raised another question: why, with one prize being unloaded in their lair, did the privateers-men let another potential prize escape them? Why not capture it, leave the hatch covers on, and unload it at their leisure?

Again his imagination wandered. He thought of warships waiting at anchor for powder hoys to arrive alongside; of dozens of merchantmen lying at anchor in the Thames after a big convoy arrived in the London river at the end of a voyage from halfway round the world. At anchor, waiting until there was a space at a dock . . . space at a dock.

Was there room enough only for one vessel where the privateers unloaded the prize schooners—and perhaps the privateers as well? Not enough room for two? Or some reason why there shouldn't be two? That made sense; it answered a question—or provided a possible answer.

Assume a schooner carried a hundred tons of cargo in hundredweight sacks—2,000 sacks. And a mule could carry, say, four sacks, a donkey two, a human being one. Five hundred mule trips, a thousand donkey trips . . .

How the devil would privateersmen—even if in league with many plantation-owners—get enough mules or donkeys or slaves to carry that number of sacks very far? Yet surely it had to be carried a good distance to get it to a port where it could be loaded again. Unless . . .

He reached up for charts rolled up in the rack above his head; charts covering the islands between Grenada and Martinique, and began looking at the bays and inlets. There were dozens: the outline of each island was irregular, like a broken piece of cheese, the bays and inlets bitten out by rats.

He decided to rule out the east coasts of the island, where the bays and lagoons took the full force of the Atlantic swell, because no privateers would dare use them: too many coral reefs, and the entrances too narrow to beat out in the prevailing easterly winds to snatch their next prize.

So the hiding places had to be on the south, north or (most probably) western side of an island. The bay he was looking for would be almost completely enclosed—for concealment. There'd probably be deep water close up to the shore—for unloading the schooners. And not too far from a larger port—for carrying the stolen cargoes overland.

The major factor was concealment. A concealed bay, or a bay in which a schooner and a privateer could hide without being seen from to seaward or being too obvious from the land. After half an hour's search of the charts he knew there was only one way of finding the likely ones—he'd have to go up the islands in the *Triton* and look. He hadn't yet paid a courtesy call on the Governor, but that would have to wait. He shouted to the sentry to pass the word for the Master.

CHAPTER FOURTEEN

As the *Triton* sailed back from Martinique, passing southwards along the west side of Grenada, Ramage stood on the larboard side looking at the mountains covering the island and reviewing the voyage. He admitted with ill grace that he was still no wiser than before.

Plenty of wide, open bays, almost enclosed bays, big bays and small bays; but none holding a privateer. Working north from Grenada, there'd been the small rocky islets just north of the island—among them the pointed Kick 'em Jenny, as aptly named a place as he'd ever come across, since the Trade winds and current flowing into the Caribbean knocked up a vicious, confused sea round it; then the large, narrow island of Carriacou, a thousand or so people living on it, and a couple of uninhabited and desolate islets just east of it.

Both islets had bays on the leeward side which could be used as anchorages—indeed were by small open fishing boats. They were picturesque; the water startlingly clear; but not only was there no sign of a privateer but the local fishermen swore they'd never seen any and Maxton, who'd done the questioning, was satisfied they'd been telling the truth.

Then the *Triton* had visited the larger Union Island to the north of Carriacou, with Chatham Bay on the lee side and several small islets on the other three sides. Again plenty of possible anchorages but all much too open for secrecy. Then Mayero and the Tobago Cays with more islets to the north, and Cannouan, larger and mountainous but hopeless for unloading schooners because of the swell.

On then to Bequia, more hilly than mountainous, with strong currents and a large open anchorage. Admiralty Bay, and a thriving whaling industry run mostly by Scotsmen. They were curious men and Ramage wanted to know more about them. From what he could gather they were descendants of former Scots taken prisoner in the fighting against Cromwell's Ironsides during the Civil War of 1648. And Cromwell had shown no mercy: these men who'd fought unsuccessfully for Prince Charles had been shipped out to the West Indies and treated like slaves. Now most of their descendants, skin burned red by the sun, many with red hair, made a living as fishermen or working on the plantations.

They had their women with them—also descendants of the women who'd elected to be transported with their menfolk —and although treated like the native slaves, refused to have anything to do with the coloured people, behaving with a pride which should have shamed many of the white plantation-owners who employed them. Already there were signs of too much inbreeding.

But whatever the rights and wrongs of their being transported to the West Indies, Ramage believed their assurances that privateers never visited Admiralty Bay.

St Vincent, a few miles across the channel to the north, was very large—much bigger than Grenada, with the port and capital of Kingstown in the south-west corner. Mountainous, fertile, a great green mass of sloping hills, terraces and forests, it had plenty of bays—among them Wallilabu, Cumberland, Château Belaire (with a small harbour)—but nothing that hid a privateer.

So far Ramage had not felt disappointed: he was sure he would find the answer in St Lucia, the last big island before Martinique. From the north end of St Vincent there was a clear view of St Lucia twenty-four miles to the north. More mountainous than St Vincent, the island seemed to attract all the rain in the Caribbean (though he remembered the prize usually went to Dominica, way to the north). At the south end, like two enormous thumbs sticking up in the air, were the cone-shaped twin mountains of the Pitons. And all along the west coast up to the capital, Castries, and beyond, were many bays.

Even before leaving Grenada Ramage had half hoped he'd spotted on the St Lucia chart the place the privateers were using—Marigot Bay. Shaped like the glass stopper of a decanter, the bay's entrance was a 200-yard-wide gap in the cliffs and it ran inland for 600 yards before a low sandspit on either side narrowed the channel to less than fifty yards.

Beyond the sandspits the bay suddenly opened out again into a circular lagoon.

Less than ten miles south of the port of Castries and completely surrounded by high hills, it had seemed an ideal spot, and as the *Triton* approached, Ramage had ordered Southwick to beat to quarters.

There was a natural platform in the otherwise sheer cliff on the south side of the entrance—a couple of guns mounted there could prevent anything approaching the entrance, and although the north side was not so sheer there were several positions where guns could be hidden.

But the *Triton* had gone right up to the entrance and hove-to, every gun of the starboard broadside aimed at the southern platform, while both he and Southwick had looked carefully, first for signs of guns, then through the entrance and across the first bay at the two sandspits which almost sealed it off from the lagoon beyond.

But the spits were low, covered with palms, and there had been no signs of a ship's masts in the lagoon. Some of the palms on the northern spit were withering, the fronds turning brown in the hot sun. Perhaps the river flowing into the lagoon had recently flooded, washing away the earth and sand from round the roots; or maybe some animal had eaten away the bark. It wasn't often one saw a dead palm tree—they seemed to live forever.

So Marigot Bay wasn't the privateersmen's nest; and as he'd ordered the yards to be braced round to get the *Triton* under way to call in at the island's capital, Castries, and then check the north side of the island before going on to Martinique, he knew why the two frigates had failed.

There'd been no clues in Castries or in Fort Royal at Martinique. Talks with the governors of both islands—and schooner-owners and captains—yielded plenty of criticisms of the Royal Navy, but no ideas; indeed, all of them talked of the privateers as if they were evil spirits manifesting themselves out of the misty rain forest in the darkness of a Tropical night. And in an atmosphere thick with voodoo, superstition, witch doctors and ignorance, it wasn't surprising.

Southwick had been unusually silent for the past hour as the *Triton* sailed down the last few miles back to St George.

Away over the starboard bow the headland of Point Saline was just coming up over the horizon, but only the caps of the smoothly-rounded hills forming the peninsula were visible so that it seemed like a sea monster wriggling along in the water.

Southwick pulled his hat forward to shield his eyes.

''Twas a waste of time, that trip.'

Ramage shrugged his shoulders. 'The only way to be sure was to look for ourselves. And now we all know what the islands look like.'

'That Marigot Bay ... I was sure we'd find them there.'

Southwick pronounced the 't' and Ramage just checked himself from correcting him yet again. Instead he nodded. 'I'd have bet on it.'

'Marigot, or the privateers coming down from north of Martinique.'

That was Southwick's particular pet idea; that the privateers were based north of Martinique and sailed down past Fort Royal, captured the schooners and took them back somewhere to the north: some isolated lair in Dominica, Guadeloupe or the dozen or so smaller islands up towards Antigua. But the authorities in Martinique had ruled it out: their only contribution to the scant information available was that there were enough fishing boats working out to leeward of Fort Royal both by day and night to be sure no privateers passed.

'What now, sir?'

Again Ramage shrugged his shoulders. 'There's only prayer left,' he said sourly.

At that moment Southwick saw him stiffen, as if stabbed in the back. He began rubbing the scar on his brow, swung round and walked aft to the taffrail. The Master watched closely, having made no secret that he was worried about the Admiral's orders: it was obvious to him—though Mr Ramage made light of it—that the Admiral had chosen the *Triton's* captain as the scapegoat. And, Southwick brooded to himself, the Ramage family have already suffered enough from the time the Government of the day used the old Earl as their scapegoat.

Southwick had lived too many years to expect justice or fair play; he'd long ago asked only that the injustices and unfairness in Service and political life should be kept within reasonable bounds. Yet to be fair to the Admiral, the two frigate captains who'd already failed to find the privateers were probably men he'd had with him since they were lieutenants: he owed them some loyalty.

When faced with an apparently impossible task maybe it was only natural to shield them by passing it on to someone to whom he owed no loyalty—Mr Ramage. Although it was bad luck for Mr Ramage, the fact was he had been lucky recently inasmuch as he'd gained a loyal ally in Commodore Nelson who, judging from his performance so far, would go a long way in the Service—if he didn't fall foul of the Admiralty through not obeying the exact wording of some order or another.

At that moment Ramage came back to Southwick. The expression on his face was an odd mixture of anger, embarrassment and happy surprise: like a child who'd been given an unjustified beating one moment and an unexpected present the next.

'I'm beginning to think we're tackling this from the wrong end,' he said quietly.

'How so, sir?'

'Well, we've been trying to find the privateers' base. But since there's never any sign of them at sea, obviously they don't patrol looking for schooners . . .'

Southwick looked puzzled. 'Then how do they find 'em?'

'They must know exactly when and where to look.'

'I don't follow you, sir.'

'Oh, wake up, Southwick: they must get secret information. If they don't go and search, then they must know that a schooner will pass a certain headland at a certain time, so they can be there to meet her in the dark. Minimum distance to sail, and a certain interception: that's why no one's ever seen them.'

'By Jove!' Southwick exclaimed. 'That *is* the only answer! And it means there's a spy at work in Grenada! But'—he paused, forehead wrinkled, nose twitching like a rabbit's—'but they sail from Grenada in darkness: it's 160 miles to Martinique and 115 miles to St Lucia. How the devil can a spy get the information to 'em quickly enough? Why—beggin' your pardon, sir,—it's almost impossible.'

'But it happens, Southwick; obviously it happens. I'm dam' sure that's how they do it. And because the privateers guess we'd think it's impossible, they succeed. Surprise, Mr Southwick: do the unexpected and you'll nearly always win, whatever the odds.'

Southwick had heard that often enough from his Captain, and seen him put it into practice. 'Was that why you left the master's mate and some men at Carriacou—so they might spot how the news is passed?'

Yet again Ramage shrugged his shoulders 'Yes and no— I'd a feeling we could do with some eyes we could trust keeping a watch from somewhere along the route, and Appleby can get down to us in a local cutter in five or six hours . . .'

'If he can keep his men sober.'

'I warned them what'd happen if they so much as touched a drop of liquor . . .'

'Aye, but whatever you threaten seamen think it's worth it.'

'Well, Appleby'll stay sober; and he has enough guineas in his pocket to hire the cutter's crew as well.'

*

Sir Jason Fisher, the Governor of Grenada, represented a new type of colonial administrator, but Ramage was far from sure he was any improvement on the old. Sir Jason came from humble origins—that much was obvious from his every action, from every sentence he spoke, from every thought he ever expressed in his whining Midland accent.

According to Colonel Wilson, who made no secret that he detested him, as a young man Sir Jason had been lucky to get a clerkship in 'John Company', and he'd worked hard and made the best of it. Like many a clever lad in the Honourable East India Company service, he'd received an excellent training, and he'd soon left it to begin his own business, so that twenty years in India changed him from a clever but impoverished and timid clerk into a rich nabob, able to retire to England at forty-four.

But Ramage guessed that the riches he'd acquired through trade had brought Sir Jason problems he'd never thought of when he'd started to accumulate his money. He was wealthy, yes; but he had no social position. Very rich nabobs returning to England with their fortunes could usually buy their way to an Irish peerage and then by sheer persistence (and a judicious marriage into an aristocratic but impoverished family who needed money sufficiently to overcome any distaste for wealth obtained through 'trade') finally become tolerated—though never accepted—by Society.

All this Sir Jason obviously had only discovered when he arrived back in England. And at the same time he'd also discovered that although he was rich, he was not rich enough. His wealth would, with some 'interest', buy him a seat in the Commons but the House of Lords would forever be beyond his grasp; even an Irish peerage was beyond his purse since the competition from other, richer nabobs was too great.

But Fisher had been shrewd; he'd recognized the problem and thought he'd found a way round it—a 'wise' marriage. Finding what to him was an aristocratic (but impoverished) family, he married the younger daughter, reversing the usual procedure by himself providing a 'dowry' in the form of a handsome settlement on his prospective father-in-law.

Unfortunately, the marriage did not open the doors to London Society; his knocks went unheeded because, as he soon discovered, his bride's family, though certainly impoverished, was by no means aristocratic.

To his dismay, he had found (and Wilson chortled as he told Ramage, who listened only because of the insight it gave him into the mind of the man he had to deal with at Government House) that in London baronet fathers-in-law were as common as coal-pits in Lancashire.

However, his father-in-law was married to the cousin of a marquis who controlled several Parliamentary boroughs, and the marquis, a kindly man, thought poor Jason deserved some reward for marrying a very distant member of the family who'd hitherto been considered unmarriageable, doomed to a nagging spinsterhood and a perpetual trial to her relatives.

And what better reward than to procure poor Jason a knighthood and give him one of the boroughs, so that he could also call himself a Member of Parliament? It mattered little to the marquis who actually walked into the voting lobbies in the Commons, providing he walked into the one that cast the vote the way the marquis wanted.

Two years of marriage, two years of voting in the Commons as the marquis dictated, two years of snubs as he persisted in trying to become 'accepted' socially had finally opened Jason's eyes, but not before it had embittered his wife, who'd shared his ambitions.

But, Wilson continued, the man with brains enough to make a small fortune in India had eventually realized what many others in a like situation discovered at about the same stage in their lives: if London Society was powerful, proud and impregnable—rating the eldest son of a cousin of an earl higher than a knight with a quarter of a million in the Funds who'd been 'in trade'—why not look elsewhere: for a smaller society where a nabob knight married to the distant relative of a marquis would count for something?

So Sir Jason had asked for, and the marquis had secured for him, the Governorship of Grenada. At this point Wilson had become scornful—the wretched Sir Jason had, of course, made another mistake: most governors came out to the islands for a few months during the dry season and were careful to leave the actual work to a deputy.

But the indomitable Sir Jason had come out (with embittered wife, servants terrified of sickness, many tons of furniture to feed the termites and a vast amount of enthusiasm) in the next available ship and stayed ever since.

Ramage, weary of the gossip, only partly listened to the rest of the tale: in nearly two years Sir Jason had established something approaching a Florentine court: he expected (and received) the obeisance of the Lieutenant Govenor, Chief Justice, Attorney General, Solicitor General, Provost Marshal, Judge of the Vice Admiralty Court and various other functionaries, right down to the Fort Adjutant and Barrackmaster, the Chaplain and the Collector of Customs.

He'd also been rewarded with the undying hatred of those who, on receiving their appointments in London, had promptly appointed deputies who had gone out to Grenada (at half the salary) to carry out the actual work while they themselves stayed in London, using the remaining half of their salaries to supplement their incomes.

But Sir Jason had put a stop to that—the same ship that

brought him to Grenada took back to London stern warnings to the absentees that in time of war all office-holders should be in the island, not their deputies. When one or two of them had not even bothered to reply to his peremptory letters, he had written directly to the Secretary of State who—according to Wilson—quickly weighed up which could make the most trouble, opted for Sir Jason and bundled the errant office-holders off to the island.

But poor Sir Jason (by this stage in Wilson's narrative Ramage was more than sorry for the Governor): after six months he had finally realized that not only did Grenada 'society' rate somewhere around the level occupied by butlers and valets in less fashionable London houses, but it was about as intelligent, interesting and vicious. His wife, who had spotted that within a fortnight of arriving, now reminded him of it daily.

The widespread revolt in the island before Sir Jason arrived, from March 1795 until March 1796, when the Frenchman Fédon led the slaves in a bloody insurrection, had only served to magnify Sir Jason's inadequacies as a Governor, whatever his skill as a man of business, and was one of the reasons why Wilson had been installed as military commander with—as he pointed out with some bitterness—the usual instructions from the Government which gave him all the responsibility for the island's defence but no powers to carry it out.

Since the Governor's mistakes and vacillations had not brought any reprimands from London, Sir Jason regarded Wilson not as the military commander but as the man responsible for seeing that all the troops were smartly turned out in the Governor's honour on every possible occasion. In fact the soldiers were known locally as 'Fisher's Fusiliers'.

'No manoeuvres allowed,' Wilson commented sourly. 'Governor's orders, of course, in case they get their uniforms torn. The damned men haven't marched five miles in the past twelve months—except to parade at the Governor's receptions.'

Out of all this, Ramage was interested in two facts: first, that Sir Jason's social uncertainty had turned him into such a snob that (according to Wilson) his constant companion was the *Royal Kalender*, with the pages containing the arms and mottoes of the peers of the realm, family names and heirs, almost worn out during the time he'd taken to learn them all by heart. And secondly, with this overbearing snobbishness went a querulousness which sprang from his complete lack of understanding of the functions of a governor.

A formidable combination.

And a moment later Wilson bore out Ramage's fears, complaining it was impossible to get Sir Jason to make any of the major decisions which only the Governor could make.

Through fear of making the wrong decision (which he hid by a pretended disdain of what he preferred to label as mundane matters beneath his notice) he made none. The result of such inaction, Wilson said bitterly, was often worse than a wrong decision . . .

Wilson had begun his story about Sir Jason in the carriage taking them both up to Government House; but the latter part had been continued in one of the Governor's drawing-rooms with Ramage standing at the window and looking down at the harbour and lagoon below. Ramage glanced at his watch and then at Wilson slumped in an archair puffing a second cigar.

Within minutes of the *Triton* anchoring off St George Ramage had gone on shore and up to Fort George to see Wilson who, in the four days that Ramage had been away, had obviously undergone a considerable change of heart.

Where Ramage had originally met rudeness, he now found genuine politeness; in place of an arbitrary 'You'll-do-as-I-say' manner he found a man anxious to hear his views, ideas and plans. And after hearing Ramage's theory that a spy was at work in Grenada he spent five minutes pacing up and down his office, heels grinding on the stone floor as he turned, and using language generally monopolized by cavalry officers' grooms in the privacy of the stables.

To Ramage's surprise he discovered—when Wilson stopped because the effort made him too hot and breathless—that the object of the Colonel's wrath was not the privateers but Sir Jason Fisher.

The reason was even more surprising—after the *Triton* sailed Sir Jason had become even more querulous (hitherto regarded as impossible) when he discovered that apart from failing to call on him, Ramage had sailed for Martinique, leaving orders endorsed by Wilson that the laden schooners waiting in the harbour were not to sail until the *Triton* returned.

Wilson was summoned to Government House where, for more than an hour, the Governor had treated Grenada's military commander more like a barrack-room orderly.

But Wilson had refused to budge over the sailing orders: as he explained to Ramage, realizing he had not the authority himself he'd looked up the regulations and discovered that among those who had was the 'Senior naval officer upon the Station' and among those who had not was the Governor—for once a fortunate oversight by the constitutional lawyer who had drafted the original regulations.

When he had pointed all this out to Sir Jason, the Governor had been outraged, swearing he could overrule an admiral, let alone a lieutenant. Could, he declared wrathfully and, damnation take it, he would.

Fortunately, after Wilson had left, the man had obviously resumed his habit of avoiding decisions, so the schooners had not sailed. In the meantime Wilson had copied out the relevant section of the regulations and later handed it to Ramage.

Now, as Ramage waited with Wilson for the Governor, he began to grow impatient: Sir Jason had received them with a chilly hauteur—or what the poor fellow thought passed for it—and, as soon as they had sat down, excused himself 'for a few minutes' on the score of 'having urgent work to attend to'. The only trouble was, as Wilson was quick to point out when the door closed behind the man, that he had sounded more like a butler excusing himself for a few minutes while he refilled a coal scuttle.

Nearly thirty minutes . . . Ramage had a lot to do. It was now three o'clock and it would be dark in less than four hours. One more schooner had finished loading and Wilson had already warned him that Rondin was making trouble, apparently offended that Ramage had not told him he intended going up to Martinique in the *Triton*.

'How long is he going to keep us waiting?' Wilson growled.

For an answer Ramage walked across the room and tugged the red bell cord. To the devil with governors; his orders came from the Admiral and time was short enough without wasting it on the Sir Jasons of this world.

'May I use your carriage?' he asked the Colonel. 'I'll send it back as soon as it's taken me to the Careenage.'

'Oh, I say—you can hardly walk out on the Governor like that!'

'Can't I, sir! The safety of the schoo——'

He broke off as the butler knocked and entered the room. Ramage glanced questioningly at Wilson, who nodded.

'Please have the Colonel's carriage brought to the door.'

The butler looked startled, knowing they were waiting for the Governor, so Ramage added, 'At once.'

The man left the room quickly and Ramage grinned at Wilson. 'I'll lay a guinea to a penny the Governor'll be here inside two minutes.'

'Not taken.'

It was a little over two minutes before the door opened again and Sir Jason walked in. If the cartoonist Gillray had drawn a skinny, defrocked parson who'd just inherited a wardrobe of clothes from a rich uncle weighing twenty pounds more, the result would have borne a remarkable likeness to His Excellency the Governor of Grenada.

He was, Ramage reflected, a man who must drive his tailor mad because Nature obviously intended that Sir Jason's physique should be a dreadful warning of what could happen to a man who worried continually.

And he had a most extraordinary gait, swinging his left arm in time with his left leg. Now his right hand was tucked inside his frock coat, as if to reassure himself his heart was still beating.

Surprisingly enough his face was almost plump—a lump of dough ready for baking and waiting to go into the oven— and from which protruded a thin, surprisingly pointed nose which twitched continuously and tiny, closely-spaced eyes glanced about with suspicious restlessness.

At their first brief meeting half an hour ago Ramage thought that the nose twitched to the left as the eyes glanced to the right, and to the right as His Excellency looked left, but he now saw this had been sheer chance. And clearly Sir Jason was a man with few friends and an overly-timid wife, because they'd all failed to warn him never to smile: when he did his narrow lips vanished, lifting like curtains to reveal a set of uneven, yellowed teeth that looked more suited to a horse trying to spit out the bit between his teeth. 'Ah—Wilson, my Lord, I'm sorry to have kept you: I'm sure you people never appreciate how busy is the life of a Governor,' he said.

'But I certainly do, your Excellency,' Ramage said uncompromisingly. 'In fact only a moment ago I remarked to Colonel Wilson how unfair it was to take up your time with idle gossip and rang for our carriage.'

The lips, which had momentarily unfolded, drew back again.

'Gossip? Gossip?' he exclaimed in his whining voice. 'Who wants to gossip? I've no time for gossip.'

'Quite, your Excellency,' Ramage said politely. 'So if you'll excuse——'

'But you've only just arrived!'

Ramage took out his watch with deliberate slowness and pressed the top so the front sprang open. After looking carefully at the face he shut it and, replacing it in his pocket, said nothing.

The Governor swung his left arm, nonplussed.

'Well—I er . . . Well, Colonel Wilson, you, er . . .'

The Colonel glanced up, startled, having been absorbed in admiration for what Ramage had just done. Obviously the Governor had expected that the two officers had come to Government House within an hour of the *Triton*'s arrival to make an official report and get his approval for their future plans.

After deliberately keeping them waiting to show his importance, he'd just been completely deflated to find they were apparently paying only a social call, and complaining how busy he was now led them both to hurry away to avoid wasting his time with 'idle gossip'.

Very neat, Wilson thought. Ramage had said nothing that could offend His Excellency; nevertheless Sir Jason was now in the humiliating position of not only having to ask what was going on, but since Wilson had told him of Ramage's authority as 'Senior naval officer upon the Station', risking being snubbed as well.

'Your Excellency . . .?' Wilson prompted.

'Oh—well, won't you stay for a drink? And you, my

Lord—surely you can spare ten minutes?'

Wilson glanced at the Lieutenant, unwilling to spoil any move, and Ramage said politely: 'You'll forgive us if we make it just ten minutes, your Excellency? We have a lot to do.'

'Of course, of course.'

He shambled across the room, removed his right hand from where it recorded his heart beat, and used it to tug the bell pull so violently that the long strip of red silk braid tore in half six feet above his hand, the tasselled end dropping back across his face.

'Damnation!' he snorted, pulling it away. 'The tropics! Everything just rots in the heat and damp!'

'I wonder if the bell rang, sir?' Ramage inquired innocently.

Sir Jason hauled his lips apart in a brave smile.

'I'm sure it did—rang it so loudly the clapper's probably broken!'

Ramage smiled but Wilson, fascinated by the Lieutenant's easy grace, just watched the two men. However, he realized that Sir Jason was learning extremely quickly and, shying from Ramage, he turned to him.

'You are coming to my ball this evening, I trust, Colonel?'

'Of course, your Excellency—social occasion of the year, what?'

'So nice of you to say so, Colonel. I trust the orchestra has been rehearsing.'

'Of course sir,' Wilson assured him. 'The bandmaster's had 'em hard at it for the past fortnight—since you gave the order.'

'And Colonel . . . I really *do* hope none of them get drunk again: it was so distressing last year and—oh, Lord Ramage, I've just realized you haven't received an invitation! You sailed so quickly and I had no idea when you would return.

'The Governor's Annual Ball is tonight—and you've just heard Colonel Wilson call it the social occasion of the year. Can I persuade you to leave your ship for a few hours?'

Ramage, thinking hard from the moment the Governor first mentioned it, realized it was a good opportunity to meet the island's leading people. And the drunker they were, he thought grimly, the more he'd learn.

He bowed slightly, 'I'm honoured, your Excellency.'

'At seven, then?'

'Thank you, your Excellency,' and he seized the opportunity to add. 'Since the invitation is unexpected and time so short, you'll forgive me if I return to the ship at once and make myself ready? There are several things I must do. Colonel Wilson...?'

'Me too,' said the Colonel, hauling himself up from the chair. 'Hadn't realized how the time had gone.'

'Please don't rush away,' the Governor protested, irritated to find that almost every remark he made was taken as an end of the visit.

Again Ramage smiled. 'Duty calls, sir: while neither of us bear the responsibilities that your Excellency does, our masters in Whitehall...'

'Quite—indeed, I understand. Until this evening, then.'

With that they took their farewell, and as the carriage clattered down the hill, Wilson said: 'Well, that went off better than I expected!'

Ramage laughed like a happy schoolboy who'd just evaded a beating from the headmaster. 'The credit's all yours, sir.'

'Mine?' Wilson shook his head.

'You discovered we had an ace—the "Senior naval officer upon the Station"—and his Excellency had to think of a way of making sure I didn't play it.'

Wilson remained silent until the carriage reached the Careenage, where one of the *Triton*'s boats waited, and then he said unexpectedly:

'Have you ever thought who our worst enemies are in a war?'

'Yes,' Ramage said promptly. 'Politicians seeking cheap victories to announce in Parliament—cheap in terms of money but usually costly in lives. Then bureaucrats—among them colonial governors. Then aged generals and admirals who should have retired long ago but hold on to power because their pride won't let them miss a chance of glory, even if they lose the battle. There are a few more. The French come about tenth on my list, the Spanish about fifteenth!'

Wilson gave the first real laugh Ramage had heard from him: a laugh that began well below the highly-polished leather belt struggling to hold in his stomach and rumbled and fought its way up to his throat.

He thumped Ramage's knee with his first.

'Seditious talk to a senior officer, young man; but I enjoy it! I've a feeling you're going to catch those privateers in a matter of days. I'll be sorry in one way because it'll mean you'll be on your way—but you're a breath of fresh air in this God-forsaken island.'

The carriage stopped by the *Triton*'s boat and as Ramage turned to thank Wilson he looked up at the mottled face, the drinker's nose, the bloodshot eyes, and wondered if he'd ever misjudged a man so much in his life.

Jackson was waiting on the quay several yards from the boat, obviously wanting to say something he did not want the other men to hear. Ramage looked questioningly.

'Evening, sir. I wanted to mention Maxton . . .'

Ramage looked puzzled, then suddenly remembered months ago asking the West Indian seaman where in Grenada he'd been born, and he'd said Belmont. Glancing at the boat's crew he saw Maxton sitting there. He had not seen his family for many years and he had neither applied for leave nor deserted. Ramage felt angry with himself and, nodding to Jackson, called Maxton, who leapt on to the quay.

'Sah?'

'Your family—where do they live?'

Maxton pointed to a group of huts on the far side of the lagoon.

'Over there, sir.'

'Do you want some leave?'

Maxton nodded, too excited to speak.

'Go now, but report back on board by dawn tomorrow: you can't have longer at the moment because we may have to sail suddenly.'

Still Maxton was too excited to speak. Ramage felt in his pocket for a guinea.

'And you'll need this.'

CHAPTER FIFTEEN

The incessant chattering of dozens of people, the air of the room seemingly solid from a damp heat, men's faces glowing red and shiny with perspiration, women's normally pale cheeks now pink despite fans fluttering like birds' wings—Ramage envied the bright-eyed chameleon clinging to the wall beside him, head poised, tail stiff and watching everything with an air of cool detachment.

The orchestra—strong on brass and percussion but excruciatingly weak on strings—were now resting for a few moments, the brass restoring themselves with large mugs of beer. And Ramage, his uniform hot and sticky, feet swollen from so much walking and his shoes seeming too small, felt none the better for a gargantuan supper where the Governor pressed his guests to just one more slice of cold turkey than they wanted and two glasses more champagne than was wise.

Ramage had anticipated becoming bored with the ball within fifteen minutes of arriving; but despite his earlier overbearing manner, the Governor was now treating him as a guest of honour. As soon as he had arrived—half an hour later than politeness dictated, because Southwick kept him busy with various problems on board the *Triton*—the Governor had seized him by the arm and insisted he made a grand tour of the enormous drawing-room which, divested of most of its furniture, this evening served as a ballroom.

And he had introduced Ramage to every guest with the phrase 'I want you to meet my young friend Lord Ramage —son of the Earl of Blazey, you know.'

Ramage was not sure which annoyed him most, the untruthfulness of the 'young friend' or the 'you know' which carried the implication that, although Sir Jason did, the person being introduced would not.

But the Governor's way of displaying his social trophy

was proving useful: within twenty minutes Ramage had met the Lieutenant-Governor, judge, leading plantation-owners and businessmen, ship-owners (Rondin among them, cool and remote, rich and intelligent enough to remain detached) and their wives and daughters. The women had several things in common—an irritatingly simpering manner and, as they were being introduced or spoken to, an equally irritating habit of coyly glancing sideways at sisters or daughters. They were, Ramage thought sourly, just about the sort of people one would expect to find at the Governor's Ball and behaved and talked with a dreary predictability.

All the efforts of the guests to keep cool were unsuccessful: the atmosphere was stifling—the difference between a Grenadan ball and a London ball, he realized, was that here perspiration replaced personality—and Ramage wished he could set half a dozen seamen swabbing down the whole room (and most of its occupants) with a few gallons of eau de Cologne.

The lighting, far too garish and hard on the older women's complexions, contributed to the heat: in addition to the great chandeliers hanging from the ceiling and winking their cut-glass eyes as the candles flickered, there were enough silver candelabra on small tables to satisfy the greed of any pirate looting a cardinal's palace on the Spanish Main.

Mosquitoes whined about his face and swarmed round the candles, occasionally dropping as they flew too near the flame and scorched their wings. And more chameleons and lizards ran along the ceiling and down the chandeliers with easy grace—unlike, he thought sourly, the Army officers in their garish and superbly impractical uniforms who by now were lurching drunkenly rather than walking and risked staggering a pace or two forward when they attempted a gallant bow.

The orchestra was tuning up, the violins plinking in preparation for the next dance. Ramage, standing with the Governor and being polite to yet another plantation-owner's fat wife, was conscious of just one person left that he had to meet.

'My Lord,' the Governor said, moving on, 'if Mrs Bends will forgive me for tearing you away for a moment, I'd like you to meet my wife's companion and private secretary,

Miss de Giraud . . .'

Ramage smiled politely at Mrs Bends and turned to the Governor and the tall woman now standing with him. For a moment she was a blur and to save himself Ramage hurriedly looked at the Governor: anything to stop the fire suddenly flooding his whole body and fight off the dizziness.

As the Governor's yellow teeth moved up and down like a horse nibbling grass, Ramage could think only of her golden skin, high cheekbones, large eyes glinting black like sparkling gems, lips full and rich, the smile friendly—or was it gently mocking? And if so, mocking him or the Governor? Or was she—well, until he looked again he couldn't be sure; but he was already certain she was the most beautiful woman he'd ever seen.

She knew she was beautiful, accepted it without arrogance, and the knowledge gave her a proud dignity. Or was it serenity? Or just straightforward confidence in her femininity so that, unlike these other stupid women, she could look a man straight in the eye without blushing, simpering, being coy, becoming tongue-tied, gauche?

He realized there was almost complete silence in the room: not just that the Governor had stopped talking, but so had nearly everyone else: he sensed they were all watching.

Something white fluttered from Miss de Giraud's left hand and dropped to the floor. The Governor moved but Ramage was quicker—he picked up a silk glove and gave it to her.

'Thank you, my Lord.'

She gave a graceful curtsy. Yes, the eyes were mocking— but gently so; her accent was entirely English; there was none of the blurring of words, the dropping of the final 'g', the sing-song lilt of a West Indian—yet it had the same depth and warmth. But somewhere in her ancestry there was coloured blood—perhaps Indian—that would account for the long, straight hair, high cheekbones and eyes . . .

As Ramage stood tongue-tied—he remember just in time to bow—the Governor unwittingly came to his rescue.

'Miss de Giraud has been my wife's companion and secretary for the past year, my Lord; but I'm afraid I monopolize her services! She's become our "Lord Chamberlain" and

"Comptroller of the Household" as well, and I doubt there's a governor in the King's service who wouldn't envy me!'

'Not a single man, your Excellency, let alone a governor!'

'No, indeed not! Why, she's considerably better at drafting my despatches than I am! When I was in India it took ten men secretaries to keep my desk clear of papers—but Miss de Giraud achieves that alone, as well as running the house.'

Still the smile; no blushing modesty and feeble protests. But Ramage pitied the Governor: he was an unlucky man that could appreciate only Miss de Giraud's efficiency as a secretary.

'His Excellency makes me seem formidable—a positive dragon!'

Before Ramage could think of a reply the Governor said gaily, 'Well now, let's dance.'

Signalling to the master of ceremonies Sir Jason looked round for his wife, waved to her and left Ramage with the admonition:

'I'll leave Miss de Giraud in your care!'

They both watched the Governor walk across the floor and, just as he reached his wife who was sitting amid a group of women gossiping behind waving fans, the orchestra struck up and the master of ceremonies cried, 'Please take your places for—the cotillion!'

It was a dreary dance but at once several women, obeying the master of ceremonies' directions, lined up on one side of the room and an equal number of men on the other.

Ramage, who hated dancing and was bad at it, regretted the fact for the first time in his life—this woman would be a superb dancer, accustomed to being partnered by men who spent every other evening dancing. The sort of——

'You have a partner waiting, my Lord?'

For a moment he thought guiltily of Gianna but heard himself saying:

'I was hoping it would be you, but I dance abominably and hardly know the cotillion. Anyway, you are already taken for this dance?'

She waved her programme and said with disarming frankness:

'No—when Sir Jason told me you were coming I kept several free.'

By avoiding looking at her, Ramage felt his confidence

226

slowly returning.

'But you didn't know I'd be so late.'

'No?' she laughed and showed him the programme. The first half dozen dances, which Ramage had missed through arriving late, had names pencilled against them. The rest were blank.

'You took a risk. For all you knew I might have had a wooden leg!'

'Wrong again, my Lord: I saw you this afternoon at Government House.'

No trace of coquettishness—or forwardness: just this frankness. Why was it so surprising? No reason—except it was so unusual.

'I must have arrived with my eyes shut: I didn't see you.'

'No, you were too busy talking affairs of state with Colonel Wilson. But come, shall we—oh no, we're too late! Henry'—she motioned towards the master of ceremonies—'will get into a terrible state if we join the line now.'

Ramage had already spotted through the big doors that there were several empty chairs on the balcony running along the entire front of the house.

'I'm a stranger to Grenada, so why don't you point out St George's beauty spots from the balcony?'

She nodded and offered her arm.

The view down on to the little town and across the lagoon was as beautiful by night as by day. Here and there cooking fires glowed red outside native huts; in the lagoon boats rowed swiftly back and forth, a man in the bow holding aloft a flaming torch to attract the fish, a second standing poised beside him like a statue, a long trident in his hand, and a third man rowing.

All round the house and down the hill fireflies winked their bright blue lights, tiny stars flashing for a second, and out here the incessant liquid croak of tree frogs almost drowned the orchestra. In the clearness of the tropical night the stars were almost too bright to be credible and over the hill on the east side of the harbour entrance Ramage could just see the uppermost star of the Southern Cross, and Sirius and Jupiter, to his left, were almost unbelievably brilliant, the brightest stars in the sky.

As they stood watching Ramage realized she had not withdrawn her arm.

'You like Grenada, my Lord?'

'Yes—though so far I've seen very little of it.'

'Of course—you left us for Martinique so soon after arriving! How did you find it?'

'More French than France.'

'And the ladies—they're very chic.'

Teasing, bantering, and her voice fascinating.

'So I'm told; but I was there only a few hours and met none.'

'Shame! Fort Royal is something to linger over—like a good brandy.'

One of the men in the boats suddenly lunged with his trident and a moment later held a large fish aloft, the red light of the torch reflecting on the wriggling body.

'I'm afraid sailors can rarely linger ...'

'A wife in every port?'

'A deliberate falsehood spread by jealous soldiers!'

She laughed. 'Another illusion shattered ... But an attractive notion, n'est-ce pas?'

'Yes—though I hardly think a wife would want to share a husband,' Ramage said dryly.

'Oh, I don't know: a woman would be more likely to share a husband with another woman—if she loved him—than a man to share his wife.'

'Indeed? This is most instructive—do go on,' Ramage teased. 'Is this an old Carib custom?'

Again that natural laugh and as if by accident her arm moved so the back of his hand rested under her breast. The material of the dress was thin, and even as she laughed he sensed she wore nothing beneath. He turned his head to look at her: the front of the dress was cut low and square; the valley between her breasts——

'Ah there you are!'

Cursing to himself Ramage turned to find Colonel Wilson beaming at them.

'Excuse me m' dear fellow, but the Governor wants to talk to you. Rather urgent, I'm afraid—they're here, your Excellency!'

Sir Jason followed Wilson on to the balcony.

'Sorry—excuse us, Miss de Giraud—but Ramage, these

blessed ship-owners have just been talking to me: fancy interrupting the ball like that. Want to sail their schooners: they say the cargoes are spoiling and they'll miss the next English convoy from Jamaica unless the schooners reach Martinique in a few days.'

'If they sail them now,' Ramage said grimly, 'they probably won't even reach Martinique, let alone ship the cargoes in the next Jamaica convoy.'

'We've told 'em that,' Wilson said, 'but they say they'd sooner risk that than let the cargoes rot.'

'They lose the schooners too,' Ramage pointed out. 'Soon they won't have any ships left.'

'They collect their insurance though,' Wilson said bitterly.

Ramage sensed the Governor's attitude had definitely changed: he was trying to persuade him to let them sail, not blustering and vowing they could go. A sudden idea crossed his mind but he dismissed it.

'Is any one owner more anxious than the rest?'

'Two are making the fuss.'

'But three are loaded. What about the third owner?'

'That's Rondin. Didn't say much—seemed more inclined to go by what you said. At least, that was my impression—agree, Wilson?'

The Colonel nodded. 'Has more sense than the rest of 'em put together.'

Ramage shrugged his shoulders. 'It's madness to sail now.' He asked Wilson: 'Have you mentioned our suspicions to the Governor?'

Again the Colonel nodded.

'Very interesting they are, too,' Sir Jason said in a flat voice belying his words, 'but it doesn't help the present situation.'

'If you'll pardon me, your Excellency, I should have thought it provided a very definite answer.'

'Well, it doesn't, I'm afraid. At least two of these gentlemen insist their schooners sail tonight.'

Tonight! Ramage tried to keep his temper. It seemed comical that you had to order men to keep their ships in port for their own safety. It'd make more sense if they were protesting because Ramage was ordering them to sail.

Wilson coughed to attract Ramage's attention. 'Lieutenant —I don't think his Excellency will mind me telling you that one owner proposes to sail his schooner tonight whatever Sir Jason or you say——'

'That's so,' Sir Jason interrupted.

'Very well,' Ramage snapped, as the idea came back more forcefully, 'just to maintain some semblance of authority—I don't imagine anyone wants me to put men on board to prevent it—I'll give permission for that one schooner to sail, though it's making a virtue out of a necessity.'

'Ah, splendid,' purred the Governor. 'Splendid, I knew you'd be reasonable.'

'But on two conditions,' Ramage said, thinking quickly and looking at his watch—eight o'clock.

Sir Jason sighed like a child impatient with its parents.

'One is that she's under way by ten o'clock and no one but the owner and the master are told after being sworn to secrecy —not even the crew must know until they're ordered to cast off the lines; second, the owner must sign a document in front of you, Sir Jason, declaring that he's sailing at his own request, at his own risk and very much against my wishes and advice.'

'And mine too, if that helps,' Wilson added.

'Very well,' the Governor agreed. 'I'll speak to him now and he'll sign the document in my study.'

'And one more thing, Sir Jason, on which I'm afraid I must insist ...'

Suddenly he realized Miss de Giraud had several minutes earlier tactfully walked a few yards along the balcony.

'... I must insist on absolute secrecy. None of the other owners must know; nor any of your staff or Colonel Wilson's. Just the owner and the master of the schooner.'

'But my dear fellow,' grumbled Sir Jason, 'are you implying——'

'Otherwise the schooner doesn't sail, sir; I'll put some of my men on board all three. And the other two owners must be told nothing—except they can't sail for the time being. They can have explanations tomorrow why one vessel left.'

'It's most irregular,' Sir Jason expostulated, 'why, they'll probably think this owner's bribed me.'

'Bribed *me*,' Ramage corrected. 'I'm permitting it to sail, your Excellency; you can make that quite clear.'

'Very well. Come along Wilson, we'll get this fellow down to my study. I'll see you later, Ramage.'

For a moment Ramage stood thinking. Had he let himself be rushed into a silly decision? There was no denying he was angry; but then he smiled. It wasn't a handsome smile; it was coldly cynical. All this could be a blessing in disguise—oh yes, he thought, very much a blessing! A spy could be caught only when he passed information; so first he had to have information. And probably the only information this particular spy sought was the time a schooner sailed.

Eventually, Ramage reflected, he would have been forced to sail a schooner as bait, knowing it would almost certainly be captured. That would be the price for just one attempt at trapping the spy, and it'd be a high price because if the owner ever discovered his schooner had been used as bait he would create the devil of a fuss. Ramage could imagine the angry letters—from the Committee of Underwriters at Lloyds, from the West India Committee and from anyone else moved to put pen to paper—streaming into the Admiralty, all blaming Lieutenant Ramage of His Majesty's brig *Triton*!

But here, by an unexpected piece of luck, was an owner actually *insisting* his schooner sailed—insisting to the Governor. And presumably prepared to put his signature to a document drawn up by the Governor that the vessel sailed at the owner's risk . . .

Ramage gave a short and bitter laugh and then turned to Miss de Giraud, but the balcony was empty. She had probably gone to—well, women did, and with much more discretion than men.

He stood a foot up on the chair and, leaning forward, stared across the lagoon. The bonfires in front of the huts were dying out. With their meals cooked and eaten, the people would be going to bed ready to rise at first light and begin their work. Only one of the boats was still fishing with a burning torch.

There was no sign of movement along the Careenage—just the dark outline of the three laden schooners secured alongside. Was the spy watching even now?

Mosquitoes hummed in his ears and absent-mindedly he waved a hand to brush them away. Itching round his wrists told him they'd already had a good meal.

St George must be one of the most beautiful small harbours in the world. Out here the breeze was cool and behind the orchestra was muted; the guests' idle chatter too was masked by the clicking of the frogs.

Yet to him the night in the tropics was always faintly menacing; always an air of mystery. Strange, almost human, animal noises from the jungle and the hysterical whine of flying insects. Scorpions moving crabwise, centipedes crawling with deceptive speed, and the sudden scurry of a lizard across your shoe. The tap, tap, tap—in the Governor's House at least—of death watch beetles steadily chewing their way through the roof timbers. Beneath the lushness he always sensed the death and decay.

And what was Gianna doing? He added four hours to the present time to allow for Grenada's distance west of Greenwich. Wherever she was she'd be in bed and asleep. But at the moment he could not remember her as clearly as he did last night. Curious, the picture was fainter, and he found it hard to recall even her voice. He must write, though God knew when any ship would leave with mail. And her letters—was she writing letters in the form of a diary and posted in time to catch the West India Packet sailing regularly from Falmouth? Would she write regularly even when she received his letters only intermittently? That was——

A rustle of silk behind him interrupted his thoughts and without looking round he knew Miss de Giraud had returned and was standing right behind him. Touching him lightly on the shoulder she whispered: 'Surely not homesick? You look so sad standing there alone and looking out to sea!'

'No, not homesick—just thinking about this and that; the view, the bonfires dying out in front of those huts ...'

'Yes, it's very beautiful: I never get tired of it.'

'But you've seen it—for a year?'

'From here for a year; from other places round the lagoon for much longer.'

'But you aren't a Grenadan?'

'No, not a Grenadan.'

It was neither a rebuff nor an evasion. Nor for that matter, an answer.

'I shall be sorry to leave Gr——'

High in the hills behind Government House a tom-tom suddenly began a rhythmic beat. No, not rhythmic: it began with a rhythm, then changed to equally spaced beats. Then stopped for a few moments, began more beats, and broke into a rhythm again.

Tum-dee-dee-tum-tum . . . tum-dee-dee-tum . . . tum . . . tum . . .

'That's the first time I've heard tom-toms here.'

'Oh? They're often beating.'

It stopped but Ramage continued listening and suddenly walked to the edge of the balcony, leaning over so his head was clear of the building. Faintly in the distance, away to the north, another drum had taken up the beat, very faintly, barely distinguishable above the croaking frogs.

'What are they doing, passing messages?'

'No—at least, I don't think so. Usually it's some voodoo rite—you know, black magic.'

'A sort of ceremony?'

'Yes—perhaps someone in a family is ill. They send for a witch doctor—though officially they don't exist—and a drummer. They have some ritual to cure the people.'

'Does it cure them?'

She shrugged her shoulders. 'I don't know. At least it can't make them any worse.'

Ramage realized several people were coming out from the doors farther along the balcony.

'We've been out here rather a long time—would you like to dance?'

'For fear my reputation would otherwise be compromised?' she whispered, laughing quietly at Ramage's discomfiture. 'Don't worry my Lord, we've been standing in front of a door all the time!'

'Nicholas, not "my Lord".'

She curtsied, again with that mocking look in her eyes. Or was it mocking? Ramage wished he could be sure.

'And I—my Lord—am Claire.'

'And may I have the pleasure of the next dance, Claire?'

'I must look at my programme.' She pretended to read it. 'By chance I am not engaged for the next dance, Lieutenant.'

They danced, paused for refreshments and danced again for nearly two hours. By then Ramage had given up trying to conceal that she was making him tremble: the silk of her dress moved so smoothly under his right hand that she might well have been naked. She knew it, she accepted it, and she responded. Time was forgotten—until a planter dancing with his plump and drab wife growled, 'It's past ten o'clock—I want a drink!'

With that Ramage jerked himself out of the sensuous little world he'd been briefly sharing with Claire. Damnation! Had the schooner sailed?

Suddenly he realized that the rest of the dancers were swirling past while he stood in front of Claire, who was watching him anxiously.

'Is anything wrong?'

'The heat—I'd like some fresh air. Would—do you think we can risk gossip and go on to the balcony?'

She laughed gaily, relieved at his explanation. 'There's no risk attached to gossip; one either accepts or rejects it.'

'Or ignores it.'

'Or ignores it,' she repeated as they walked to the door.

'Which do you do?'

'I've never been thought important enough to be gossiped about!'

'The Governor's "Lord Chamberlain" is too modest. But——'

'But if I was? I'd ignore or reject: it's the same either way.'

As they reached the balcony he saw the schooner had sailed. The last bonfire was nearly out; the last torch fisherman had gone home. The lagoon and the harbour looked like glass; just a breath of wind rippled the surface and there was only an occasional tiny green splash as a fish jumped and stirred up phosphorescence. His watch showed it was eleven minutes past ten.

And a tom-tom, which had been beating as they came out on to the balcony, gave a few more desultory beats and stopped.

'There's more music in a tom-tom than in the Governor's orchestra,' he commented.

She shivered unexpectedly. 'It's cold out here!'

'But wait a few moments—you enjoy this view year after year. In a couple of months' time I might be in a snow storm off Newfoundland!'

There was no one else on the balcony and he kissed her, and what seemed hours later, when she'd whispered 'Will you remember me when the snow is falling?' the distant tom-tom had long finished beating out its message to whichever heathen god was listening.

234

CHAPTER SIXTEEN

The shout of a sentry roused Ramage before daylight. A few moments later, with more shouted challenges—apparently to an approaching boat—and the sound of men running along the deck, he was wide awake, leaping out of his cot and grabbing a pair of pistols. He flung open the cabin door just as the Marine sentry outside shouted 'Captain, sir!' and reached the quarterdeck in time to meet Jackson running aft to report.

'It's Mr Appleby, sir: he's just arrived from Carriacou!'

A few minutes later the boat, a half-decked fishing drogher, was anchored to leeward of the *Triton* and Appleby was coming up the side. Then Southwick appeared, still half asleep, and the Corporal of Marines with four of his men stood round with lanterns, uncertain what to do.

Appleby reached the deck, saw Ramage in the lantern light and saluted.

'Good morning, Appleby! What brings you back? Something interesting to report?'

Appleby grinned uncertainly, as if he was having second thoughts.

'Good morning, sir: yes—at least, I hope you'll think so.'

'Very well—you haven't eaten, I suppose? No? Steward—tea at once, and breakfast in ten minutes!'

In the cabin Ramage paced up and down, shoulders hunched to avoid bumping his head on the low beams, while Appleby sat nervously at the table. It had taken Ramage two or three minutes to get him started off on his story—he'd suddenly become nervous, apparently afraid at the last minute that Ramage would think his report ridiculous and blame him for leaving Carriacou.

'We were keeping a sharp watch on the islands and the north end of Grenada, just as you told us, sir. Then last night at 8.42 exactly we saw a bonfire suddenly light up on a hill above Levera—that's on the north-east side of Grenada.'

'I know it,' Ramage said. 'Could you make out how big?'

'Through the "bring 'em near" it looked much more than a bonfire: as if several big trees were burning.'

'And then?'

'Well, I wouldn't have thought much about it—after all, sir, it could have started accidentally—but about ten minutes later another bonfire started on the north side of Kick 'em Jenny. That wasn't so big but easy to see because it was much nearer.'

'The Levera bonfire—could you have seen that easily from Carriacou without a telescope?'

'It'd have been chancy, sir. Probably missed it if there'd been a bit of haze, rain squall—even a bright moonlit night.'

'But the one on Kick 'em Jenny?'

'Could see that plain as anything, sir, without the glass.'

Ramage nodded as he tried to recall some of the events of the previous evening at Government House.

'Then the drum started, sir,' he added, almost as an afterthought.

'The *what*?' Ramage almost shouted.

'The drum sir—tom-tom, I mean. At the south end of Carriacou. It was about five minutes after the bonfire started at Kick 'em Jenny that this tom-tom started—well tomtomming. As soon as it stopped another one started about six miles away—I reckon it was somewhere in the middle of the island. Seemed to beat the same sort of tune. When that one finished we thought we heard a third one at the north end, but none of us was sure.'

'No bonfires to the north?'

'Well, sir, that's what bothered me. It was the first thing I thought of when I realized these tom-toms might be passing a message across the island, so we dashed up the hill and looked. We saw a red glow—just a reflection really at the north end of Carriacou, that's for sure.

'Then about five minutes after that I *thought* I could see the reflection of another bonfire on the north side of Union Island—you remember sir,' he continued, 'that's the one between Carriacou and Bequia. But to be honest, I'm not absolutely sure. We'd all got a bit excited by then and I might have been imagining it. The men weren't sure, either. Afraid we let you down there, sir.'

Ramage shook his head. 'Don't worry about that: I'd sooner know you weren't absolutely sure than have you tell me you were when you weren't. Go on, then.'

'Well, we got a boat and sailed for here.'

The steward knocked and brought in two mugs of tea. 'Breakfast's ready now, sir.'

'Very well—ask Mr Southwick to join us.'

As soon as the Master came down, he told Appleby to repeat his story and, sipping the tea, Ramage reviewed his evening's activities at Government House with a mixture of shame, anger and irritation. Instead of using every minute of the time he was at the Governor's Ball to watch and listen, he'd spent most of the time flirting with a woman—more than flirting, he thought, growing hot with the memory—just like some sailor given a night's shore leave. Trying to dismiss the memory he pictured the scene from the balcony and suddenly remembered the schooner.

'Did you pass a schooner going north as you came down?' he interrupted the master's mate.

'Yes sir, about two o'clock this morning we passed one off Kick 'em Jenny.'

'The wind?'

'Stiff breeze from the east, sir—though the island blanketed us once we were in the lee.'

Moodily Ramage resumed sipping his tea, picturing the scenes on each of the islands during the night. While he'd danced at Government House, men had watched for a bonfire on their neighbour to the south, and as soon as they spotted it, got out tom-toms and passed the news northwards across their own island to other men waiting on the north side ready to light another signal fire. No wonder news travelled so fast!

He continued thinking as breakfast was served and Southwick, seeing him occasionally rubbing the scar on his brow, kept silent. When he'd finished the meal Ramage glanced up and said, 'No doubt you'll want to wash and shave, Appleby?'

The master's mate took the hint, thanked Ramage and left the cabin.

As soon as the door shut Southwick asked. 'What do you make of it, sir?'

'It's pretty obvious, isn't it?'

Unperturbed by Ramage's surly tone, Southwick persisted.

'It's obvious until the news gets to the north end of St Vincent, sir. But from there it's a long way across to St Lucia—twenty-four miles. Have to be a big bonfire for anyone in St Lucia to see it!'

'Needn't be a bonfire. It took Appleby five hours to get here from Carriacou in his fishing boat. That's nearly six knots. There's nothing to stop a fishing boat leaving St Vincent and crossing the channel to St Lucia in four or five hours. Then the tom-toms pass the message the length of St Lucia. In the meantime the schooner's hardly reached Bequia.'

But Ramage knew he was still ignoring the vital question, and it probably hadn't even occurred to Southwick yet. Briefly he told the Master about his previous evening's conversations with the Governor, and the schooner-owner's determination that his vessel should sail.

'He deserves to have her captured,' Southwick growled. 'Underwriters'd never pay up if they knew.'

'They'll get to know eventually.'

'Do you suspect him, sir? Some sort of fraud with the insurance?'

Ramage shook his head.

'It wouldn't make sense. Just think what's shipped out of Grenada in a year—about 12,000 tons of sugar, more than a million gallons of rum, 200 tons of cotton, 100,000 gallons of molasses ... with freight rates so high a schooner-owner makes an enormous profit—more in six months, I should imagine, than he could claim on the insurance for a total loss.'

'But they're not making profits because the schooners are being lost,' Southwick pointed out.

'Yes, but they'd sooner make the profits. That's what convinces me there's no fraud.'

'Then where the devil *do* the privateers hang out?' Southwick exclaimed bluntly. 'Until we find their nest I don't see we can do much.'

'Our next job is to discover how the spy found out when the schooner was going to sail.'

Southwick shrugged his shoulders. 'Anyone could have seen her leaving.'

'At ten o'clock, yes!' Ramage snapped. 'But Appleby's already told us that the first signal he saw was at 8.42. So the spy knew beforehand. Why, they knew in St Vincent by nine o'clock.'

'I still don't see it matters, sir,' Southwick said doggedly. 'If only we can catch the privateers the spy's out of business.'

'Yes,' Ramage said patiently, 'but we don't know where they're based and no one's ever seen them!'

'True,' the Master admitted, scratching his head, 'but I still——'

'I don't either at the moment. But you're looking through the wrong end of the telescope.'

Southwick looked startled. 'How do you mean?'

'Well, the spy's given himself away.'

The Master grunted his disbelief.

'Of course he has. Why didn't he wait until the schooner sailed before passing the signal?'

'Can't see it matters, sir.'

'Nor can I—and that's the clue. He passed the signal soon after eight o'clock last night and the schooner sailed at ten, so he gained two hours. But two hours can't matter to the privateers.'

'I still don't——'

'Exactly! Those two hours don't matter. So why didn't the spy wait?'

Southwick shook his head but said nothing.

'Because he was too confident. He didn't think we'd ever guess the trick. He and privateersmen have been getting away with it for months. Tom-toms and bonfires—and no one's ever noticed them!'

Southwick nodded, then said questioningly: 'I can see that, sir; but I can't see he's given himself away—that's what you just said—by making the signal before the schooner sailed.'

'You weren't listening properly when I told you what happened at Government House.'

It was an unfair thing to say and Ramage knew it, because he'd only realized the full significance of the timing a few minutes ago.

'What did I miss then?' The Master's voice was almost truculent.

'You missed me saying that only four people knew the schooner was going to sail.'

'Only four? Why, it'll be easy——'

'No it won't,' Ramage interrupted bitterly. 'Those four

people are the Governor, Colonel Wilson, the schooner's owner and, later on, the schooner's master. Four people. Which one would you suspect?'

'Phew! The Governor, the Colonel, the owner . . . Well, we're almost back where we started!'

'Almost. We take ten steps forward and slide back nine.'

'The schooner-owner: must be him. It's an insurance fraud.'

Again Ramage shook his head. 'No—if it was, the owners of all the schooners lost so far would be in it. And they're the losers because soon there won't be any schooners left. Apart from that this owner signed a document taking full responsibility. That alone rules out insurance because the underwriters could refuse to pay. It means he wants the profits from the freight—and is prepared to gamble.'

'I suppose so,' Southwick said grudgingly. 'But surely you don't suspect the Governor or Colonel Wilson?'

'Hardly. That's what I meant about slipping nine steps back.'

Idly he tapped the table with a knife. The sky through the skylight overhead was turning from black to grey. An idea was floating round in his brain, the details for the moment blurred.

'By the way, I gave Maxton leave yesterday afternoon. Jackson told you?'

'Yes sir: he's due back at dawn, I believe.'

Ramage nodded.

'It'll be interesting to see if he deserts,' Southwick added.

'You think he will?'

'No, I'm sure he won't. I hope not, anyway.'

The idea was beginning to take shape and he started rubbing his brow. Southwick misunderstood the reason and said: 'It'd be disappointing, after all he went through with you in the *Kathleen.*'

'I wasn't thinking of that. Listen, Southwick—those damned tom-toms *talk*. But who can read what they say? I wonder if Maxton can.'

'Is it important? Surely we can guess. Last night they said the schooner was sailing!'

Ramage grinned. 'Ever thought hard about a tom-tom, Southwick?'

The Master looked puzzled. 'Not really. It's a sort of drum, and these fellows use it to signal with, like shouting a long distance.'

'Yes, but with this difference. You can recognize a man's voice when he shouts. Can you recognize a tom-tom? Recognize whether one particular man's beating it or another, even though the message is the same?'

Southwick shrugged his shoulders. 'They all sound alike to me.'

'Exactly. And I'm wondering if they sound alike to the natives.'

'By Jove,' Southwick exclaimed, banging the table with his fist. 'You mean, we could get a native to pass some false signals? Throw the whole system into confusion? Why, we could drive this spy mad! Just think of him listening to us drumming out false information about a schooner sailing. He has to get *his* drummer to thump out "Annul previous signal"; then we follow up with another "Annul..."'

He roared with laughter at the thought, thumping the table to simulate a tom-tom, but then his face fell. 'Still doesn't find the privateers, though!'

'No, but it's a good idea: we may be able to use it—if we can find someone who talks the language of the drums. Send Maxton down to me as soon as he comes back on board: he might know something.'

*

As the sky lightened and the *Triton*'s ship's company were busy scrubbing the decks, polishing brasswork and going through the dozens of jobs carried out at daybreak on board every British ship of war, Ramage slowly shaved himself, deliberately taking his time, trying to find a flaw in his conclusions. They were simple enough to worry him.

First, the spy was so sure his tom-tom and bonfire method would never be discovered that he revealed his knowledge by passing the signal before the schooner sailed. Very well, that probably wasn't over-confidence on his part—tom-toms were beating most nights, and the two frigates didn't spot the bonfires.

Secondly, suppose the spy was caught. He might be doing it for money—the privateers would pay well for information. Or he might be French and doing it to further the Revolution —Grenada was only just recovering from Fédon's Revolt. Once captured, could the spy be forced to reveal where the privateers were based? It was possible. But would it help that much, with only the *Triton* to tackle them? These privateers would be among the fastest vessels in the islands. Going to windward they could sail rings round the *Triton*.

Yet—he ran his hand along his jaw: the razor was blunt—perhaps they could be trapped in their base. The fact that it was well-hidden might also mean it was hard to get out of: maybe the privateers had to use boats to tow themselves out . . .

There was a knock on the door and Southwick called, 'Maxton's here, sir.'

'Send him in.'

Ramage made the last few strokes with the razor, wiped off the remaining soap, and looked at his face. His eyes were more sunken than usual; his cheeks too. That meant he was worrying more than he realized; a few late nights didn't do that. He must have lost six or eight pounds in weight. Yet he wasn't conscious of worrying overmuch.

He walked into the day cabin and saw Maxton standing just inside the door, obviously overawed at his first visit to the Captain's quarters.

'How were the family, Maxton?'

'Glad to see me, sah.'

'Your parents alive?'

'Yes sah! My father's a freed slave.'

'Brothers and sisters?'

'Four brothers, three sisters, sah. And twenty-seven nephews and nieces.'

'Congratulations,' Ramage said, smiling as he tried to average it out. If all seven had wives or husbands, it was nearly four children each. He brushed the irrelevance aside: his approach to the seaman was going to be unorthodox.

'Ah—Maxton, I need your help.'

'Yes sah?'

'You heard the tom-toms last night?'

Maxton's eyes seemed suddenly to become opaque before he looked away.

'No sah, I didn't hear no drums.'

Interesting—he called them 'drums'.

'Nothing? You heard nothing?'

'Nothin', sah.'

The man moistened his thick lips; his hands wrestled with each other. Perspiration was beading his upper lip and brow, and he looked down at the deck.

'Well, someone was beating them last night, Maxton.'

'If you say so, sah.'

'And the drums were talking, Maxton.'

'Yes, sah.'

'But you didn't hear them?'

'No sah, I heard nothin'.'

'Well, I heard them, Maxton. Shall I tell you what they said?'

Maxton's eyes flickered at Ramage for an instant before looking down again. He was terror-stricken: that much was clear, though Ramage could think of no reason nor guess the man's thoughts.

'They were passing a signal, Maxton. They said that a schooner was sailing from St George for Martinique.'

Ramage thought for a moment, suddenly realizing something he had not thought of before—an ordinary bonfire could only signal one fact, unless someone hid the light for a moment or two and showed it again, as the Red Indians did. But Appleby had reported that several trees were burning to make the bonfire, so obviously that was impossible. But hold on—did it mean the bonfires were lit a certain time before the schooner sailed? Two hours before? Was that the pre-arranged signal? It was worth trying.

'The drums also said the schooner would sail at ten o'clock, Maxton. And you heard it and you knew what it said.'

'No sah,' the man exclaimed, his hands held out as if imploring Ramage to believe him. 'No sah, I didn't hear nothin'.'

'You heard the drum, you knew what it said, and why it was saying it, yet you didn't warn me. You knew that drum was helping the enemy, Maxton. An enemy you know we're trying to stop capturing the schooners. The same enemy who tried to kill us several times when we served in the *Kathleen*.' Then he added as an afterthought: 'An enemy who is trying to kill me now, Maxton.'

'Oh no he's not, sah: he's just tryin' to capture the schooners. You see, the freebooters——'

He broke off, realizing he'd just given himself away.

'Maxton,' Ramage warned quietly, 'I won't bother to warn

243

you about the Articles of War: you know the penalties for helping the enemy by not passing on information to the officers. I'm just sad that you care so little about me and the rest of your shipmates that you'd let us all get killed by walking into a trap.'

For a minute or two Maxton just stood trembling, his eyes large, perspiration running down his face, lips quivering; a man in the grip of a great, perhaps nameless fear. Suddenly he seemed to get control of himself and with an enormous effort of will he said:

'If I said anythin' about the message sah, they'd kill all my family and me too.'

'Who would?'

'Why, the loogaroos sah,' he exclaimed, as if surprised Ramage did not know.

The *loupgarou*, the vampire: Ramage remembered the natives' twin fears, jumbies and *loupgarous*. Of the two, jumbies were less fearsome—evil spirits that could be kept at bay with jumbie beads, which were talismans or lucky charms. Jumbies could be bought off with offerings of money and other things and were mischievous rather than dangerous.

But not *loupgarous*. They came out only at night, flying around unseen in the darkness to attack unsuspecting people and drink their blood, leaving them maimed or dead. And no one knew who they were, for they were really human beings whose spirits emerged from their sleeping bodies and changed into vampires.

They spent the night going about their dreadful business and before dawn returned to the sleeping bodies so that these particular men never knew that, as they slept, they turned into *loupgarous*.

And only the witch doctor could summon up the *loupgarous*; only a witch doctor could order them to attack a particular person. More important though, Ramage realized, no white man could ever persuade a coloured man they did not exist; that they were a lot of nonsense invented by witch doctors. Oh, what was the use, he thought: this was voodoo; black magic practised in Africa for centuries and then transported to the West Indies. It'd be as impossible to persuade a West Indian that *loupgarous* did not exist as to convince a Scots Calvinist that Christ never existed.

But for all that, Ramage knew he needed the information; he needed it so desperately that he had to use questionable methods to get it.

'Maxton, you believe the witch doctor can order the *loup-garous* to kill you and your family, so naturally you're frightened of him.'

The West Indian nodded. Suddenly Ramage snapped:

'Are you frightened of me?'

The man shook his head vigorously, surprise showing on his face. 'No sah!'

'Why not? I too can kill you—you've broken one of the Articles of War and I can have you hanged. And the Governor can hang your family for abetting you in treason.'

To Ramage's amazement the West Indian suddenly dropped to his knees, muttering—gabbling, almost—a prayer in what Ramage recognized was crudely-pronounced Latin: a Catholic prayer.

Then sickened by what he was doing and what he had to do, he realized Maxton's terrible predicament. The Catholic priest had, in his childhood, made Maxton a Christian and frightened him to death with visions of Hell's fire and eternal damnation; at the same time the witch doctors had been busy with equally horrifying voodoo threats; of *loupgarous* and jumbies and nameless evils of darkness and ignorance, the extent of which Ramage could only guess.

Maxton's predicament was in fact worse than Ramage guessed: soon after he had heard the drum and realized what it was saying he had been approached by the witch doctor, who heard he was from the *Triton* and warned him to be silent. But Maxton had earlier planned to go to the white priest that night for a routine confession. It was to have been a long confession—the first for two years. There were many sins for which he sought absolution and which to Maxton seemed grave: killing men, although they were the enemy; swearing, blaspheming and drunkenness. To the priest, a worldly man, when Maxton visited him late at night, they had seemed minor compared with the almost daily stories of knifings, wife-beating, murder and theft.

Maxton had overcome his fears enough to finish his confession with an account of the witch doctor's visit earlier that night, admitting he was too frightened to warn his captain of the drums' message. But the priest, not knowing the actual significance of the message and too sleepy to ask, took little notice: he was more concerned at Maxton's admission that he had not regularly said his prayers and that he had blasphemed with a monotonous regularity for more than two years.

So, his ears ringing with admonitions, Maxton had left the priest's house no wiser than when he entered, except that the priest had almost brushed aside the drums' message while the witch doctor threatened him with death over it. And he'd arrived back home to find the witch doctor had been back in his absence and reduced the whole family to a state of terror; so much so that one brother and two sisters swore they'd already seen two *loupgarous* flying among the trees, watching and obviously waiting for them to go to sleep before they began their bloody work.

But none of the others, priest, witch doctor, mother, father, brother or sister, thought of the third factor. Maxton feared the God of the priest; he did what the priest told him because the alternative was Hell fire and damnation. And he also feared the gods of the witch doctor.

Ramage, as he watched Maxton, saw the direct conflict between the priest's orders and the witch doctor's and guessed Maxton would obey the witch doctor for the very practical reason that whereas the priest only threatened eternal damnation after death (but without any threats of instant death) the witch doctor's threats were very much more positive and immediate: he promised prompt death at the hands of a *loupgarou*, not only for Maxton but for the whole family.

Yet neither witch doctor nor priest—and least of all Ramage—knew that there was this third factor in Maxton's life; almost a third god, a man whose orders he obeyed not because they were accompanied with terrible threats, but because he wanted to.

And that man was Lieutenant Ramage.

So now, on his knees in the Captain's cabin, his mind a whirl of conflicting fears and loyalties, Maxton was terrified. Not for himself, he now realized, but for his family and for his Captain, both threatened by the same dreadful powers.

Ramage looked down at the man and, recalling how Maxton had grinned at the approach of the Spanish Fleet at the Battle of Cape St Vincent and watched Ramage steer the little cutter *Kathleen* straight for the *San Nicolas* with the same grin, knew that whatever terrified the West Indian was now beyond the comprehension of a white man.

'Maxton,' he said gently, but speaking slowly and clearly, 'there's a way out of this which can save us all. Tell me honestly, can you read the drums?'

Maxton nodded dumbly.

'Very well: is it difficult to learn the language they talk?'

The man shook his head.

'Could Jackson learn enough to send a particular message —not read one—in an afternoon?'

The head nodded.

'The witch doctor didn't say you couldn't teach Jackson, did he?'

'No sah.'

'Will you, then? And show him how to make one of these drums?'

Maxton scrambled to his feet: the fear had gone and in its place was enthusiasm. With the speed of a Caribbean thunderstorm clearing to reveal bright blue skies, Maxton had stopped trembling and was eager to help.

'Yes sah!' he exclaimed eagerly. 'But the witch——'

'The witch doctor will never know—or guess. And rest assured, Maxton, my ju-ju is stronger than his: that I promise you. Now, you'd better report to Mr Southwick.'

★

After making sure that Maxton was provided with the barrel he needed to make the drum, and that he and Jackson were down in the orlop where the American could begin his first lesson in complete secrecy, using the Marine drummer's drum, Ramage had gone on shore to visit Fort George.

The Colonel was in his office and greeted Ramage with as much enthusiasm as a considerable thick head from too much rum would allow.

Ramage had given a lot of thought to how he would tackle the task of finding the spy. He'd also thought a lot about Wilson. The Colonel had been very free in his talk about the Governor—but was that because he was an old gossip or because he was shrewed enough to realize Ramage needed to know all about Sir Jason if he was to be able to handle him? Ramage had decided it was the latter.

And for that reason his first call was on the old soldier who looked askance at Ramage's first request—that one of his most trusted soldiers should, as secretly as possible, buy a cured goatskin.

Maxton had specified the size and quality needed for the drum and Ramage passed them on to the Colonel, but to preserve secrecy offered no explanation for the strange request. Wilson asked no questions, sent for an aged corporal and despatched him on the errand, explaining the man had a native wife.

'Well,' he said to Ramage, 'now we've sent the best man in my little army on the trail of goatskin, what's the Navy doing this fine morning—apart from not sleeping off the after-effects of the Governor's Ball?'

'The Navy's brought bad news: the privateers will capture that schooner within the next twelve hours.'

'Will they, by Jove! And why can't you stop 'em?'

'Because they've a head start of a couple of dozen tom-toms, a dozen bonfires—and a spy who was probably a fellow-guest at last night's ball,' Ramage said flatly.

Wilson looked up calmly at Ramage to make sure he was not joking and saw the brown eyes were alight with what might have been anger or excitement, but was certainly not amusement.

'Hmmm. Well, I've spent enough years out here not to let anything surprise me; but the King's enemies have recruited some damned odd allies, I must say!'

It took Ramage less than five minutes to tell Wilson how he'd heard the tom-tom while the Governor's guests danced, followed by Appleby's arrival from Carriacou before dawn reporting the signal bonfires.

Ramage, concentrating on his story, did not look up at Wilson until he'd finished, and was startled at the change in the man's face: the puffy look had vanished; the watery eyes were now sharp. His face was different—and so was his posture. The whole air of flabbiness had vanished: Wilson was once again a soldier, mentally and physically alert. And his first few words were spoken with a new briskness.

'Glad the Admiral sent you, m'boy. Misjudged you at first —I admit it. Admiral's son and all that: thought you'd got your command through "interest"—not unknown, you know!'

He grinned with an affection Ramage did not notice and continued:

'Now m'eyes are opened. You were quick enough to spot the tom-toms—and you had the wit to leave lookouts at Carriacou. Never occurred to me—nor to those two nitwit frigate captains the Admiral sent earlier.'

He took a quill, knife, bottle of ink and sheets of paper from a drawer and put them on the desk. He spent a few moments sharpening the quill—not because it was blunt, but because he obviously wanted time to think. Dipping the quill in the ink and squaring up the loose pages, he wrote several words one beneath the other and then read them aloud:

'Colonel Wilson ... Lieutenant Ramage ... Sir Jason Fisher ... Edward Privett ... and the schooner's master. Now, who else knew you'd given permission for the schooner to sail at ten o'clock?'

'No one, if Edward Privett's the schooner-owner. But that document I asked Sir Jason to draw up for him to sign: I wonder if Sir Jason wrote it, or if a clerk made a fair copy?'

Wilson's brow furrowed. 'No, I was in the study all the time. Just me, Sir Jason and Privett. Sir Jason—yes, he sat down at the desk and wrote it himself, then read it out aloud. Privett took the pen and signed it. The door was shut. No, only the three of us heard—or saw.

'The signed document?'

'Sir Jason locked it in his desk.'

'What did Privett do after that?'

Wilson scratched his nose with the tip of the quill.

'We talked for a few minutes; then Privett wrote a note to his captain telling him he was to sail at ten but impressing the need for secrecy. He read the note aloud and sealed it. I had it sent down to the schooner by one of my officers.'

'The officer?'

'One of my A.D.C.s. Knew nothing about it. Just called him in and told him to deliver it into the captain's hands and get a receipt. Came back half an hour later, reported he'd done so, gave me the receipt.'

'Half an hour?'

'Yes—takes fifteen minutes to the careenage by carriage.'

Ramage rubbed his brow. 'That means the schooner captain's definitely cleared.'

'How so?'

'The tom-tom was sounding less than ten minutes after you and the Governor left me and went to the study. We allow ten minutes for signing the document and writing the note—more perhaps? Plus fifteen for your officer to deliver it. That means the tom-tom couldn't have started until at least twenty-five or thirty minutes after you left me on the balcony . . .'

'So we're back again at Government House,' Wilson said.

'What did Privett do after you'd sent the officer away with the note?'

'I was just thinking about that. Now—the three of us in the study, the document signed and the note written. Then I rang for the butler to fetch my A.D.C. He came in, I gave him the note and off he went. Privett started making a flowery speech of thanks; then the Governor rang again for drinks. Yes, by Jove—we talked there for at least fifteen minutes. More like twenty-five.'

'What about?'

'You,' Wilson said blandly. 'Privett expressed a doubt about your abilities—based on your youth. We dispelled them. Don't blush; neither of us perjured ourselves on your behalf.'

Ramage gave a mock bow.

Wilson nodded slowly and, looking directly at Ramage, said: 'Think seriously about this. I trust you because it's your plan that's gone astray and you've got to account to the Admiral. But Ramage, make no mistake—it's your duty to satisfy yourself that both the Governor and myself are trustworthy.'

'I've already done that, sir.' Ramage said dryly.

'You have, by Jove?'

'I can check your story with the Governor, and you know that. And with Privett, for that matter. And all three of you hadn't left the study before the drum began. So obviously all three of you are beyond suspicion. You couldn't have done anything even if you'd wanted to!'

Wilson sat back in his chair and roared with laughter.

'You don't miss much, Ramage! But'—his face became serious again—'where does that leave us?'

He glanced down at his list, and wrote in another name. 'I've put down my A.D.C. I'd trust him with my life—indeed, have. He *could* have opened the letter. But,' he added as an afterthought, 'your timetable already cleared him.'

Ramage nodded. 'Yes, if he'd opened the letter as soon as he'd left you he couldn't have given the information to the spy before the drum started.'

Both men sat alone with their thoughts. Wilson watched the young Lieutenant rubbing his brow gently and staring at the table. The lad looked drawn, but that was hardly surprising. This sort of thing smacked of ju-ju and voodoo. How else could secret information get out of a closed room? And soon Ramage would have to send a report to his Admiral— a report which said that a schooner he'd allowed to sail had been captured, because Wilson had no doubt Ramage's forecast would prove correct. And an Admiral sitting in Barbados was unlikely to be very sympathetic, particularly, as Wilson had guessed earlier, if the Admiral was obviously using him to cover the two frigate captains who'd already failed.

But in fact Ramage was not thinking of the Admiral, nor particularly of his own responsibility for the schooner sailing: he'd deliberately agreed to let her sail because it suited him to use her as bait. Very well, the bait had been taken, which surely meant that somewhere during last night's ball there must be just one clue which would lead to the privateers?

And he'd met enough difficult situations in his life to know that an answer rarely came when you sat down at a desk and tried to think; it was more likely to emerge as you walked along a street, or reached across the table for a sugar dredge.

But anyway it was comfortably cool in this room. So just run through the evening's events once again. At about eight o'clock he was talking on the balcony to Cla—to Miss de Giraud. Then Wilson came out and said the Governor was looking for him and almost at once Sir Jason joined them. Miss de Giraud had discreetly moved away; he'd told the

Governor the conditions under which one schooner could sail at ten o'clock. Sir Jason and Wilson had then gone to the study.

Was anyone lurking on the balcony? No, there'd been only himself and Claire. After the two men had gone he'd begun talking to Claire again—after she'd returned from powdering her nose, or whatever had taken her away for a few minutes.

Suddenly he stood up. 'May I borrow a carriage, sir?'

Wilson, startled by Ramage's white face and blazing eyes, agreed and shouted to an orderly.

'Anything wrong, Ramage? Look as though you've seen a ghost! Don't say you've got one of these damned fevers?'

Numbly Ramage shook his head and turned to the door.

CHAPTER SEVENTEEN

Both the coachman and the soldier in the blue and gold uniform of the Grenada Volunteers sitting in front with a musket, eventually protested as Ramage cursed and swore as he goaded them to go faster. The road up to Government House was steep; but Ramage had almost lost control of himself in a turbulent mixture of rage mingled with disbelief at what now seemed all to obvious.

Finally, with the horses' flanks running with sweat and their mouths flecked with white, the carriage swung up the driveway to Government House and even before the footmen had time to open the door and unfold the ladder Ramage had jumped down and was running up the wide stone steps.

The two soldiers on guard at the big doors hesitated, unsure whether to challenge or salute the naval officer running towards them, one hand clutching his sword scabbard and the other his hat, and finally saluted.

Catching sight of the butler as he entered the house, Ramage called to him to find the Governor urgently, and when the man walked ponderously towards him with a pompous request to state his business, he received an angry retort from Ramage that he didn't discuss the King's business with butlers and to take him to the Governor at once.

But the clatter of galloping hooves, carriage wheels and pounding feet had brought Sir Jason into the hall, and hearing the last of the exchange he called to Ramage and together they went back into the study.

'My apologies, your Excellency, but there's some urgency in all this!'

'Oh indeed?' Sir Jason said coldly. 'I must admit I'm not used to people bursting into Government House, especially without an appointment.'

Nettled, Ramage snapped rudely: 'Fédon was not so punctilious.'

'Don't be insolent, Ramage: I shall report this to the Admiral.'

Ramage was far too angry—with himself more than the Governor—to care what was reported, although he admitted Sir Jason was justified in being surprised at his hurried arrival. But (had he not been a colonial governor) that alone should have warned him of an emergency.

'What you report, and to whom, is your affair, your Excellency. I have come to warn you that you're probably employing someone who's also a spy, and the schooner that sailed last night is likely to be in the hands of the privateers within the next few hours.'

'But—but this is preposterous! Do something, man! You must stop it being captured! Why, I shall——'

'If I could fly through the upper regions with the speed of a bird, I could possibly save her. Since I can't, she'll be captured . . . sir.'

'And what's this outrageous nonsense about me employing a spy? That's tantamount to accusing me of being a traitor and——'

'I said "You are probably employing someone who is also a spy", your Excellency: I don't suggest you know this person's a spy.'

'Well, thank you for that qualification,' Sir Jason growled. 'What am I supposed to do about it?'

'Nothing, unless you wish,' Ramage said quickly, seizing his opportunity. 'I'd prefer to deal with it myself—with your permission, of course.'

The Governor had clearly lost control of the situation and was only too willing to agree, though still anxiously clinging to the outward trapping of authority. 'Very well, you have my permission; but I hold you responsible.'

Ramage couldn't be bothered to ask for what he was being held responsible. Instead he said: 'Where is Miss de Giraud?'

'In her room—she has a migraine, though I can't see what she has to do with all this.'

'Very well: I wish to be taken to her room at once. I have to talk to her alone, though if your Excellency wishes to accompany me and make sure this meets with her approval . . .?'

'Dammit!' expostulated Sir Jason, 'this is most irregular! Prying into the private quarters of my staff? I simply——'

'The consequences of your refusing, sir, are much graver than you can possibly guess.'

Ramage had tried to sound pontifical and was pleased with the result.

'Oh very well, come along then. I don't approve, though. I'm acting under protest—remember that, Ramage.'

'I'll remember, sir,' Ramage said, taking little care to keep the ambiguity out of his voice.

She was sitting in a wicker armchair when they entered the room and wearing a severely-cut lime-green dress, her face pale. Ramage watched her closely as she looked up at Sir Jason, who stammered out an embarrassed, vague explanation for their visit. She was holding what looked like a religious book and her hand was trembling. Her eyes were slightly red, as though very recently she had been crying, and Ramage wondered the reason.

'Of course I have no objection to his Lordship asking me questions, Sir Jason,' she said easily. 'I'm flattered that he's interested in any answers I could give. So far he has only asked me to dance with him.'

Her smile was genuine but Ramage suspected it took more effort than it should and Sir Jason, who had obviously expected to find her indignant, stood nonplussed.

'Perhaps you could spare me ten minutes in your study later, Sir Jason?' Ramage asked.

'Oh yes, by all means. Oh indeed, any time.'

He backed out of the room and shut the door. Ramage walked over to the window and looked out. A tiny humming-bird hovered almost motionless before the bell-shaped blossom of a golden alamanda, the sun catching its dark green plumage.

Ramage could hear Sir Jason's footseps receding down the corridor, and he waited two or three minutes, still watching the humming-bird and irrelevantly noting he'd never really appreciated the beauty of the blossom.

Slowly he turned and faced her, deliberately keeping his back to the light so that his face was in shadow.

'You came in a hurry, Nicholas. I heard you swearing

from half-way up the hill. You shouldn't make horses gallop in this heat—it's cruel. Is there some sudden emergency?'

'No,' Ramage said casually. 'But it's sometimes useful to let people think you usually ride slowly. Then they're more likely to be surprised when you suddenly gallop.'

She smiled and shook her head. 'I'm afraid the significance of that profound remark is beyond the comprehension of a mere woman!'

Ramage smiled back reassuringly, hating his necessary hypocrisy.

'The Governor says you have a migraine. Isn't a darkened room the treatment for that?'

'Yes, but don't tell the Governor; otherwise he won't believe my excuse for not working today. The truth is I found last night's ball rather exhausting. Obviously you didn't!'

Although there was a wealth of meaning in the last two sentences there was neither coyness nor modesty; just a plain statement. For a moment Ramage was uncertain if she was genuinely and naturally resuming their strange and briefly passionate relationship where it had left off only a few hours earlier. But the hand holding the book was still trembling—why didn't she have the sense to put it in her lap?—and her upper lip and brow were now covered with fine beads of perspiration, yet the room was cool.

'Exhausting? No, not at all. Enlightening, though.'

She glanced up suddenly, looking him straight in the eye. Although there was no embarrassment, Ramage thought he detected fear. Yet he wasn't sure because she was unlike any woman he'd ever met. To her, he suspected, the normal usages of polite conversation, the white lies and gentle hypocrisies of society, were foreign or abhorrent. Or maybe she was just brazen; a consummate actress. It was one or the other; there was no middle path.

She said quietly, 'Nicholas, say what you have to say, because remarks like that are wounding, and you're watching me like a tiger.'

For a moment her eyes seemed to—he turned back to the window, deeply puzzled. 'Wounding,' she'd said. He gripped the sill and stared at the blossom without seeing it. The anger and bitterness which had exploded inside him like a volcano in Colonel Wilson's office had suddenly gone. On the one hand he was thankful because now he was thinking more clearly; but on the other hand he realized it was making his task harder.

Although certain his suspicions were well-grounded, he now wondered if it was as straightforward as he'd thought. He sensed some powerful, complicated reason behind it all; something as weird as voodoo and equally inexplicable.

Or was that what he hoped? Was that what he wanted to be told because he'd fallen in love with her? He brushed the idea away impatiently: of course he had! Of course that's what he'd hoped to hear! That's why he'd been so angry. Why, he thought bitterly, he'd behaved like a cuckolded husband confronting the unfaithful wife. And he wasn't even married.

He glared at his knuckles, which were white from his grip on the window sill. Admitting it all to himself seemed to make it easier: at least he now admitted he'd fallen in love with her, and warned himself of the danger that private emotions would interfere—were interfering, up to this moment—with his duties.

And still were: there was no point in glossing over it. What did he do now? How was he going to get from her the secret of the drums? Bully her, reduce her to tears, frighten her into revealing everything she knew and had done? Or did he try—well almost seduce her, using her feeling for him (if she had any: he was sure she had—but she might be a superb actress) to get the information he wanted?

He turned to find her weeping silently, sobs shaking her whole body. He took a step to hold her, then drew back. Trying to push his emotions to one side he told himself coldly that first he needed to know if she was genuine or just acting a part. And he needed to know for two reasons—because he was in Grenada on the King's business, and because—well, because he'd fallen in love with her.

But where to begin? Are you a spy? Do you love me? If a spy, why? If you love me—damnation! Ridiculous questions—yet he had to know the answers.

She looked up at him and whispered: 'Ask the questions!'

He found he could say nothing, and after a few moments she said: 'You're afraid to hear the answers.'

He nodded dumbly.

Still speaking quietly but with what Ramage was startled to realize was bitterness and contempt for herself in her voice, she pleaded: 'Oh for the love of God ask! If only I'd had the strength this morning I would never have heard them!'

'What do you mean, "strength"?'

She shook her head despairingly.

'I've spent the morning trying to find the courage to end my life—and I couldn't. Now you know why I must hear the questions: that they come from your lips is probably part of my punishment.'

Although almost numbed by her words, Ramage knew she'd already told him all but the details: she was the spy, she was not a consummate actress—and perhaps she did love him.

He knelt beside her, took one of her hands in his and, cursing the banality of the phrase, said: 'Tell me what happened.'

'No! Just ask questions!'

Her vehemence startled him, but she avoided his eyes.

'How can I? I don't know where to begin.'

'Oh *please* don't make me sound as if I was confessing everything to a priest. Just ask questions—then perhaps you'll begin to understand.' But she shook her head as she added. 'No, you can never do that.'

By now Ramage knew that question-and-answer was the only way and he remained kneeling. It'd be easier for her to answer if he wasn't towering over her, and he had no doubt now that everything she would say would be the truth.

'Claire, if I must ask questions, the first one is obvious: did you hear me tell the Governor last night that the schooner could sail at ten o'clock?'

'Yes,' she whispered. 'I heard.'

'It was about eight o'clock, wasn't it?'

'I don't know—I suppose it must have been.'

'While I was talking with Sir Jason and Colonel Wilson, you left the balcony . . .'

'Yes.'

'And you went away to pass on that information to someone?'

'Yes,' she whispered.

'And then the tom-tom signalled it to the north?'

'Yes.'

'What did the tom-tom say—just that the schooner would sail that night?'

'Yes—that it would sail about two hours later.'

'To whom did you pass the information?'

Suddenly he felt her body go rigid: the hand he was holding tensed. The room seemed cold, as though an invisible fog had swirled in through the window. It wasn't the question: it was something else. He felt his senses sharpening: colours were brighter, he heard noises more sharply.

Someone had come into the room: someone of whom she was terrified. Someone who would kill them both to keep the secret.

Ramage's mind started racing and to gain the vital few moments he needed he said, with studied casualness, trying hard to keep his voice at the same pitch:

'Leave that for a moment—a more important question is do you think the schooner has already been captured?'

'Yes.'

Her voice was almost a sob: the tips of her fingers moved slightly in his hand as if trying to warn him of the other person's presence.

Ramage moved slightly as if his right leg was cramped from kneeling, and apparently absent-mindedly rubbed the shin muscle—at the same time managing to flick up the strap over the top of the throwing-knife nestling in its sheath inside the boot.

He tried to sense exactly where the person was standing as he asked: 'Will the next schooner be captured if I let it sail?'

'I expect so.' Then, as he gently squeezed her fingers to show he'd understood her signal, she added. 'I'm certain.'

'So there's nothing we can do to save the first one? Think carefully before you answer.'

There was the edge of a shadow to his left: the shadow of the top of the man's head. Ramage's back was square to the door and the sun was shining in from the window to his left, so the man must be standing almost directly behind him. And there was a draught blowing through the room. The man had come through the door—that accounted for the sudden chill a minute or two ago; and it meant whoever it was probably had a right to be in Government House.

'Nothing,' she said. 'It has already——'

Ramage was on his feet like a spring uncoiling, throwing knife in his hand, and facing the man. Sir Jason's butler was holding a pistol in his hand, aiming it at Ramage's stomach.

Surprise—create surprise! The words hammered in Ramage's brain. But how? Then without consciously thinking, he said, as if in a casual reproof:

'I didn't hear you knock.'

For a moment the butler was startled. Obviously he'd been expecting either an attack or angry shouts; but his natural politeness made him begin to reply automatically with an apologetic:

'Well, sir——'

'Close the door!'

The hand holding the pistol moved indecisively—and the muzzle swung a few degrees.

At the same instant Ramage's right hand jerked up and forward, there was a flash of metal and the man spun round with a stifled grunt of pain.

The pistol dropped to the ground and, even as the man's left hand clutched the black-hilted knife sticking in his right shoulder, Ramage leapt, knocking him flat on his back and jumping down astride his chest.

In the same movement he'd wrenched the knife from the man's shoulder and now held the point in one hand, the hilt in the other. As he called to Claire to pick up the pistol he pushed the blade down horizontally across the man's throat.

'Don't move!' he snarled. 'Before you die *you* can answer some questions!'

'But I'm bleeding to death!' the man croaked. 'My shoulder—for pity's sake, sir—oh for pity's sake——'

'I don't give a damn whether you live or die.' Ramage hissed. 'I know all I need to know, but you can fill in some details.'

Suddenly the man gave a convulsive heave up with his stomach in an attempt to pitch Ramage forward over his head. The jerk was so unexpected that Ramage, almost losing his balance, had to press down to avoid being flung on his face, his whole weight coming on to his hands.

A hissing and gurgling as he regained his balance astride the man made him look down. The knife had cut the man's throat; even as he watched a bright red river of blood pumped in an ever-widening pool across the polished wooden blocks of the floor.

Ramage felt no regret; instead, as the pumping and the stertorous breathing stopped, he simply thought bitterly to himself that he didn't know all he needed to know; that many details had to be filled in.

He stood up and turned to Claire. Still clutching the pistol, she had fainted.

CHAPTER EIGHTEEN

More than an hour later a carriage drew away from Government House and headed down the hill. A large trunk on the rack behind contained the body of the butler, while Ramage and Colonel Wilson sat inside, hot and exhausted.

Neither man spoke until the carriage arrived at Fort George, the trunk had been unloaded and taken to the magazine, and they were both sitting in Wilson's office.

Only then did the Colonel—who, since he'd arrived at Government House after an urgent message from Ramage, had simply done what the Lieutenant told him—ask his first question.

'Why didn't we leave a guard over the dam' woman, Ramage? She could be up to some more mischief this very minute!'

'It isn't necessary, sir: she was being blackmailed. The butler was our man.'

'But there must be others: what happens when they find he's missing?'

'The only one that mattered was a gardener: he took the butler's messages to the drummer.'

'What about him, then?'

'He won't trouble anyone,' Ramage said shortly.

'And the drummer?'

'We still have to find him. I know his name but not where he lives. He never goes near Government House, though, and won't be expecting to hear from the gardener until the next signal's to be passed.'

'Sir Jason seemed mightily upset,' Wilson said, not troubling to disguise the satisfaction in his voice.

'Hardly surprising, sir; imagine how it'll look in a despatch to London: the Governor's butler a spy who was blackmailing the Governor's wife's secretary into betraying secrets.'

'Well, I'm not going to gloss over it in my report to the Secretary at War,' Wilson said crossly. 'Ever since the Insurrection I've been convinced there's been a leakage of information from Government House. When Sir Jason arrived I begged him to change all the servants—that damned butler particularly; I couldn't stand him. But Sir Jason wouldn't hear of it. In fact he thought the world of the butler.'

'I wonder what else he discovered over the years and passed on to the French.'

'Beggars the imagination to think of it. Must have been a rich man by now—they'll have been paying him well.'

Ramage shook his head. 'He didn't get a penny.'

'What?' Wilson almost shouted. 'Did he—dammit, you mean to say he played traitor for nothing?'

'No,' Ramage said wearily, for the heat and excitement were taking their toll, 'he wasn't a traitor. No'—he held up a hand hastily to stop Wilson, who seemed likely to explode —'he was a French national. French father, British mother. Spoke both languages fluently.'

'How d'you know all this?'

'From his daughter.'

Ramage had optimistically hoped that in the excitement no one would ask the question, but there was no avoiding it.

'Daughter? Who ...' Wilson paused as he saw the misery in Ramage's face. 'Oh, hmm, deuced sorry about that, m'dear fellow. I ... How much does old Fishpot know about this?'

'Nothing, sir. I had a long talk with Miss de Giraud while I was waiting for you to arrive. You know as much as Sir Jason because you were there when I told him. And a little more, now.'

'So you and I—and the lady—are the only ones that know?'

Ramage nodded. 'And now you have a duty to do, sir, so ...'

'Lookee young Ramage. I've my duty to do, yes. But answer me this honestly—as far as I can make out she was answering your questions openly when you realized that fellow had come into the room with a pistol?'

'Yes—she was anxious to. She'd spent the morning trying

to pluck up courage to do away with herself.'

'She told you that?' Wilson exclaimed.

'Yes—you see, I'd asked her to tell me the whole story but she couldn't bring herself to; not starting at the beginning, as it were. She wanted me to ask questions.'

'Right—now you answer two questions for me. Forget any feelings you have for her—don't get embarrassed; I envy you—and tell me if you, as a King's officer, are certain she was telling you the truth all the time.'

'Yes, and apart from that, her answers tally precisely with what we already knew.'

'Very well, Second question—if she hadn't answered your questions, could you have found out about the butler and all that business?'

Ramage shook his head.

'Definitely not. After all, we only discovered about her by eliminating everyone else. But the trail would have stopped there.'

'So in effect she's turned King's evidence: she's helped us trap a spy?'

Suddenly Ramage realized what the old Colonel was driving at.

'Yes, and willingly.' Then, after a moment's thought, he added, 'But from your point of view, sir, since you're responsible for the internal security of the island, you mustn't forget that if she'd committed suicide this morning . . .'

'I'm only concerned with what she did; not what she might have done,' Wilson said crisply. 'By the way, what's the Governor proposing to do?'

'His last words to me, while you were seeing the trunk loaded on to the carriage,' Ramage said dryly, 'were that he was going to write a strongly-worded protest to Admiral Robinson and the Admiralty about me.'

'Protesting about what?'

'I don't think he was too sure. Probably because I deprived him of his butler . . .'

Wilson laughed.

'A serious offence. But just one more question about Miss de Giraud: what made her—well, obey her father and give away secrets?'

'Sheer terror. He was a fanatical revolutionary—one of

Fèdon's right-hand men. During the Insurrection he took her to see some voodoo nonsense—the ritual murder of a negro accused of helping the British, and the negro's wife. It was five hours before they were dead. The drummer who beats the tom-tom was one of the murderers. She was eighteen years old when she saw that. When she went to Government House, her father simply told her if she didn't do what he told her, she'd be handed over to this man. She believed he'd do it—and so do I.'

'Did the Governor know she was the butler's daughter?'

'No, nor was the man really a butler. Came from an old French family. Some row at Court and he was exiled. It embittered him, so he was ripe to become a revolutionary. When the war began, he was sent to the West Indies as a spy because of his perfect English, and his daughter, too.'

'Why, isn't the daughter a Jacobin, then?'

'Her mother—she was English, remember—left him years ago in France and took the girl to England. After the Revolution but before the war began the father forced her to go back to France, though she regarded herself as English.'

'And the Governor knows none of this?'

'Not a thing. Just that I had to kill his butler because he was a spy, and that the whole thing must be kept secret.'

'Very well, that closes the affair. What do you intend doing now?'

'About the privateers? Frankly sir, my head's still in a whirl: knifing a man accidentally like that leaves a nasty feeling . . .'

'You'd have an even nastier feeling if he'd shot you, which he obviously intended doing. Don't become one of those people who cheerfully kill a man with a cannon at a mile range but baulk at killing the same man with a sword at one yard.'

'Just as lethal, but less personal. No, I really meant killing him in front of his daughter. Although I think he intended shooting her as well.'

'Upsetting,' Wilson admitted, but without much conviction. 'Now, what else is to be done about the butler?'

'Well sir, to be honest I don't think I've the patience to try to deal with Sir Jason. We'd be unwise to tell him any more than he knows already. If he knew the whole truth he'd probably talk. Or his wife would.'

'Leave that to me,' Wilson said flatly. 'I'll go up and see him. Now for Miss de Giraud—I don't like leaving her there. A shot through her window... There are plenty of French sympathizers on the island. We don't know how many knew what the butler was doing. Now he's vanished, as far as they're concerned they might get frightened.'

Ramage nodded. 'That's crossed my mind, but——'

'She can stay at my house. My wife likes her and the place is always guarded. I can get her there this evening without anyone knowing. All the servants are soldiers' wives and been with us years.'

'Thank you, sir. Now if you'll excuse me I'd like to get back on board.'

'Fine—leave Sir Fishpot to me. And let's hope we think of a way of smoking out those privateers. Pity the *Triton*'s not a Trojan horse!'

★

Ramage was drafting a brief report for Admiral Robinson when Jackson knocked on the door and came into the cabin, handing him the throwing knife.

'All cleaned up and re-sharpened, sir. Nasty nick just to one side of the point; must have caught the bone.'

'Probably,' Ramage said, cutting short the American's curiosity. 'Now, how are your lessons going?'

'Maxton says pretty fair, sir. He's softened up that goat-skin for the tom-tom and we're using a butter firkin, not a cask. More like the real thing, so he says. It'll be ready in an hour or so.'

'You've got the rhythm right?'

'Yes—leastways, he reckons so, though it's difficult to tell with a Marine drum 'cos the skin's stretched differently.'

'Have you got out of Maxton what that signal was?'

'Yes. They don't beat out words or numbers apparently; just pre-arranged sort of tunes. They all have different meanings.'

'Right. Now listen carefully, Jackson. When you're next practising I want you to say something casually to Maxton. Just say it conversationally, and watch his reaction.'

'I follow, sir: catch him unawares.'

'Exactly. Now I think I know the name of the man who

uses the tom-tom and we've got to catch him. I don't know where he lives, but Maxton probably does. If he *does* know the man—and you'll have to judge that from his reaction—he's got to tell us. Tell you, preferably.'

'Leave it to me, sir,' Jackson said confidently. 'He's a good lad. Just that the witch doctor put the fear of—well, I don't know what—into him.'

'I understand. Now, this tom-tom fellow is called Josiah Fetch.'

Jackson repeated the name and left the cabin, saying his next lesson with Maxton was due at two o'clock.

Footsteps on the companion ladder and the clump of the Marine sentry's boots as he saluted warned Ramage that Southwick had at last finished his duties on deck.

As the old Master sat down in a chair, tossing his hat on to the settee and running his hand through his bushy white hair, Ramage was surprised how much had happened in the four hours or so he'd been away from the ship. As far as Southwick knew at present they were probably four hours spent drinking rum punches with Colonel Wilson or the Governor.

Briefly Ramage retailed the morning's events, omitting only the father-daughter relationship, and Southwick acknowledged the various episodes with a nod of his head. When Ramage had finished Southwick said slowly:

'Glad you weren't out of practice with that knife of yours, sir. But now this butler's dead we've—well, reached a dead end!'

'As you say, a dead end.'

'Looks as though we'll have to let another schooner sail and shadow her with the *Triton*, or send off a false signal and hope they take the bait, sailing the *Triton* instead of a schooner.'

'That'll never work. You know how the privateer schooner can work up to windward. Apart from that, we'd be spotted sailing: the butler, gardener and drummer can't be the only ones involved.'

Southwick sighed. 'I knew there was a catch in all this—told you so, didn't I, sir? As soon as I heard those two frigate captains had failed and you'd been given the job I knew the Admiral was up to something.'

'You don't think I imagined he was selecting me for promotion do you?' Ramage said sourly.

'Did that Colonel have any ideas, sir?'

'I didn't ask him—hardly his field. All he contributed was a Trojan horse.'

'What do we want horses for?'

Ramage looked so puzzled that Southwick added hurriedly, 'Sorry, sir, is it some special sort of horse?'

Ramage laughed and began to tell Southwick the legend. Suddenly he broke off. 'I'll tell you the rest some other time —I've just remembered something. Have the jolly boat manned—I'll be on shore for a couple of hours.'

* * *

Wilson was at first sceptical of Ramage's plan because of the danger it involved: it was impossible to guess the odds against Ramage and his men, he protested, but likely they'd be at least three to one.

'Always assume the odds'll be greater than you expect— you'll never be disappointed,' he warned.

But apart from the heavy odds, he finally agreed the plan was for the moment the only possibility. Like Ramage, he was disappointed that Claire de Giraud had no idea where the privateers were based except that it was at one of the islands to the north.

Surprisingly, Wilson had agreed with Ramage that of all the ship-owners to choose, Rondin was the most trustworthy, as well as being the most intelligent. Ramage was even more surprised when Wilson advised that Rondin should be brought to the Fort, instead of Ramage visiting the man's house.

'We don't know who our enemies are,' Wilson declared. 'If anyone sees you going to Rondin's house, who knows what they can guess? But he's in the country today. I'll arrange it for tomorrow morning.'

* * *

Next morning Wilson's carriage brought a puzzled Rondin to the Fort. He listened attentively as Ramage began by telling him the schooner that sailed two nights earlier had almost certainly been captured.

'I'm not surprised,' he commented. 'The owner was a fool to make the Governor persuade you, and to do it in the midst of a ball ... Now, you want me to do something?'

Ramage liked his direct manner. He did not ask questions; merely listened to what was said, as if sensing he was being told all he needed to know. When Ramage finished outlining what he wanted of the ship-owner, Rondin shrugged his shoulders and smiled.

'You're doing me an honour: to show you trust a man these days is to honour him. But schooners are expensive, and if this one is lost——'

'She's insured,' Wilson interrupted. 'And if we don't catch these blasted privateers you'll probably lose her anyway—and others.'

Rondin nodded. 'She's insured all right, though I imagine the underwriters would quibble if she was lost through being involved in Lord Ramage's plan. Still, that's not why I'm hesitating.'

'Why, then?' Ramage asked.

'I'm a rich man, my Lord. I could lose half a dozen uninsured schooners without worrying too much ... No, I'm more worried about you and your men.'

'Me and my men?'

'One doesn't become a successful plantation-owner and ship-owner, my Lord, without weighing up odds and taking a long view. Sometimes I've found it worth taking a short-term loss to make a long-term gain. But you naval officers rarely have the choice: when you sight the enemy you have only two alternatives—to attack or not—and only a matter of minutes to decide.'

Wilson interrupted: 'All that's obvious, if you don't mind me saying so, Mr Rondin.'

'Of course, my dear Colonel; I'm merely mentioning it as a preface to explaining my reluctance.'

Ramage was beginning to share Wilson's impatience.

'If you're reluctant, Mr Rondin, then I can only ask that you keep secret everything you've heard here this morning and we'll approach someone else.'

'You misunderstand me, my Lord: I'm reluctant, but I'm certainly not refusing.'

'Come on, Rondin, explain yourself,' growled Wilson.

'I'll address my remarks to you, Colonel, to avoid embarrassing this young man. You'll remember Admiral Robinson

269

sent two frigates which sailed up and down for a couple of months . . . ?'

'Yes, I remember well enough.'

'Well, without meaning any disrespect to the Royal Navy, we still lost schooners. But the two captains were dull-witted men. They regarded their task—at first, anyway—as a simple one. But as the weeks went by with no success, they just regarded themselves as unlucky. They didn't real-ize it wasn't simple; they didn't revise their original view. . .'

'Go on, go on,' Wilson said impatiently.

'Very well, I think we can agree they were stupid men. But then we were lucky enough to be sent Lord Ramage who realized from the start it wasn't an easy task because he has the imagination the others lacked. He has moral courage—more than enough, from what I hear—to stand up to his Excellency . . .'

Rondin had a habit of tailing off his sentences, his voice dropping and giving the impression to his listeners that they had gone deaf.

'I wish the Governor was as terrified of me as he is of the Lieutenant,' Wilson said with a broad grin, 'but do hurry up!'

'Bear with me a moment, Colonel. My only objection is this: privateers carry enormous crews. Any two privateers have four times more men that the whole ship's company of the *Triton*. You're likely to meet odds of about seven to one. I'd put my money on you and your men at two, perhaps even three to one. But above that . . .' He turned his thumb down.

'I've already pointed out all this to him,' Wilson said, nodding in agreement.

'I would have bet on *that*, Colonel,' Rondin said, 'because you're a brave man concerned with the safety of another brave man. No, don't blush like a girl, my Lord; one's either brave or one isn't; it's as simple and as complicated as that. No, just listen to the reasoning of a businessman.

'If you go ahead with your plan you stand perhaps a ten per cent chance of success. That kind of percentage rules out the whole thing from my point of view.'

'But——' Ramage started to protest.

'Listen carefully: no businessman would risk his whole

capital for a ten per cent gain. If he loses, he's lost everything; he can't start again. Even a gambler would only risk his whole capital if he had a chance of a hundred per cent gain.'

'But I still don't——'

'No, because you aren't a businessman. Now, to be blunt, you're our only chance of destroying these privateers. Very well, I want you to succeed. Apart from my personal regard for you, my profits will quadruple if the privateers are destroyed—and be quartered if they're not.

'So I'd rather you waited for a better chance of succeeding. If you're killed we can resign ourselves to another six months or a year of losses. That means ruin: we'll have no schooners left. Not a hundredweight of produce can be shipped to England. Grenada will collapse.'

'But there are frigates,' Ramage protested. 'Admiral Robinson——'

'Can do nothing: it's men that matter, not ships,' Rondin said. 'No ship of war is better than her captain.'

Having spent most of his life in the Navy, his contact with men of business had been small, so Ramage was fascinated by Rondin's honesty in weighing personal against business feelings.

Wilson asked bluntly: 'For all that, you'll let us use one of your schooners?'

'Of course! But I hope I've persuaded him to wait for a more propitious opportunity.'

Ramage shook his head.

'The big difference between a businessman and a fighting man, Mr Rondin, is that the businessman can rarely surprise his competitors. He gets a higher price for his goods only if he gets to the market first selling something everyone wants.'

'True enough,' Rondin admitted, 'and in wartime the convoy system means all our produce arrives on the English market at the same time, so that overnight scarcity becomes a glut, and prices drop accordingly.'

'Exactly, but a fighting man can often surprise his enemies. I'm hoping surprise will give us a considerable advantage—bringing the percentage down to something more acceptable to an investor!'

Rondin smiled. 'The schooner's yours, my Lord. Now,

tell me again exactly what you want me to do.'

★

Jackson and Maxton reported promptly to Ramage on the quarterdeck.

'Well, Maxton, how's your pupil coming along?'

'Fine, sah,' the West Indian said enthusiastically. 'We've made the drum and it's just right. Jacko's been practising. You won't be able to tell the difference.'

Knowing a West Indian's two faults were the habit of saying what he thought the other person wanted to hear, and an incurably optimistic approach to all problems, Ramage said sharply:

'It's not whether *I* can tell the difference, Maxton, but whether that fellow listening up to the north can.'

Maxton shook his head, as if guessing what Ramage was thinking. 'Even I wouldn't be able to tell the difference, sah.'

'Very well, you've obviously been a good teacher. I appreciate it.'

Maxton looked embarrassed, knowing there was more behind his Captain's words than most people realized.

'Jackson,' Ramage said, 'I want to see you in my cabin in five minutes. Mr Southwick! If you can spare me a minute.'

Down in the stuffy cabin the Master listened with his usual cheerfulness as Ramage described the latest developments, nodding at the prospect of action at last.

'M'sword's been getting rusty!' he exclaimed.

'I hope it'll stay rusty,' Ramage said. 'I'll be leading the boarding party and you'll be commanding the *Triton*.'

'Oh, sir!' Southwick sounded like a disappointed schoolboy. 'The boarding party's really my job. After all,' he added slyly, 'you command the *Triton*, sir: she's your responsibility...'

'Not if I leave you in command,' Ramage countered.

'Seems to me you're taking advantage of your position, sir,' the Master said in mock protest.

'That's the sole advantage of seniority, Southwick. It starts with the Prime Minister, who bullies the First Lord, who bullies the Commander-in-Chief...'

'Down to lieutenants commanding brigs who bully masters of brigs,' Southwick added.

272

'Who bully quartermasters of brigs...I can't see what you're complaining about, Southwick!'

'All right, sir,' Southwick said, 'I submit only because I know Admiral Robinson's doing the same thing to you!'

'As good a reason as any.'

There was a knock on the door and the sentry called that Jackson wished to be admitted.

The American came in and stood at attention, shoulders hunched, head bent forward to keep clear of the beams overhead.

'Ah Jackson—how did your conversation with Maxton turn out?'

'Well enough, sir. You see, he was frightened when he began giving me lessons; kept muttering and grunting words I didn't understand, and crossing himself the way Catholics do. But he didn't today, and when I——'

He glanced at the Master and Ramage nodded.

'—when I said I'd heard the best drummer in Grenada was a man called Josiah Fetch, Maxton just swore. Never heard him carry on like that before, sir. Three or four minutes he was, just cussing and blaspheming——'

'Did he cross himself?' Ramage interrupted.

'Never once, sir. When he calmed down I asked what'd put him about so, and he said this man Fetch was the wickedest man in the Caribbean; that he wished him dead.'

Ramage nodded. 'Did you get the impression he'd help...'

'Yes, sir. To be honest—I hope I didn't over-step the mark, sir, but I thought you might have the same idea—I sort of hinted that it shouldn't be too difficult to do him in.'

'What did he say to that?'

'Went quiet for a minute or two and his eyes went glassy —you know how I mean, sir. Then he asked if I'd help, and if I reckoned Rossi an' Stafford would join us, I said I knew they would.'

'Does Maxton know where he lives?'

'Yes, apparently he's a sort of witch doctor and terrorizes all the local people, Maxton's father included, and makes 'em pay him so much a week from their crops. Maxton says he was mixed up in the big rebellion a year or so ago.'

'Thank you, Jackson; that's all we need to know. You'd

better sound out Rossi and Stafford about this Fetch fellow. Don't go into a lot of detail, though.'

As soon as Jackson left the cabin, Southwick said: 'How many men are you taking, sir?'

'Say twenty. Water and food for forty-eight hours. Swords, pikes, tomahawks and pistols. No muskets—too crowded for them.'

'Twenty? Can't you squeeze in more?'

'I doubt it, but have another twenty standing by when you rendezvous with us. Oh yes, some grenades might be useful—you'd better see to it that half a dozen men know how to use 'em and make sure they've flints and slow matches. And I want false-fires and rockets, at least a dozen of each.'

Southwick had already taken pen and paper and was noting down Ramage's requirements.

'Call for volunteers, sir?'

'No—they'll all volunteer. Just pick twenty steady men for the main party, and another twenty to stand by. Don't leave yourself short of topmen. I'd like Jackson, Maxton, Rossi, Stafford, Evans, Fuller, John Smith the Second ... You keep Appleby; you'll probably need him.'

'Although you don't want muskets, sir, there's those half dozen musketoons. They fairly cut a swathe through a crowd o' men.'

Ramage nodded. 'I'd forgotten—yes, we'll take them. One each for Jackson, Stafford, Evans, Fuller and Smith the Second, and you choose the other one.'

'Very well, sir. I'd better make a start on this, and the station bill will have to be changed.'

With that Southwick bustled out, and Ramage took up the pen, jabbed it in the ink, and scribbled a few lines in his daily journal. With so much happening, one day was merging into the next, and he'd need the notes when he came to write his report.

Just before leaving the Fort, the Colonel had given him some advice. Wilson began by pointing out what was already obvious, that Admiral Robinson had given Ramage his orders for a particular reason, because whoever received them was likely to fail, and would be a convenient scapegoat.

It was what followed that surprised Ramage.

'Suppose you don't come out of this alive, m'lad,' the Colonel had said with his usual bluntness. 'I'm the only one in any authority who knows what you're going to attempt tomorrow night. So why don't you write a report to his Excellency explaining exactly what you intend doing and why. You can leave it with me, and I'll deliver it the following afternoon, when it's too late for him to countermand anything—or, for that matter, accidentally reveal anything that's secret.'

Although he'd shrugged off the idea at the time, Ramage had since realized it was sound advice. Well, if he didn't write the report now he never would, because there wasn't much time left. He closed the journal, took out some sheets of notepaper, dipped the pen in the ink and began writing.

Triton, St George Roads, 1st June, 1797

Sir,

Having failed to discover the precise whereabouts of the privateers' base by making a reconnaissance in H.M. brig under my command, but having discovered the means by which advance news of the sailing of schooners is passed northwards through the islands to the privateersmen, I am putting into execution a few nights hence the only plan which, upon mature consideration, offers any chance of speedily securing the safety of the schooners upon which the trade of the island of Grenada so largely depends.

The plan fell into four parts, Ramage wrote, and described it briefly, concluding:

The operation depends for its success upon the amount of surprise that can be achieved. If surprise is lost, the operation will fail since the privateersmen will outnumber the British seamen by a considerable margin. However, this is a factor against which it is impossible to plan in detail.

I am, sir, &c,
Nicholas Ramage,
Lieutenant and Commanding Officer

His Excellency Sir Jason Fisher, Knt,
Government House,
Grenada.

Calling for his clerk and telling him to copy the letter into the letter book, and make another copy for Colonel Wilson, Ramage then went up on deck, thankful to get into the cool breeze.

*

The next afternoon, by which time, Ramage estimated, the privateers would have unloaded their prize, he went on deck to give orders to Southwick to get under way.

'I have to report that four men have deserted, sir,' Southwick said solemnly.

'Deserted? Who the——'

Southwick laughed at Ramage's dismay.

'The tom-tom, sir—difficult to smuggle something like that on shore. I thought the best thing was to send in the Master's Mate with a boat to fill water-casks. Jackson put the tom-tom in a kitbag and while Appleby turned his back he and Maxton and the other two slipped away. Anyone watching would've thought it was a regular case o' men deserting.'

Ramage felt childishly annoyed: to begin with he'd completely forgotten to arrange for the four men to be landed to carry out their part of the night's work; and he was—he admitted it—jealous that Southwick had, without reference to him, thought up an ingenious way of doing it.

'I hope you explained what they're supposed to do,' he said tartly.

Southwick related in detail what he'd said.

'Fine—they didn't forget to take false-fires, I hope?'

'Took three, sir, just in case one gets damp.'

'Hmmm,' Ramage grunted.

Now he had nothing to do he was getting jumpy. Too much depended on too many people doing things upon which other things depended. Jackson was reliable—but had Maxton *really* trained him with that damned drum? Would the four of them carry out their orders properly? Could Rondin really be trusted, or had he already passed a warning to the privateers?

Was—he forced himself to think about it now, though he'd been avoiding it most of the afternoon—Claire really to be trusted? He felt ashamed at his doubts; but he'd fallen in love with her and that alone might warp his judgement, leading him to wasting men's lives. That worried him more, he admitted, than if she'd been married and he'd cuckolded her husband while a guest under his roof. And what if the schooner——

'Everything'll go all right, sir,' Southwick said quietly, sensing Ramage's doubts. 'It's the waiting that plays old Harry with all of us.'

'Not with you,' Ramage said.

'You'd be surprised, sir. I'd sooner be leading a boarding party than trying to conn the *Triton* round reefs in the dark into some damned bay I've never seen before and where the chart gives no soundings.'

'Better to run the ship aground than get a pike in your stomach.'

'No,' Southwick laughed, 'when you've a stomach the size of mine'—he patted it proudly—'you'd sooner take your chance with a pike than a reef.'

At that moment the clerk came up with Ramage's letters to the Governor and Wilson. Both were plastered with red seals, and Ramage said:

'Have these delivered to the Colonel at the Fort, Mr Southwick, and we'll get under way as soon as the boat returns.'

CHAPTER NINETEEN

The *Triton* had sailed in broad daylight with all the ritual attached to a final departure, including a farewell salute fired in honour of the Governor, and rounded Point Saline. To a casual onlooker or a watchful spy, she was obviously bound for Barbados or Trinidad.

And, as planned, when darkness fell with its usual Tropical suddenness, Ramage had given the order for her to wear round and steer for the rendezvous with Rondin's schooner, the *Jorum*, at midnight four miles off Gouyave, a small village on the northwest side of Grenada ten miles from St George.

From several minutes before ten o'clock he and Southwick had watched Point Saline for signs of the blue flame of a false-fire. At ten minutes past ten Ramage shut the night-glass with a snap, having taken three bearings.

'Well, Jackson must have done the job. Fetch must be dealt with and the signal passed.'

'Unless they all got drunk—or walked into a trap. Or that Fetch fellow was too smart for them,' Southwick growled.

Since the remark merely emphasized his own unspoken fears and it was unlike the Master to be depressed, Ramage snapped:

'Or the wind might drop and we'll miss them at the rendezvous.'

'It might,' Southwick said, missing Ramage's sarcasm. 'Often does drop at night.'

Ramage made no reply: he'd lose his temper with the old fellow if he wasn't careful. He opened the night-glass again and looked up towards St George.

Over there at this moment, within the circle contained by the telescope's lens, Claire was at Wilson's house and probably making polite conversation with the Colonel's lady; Sir

Jason would probably be playing whist—had he found a new butler yet?

Ramage shivered. He'd left his coat in the cabin and although chilly it was not entirely the wind. But he was thinking of Rondin's words. When spoken, the praise and businessman's cold-blooded approach had alternately embarrassed and surprised him. But now their significance was sinking in. Rondin had tried to deter him because he thought a better opportunity of destroying the privateers would come along. But Ramage felt instinctively it would be foolish to miss the present one.

Although their spy in Government House was out of action, the privateersmen had too much at stake to shrug their shoulders and go elsewhere. No, they'd quickly set up a new system, and it wouldn't be difficult: someone watching for a schooner sailing, beating a drum for a few moments from a high hill over the harbour—and vanishing into the rain forests until the next schooner sailed. Not as effective a spy as the butler—who obviously found out many other secrets—but equally effective as far as catching the schooners was concerned.

Ramage knew it was his only chance. And all the while Admiral Robinson waited in Barbados. In London the Admiralty, the West Indian Committee and the underwriters would soon be needing scapegoats to placate them. Rondin was right—if one had plenty of time. But Ramage knew time was the only thing he lacked.

'Keep on imagining I can hear tom-toms,' Southwick grumbled.

'It's that stomach of yours: you ate too much for supper.'

'I did, too,' Southwick admitted. 'But it'll be a few hours a'fore I can sit down to a quiet meal again without fretting about whether the quartermaster's gone to sleep.'

'You haven't much to grumble about,' Ramage said unsympathetically. 'You'll have twenty-four hours at the most. What about me—twenty-four months of it. Well, nearly twelve anyway.'

'You're welcome to every minute,' the old Master said with a sudden cheery frankness. 'Just don't go and get yourself killed and leave me to take the ship back to Barbados!'

'Barbados? I thought you said you were going to run her

279

up on a reef in the dark?'

'Aye, that'd take a load off my mind. Then I can hire a schooner for the King's service and go back to Barbados as a passenger——'

Ramage cut him short. 'If you can spare a moment of your fast-vanishing leisure to order a cast of the log—and repeat it every fifteen minutes—you'll avoid having me fretting.'

'Aye aye, sir.'

'I'm going below for half an hour. Keep an eye on the course steered.'

'Aye aye, sir.'

'And keep a sharp lookout.'

This time Southwick made little attempt to keep the irritation out of his voice, 'Aye aye, sir.'

Moodily Ramage walked to the companionway, not knowing Southwick had deliberately pretended irritation because he knew his young captain's nerves were bar taut and the reply would make him realize it by the time he reached the cabin.

No sooner had he sat down to write up the log than Ramage remembered he'd forgotten to bring the slate with him and angrily shouted through the skylight for Southwick to pass it. As soon as it was passed down he copied the details and handed it back to the seaman waiting overhead.

Then he went over to the chart spread out on the table, each corner held down by a weight to prevent it rolling up again. He plotted the three bearings, pencilled in a tiny cross and wrote the time beside it. From the cross he checked off the course he'd given Southwick to steer, knowing it was a waste of time since he had already checked it several times earlier, long before darkness fell, and the *Triton* had been in the precise position he had intended when he had given the order to alter course.

Irritated at his own jumpiness he flung down the pencil, went over to a cupboard and took out his case of duelling pistols. They were a gift from Sir Gilbert Elliot, the former Viceroy in Corsica, to mark the day when Ramage was given his first command, and were a splendid example of the gun-maker's art: each stock was of richly-grained walnut; the hexagonal barrels, shining blue in the dim light from the lantern, were long—too long for the rough and tumble of

280

fighting, but ensuring accuracy—and the upper flat surface was ideal for aiming quickly.

He picked up one of them, flicked up the appropriately-named hammer to expose the priming pan, blew into it to make sure there were no fine grains of priming powder still in the pan or touchhole, then pushed the hammer down again so that it covered the pan. Then, after checking that the jaws of the cock gripped the flint tightly, he cocked the gun and squeezed the trigger. The cock arched over faster than the eye could follow, the flint in striking the curved face of the hammer lifting it from the pan and making a satisfactory spark.

After repeating the procedure with the second pistol, he shook out lead shot, each the size of a schoolboy's marble, from a green baize bag, and took some cloth wads from a compartment in the case.

Selecting two shots he rolled them on the desk and then held each of them up to the light. They were well-cast and, as far as he could see, perfectly spherical. Not that it would matter much at the ranges he'd be firing.

Holding one of the pistols with the muzzle pointing upwards, he took the larger of the two flasks from the case, put the funnel-shaped end in the muzzle and pressed the catch at the side which automatically allowed the correct amount of powder to drop into the barrel.

It took only a few moments to ram home both shot and wad, pour priming powder from the smaller flask into the pan and shut the hammer down again, making sure it was a tight fit and none of the priming powder could shake out.

After loading the second pistol he took his jacket and put a couple of dozen shot and wads in one pocket and the two powder flasks in another. A sudden thought struck him as he put the coat down on the settee, with the two pistols on top, and looked round for his hat.

Quickly he went up on deck and found Southwick.

'In the dark,' he said, 'we can't be sure of identifying each other. A fraction of a second might save a man's life. Get the boatswain's mate to cut up forty strips of white cloth—wide enough for each man to tie round his head. Explain the reason to them—anyone without a headband is fair game. Have someone take four over to the schooner for

Jackson's party.'

'Don't forget to wear one yourself, sir.'

'What? Oh yes, of course.'

And Ramage realized he was more jumpy than he cared to admit; but for Southwick's warning he'd have crammed his hat on his head when he went on board the schooner. If it had sailed, and if they could find it in the darkness.

★

A sudden yell from a lookout sent Ramage dashing up the companionway. Southwick pointed over the larboard side, where several small objects bobbed about, black on the dark grey of the sea.

'Dozens of 'em,' Southwick growled. 'Thought they were rocks for a moment! Can't make out what they are, even with the glass.'

Ramage called to the lookout who reported that they stretched diagonally across the brig's bow from the larboard beam.

'Back the foretops'l, Mr Southwick!'

Within moments of Southwick's bellows the foretopsail yard was being braced round and the sheets trimmed again so the wind blew on to the forward side, trying to push the brig astern in opposition to the maintopsail trying to thrust her ahead. The opposing forces, balancing each other, stopped the ship within a few yards of the line of objects.

By then Ramage was on the fo'c'sle with the night-glass jammed to his eye. He snapped it shut and went aft to tell Southwick.

'Casks and sacks—the *Jorum*'s ahead of us and to windward and has dumped some of her cargo.'

'She got up here faster than I expected!' Southwick exclaimed.

'I told you these schooners were slippery. Let's get under way again!'

Southwick shouted the orders which set the men bracing the foretopsail yard round again and the sail filled with a bang. Almost at once the brig stopped pitching gently, and the splashing as her stem and counter alternately slapped down on to the waves gave way to the steady sluicing of water as she gathered speed.

282

But more than ten minutes passed before Ramage was certain he had identified the mountain peaks that let them identify the few bonfires on shore as the village of Gouyave, while it took a timed run of fifteen minutes to establish their exact position and discover they were half a mile inshore of the rendezvous. By that time Ramage had the ship cleared for action and the carronades run out, using only the depleted crew.

Southwick's cursing at their slowness was interrupted by a hail from the lookout on the starboard bow:

'Sail ho! A point on the larboard bow, sir; about a couple of cables distant.'

'Very well,' Southwick acknowledged, jumping up on to a carronade with an alacrity which belied his age and bulk.

'No sail set, sir: seems to be just lying there!' the man added.

Again Southwick acknowledged and Ramage said: 'Remember to check why the larboard lookout didn't sight it,' and warned, 'Make sure there's nothing else around.'

The chances of a trap were slight. But it wasn't until all the lookouts spaced round the ship reported nothing else in sight that Ramage ordered Southwick to heave-to a cable's distance to windward of the schooner.

For the past hour the two boarding parties had been kept below, the ship being sailed and cleared for action with the reduced crew. Now Ramage told Appleby to assemble the first party aft. While that was being done, he went down to his cabin, put on his coat, stuffed the two pistols into the top of his breeches, slung a cutlass belt over his shoulder and jammed his hat on his head.

As he took a last look round the cabin he saw a strip of white cloth lying on his desk. Cursing his memory he threw his hat on to the settee and tied the strip round his head. Hell, his forehead felt sore; God knows how many times he had rubbed the scar this evening, like a baby sucking its thumb.

Up on deck he found the men grouped aft by the taffrail with Appleby bending over the binnacle light reading out their names from a sheet of paper. Finally, the last of the men answered and Appleby reported:

'All sixteen men present, sir.'

Sixteen? Ramage was puzzled for a moment, then realized the other four were already in the schooner.

And where the devil was the schooner now? He turned and saw her black shape close by to leeward. Even as he looked Southwick hailed it through the speaking trumpet.

'What ship?'

'The *Jorum* schooner, Mr Southwick, sir, lying to and awaiting orders.'

Ramage almost sighed with relief: Jackson's voice and answering in the pre-arranged manner.

'Ready for the boarding party?'

'Aye aye, sir.'

'How many?'

'No more'n twenty, sir, and even then it'll be a tight fit.'

Southwick swore and from below Ramage heard yells of disappointment from the other twenty men standing by.

'All right, Jackson, I'm sending 'em over now.'

Ramage noted Southwick's confident 'I'. They'd already agreed that the Master took command from the moment the *Triton* hove-to near the schooner.

The jolly boat which had been towing astern was hauled alongside and ten of the boarding party were ferried over to the schooner. When it returned for the rest Ramage moved over to the ladder and, as soon as the last of the men disappeared over the side, reached out to shake Southwick's hand.

'Best o' luck sir: Hope to see you back on board very soon!'

'Thanks, Southwick. If not, go round St Lucia and just steer east—you can't miss Barbados; but even if you do, you'll soon sight Africa!'

Southwick gave a full-bellied laugh and the men in the boat joined in.

A few minutes later Ramage was scrambling up the lee side of the schooner, followed by the boarders, to be greeted by her Captain, a young white man who introduced himself as James Gorton.

'All of Mr Rondin's instructions have been carried out, sir,' he reported. 'But I daren't jettison any more cargo to make extra room or we'll be floating so light the privateers'd get suspicious.'

'But we can get twenty men in the hold?'

'Yes, sir. Not much room and it stinks o' molasses and is running alive with cockroaches. No rats though—well, not many.'

Ramage saw that the canvas hatch cover had been rolled back and several of the wooden beams covering the hatch had been lifted off. From the hold there was the faint glow of a lantern.

'Right,' Ramage said crisply. 'Let's get my men below out of the way. Come on, boarders—down you go. Careful with those grenades and false-fires!'

The men moved silently across the narrow deck from the bulwark.

'Jackson?'

'Here, sir!'

Ramage moved forward, followed by the American, to be out of earshot of the schooner's crew, who were gathered around Gorton at the hatch.

'Did everything go off all right?'

'Perfectly, sir. Found Fetch's hut without any tacking back and forth. He was getting drunk with rum.'

'Tie him up?'

'No, sir.'

'What then?'

'There was a fight of it. We left him for dead.'

But Ramage knew Jackson too well: the American's voice was too glib, too well rehearsed. It was the true story, but not the whole one.

'You mean Maxton killed him.'

'Well, that's about the size of it, sir. Can't say I blame him. Never came across such an evil man in my life.'

Ramage sensed that Jackson, who had fought and killed many times, was shuddering at the memory of it.

'What happened?'

'Well, we got to his hut. All round were these horrible dolls with evil faces. Some were made of cloth wrapped round bones—human bones, I swear, shins, thighs and arms. And he had beads and things laid out in circles on the ground, and squares and diamonds. Well, we crept up and then dashed into the hut.'

'How could you see?'

'Bonfire burning—the hut's just a three-sided shelter

285

with a thatched roof. He was just crouching there on his haunches, drinking from a gourd, and when he saw us he asked what we were doing. Maxton—I didn't get time to speak—said he'd come to cut him. That's the word they use for attacking anyone with a knife——'

'I know, I know,' Ramage interrupted impatiently.

'Well, this fellow started cussing him and saying he'd strike him dead and set the loogaroos, or some such thing, on to his family. Maxton said something I didn't understand—defying him, I reckoned—and this fellow said he'd already set the loogaroos on scores of families; and as for white men—he said this to me—well, when Fedding was ruling the island——'

'Fédon,' Ramage corrected. 'The Frenchman who led the rebellion a couple of years ago.'

'Well, when Fédon was alive he'd eaten a white man a day—Fetch, that is—and he knew a wicked white man had sent us now. Maxton asked him what if a white man had, and Fetch picked up a piece of wood—a Y-shaped stick with hair and beads tied to it, and pointed it at me (he'd guessed I was the leader) and said he was going to put the loogaroos on me and my master that very minute. Well, that did it for Maxton: it was so fast I couldn't see exactly what happened, except that suddenly Fetch was falling over backwards and Maxton's knife was in his throat.'

'What about the tom-tom?'

'Ah, that went off a treat,' Jackson said proudly, glad to change the subject. 'We found Fetch's and used that in the end. I thumped away, and three or four minutes after I'd finished we heard another one over to the north begin to beat out the same tune. That was the seven-thirty signal, sir.'

'Good,' Ramage said. 'How was Maxton after that?'

'Funny you should ask that, sir. Very quiet the whole time after the Fetch business. No laughing or joking; hardly answered questions or anything. But he didn't miss anything. Heard the tom-tom before any of us. He was—well, sort of all taut, like a backstay in a gale of wind.'

'Very well. Now you'd better get below with the rest of them. You did a very good job, the four of you.'

Jackson grunted. 'Tell you the truth sir, I don't know why someone didn't do in that fellow Fetch a long time ago.'

Ramage found Gorton aft, standing by the schooner's heavy tiller.

'I think we might get under way, if you're ready,' Ramage said politely, careful to indicate he knew he was a passenger—for the time being anyway.

'Aye aye, sir,' Gorton answered smartly, and shouted for hands to man the halyards.

The crispness of the 'Aye aye, sir!' told Ramage that, while Gorton might not be a deserter from the King's service, he'd certainly spent some of his life in the King's ships. Well, deserter or not, it probably meant the man wouldn't get in a panic at the smell of burnt powder . . .

The men grunted in unison as they swigged on the halyards, the blocks squeaking as the ropes rendered through them, and the big heavy gaff of the mainsail slowly climbed up the mast, followed a minute or two later by a headsail, and then the big foresail.

As the *Jorum* gathered way Gorton leaned hard against the tiller, obviously waiting for his men—they couldn't number more than a dozen—to trim the sheets before anyone relieved him. Ramage moved over and helped push.

'Bit short-handed, sir,' Gorton apologized, 'but it's hard to get anyone to sign on these days, the way things are. All these scallywags are getting four times the normal wage. All except me, that is.'

Ramage grunted sympathetically. 'Reliable men, though?'

'Oh yes—they aren't the *Jorum*'s regular crew: Mr Rondin told me to pick the best I could find. And I did: my own neck depends on 'em, as well as yours!'

Two men came out of the darkness and Gorton told them to take the helm, giving them a course to steer.

'P'raps you'd like to step down into my cuddy, sir? T'aint no bigger'n a dog kennel, but we can talk there.'

Ramage looked back at the *Triton*, now receding on the schooner's larboard quarter. He hoped Southwick didn't try to shadow too closely and scare off the privateers; on the other hand he didn't want him to let the brig off so far to leeward it'd take hours to get up to windward again when he saw the rockets.

'Yes,' Ramage said absently, 'we'd better just run over the plan.'

CHAPTER TWENTY

Standing on deck and looking down into the hold, Ramage marvelled at the adaptability of seamen. The twenty Tritons were crammed into a space not much bigger than that needed by a bosun's mate to swing a cat-o'-nine-tails, and all of them were asleep. Some were lying in the valley formed by two casks of molasses stowed side by side; others were curled up on sacks; at least three, bothered by the fetid heat, were standing up, propped only by the protruding ends of sacks, just below the gap where two of the hatch boards had been pulled to one side to let in fresh air and light.

The sun was hot: beating down on the deck overhead, it must be making the underside of the thick planking like the inside of an oven. Cockroaches as long as a man's little finger roamed across casks, sacks and sleeping men with an easy nonchalance; the tiny fruit flies swarmed thickly like puffs of black smoke. The stench seemed less strong now, presumably because his nostrils had become used to it—numbed, more likely.

For the hundredth time Ramage cursed the two small open boats which stayed a few hundred yards up to windward of the schooner. At daybreak they had borne down on the schooner and then luffed up, keeping station on her as if she was a flagship and they the two frigates. Each boat carried four men, all of them sitting out along the windward side acting as human ballast.

Although the boats' sails were made of flour bags—using Gorton's old and battered telescope Ramage was able to read the miller's names painted on them—they skimmed across the sea like flying fish, rising up the crests, swooping down into the troughs, and occasionally one of the men would bend down and bail vigorously for a few minutes, using half a calabash husk.

Because of the boats Ramage dare not let the boarding party on deck. He allowed two men to come up at a time after warning Gorton to get two of his own men out of sight: one of the things that interested the boats was undoubtedly how many there were in the *Jorum*'s crew.

In a stiff breeze lasting through the night the *Jorum* had swiftly dropped Grenada astern and long before noon Bequia was abeam and, an hour later, the southern end of St Vincent. Ramage was sleeping in Gorton's cuddy when the schooner captain woke him to report two boats from Bequia had now joined while the first pair were bearing up, sailing hard on the wind and apparently bound for the southern end of St Vincent.

'Reckon they're going to report there?' Gorton asked.

Ramage nodded sleepily. 'I wonder where the new chaps will be relieved . . . Is the *Triton* in sight?'

'Made out her royals once or twice over to the south-west, but they wouldn't have seen her from the boats. Even if they had, she's so far down to leeward no one'd think she was bound our way.'

'Thanks, Gorton: pass the word if anything else turns up.' With that Ramage turned over and fell asleep.

He woke again and realized, with a guilty start, it was late afternoon. Then, remembering he'd had no sleep the previous night and was unlikely to get any tonight, he stretched out in the narrow bunk and dozed off again. The sun was setting when he woke again, hungry and thirsty.

Hurriedly he pulled on his coat and went on deck to find Gorton sitting on the hatch talking to Jackson. A couple of the Jorums were squatting out of sight behind the bulwarks, while two Tritons paced up and down. The two little boats were still out on the starboard bow.

Ramage was about to excuse himself but decided against it just as Gorton said:

'Glad you had a good sleep, sir: expect you'll need all your energy for tonight!'

'Yes. I see our friends are still with us.'

'Aye, I've been tempted to have a bit o' target practice with 'em—you see my massive guns.'

He gestured to the small brass guns mounted in swivels

which fitted on top of the bulwarks and fired one-pound shot.

Ramage thought for a moment. Would the fact the *Jorum* hadn't fired at them make the men in the boat suspicious?

'Do they often keep up with you like this?'

'Sometimes, sir. Normally just one boat, and never for more than a couple of hours. They're usually fishing and try to sell us anything they catch. We often buy, too—don't get much luck towing a line ourselves.'

'So they wouldn't be expecting you to fire at 'em to keep away?'

'Why of course not! Oh, I see what you mean. No sir, but these two'll know we are wondering what the devil they're doing it for.'

Ramage rubbed his chin and the rasping irritated him.

'If you'd like to borrow my razor,' Gorton said, 'there's a basin and a jug of water in the cuddy.'

There was just enough light left for Ramage to shave; by the time he had finished washing it was almost dark, but even as he reached for his coat Gorton called:

'The boats are bearing up!'

In a few moments Ramage was standing with him at the bulwark. Now just grey smudges with the sails foreshortened, the boats were heading towards the twin peaks of the Pitons at the south-western end of St Lucia. From this distance both mountains looked like large bungs from casks upended on the horizon.

It was half past six, and Ramage motioned to Gorton to pass the telescope. Slowly he swept the horizon from the tip of St Vincent to the south and then right across the wide channel northward to the Pitons. Apart from the departing boats there was nothing in sight and he searched along the coast of St Lucia over on the starboard bow. There was no sign of other boats coming out to relieve the pair which were fast disappearing, their shapes merging into the land.

That could only mean they knew all they needed to know. And, more significant, that nothing the schooner did now could affect the privateersmen's plans. And in turn that meant they would attack within a few hours; probably soon after nightfall. The trap was set; the *Jorum* was in it; the only question was when it would be sprung by the freebooters.

Swinging the telescope round to the south-west, Ramage

searched for and then finally sighted the *Triton*'s royals; two narrow strips of sail—the rest of the ship was below the curvature of the Earth—lit by the last rays of the sun which was already well below the horizon. Southwick was being sensible. Instead of keeping abeam of the schooner he was staying well back on her larboard quarter and, Ramage guessed, as night fell he'd haul his wind and beat up towards the coast, unseen in the darkness, and with a bit of luck he would be able to lay the island's capital and main port of Castries on one tack, whereas if he was dead to leeward he would have to make several tacks.

The *Jorum* was now steering north parallel with the coast and making better than six knots. If the privateers came from the north they too could make six, since the wind was east, so they would be approaching each other at twelve knots.

The puzzling thing was that there were no suitable bays anywhere along the west side of St Lucia where the free-booters could be hiding—unless they'd moved into one from somewhere else as soon as they had the signal. Sweeping the coast with the telescope he could not make out anything resembling a sail. He could still see more than twelve miles —so they were unlikely to meet anything for an hour.

He suddenly noticed a smell of cooking, and Gorton said:

'Thought your men'd like a good meal a'fore tonight's work: nothing like a warm lining for a fighting man's stomach!'

'They'll appreciate it,' Ramage said vaguely, still thinking of distances, speeds, the chances of wind changes.

'They wouldn't let me serve 'em lunch—said they had grub with them.'

Then Ramage remembered there was no reason why the men should still remain below. After mentioning it to Gorton out of politeness, he called the Tritons up on deck.

*

Breathing steam straight from a kettle while squatting in a large oven must be something like this, Ramage thought miserably. The last of the heavy planks covering the hatch had thudded into position an hour ago and the canvas cover stretched over them, the battens holding it down kept in position by wedges driven home with a mallet.

One of the seamen belched contentedly, announcing: 'Got a fine supper out o' this, anyway.'

'Aye,' another man agreed. 'Dunno what it all was, but that spinach stuff was good.'

'Not spinach—that's callalou,' Maxton corrected.

'Don't spoil it wi' a name like that!'

The first man belched again. 'Bananas good, too.'

Maxton grunted. 'Not the best. Tasted more like bluggers.'

'Like *what*?'

'Bluggers.'

'Thought you said summat else. What's "bluggers"?'

'You'd think they were bananas,' Maxton said, enjoying his knowledge. 'For eatin' raw we have figs—you call them bananas. Then plantains—bigger'n bananas, and we cook 'em. No good for eatin' raw. Then there's bluggers. Cook them, too.'

Ramage, realizing Maxton's 'bluggers' were in fact 'bluggoes,' interrupted: 'Belay that, now; I want to check off everything. Everyone's wearing a strip of cloth round his head?'

There was a chorus of agreement.

'Very well then; don't forget, anyone without a white band is an enemy, except for the Jorums, but they'll be shut up out of the way, I expect. Now, those men with musketoons should have them loaded and on half-cock. Report as I call your names.'

Starting with Jackson he called out the six names.

He then named the men who had been issued with grenades and each replied that his grenades were ready.

'Now, all pistols loaded and at half-cock. Report any not loaded.'

There were no replies.

'And rockets and false-fires?'

'Here, sir,' two voices answered.

'Very well. Once I give the word, not a sound. And when I shout "Get 'em!" you know what that means?'

There was a deafening 'Aye aye, sir!'

'And the challenge . . . ?'

'"Triton!"' the men roared.

'And the reply?'

'"Jacko!"'

'*Mister* Jacko,' Jackson said in mock protest, and again the men laughed, knowing Ramage had deliberately chosen the American's nickname, although not to honour the American, but because, like the word 'Triton', it was distinctive; easily shouted and easily distinguished.

'Very well then,' Ramage said. 'And don't forget, from the time we're boarded and until they start taking the hatch covers off and I give an order, not a word. Anyone wanting to cough or sneeze must shove his head under a sack.'

That had been a good idea of Gorton's, and throwing several hundredweight of cocoa beans over the side to provide the empty sacks gave the men a little more room, too.

Ramage estimated it was now eight o'clock, so it would have been dark on deck for more than an hour. Twisting round his legs to make himself more comfortable as he sat across two casks, he grunted as the butt of a pistol dug in just below his ribs.

He'd thought that once all the hatch covers had been put back on, the waiting would have been worse than during the day; but the men were so cheerful his fears had almost vanished. To them the prospect of a good fight was as good as a night on shore in Plymouth with five gold guineas in their pockets. Better, as he had heard one of the men comment, since they wouldn't have thick heads in the morning. Not thick heads, he had reflected gloomily; but several of them might be dead or badly wounded.

*

Someone was shaking him and he woke with a start to find Jackson whispering hoarsely, 'Did you hear the knocks, sir?'

Blearily Ramage said: 'No—how many?'

'Two double knocks.'

'Vessel in sight!' Ramage was thankful Jackson had been with him when he had arranged the code by which Gorton would signal, banging the hatch coaming with a belaying pin.

Suddenly there were four evenly spaced knocks.

A single knock after sighting meant the vessel was ahead, two was to larboard, three to starboard, four astern ...

So the vessel was coming up astern.

'Don't shout, but make sure everyone's awake. Each man shake the one nearest him!'

Ramage felt the familiar symptoms of fear fighting with excitement.

Shouting on deck—too loud for orders. A hail to another ship?

A full minute passed and then suddenly a sharp double knock: another vessel! Two even knocks—to larboard!

Keep the men informed, Ramage remembered.

'Listen,' he whispered loudly. 'Two vessels in sight—one astern, one to larboard.'

More shouting, then a sudden brief tattoo from two belaying pins: the agreed signal for 'Vessel or vessels are definitely enemy.'

'Both privateers,' Ramage whispered and heard a few contented growls from the men.

Shouts on deck, the noise of sheets being hauled, a metallic rumble as the tiller was put over, the heavy rudder's pintles grinding on the gudgeons.

The shouting on the *Jorum*'s deck sounded desperate now: Ramage had warned Gorton that his men should simulate panic, and they were making a good job of it.

Suddenly the whole ship shuddered from an enormous rasping crash along the larboard side: one of the privateers had run aboard, and shouts and the thudding of feet just above their heads told the Tritons that the freebooters were swarming over the *Jorum*'s bulwarks.

'Lubberly crowd,' Jackson whispered.

Ramage said nothing; his imagination already working hard. In the darkness the privateer had obviously misjudged the distance and in coming alongside her prize had hit harder than intended. Ramage thought of a plank split—maybe even the butt ends of a plank or two sprung at the waterline. Water beginning to pour in and the hold slowly filling, perhaps unnoticed on deck until the schooner became sluggish in the water. The privateersmen, probably unused to the way she handled, would attribute it at first to the fact she was heavily laden with cargo . . . And in the hold, battened down, the Tritons.

Even if Gorton noticed and, to save them, told the privateersmen the Tritons were trapped below, the privateersmen would be foolish to release twenty fully-armed men: no, they would just quit the schooner and leave them to drown!

Ramage realized most of the shouting on deck had stopped: what there was seemed to be between the privateer alongside and her consort nearby.

The sluicing of water past the *Jorum*'s hull had stopped, leaving an eerie quietness round them, and she began rolling heavily, while above them the mainsail, foresail and head-sails slatted viciously, shaking the masts.

Obviously the capture was complete. For the freebooters the hunt was over; all that remained now was to carry the carcass home. He heard someone giving orders—the man seemed to be standing just above him—in a mixture of French, English and patois.

Hard to be sure of the speaker's nationality.

The squeaking and rumbling of the sheets rendering through blocks; the metallic rasping of the rudder fittings as the tiller was put over; the change in the *Jorum*'s motion, and then once again the noise of water swirling past: the privateersmen had the schooner under way.

A few minutes later, conscious his clothes were soaking with perspiration caused as much by excitement as by heat, Ramage reckoned the *Jorum* was now sailing on much the same course as she was before the capture. The privateers' base was still to the northward.

So the two ships most probably sailed south to intercept the *Jorum*, keeping a certain distance apart to widen their field of view, spotted her before they were themselves sighted, and then turned on to her course. Neat—the one astern stopped her escaping to the south, forcing her to keep going northward if she tried to make a bolt for it; the one to larboard trapping her against the land, preventing her escaping to the open sea to the westward.

He whispered to Jackson as he pulled out his watch, and as the American snapped a flint he saw in the light of the spark it was half past eight. He tried to concentrate because he could rarely solve a mathematical problem without pencil and paper.

Now, when the last two small boats left, they would reach the land near the Pitons at about seven. They might pass a signal, but more likely they were supposed to make a signal only if the schooner did anything unusual. So, by half past six the men in the small boats were certain the *Jorum* was going to continue her course. At that time, as they disappeared from sight in the gathering gloom, Ramage had been able to see about a dozen miles up the coast and the *Jorum* was making six knots.

Now for the hard part, and he tried to shut out the noise of the sea, the noise from on deck, and the creaking of the schooner's hull as she rose and fell on the slight swell waves.

Just as darkness fell, at seven, there were no ships in sight. But the privateers had intercepted about quarter past eight, so assuming they and the *Jorum* had been converging at twelve knots—allowing for them to manoeuvre into position—they had probably sailed from a bay twelve miles to the north.

Twelve miles? But that was almost at Castries! Obviously he'd made a mistake. He started all over again, but for the second time came up with the same result. Well, his reasoning was wrong somewhere because there were only a few shallow bays before Marigot, into which he had looked carefully from the *Triton*, and then Castries itself and some rocky islets which couldn't conceal an open boat, let alone a privateer ... Oh, the devil take it; the privateers could have come from anywhere—from the south side of St Lucia, he suddenly realized; in fact the two small boats might have met them after dark off the Pitons!

A sudden clatter on the hatch cover made him sit up with a start; then he leaned back, feeling foolish. The privateersmen must have put down some muskets or cutlasses—if they had been opening the hatches he'd have heard them hammering out the wedges.

Jackson whispered. 'I hope the skipper's all right.'

'Should be; I told him to surrender the ship as soon as he could without making them suspicious.'

'He's a good man.'

'You ever served with him?'

'No,' Jackson said after a pause. 'How did you know he'd "run", sir?'

'He's got "R" written all over him.'

'No, seriously, sir?'

'Jackson, it's always obvious when a man's served in the Navy. Phrases he uses, the way things are done—there aren't many schooners out here run Navy fashion. And I doubt if Gorton is his real name.'

The American thought for a while, then whispered: 'He "ran" before the war, sir.'

'It doesn't matter much whether an "R" is put after a name in peace or war, Jackson. Court martial and four hundred lashes through the Fleet—that's if he's not hanged at the foreyardarm.'

'But you won't——'

'I'll probably inform the Admiral, yes.'

'But, sir!' Jackson's whisper was almost explosive.

'I'll probably inform the Admiral that Mr Gorton, skipper of the *Jorum* schooner, rendered exceptional service...'

'Phew, sir, for a moment I thought...'

'Stop thinking, Jackson; you'll make yourself hoarse.'

*

The *Jorum* sailed on without any sail trimming and, judging from the regular pitching and rolling, without changing course. Then, as Ramage heard shouting and, a few moments later, the noise of sheets being hauled and the squeaking of the rudder going hard over, he whispered:

'Quick, Jackson—flint!'

The sparks flashing over the watch face showed it was just an hour and a half since the schooner was boarded.

More shouts, then bare feet scuffling across the deck; soft thuds which Ramage recognized as coils of rope being dropped on the deck—halyards for sure, the coils taken off the belaying pins and then overhauled ready to run.

The schooner began to pitch more frequently as she came hard on the wind, butting into the waves which were shorter in the lee of the island. In fact——

'Listen, sir!' Jackson whispered. 'Think I can hear breakers!'

Ramage heard them at the same instant; the thud and scurry of seas hitting the foot of a cliff, breaking and swirling back, the sucking noise echoing.

And several high-pitched squeaks from beyond the ship. Shouts—both distant and from the deck above. Oars creaking! Yes, several boats were rowing near-by, and the privateersmen calling to them—not angry or hectoring yells; more like greetings and replies.

Sudden shouts from the deck and the slatting of canvas

and banging of blocks as sails were lowered. The *Jorum* lost way and began to wallow. More shouting, from forward now, and then the heavy rasping of something being dragged across the deck.

'They're passing a hawser,' Jackson whispered. 'Maybe the boats are going to tow us in.'

And they'd only do that if the schooner had to be manoeuvred into a berth or anchorage impossible for her to reach under sail, either because it was dead to windward or the channel too tortuous. Maybe both. Or perhaps high cliffs were blanketing the wind. Yes, Ramage thought, that was more likely.

High cliffs? Well, nearly all the west coast of St Lucia was high cliff, and the only bay he could think of was Marigot—the entrance to that was narrow. He recalled the view through his telescope as the *Triton* was hove-to a hundred yards off the entrance: the parallel-sided bay at the opening which narrowed suddenly with a sandspit jutting out from either side and the circular lagoon beyond. On the chart it looked, he remembered, like the stopper of a decanter. Yet although Marigot had seemed an obvious place—particularly on the chart—it had been empty . . .

The creaking of many oars in their rowlocks—the tow had started. Occasional shouts from forward, replies from aft. Someone in the bow was conning the ship, shouting directions to the men at the helm.

Claire in St George, Gianna in London—or perhaps staying with his parents in Cornwall. The Governor would get his letter in a few hours. Southwick would be conning the *Triton* up towards the coast now—Ramage pictured him standing on the fo'c'sle, night-glass to his eye, scanning the black sprawl of the coastline, hoping for the sight of a sail, his brain automatically correcting for the fact a night-glass gave an inverted image so the sea and coastline, upside down, would look like the sky with black clouds low on the horizon.

Two privateers—probably fifty men in each. And how many more at their base, into which the *Jorum*, the Trojan sea horse, was now being towed? Probably not more than twenty. More important though was how many privateers-men were on board the *Jorum* at the moment, and if Gorton and his crew had been taken off?

More shouting and slowly the *Jorum* lost way and came to a stop, now neither pitching nor rolling; she was motionless, obviously lying in some quiet bay.

Would the privateersmen start unloading the cargo immediately or wait until daybreak?

'For wot we's about to receive...' whispered one of the men.

CHAPTER TWENTY-ONE

The thud of a mallet slamming on wood just above them, a muttered oath and a second thud, followed by the sound of the wedge falling to the deck, warned the Tritons that in a minute or two they'd be fighting for their lives. Another couple of thuds farther along and another wedge fell out. As the third was knock out Ramage knew that completed the starboard side. The two on the fore side were then driven, followed by three on the larboard side and, with every one of the Tritons tensing, the first, then the second on the after side.

'They're using a lantern,' Jackson whispered.

'Must be,' Ramage said humorously, '—only one bout of cursing.'

'Means we'll have the advantage—our eyes accustomed to the darkness.'

For a moment Ramage weighed the advantages of kicking over the lantern as soon as they leapt out, then decided that the surprise and confusion outweighed it.

A rasping as the four battens round the hatch were slid out, then the heavy canvas tarpaulin was dragged off.

The tingling, as though his arms and legs had pins and needles; stomach shrinking, full of cold water; arm and leg muscles tensing but feeling weak, as if they'd let him down when the moment came for a supreme effort. Ramage's breathing was shallow and perspiration felt cold now on his forehead.

I have to lead these men, he told himself coldly: they look to me. He bent down and flipped open the strap over the sheath of his throwing knife, then methodically picked up his pistols, checked each was at half-cock, and stuck them in the waist band of his breeches. Quietly he drew his cutlass.

'Stand by, Tritons!' he whispered hoarsely, his voice

almost drowned as one of the big beams was suddenly lifted and dragged clear, exposing a long narrow slot through which he could see stars shining. The weak flame of the lantern lit the underside of furled sails and part of the rigging, so that it looked like long spiders' webs covered with hoar frost.

Another plank lifted and was dragged clear, and the sight of a man's head outlined against the sky. A second man standing astride the gap and bending down to lift an end of the next beam. And a third and a fourth man helping, lifting and hurling it clear so it fell to the deck with a crash.

Six more beams to be lifted out. Would someone pick up the lantern and peer down into the hold to see what the *Jorum* was carrying before the last was hoisted clear?

Ramage's question was answered by one of the men calling to someone several yards away. 'Tell Dupont and the rest of 'em we're nearly ready.'

Footsteps receding? Ramage was certain he heard the tread of someone walking along a wooden jetty. But where on earth could they be, with a jetty? Damnation! So concerned about the jetty, Ramage had wasted several seconds before realizing he must attack immediately, before 'Dupont and the rest of 'em' arrived, and promptly bellowed:

'Get 'em, Tritons!'

As he grabbed the edge of the coaming and swung himself up it seemed the entire hold erupted with hundreds of men screaming 'Tritons! Tritons! Tritons!'

The four men lifting off the beams ran for the bulwark yelling wildly in fear and surprise. A pistol exploded just beside Ramage and one of the men sank slowly to the deck, as if overcome with weariness. The second hesitated a moment, standing on top of the bulwark, and another pistol fired, toppling him over. By now the third and fourth man had leapt clean over the bulwark and were running along the jetty towards the shore.

Ramage turned and ran aft, surprised to hear himself screaming 'Tritons!' and instinctively striking sideways as a sword blade gleamed momentarily in the darkness. Sensing rather than seeing there was a group of four or five men standing near the tiller, he slashed at the dark shape of his attacker with the cutlass while trying to drag a pistol from his waistband with his left hand.

A surge of Tritons overwhelmed the men by the tiller and, as Ramage realized his opponent was a better than average swordsman the man suddenly flung his cutlass at Ramage's head and leapt over the side into the water.

Within a couple of minutes there was almost complete silence on the schooner's deck and the croaking of frogs and screams of frightened birds was all Ramage could hear as he hurriedly checked his men. No one had even a scratch to report. The first two privateersmen were dead beside the bulwark; two of the five standing aft were dead, the rest dying.

'Jackson! Make the prisoners say what happened to Gorton. Evans, you ready with those signal rockets? Right, fire one and make sure it doesn't foul the rigging!'

Even before Jackson had time to start, one of the Tritons was calling that Gorton and the rest of the *Jorum*'s crew were tied up in the cuddy, and a minute later, while Ramage peered around him, trying to make out where the schooner was and if the two privateers were near-by, Gorton came up, swinging his arms as if he was cold.

'You've got the ship back then, sir!' he exclaimed. 'Sorry about this slapping but the ropes numbed my arms. We're in Marigot, sir. They didn't make any secret of it. As soon as someone called Dupont came on board—he's their leader—we were going to have our throats cut!'

Ramage peered round, still trying to spot where the privateers were anchored, and Gorton said, 'There's one of them over there...' pointing to the east, where Ramage could just pick out the shape of a vessel dark against the mangroves growing to the water's edge. 'And the other's just beyond.'

'Find a——'

He spun round with an oath as a sudden hissing roar and a flash behind him seemed a prelude to the schooner blowing up; but a rocket snaking up into the sky to burst into five red stars told him Evans had carried out his orders.

'Gorton—keep an eye on those privateers: watch for boats pulling over towards us. Can you find your night-glass?'

'Aye aye, sir!'

'Jackson—take all the men with musketoons and half a dozen more and get out along that jetty: stop this fellow Dupont and his men!'

What now? Everything was happening so fast and not at all the way he had expected: instead of all twenty of the Tritons fighting a sudden, short and savage battle with all the privateersmen, it might now turn into a long-drawn-out siege, with the *Jorum* a fortress.

Could the *Triton* ever get into here? If the privateers put springs on their cables and hauled themselves round they could train their broadsides on to the *Jorum* . . .

Jackson had already assembled the men with musketoons and had them scrambling over the bulwark on to the jetty, but he was arguing with several other men who wanted to be among the other half dozen.

'Take more, Jackson!'

'Aye aye, sir!' With that Jackson and the rest of the men were scrambling over the bulwark and running along the jetty.

Gorton called: 'Boats leaving both privateers, sir.'

Ramage acknowledged. Would they try to board, or land on the shore and attack along the jetty?

But what was puzzling him was Gorton's certainty that this was Marigot Bay. It seemed completely landlocked.

'Where's the entrance?'

Gorton grunted. 'That's what's puzzling me, sir. There's the high hills to the south—they're clear enough. And to the north—that's the ridge there. Well, the entrance is between the two.'

'But it's closed off completely—why, you can see palm trees growing across.'

'I know, sir.'

Suddenly a loud popping and flashing of flame at the land-ward end of the jetty showed that Dupont and his men were attacking. The musket flashes seemed almost continuous from landward, punctuated by the occasional heavier boom of one of the Tritons' musketoons firing. Jackson's men were heavily outnumbered—and they hadn't much shelter. Even worse, they were having to stay close to the jetty so Dupont's men couldn't cut off their escape route back to the schooner.

Ramage rubbed his brow. From the other side the priva-teers' boats were approaching fast. No shooting—obviously they were hoping they wouldn't be seen; hoping that Dupont and his men attacking along the jetty would occupy the

Tritons' attention.

And in the meantime the *Jorum* was secured alongside the jetty, no longer a Trojan horse but a bullock tied up in a stall at the slaughterhouse. And the French call us *rosbifs*, Ramage thought irrelevantly.

Although the musket-fire on shore was easing, it was now interspersed with the challenge 'Triton!' showing it was almost hand-to-hand. The privateers' boats were perhaps fifty yards away. And he felt a slight breeze on the back of his neck, from the north-east he noted automatically, and then nearly jumped with the realization it was blowing towards the palm trees on the sandspit...

Should he or not? Out of the frying pan? Well, the pan was pretty hot... He yelled out a string of orders: for the grenade men to wait on the larboard side, others to stand by to cut the mooring warps, with more ready to push the *Jorum* clear of the jetty. The remainder, he shouted, were to stand by at the schooner's taffrail with pistols, ready to fire along the jetty.

Who to send to Jackson?

As if sensing the thought, Gorton said: 'What can I do, sir? I'm standing here like a spare topsail halyard.'

'Get along the jetty to Jackson. Tell him as soon as I shout "Tritons!" he's to get his men back on board. We'll try to cover them with pistols.'

'What about——'

'Get moving, Gorton!'

The man cleared the bulwark in one leap; a moment later Ramage heard him running along the jetty. Then he cursed —he'd forgotten to tell him to shout when Jackson was ready...

The privateers' boats—five of them—were closing fast, moving silently like water beetles across a village pond, silent but heading directly for the *Jorum*. Each one of these freebooters knew more about boarding an enemy in the dark than any twenty men in one of the King's ships. If only Jackson arrived back as they... No, that was asking too much.

Five boats, twenty or more men in each. A hundred men, and Dupont had—forty or fifty? He felt sick. Trojan horse! It'd been a wild idea and Wilson had known it—that was why he had wanted that report written for the Governor. An obituary. A two-page obituary for twenty Tritons.

As he stood frightened and despairing that once again he had acted without enough thought, he felt the wind chill on his cheek. The offshore breeze had begun, and a few moments later he saw the fronds of the palms moving gently as it reached them.

But better the *Forum* stranded on the beach by those palms, where they would have something of a moat all round them, than stuck here at the end of the jetty.

He filled his lungs and shouted: 'Jackson! Are you ready there?'

'Aye aye, sir!'

'Tritons!'

He was almost screaming now with excitement and relief.

'Aft there—ready with your pistols! Shoot down anyone without a white headband—but watch out for Gorton!'

Feet thundering along the jetty, pursued by musket shots. The dull flash and crack of a musketoon as the Tritons covered their retreat.

'Cast off all lines!'

Ropes splashed into the water forward, and then aft.

A quick glance round showed the privateers' boats were twenty yards off.

'Grenade men—stand by to light your fuses!'

Then he thought of Evans and shouted for him, hoping he hadn't gone with Jackson.

The Welshman was standing near-by.

'Quick—light a false-fire!'

Seamen scrambling over the bulwarks from the jetty, white bands round their brows; pistols whiplashing as the Tritons at the taffrail fired along the jetty. Sparks close by, then suddenly Evans's false-fire lit up the whole schooner in its ghostly blue light.

'Grenade men—crouch down! The boats are coming alongside. When I give the word light your fuses from the false-fire and drop the grenades into the boats!'

He was thankful the grenades had no more than five-second fuses. Two wounded men being lifted over the bulwark. Then Jackson standing in front of him, wild-eyed in the light of the false-fire.

'Dupont's got fifty men or more, sir. We lost two dead,

and two wounded.'

'Very well. Five boats approaching on the larboard side. Get your men ready but keep clear of the side until I give the word. We've cast off from the jetty.'

He looked over the larboard side: damn, he'd left it late.

'Grenade men: light and drop 'em in the boats—smartly now!'

The men crouched round the false-fire with the grenades, holding them so the fuses, sticking out like wicks, were in the flame. As soon as the fuses sparked the men ran to the side, paused a moment—Ramage realized the bright light had dazzled them—and then dropped the grenades. Almost at once there were shouts from the boats and the crack of pistols fired upwards. One of the Tritons slowly toppled backwards without a sound, a dark stain on his headband.

'Start bearing off!' Ramage yelled. 'Heave her off the jetty!'

A great flash and a deep, sullen roar on the starboard side, then another. Screams of men in terrible pain, screams of men almost witless with fear. It was raining, and pieces of wood were falling on deck. Two more explosions, then a third. Ramage realized the grenades had not only blown up the boats but the explosions were showering water and wreckage over the schooner's deck.

Then Jackson was yelling something from the rail but Ramage couldn't hear from where he was standing at the starboard side exhorting the men to shove harder at boat-hooks—some had even snatched up the hatch beams—to get the schooner away from the jetty.

More yells from the taffrail. What the devil were they shouting about? Glancing back along the jetty it wasn't hard to guess: a black mass, a giant caterpillar, was advancing slowly along it—Dupont's men, and the Tritons at the taff-rail were hurriedly re-loading their pistols.

'Jackson! Musketoon-men aft—sweep the jetty. Smartly now!'

Conscious that Gorton was working feverishly at the bul-wark, Ramage then heard Jackson's wail that there'd been no time to re-load the musketoons. Dupont's men were twenty yards away. Although the *Jorum* was slowly moving along the jetty, its angle to the wind was too small to stop her bumping back against it. But every moment she was clear she was drifting farther towards the end.

Flashes of musket-fire from Dupont's men: very wary now, firing and re-loading as they came; not realizing there wasn't a loaded pistol or musketoon in the schooner. Maybe those terrible explosions had scared them.

Again the *Jorum* was shoved away from the jetty, moving four or five yards and then beginning to drift back towards it as the Tritons hurriedly tried to push her off once more.

Dupont's men were almost level with the taffrail. Ramage turned to snatch up the false-fire but found Jackson crouched over it, a grenade in one hand. A moment later he stood up and Ramage could see the fuse spluttering.

The American ran to the taffrail, stood for a few moments —again Ramage saw he was dazzled—and then with an ear-splitting shriek of 'Tritons!' tossed a grenade into the middle of the men on the jetty.

Then he promptly dropped down below the level of the taffrail, shouting a warning to all the men near him.

A flash, deep red against the blue light of the false-fire, and simultaneously a heavy explosion which merged into the sound of splintering wood and the yells and screams of men, and echoed round the hills.

'I got the swivel ready, sir!'

Ramage, startled as he pictured the grenade's effect, jerked back to see Gorton standing a yard away, gesticulating at the small swivel gun fitted into the top of the bulwark and which he now had trained on the jetty.

'Wait a moment—may not be necessary!'

Beginning to feel a little more optimistic, Ramage peered along the jetty and saw there was still a black mass of men there. Not so many though, and none moving. Dupont had quit, leaving his dead and wounded behind. Quit to re-group, re-plan, give new orders.

'Just stand by that swivel, Gorton, and get the others loaded! Now you men, put your backs into it and get us clear!'

And once again the *Jorum*, pushed bodily away from the jetty, drifted a few yards and then bumped again as the wind pressed against her hull, masts and rigging.

In the last of the light from the dying false-fire Ramage

saw the end of the jetty was now abreast her foremast.

'Come on lads, one good heave and we're clear!'

The wind backed a few degrees in a sudden gust, just enough to blow the schooner clear, then it dropped and veered again. Ramage watched the *Jorum*'s stern clear the end of the jetty and almost sighed in relief.

Well, adrift in the bay they were safe from Dupont's crowd for the moment. But now what? No point in trying to sail the schooner out—even if he could see where the devil the entrance was—because the privateers could sneak out and vanish if the *Triton* didn't arrive in time to blockade them in. So he had to stay and try to destroy them. A forlorn hope.

Now what? Time and again the question repeated itself, and the schooner slowly drifted towards the palm trees, which he realized were growing on a narrow sandspit. He was rubbing his brow as if some magic would make his brain work, and perhaps it did. Since he couldn't sail the schooner out, there was no choice: he had to stay in the bay, and if he stayed he had to fight . . .

He turned away from the bulwark. The first thing was to get the *Jorum* into some sort of fighting trim again—the two privateers were still there and Dupont had plenty of men on shore who'd be swarming on board the moment she ran aground on that sandspit.

'Gorton! Are your swivels loaded yet? Jackson! Every musketoon re-load, and pistols too. Aft there! Leave your pistols with Jackson and man the jib and foresail halyards!'

Again he looked round. The schooner was barely moving —but he suddenly realized she was drifting into the arcs of fire of the privateers' broadside guns and any minute would be in effective range of their swivels.

He knew panic wasn't far away and was surprised enough to try to guess why. He was even more surprised when he realized the answer. The high hills—mountains, in fact, covered with a thin layer of soil on which scrub bushes had a hard fight to survive—formed a complete amphitheatre with the water as the arena. The effect was heightened because he couldn't see the entrance. He felt trapped, much as a Christian must have felt trapped in a Roman stadium when thrown to the lions . . .

He shook his head to get rid of the thought and bellowed

for the jib and foresail to be hoisted, moving aft to take the tiller himself. As the halyards creaked and the sails crept up the mast, showing themselves only as they hid the stars, the gentle gurgling of water under the stem increased and he leaned against the tiller, steering for the middle of the row of palms along the sandspit.

The *Jorum* slowly swung to starboard: too slowly—she needed the mainsail, and he shouted for it to be hoisted. It was barely halfway up the mast when he felt the wind's effect, pushing round the schooner's stern and helping the rudder which, because of the ship's slow speed, could hardly get a bite on the water.

Flashes over the larboard quarter as the privateers opened fire with their swivels; the thumping of metal on wood—on the hull and spars of the *Jorum*. Five swivels a side in each privateer; twenty musket balls in each gun. Two hundred balls had been fired at the schooner; none had hit a man— there hadn't been a shout—nor were the masts or sails damaged, since everything was still up and drawing.

A minute to re-load. He leaned harder against the tiller. All very interesting. Plenty of steerage way, but where to steer?

The palms stretched in a wide barrier ahead, a thick clump to starboard and another clump to leeward, and dead ahead they were evenly spaced. And—yes! Beyond them he could just see the twinkling of stars reflecting on the water, so that was probably the narrowest part of the sandspit blocking the way out.

Yet he still couldn't see how the devil the privateers got into the lagoon in the first place . . .

Run her bow straight up on the sand? Or luff up and furl all the canvas, letting the *Jorum* drift broadside on to the sandspit? That way the swivels on one side could cover the sandspit and those on the other the privateers. But that way also meant Dupont and his cut-throats could board along the whole length of her side!

That decided him—he'd run her stem up on to the sand so Dupont's men could board only over the bow, where they would be crowded together and a good target for the swivels and musketoons.

'Tritons!' he yelled. 'Hear this: I'm going to beach the

ship bows on. Stand by for the shock and come aft—both masts might go by the board. As soon as we hit—not a moment before—let the halyards run. If we still have any masts standing!'

Now he had made up his mind and there was plenty to do he felt the panic slipping away as quietly as it came. Jackson was helping him with the tiller—Ramage hadn't noticed him moving in the darkness—and the American said:

'How the hell did they get us in here, sir?'

'I wish I knew! No sign of a channel. The chart shows a sandspit either side with a channel between.'

'Gorton's certain it's Marigot Bay.'

'So am I; but it doesn't square up with the chart.'

'Charts could be wrong, sir.'

'I know that, blast you!' Ramage snapped. 'But not *that* wrong. Anyway, we've looked into the place with a telescope twice from seaward.'

'Sorry sir.'

Clearly he wasn't; nor did Ramage's short temper at times like this upset him.

They were approaching the palms fast now.

'It's a narrow spit, by God!' Jackson exclaimed. 'Why, it isn't four yards wide!'

Through the palms Ramage could now see the star-speckled water of the outer bay extending for several hundred yards, with mountains on both sides. And then he saw the mountains almost meeting to form the slot in the cliffs that was the entrance from seaward. It was dead ahead, and Jackson saw it a moment later, just as Gorton ran back to report it.

But there was no way to it: the palm trees cut it off!

With a growing sense of desperation, knowing the spit was barely forty yards away, Ramage forced himself to look slowly from side to side, eyes straining in the darkness for a glimpse of a channel. But there was nothing; just mountains to starboard sloping down to the spit which stretched across to join the mountains on the other side. He shrugged his shoulders. Twenty yards, fifteen, ten . . .

'Stand by!' he shouted. 'Brace yourselves!'

The initial shock shouldn't be too great: the *Jorum*'s fore-foot would ride up the sloping sand until it could force its way no farther.

Five yards ... any second now: her bowsprit was almost between two palm trees. And—but it *was* between two palm trees and still going on: the bow wasn't lifting as she rode up on the sand, nor was she slowing.

Both Jackson and Gorton swore in disbelief.

A violent crash shook the *Jorum*, timber wrenching against timber, but she kept going: one palm tree toppled to starboard, another to port. Somewhere ropes were parting, slashing into the water on either side like great whips.

'Take the helm, Jackson!'

Ramage leapt to look over the side as the *Jorum* swept on in the darkness, more palms toppling—one hooked in the bowsprit was being carried along—until she was sailing through the middle of the spit, with the sound of timber scraping along her hull.

And in the water, swirling, turning, lit by patches of pale green phosphorescence, Ramage could see baulks of timber, lighter planks, and several palm trees floating.

The cunning devils! No wonder no one had ever seen in —or out—of the lagoon!

But now what? As he jumped back to the tiller he saw the seaward entrance clearly, dead ahead and about 750 yards away. To larboard a narrow sandy beach ran round the edge of the bay; to starboard more sand at the foot of the hills but the pale green of phosphorescence showing where the sea lapped round isolated rocks.

Do something, you damned fool, he told himself; otherwise you'll be out to sea again! Astern there was a clear gap in the spit where the *Jorum* had burst through.

'Hard over!' he hissed at Jackson. 'We'll beach her on the larboard side there, abreast those two rocks!'

'Aye aye, sir,' Jackson said cheerfully. 'That'll leave Dupont's crowd on the other shore!'

'Stand by!' Ramage shouted, 'we're going to beach. This time we'll do it properly!'

Several of the men cheered and others laughed; then as a few of them began chanting 'Tritons! Stand by the Tritons!' the rest took it up until every man in the *Jorum*, Ramage included, was shouting it at the top of his voice.

Even as he bellowed Ramage felt an insane urge to giggle:

how many ships had ever been run aground deliberately with their crews yelling what was almost a battle cry?

Then she hit: her bow rose slightly, canting up the bowsprit as though she was meeting a sea, and she stopped Timber creaked, then there was a crunch as the foremast slowly leaned forward, ropes twanging as they parted under the strain, the foresail flapping as it went with the mast. For the last part of its fall the mast seemed to speed up; then it crashed down on the starboard bow, splintering the bulwarks.

The sudden silence was broken first by the squawking of birds disturbed by the schooner's unexpected arrival: then the frogs, frightened into a momentary silence, resumed their usual chattering.

Ramage called: 'Anyone hurt?' but there was no reply.

'Jackson—take half a dozen men and search through the wreckage of the foremast in case anyone's trapped.'

As the American ran forward Ramage turned to Gorton:

'Man the swivels: larboard side cover the beach, starboard side the rest of the bay.'

'But what happened, sir?' The man seemed dazed.

'What d'you mean?'

'The spit—we just . . .'

'Both spits are still there—look, there's the one on the north side with the clump of palms, and there's the southern one, with the other clump. The channel's between the two—where we came through.'

'But—so help me, sir,' Gorton burst out, 'there were palm trees right across there. You saw them!'

Ramage laughed, realizing Gorton hadn't understood the privateersmen's trick.

'Yes, plenty of palm trees. Only they were growing in a great raft. Haul the raft to one side, two privateers and their prize go in through the gap; haul the raft back and close it again, and there's a complete row of palm trees hiding the inner bay. If you're looking through the entrance with a telescope from seaward you'd simply think your bearing made it appear the tips of the spits overlapped slightly; you'd never dream the "overlap" was a raft of palms hiding a jetty and a couple of privateers!'

Gorton swore softly.

With the *Jorum* hard aground and no chance of floating off on a rising tide—the rise and fall here was only a few inches—Ramage gave the order to furl the mainsail, and then posted lookouts.

Then he sat down on the tiller, thankful for a few minutes in which to collect his thoughts but realizing that being aground on the southern shore of the outer bay was not really much different from being secured alongside the jetty on the northern shore of the lagoon, except that Dupont and his men now had a couple of miles' walk to get at them, unless they had more boats.

In a few minutes, he thought to himself, he'd send some men on shore to climb up the hills at the entrance to see if the *Triton* was in sight. It was time to light a bonfire and fire another rocket to help Southwick before Dupont arrived or the privateers tried to make a bolt for it,

CHAPTER TWENTY-TWO

With his lungs feeling they were about to burst and the muscles in his shins aching so much he was almost crying with pain, Jackson hauled himself up to the rock on top of the cliffs forming the southern entrance to Marigot and looked seaward. For many seconds the darkness was just a red haze, the air whistling in his throat as he struggled for breath and perspiration running into his eyes despite the white cloth round his head.

Gradually, as he regained his breath and his head stopped throbbing, the horizon took on a definite outline. And to the south-west, a small dark shadow in the distance, he saw the brig.

He was too weary to be impatient with Mr Ramage: he knew Mr Southwick would be there. The swearing and grumbling behind him grew louder, then the crackling of twigs as men barged their way through the low bushes. A moment later Gorton, followed by several Tritons, joined him.

'Ah—just nicely placed to catch the offshore wind, Jacko!' he commented. 'He'll be up here in an hour. Wonder if he saw our rocket?'

'Doubt it,' Jackson said. 'Is Evans here?'

'Aye and m'rockets.'

'The rest of you men—start collecting stuff for bonfires,' Gorton said. 'One here, one there and a third just beyond.'

Gorton pointed down to the entrance to Marigot and said to Jackson. 'Not very wide . . .'

'No—I'm not surprised they towed us in.'

From up here Jackson could just make out the gap where the *Jorum* smashed through the raft, showing the channel between the sandspits leading into the lagoon. And almost directly below where he stood was the dark shape of the

Jorum, like a stranded whale thrown up on a beach.

The two privateers, which had been anchored at the inner side of the lagoon, were indistinguishable against the background of mangrove swamps, showing they were very close in because the water of the bay was smooth and shining in the darkness.

'What d'you reckon Mr Ramage plans to do, Jacko?' Gorton asked.

'Don't reckon he has a plan. Can't have, if you think about it. We can't start anything; just wait to see what the privateers do and hope the *Triton* gets here in time. We've done our share—it's up to her now.'

'How so?'

'Well, we've found the privateers' base and they're still in it. Until the *Triton* gets here we've got to stop 'em getting out if they try to bolt, because if they get to sea we'd never catch them. But that's all, as far as I can see.'

'Is that why he beached the *Jorum* just down there?'

'Yes, though if they really try to sail we probably can't stop them with your swivels. Knowing Mr Ramage, my guess is he reckons the privateers won't try to because they think we *can* stop 'em!'

'He's a cool one,' Gorton said. 'I was still trying to puzzle out why we went through the spit like that when he beached her.'

Gorton's admiration was genuine and frankly spoken, and Jackson said, 'He's a cool one all right. You get used to it, though! You ought to have been with us when we rammed a Spanish sail of the line in our last ship—a cutter not much bigger'n your schooner!'

'What?'

'Tell you later—we'd better start getting back to the *Jorum*. Old Dupont could be paying us a visit soon!'

Gorton nodded as he looked round and saw the men had built up three piles of brushwood and were having to scramble down the side of the hill to cut more. And the *Triton* would have no difficulty in laying the entrance on this tack.

'Evans—loose off one of your rockets.'

He saw the glow of a slow-match as Evans blew on it; then the rocket spurted flame for a moment before hissing up into the sky, to burst high over their heads.

He looked over at the *Triton*, and a couple of minutes later a white rocket rose lazily from the brig and burst into several white stars. He knew Southwick would already have taken a bearing of Evans's rocket and even now was probably bending over the chart, working out whence it had been launched.

Gorton gave the men their instructions. 'Light one bonfire in fifteen minutes' time. Watch for any rockets from the *Triton*—they might send one up just to make sure it's our bonfire and not one lit by the privateersmen. If you see one, then Evans is to fire one. Is that clear?'

'Aye aye.'

'The bonfire may last ten minutes. Now use your common sense how soon you light the second and third, but the third one *must* be burning when the *Triton*'s very close. Mr Ramage may send a boat to meet her, so make sure a man comes down to tell him when she's a mile off.'

'What if we spot anything back there—where the privateers are, or Dupont's men?' Evans asked.

'Good point. Three pistol shots for privateers moving, two for Dupont's men. And send a man down with a message as well—fast!'

*

Ramage suddenly realized he'd made a bad mistake when Evans's rocket soared up and later he glanced up at the hill to see the glow of the first bonfire, a bright beacon signalling his stupidity.

He sat down on the hatch coaming, cursing softly. Up to the moment the rocket was fired from the top of the hill all the privateersmen knew was that their prize schooner was a trap. There was nothing to make them suspect one of His Majesty's brigs of war was in the offing.

Most likely they would try to destroy the *Jorum* by boarding from the beach—probably waiting until daylight—and then sail both privateers to some other hiding place.

It was unlikely the rocket fired from the *Jorum* when she was alongside the jetty would have alarmed them: an hour had passed without anything happening. But now the rocket from the hilltop and the bonfire was a clear warning that one of the King's ships was close enough to need a beacon . . .

And, Ramage told himself angrily, if Dupont—or whoever leads them—has any sense, he'll make a bolt for it now: he'll try to get both privateers to sea at once, before a warship arrives off the entrance to blockade him in.

Ramage jumped up and walked along the deck cursing aloud, men scattering out of his way, startled at his behaviour. Suddenly his foot caught on a rope and he pitched flat on his face.

Scrambling up and livid with anger he bellowed: 'Jackson, why the devil's this rope lying all over the deck?'

'Dunno sir, I didn't put it there.'

'Who did?'

Jackson hesitated, then said flatly, 'Dunno, sir.'

'Tell me, blast you, or I'll have you flogged!'

'Well sir, it's part of the foremast shrouds, so in a way you . . .'

It was farcical and Ramage knew it, suddenly bursting out laughing. The more he laughed the more farcical it seemed and everyone on board joined in. By the time he had managed to stop, Ramage thought of the men shouting their makeshift battle cry as the *Jorum* ran aground, and that set him off again until, hiccoughing and with tears streaming from his eyes, he staggered back to the coaming and sat down again.

Gradually the laughing died down, and soon Jackson was standing in front of him.

'Ship's cleared for action, sir, and I've had the boat hoisted out, too.'

'Good. Are you proposing a fishing trip with Fuller?'

Jackson laughed. 'Well sir, Fuller did bring his fishing line.'

'Is that true?'

Ramage knew the Suffolk man lived for fishing, and Jackson sounded serious.

'Yes sir—he never moves without his line.'

'Pity he's up the hill, then, because you're in for a long row soon.'

'Can I pick my men now, sir?'

'Yes—but you're not going for a while.'

As Jackson walked away Ramage looked at his watch. More than an hour since the *Jorum* broke through the raft— more than time enough for Dupont to lead his men round the bay—even allowing that he would have to climb into the hills to avoid the mangrove swamps. Or had Dupont boarded one of the privateers?

Yes—that was a possibility. Each privateer was short of the fifty or so men, not to mention the boats, who had been killed with the grenades. Had they more boats? Unlikely—Ramage knew if he had been a privateer skipper faced with boarding the *Jorum* he would have sent off every available man and boat. Which also meant that if Dupont hadn't a boat at the jetty, they'd have to make a raft to go on board the privateers because few of the men would be able to swim; certainly none would risk sharks by swimming in the dark.

The devil take it; if only he could calculate all the possibilities at the same time, instead of having a series of afterthoughts which meant it was ages before he managed to make the right decisions. And his present tiredness didn't help.

All right, assume the privateers will make a bolt for it. To stop them the *Jorum* has the five swivels, half a dozen musketoons and a few pistols. And twice that number wouldn't stop them—not desperate men always living in the shadow of the noose, knowing no one would show them mercy, that capture meant trial and the death sentence as pirates, whether or not they carried letters of marque.

Very well. It was three hundred yards from the *Jorum* to the other side of the bay. How wide was the channel? How close did the privateers have to pass to get out? A couple of ideas drifted through his mind, but he had to concentrate on overcoming his weariness before he could hold on to them long enough to examine their possibilities.

He called for Jackson and told him:

'Find a leadline—or make one up. Then take the boat and run a line of soundings from here to the far shore over there. I want to see where the channel is, so we know how close the privateers have to pass.'

Within twenty minutes Jackson was back to report that although the channel was fifty yards wide, the deepest part was close to the *Jorum*, which was lying right on the southern edge where the water shoaled suddenly from five fathoms to one. On the north side it shoaled gradually, he said, adding:

'Plenty of nasty little rocks sticking up, too, all along that side of the channel—like buoys at Spithead, sir!'

'Could you drop a bight of the anchor cable over one of them?'

Jackson slapped his knee. 'To make a snare? Easy, sir!'

'Carry on and do it, then. Pass it through the *Jorum*'s hawse first and we'll haul in the slack later.'

Jackson ran forward, calling for men.

The first bonfire up on the hill had gone out. Orion's belt, Sirius, Castor and Pollux ... The stars were moving across the sky on their pre-ordained curves. Curious that Betelgeuse was so red and Sirius so sparkling white. As he looked down again he found he was almost dazzled by the stars, the hillside across the bay seeming speckled with fireflies.

Partly dazzled ... again an idea slid through his mind. Dazzled! The men at the privateers' helm, the captain probably standing in the bow conning her, anxious in the darkness to keep in the channel yet avoid the *Jorum*, and equally watchful for a sudden windshift or eddy off the cliffs.

And as he gets abreast the *Jorum* ...

*

As the seamen heaved down on the windlass bars to turn the drum, which looked like an enormous cotton-reel, Ramage watched the cable curving upwards out of the sea, dripping as the strain squeezed out the water from between the strands.

From the schooner the cable stretched right across the channel to the rock on the far side where it was secured, and forming a gigantic trip rope which would be invisible in the darkness.

'Pity we can't get a bit higher, sir,' Jackson commented. 'It'd take out their foremast for sure.'

'I doubt it,' Ramage said, 'but anyway we can't.'

'Reckon it'll damage them much?'

'No—I doubt if it'll damage them at all.'

Jackson was silent for a minute or two, puzzling out its purpose if it wasn't going to do any damage. He finally had to admit defeat.

'May I ask ...'

Ramage, surprised at the American's bewilderment, said, 'After we broke through the raft, we had a devil of a job trying to see where the channel was, didn't we?'

Jackson agreed.

'But they've been in and out dozens of times and know where the channel is,' Ramage continued. 'Very well, they get abeam of us, nicely in the middle of the channel, but jumpy because we're firing on them with the swivels . . .'

Unintentionally Ramage paused, visualizing its happening.

'. . . Suddenly the ship hits something. If you were the skipper what'd be your first reaction?'

'That we'd hit a rock!'

'But you know you're in the channel.'

'Then I'd be damned uneasy, sir!'

'What would you do?'

'Well, I'd take a quick look over the side and make sure!'

'All of which,' Ramage said dryly, 'would have wasted several seconds just as you're abreast of the *Jorum*.'

'True enough!' Jackson said emphatically.

'But you'd be even more jumpy if in fact the *Jorum* hadn't, up to that moment, so much as fired a pistol at you.'

The American waited, then knew that was all he was going to be told. He'd been through many adventures with his captain; on more than one occasion he'd known—or, he corrected himself, thought he knew—they'd be killed; but each time Mr Ramage had produced some apparently crazy idea which saved them.

And yet, Jackson realized, the ideas usually revolved round one sort of—well, almost a rule, which Mr Ramage was always trying to din into him: surprise. You could nearly always lessen the odds by surprising the enemy.

It had become a sort of game between them, too. All right, he thought, Mr Ramage had explained the purpose of the cable—just to make sure the first privateer captain is jumpy, so the cable's only part of the plot. But as usual Mr Ramage had given him a clue—if the *Jorum* had not, up to that moment 'so much as fired a pistol . . .'

Suppose the moment Mr Ramage felt the privateer hit the cable he opened fire with the swivels, musketoons and pistols? No, that was too obvious; he had something else up his sleeve, and Jackson couldn't fathom it.

Ramage looked at his watch and then glanced aft. The three men standing there as lookout were reliable and one of them had the night-glass. Surely Dupont had managed to get on board one of the privateers by now? Ramage felt confident the man didn't intend attacking the *Jorum* from the beach. He walked over to Gorton, calling to Jackson: 'Muster the hands aft; I want to have a word with them.'

As soon as the men were gathered round, with the three lookouts listening, Ramage stood with Gorton and explained his plan should the privateers try to sail out. As soon as he finished he asked if there were any questions, but there was none, and as he dismissed them the men scurried off in the darkness to prepare themselves.

A few minutes later Ramage heard one lookout speak sharply to another and saw he now held the night-glass to his eye.

Suddenly he turned.

'Captain, sir: the nearest privateer's weighing and she's just hoisting a headsail!'

CHAPTER TWENTY-THREE

As Ramage stood at the taffrail, night-glass to his eye and watching the opening where the *Jorum* had smashed through the raft, Jackson murmured:

'Like a ferret watching a rabbit hole!'

'Mutinous words, Jackson. Five dozen lashes at least.'

Jackson chuckled. 'Well, I'd sooner be on the ferret's side . . .'

'And flattery doesn't get promotion in this ship.'

Seeing the first privateer was now fifty yards from the gap but there was no sign of movement in the second, Ramage said: 'You'd better check that the lads in the boat are ready and their slow-match hasn't gone out.'

The privateer was now hoisting her mainsail and foresail. The wind was easterly, eight or nine knots.

And Ramage's hand was trembling with excitement, making it doubly difficult to follow the movements of the privateer in the night-glass, which inverted the image. But, he warned himself, the minutes it took that privateer to reach the *Jorum* were going to be among the most important in his life.

There was a hail from the shore. He swung round and answered.

'From Evans, sir: the *Triton*'s a mile off, just south-west of the headland and he's going to loose off a rocket—Gawd, there it goes now!'

'Very well, tell Evans——'

'An' he's lighting the bonfire—we got a lot more brushwood to keep——'

'Very well, get back to Evans and tell him the first privateer's trying to get out. Smartly now!'

'Aye aye, sir!'

As Ramage turned back to watch the privateer his body went rigid: blast! Another mistake. The *Jorum*'s boat should be setting off to warn Southwick. Who to send? He wanted to hold on to Jackson . . .

The privateer was two hundred yards off, the phosphorescence of her bow wave giving her a pale green moustache. Neatly trimmed.

'Stafford! Jackson! Lay aft here!'

Both men were beside him in a moment.

'Jackson—I'm changing the plan. Stafford—you've got to go at once in the boat to Mr Southwick. You see the privateer? Good—well, the *Triton*'s a mile south-west of the entrance. Get out to her as fast as you can, tell Mr Southwick the position here and—listen carefully—tell him to heave-to right off the entrance. If there's shooting going on, he's to wait for daylight. But if he sees two white lights at our bow, one above the other, send a boat in for orders. Take a false-fire and a slow-match so Mr Southwick sees you. Hurry!'

'Best o' luck, sir!'

'Thanks, Stafford. Now, Jackson, you do your job here on board: get the gear out of the boat!'

The privateer was now a hundred yards off, approaching fast: she'd picked up a puff of wind and was bringing it with her. Hell fire, she was making four or five knots . . . The cable —she'd barely feel the bump.

'Jackson—you ready?'

'Aye aye, sir, here at the mainchains.'

'Very well. Everyone else standing by?'

A low chorus told him the men were ready and waiting, several of them crouched below the bulwark holding the slow-matches which looked like red glow-worms.

'Swivels!' Ramage called softly. 'Not a man to fire until I give the order. Aim at the quarterdeck.'

Fifty yards—and doing more than five knots. No, less— hard to tell because she was foreshortened. Her sails, broad off with the sheets eased to catch every scrap of wind, seemed enormous.

Would she open fire? He imagined privateersmen sighting along the barrels, each gun loaded with many grapeshot, each one a piece of solid iron the size of a hen's egg. Men sighting and ordering their crews to train a few degrees this way or that, preparing to fire right at the *Jorum*'s quarterdeck, just where he was standing: just the position he had told his own

323

men to aim for in the privateer.

Bile tasted sour in his throat as he almost vomited: he was
cold, perspiration like ice on his forehead, his mouth full of
saliva now and more coming every second, welling up under
his tongue, his teeth furred. Just fear, and his duty to hide it
from the men...Too close now for the night-glass and he
put it down, wrenching out his pistols.

Stretching out each thumb to cock them helped steady his
nerves. Click, click. Two duelling pistols ready for action
against a privateer. Each lead ball might dent the paintwork,
but holding them helped him. Nothing like a firm grip on a
pistol butt to instil bravery.

Twenty-five yards—barely her own length. Blast, how long
did it take for a——

And he shouldn't be standing there anyway! He turned and
sprinted forward, almost weeping at his stupidity. As he
reached the bow and stood with his foot on the cable, he
looked hurriedly across at the black bulk of the privateer
gliding along, the silence broken only by the lapping of water
at her bow.

She'd almost reached the cable: her stem must be within
a few yards.

Why didn't they fire into the *Jorum*? Stupid question—
the flash of the guns would blind the privateer's captain.

The sudden jerk on the cable so startled Ramage that he
leapt back and it was a second before he yelled:

'Jackson! Light up!'

Almost at once the unreal, bright blue glow from the false-
fire lit up the whole bay.

And slowly the privateer slewed round until she was heading for the opposite shore, her booms and gaffs crashing as
they gybed over.

'Swivels—fire!'

And all along the *Jorum*'s side the flash-crash of the guns
firing—one, two-three-four, five. The uneven spacing showed
each man was aiming carefully, not firing just because the
next one did.

'Into their rigging now—rockets!'

Blast, if he had the night-glass he'd be able to——

Suddenly the unearthly hiss and meteor-trail of two signal
rockets racing almost horizontally across the bay straight at

the privateer, exploding in showers of sparks as they hit, large red pieces ricocheting in all directions—red pieces which suddenly burst into red stars. And a few moments later he saw tongues of flame as burning fragments lodging in sails and rigging were fanned by the wind.

Jackson was tugging his arm. 'She's aground, she's aground, sir!'

Ramage nodded numbly: he hadn't noticed. Yes, her bearing wasn't changing: she was lying at the same angle to the north shore as the *Jorum* was to the south. And with a bit of luck she'd bilged herself on a rock! *Had* she taken on a list, or was it an illusion caused by her sails swinging? And down by the stern? Hard to tell with the false-fire throwing such weird shadows.

But she was still full of privateersmen: full of men who, if they could get on board the *Jorum* (and they might yet), would slit their throats and enjoy doing it.

'Swivels!' Ramage snapped. 'Fire!'

As the whiplash crack of the five guns echoed back and forth across the bay Ramage turned to Jackson and snarled:

'What happened to the musketoons?'

'All ready, sir.'

'Musketoons—open fire, smartly now!'

Damn and blast, what——

'Jackson, get aft and see if there's any sign of the second privateer weighing. The night-glass is on the rudderhead.'

One by one the musketoons added their quota of musket balls. The false-fire, spluttering away by the mainchains with two men standing near with buckets of water in case it set fire to the ship, was dazzling him, but it helped the men aiming.

He saw that one by one the swivels were being re-loaded, but his anger was ebbing. There were few seamen who'd show a moment's mercy to privateersmen, but somehow this seemed like cold-blooded murder.

'Lookouts report no sign of movement from the second one, sir,' Jackson reported, handing him the night-glass. 'I had a good look. Men on deck—all crowded up trying to get a sight of what's happening here.'

'Very well.'

'Swivels are loaded, sir.'

'Very well.'

'And the musketoons.'

'Very well.'

'They'll finish us off to a man if they get the chance, sir . . .'

'I know,' Ramage said dully. 'Five more rounds each from the swivels and the musketoons. We've got to save some powder and shot for the other one . . .'

'Aye aye, sir,' Jackson said, and because he knew his captain he took a few paces before giving the order to resume firing.

The bonfire was burning brightly on top of the hill. Had Stafford managed to reach the *Triton*? Through the glass he saw the privateer's transom had been smashed in by the *Jorum*'s swivels. There were a few men at her bow and some others in the water, swimming towards the beach.

★

The moment Jackson woke him, Ramage realized it was dawn: the few stars still visible were disappearing in a cold grey light. He was cold and stiff from lying on deck in the lee of the taffrail.

'The *Triton*'s still hove-to just off the entrance. No sign of life on the privateer opposite but there's movement on the other one in the lagoon.'

Jackson helped Ramage stand up. 'Hope you feel fresher now, sir.'

'I feel like a corpse. And you?'

'Fine sir, but I had an hour's more sleep than you.'

'Where's a tub?'

Jackson pointed to a wooden bucket by the hatch coaming. Ramage walked over, knelt down and ducked his head into it. Suddenly he stood up, rubbing his eyes and swearing.

'Jackson, you damned fool! I meant fresh water!'

'But it was, sir—someone must've emptied it and refilled it from over the side!'

Although his eyes were stinging. Ramage was now certainly wide awake. He blinked a few times and then looked seaward. And there was the *Triton*, foretopsail backed, lying hove-to just outside the entrance. The privateer opposite, sails still hoisted, seemed deserted.

In the few moments before he had fallen asleep an hour

ago, leaving Gorton in command while he had a brief rest, he'd had an idea and was thankful sleep hadn't erased it from his memory. Now to test it.

'Gorton, Jackson—here a moment.'

Without any preliminaries he abruptly asked the schooner captain: 'Just imagine you command the second privateer. Would you have guessed why the first one went aground?'

'From that distance, I'd have reckoned the false-fire dazzled 'em and they missed the channel.'

'You wouldn't have guessed the cable was there?'

'No, sir,' Gorton said emphatically. 'And the rockets went off after they'd turned.'

'Very well. You're still the second privateer's skipper. What would you do now?'

Gorton thought for a moment, then said emphatically: 'Wait for daylight—say another half an hour—and then make a bolt for it.'

'And you think you'd succeed?'

Gorton nodded.

'Why?'

'Because I'd reckon there's nothing the *Jorum* can do to confuse me—I'd be able to see the channel. And what's more, I'd keep shooting at her—which the first one couldn't do for fear of dazzling herself.'

'So the fact the *Jorum*'s here wouldn't bother you.'

'No sir. After all, the privateer carries six-pounders. She knows we've only got the swivels.'

'But she can see the *Triton* hove-to at the entrance,' Ramage pointed out.

'Wouldn't bother me, sir—with due respect,' he added quickly. 'Let's see—the privateer gets out on this easterly wind. But that's a head-wind for the *Triton*. To cover the entrance the *Triton*'s got to stay hove-to, heading north-east on one tack or south-east on the other. Either way that means she's got the entrance fine on one bow or other.'

'So?'

'So I'd steer straight for her—don't forget the privateer's fore-and-aft rigged—making sure I keep out of the way of her broadside guns.

'Now,' Gorton said excitedly, waving a finger. 'The *Triton* wont' know which tack to fill on to stop me 'cos she doesn't know if I'm going to pass across her bow or under her stern. But whichever I do, in this light wind, she won't get round in time!'

Gorton sounded utterly confident and Ramage knew he'd spoken honestly—and sensibly. He nodded. 'I agree; not a thing she can do to stop you.'

'My oath!' Jackson interjected. 'After all this we've got to let one of 'em slip through our fingers!' Then, seeing Ramage glowering at him and rubbing his brow, he added hastily, 'I mean it'd be a pity if we did, sir.'

'Jacko's right, sir,' Gorton said. 'Surely——' he broke off, correctly interpreting the American's expression, and added cautiously: 'What had you in mind, sir?'

'The quickest way of getting yourself killed is to assume your enemy can't work out what you'll do. Particularly as—in this case—you've only one course of action yourself. What you've described is the only thing the privateer can do.'

Both Jackson and Gorton nodded like penitent schoolboys, but a few moments later Gorton said:

'I can see that, sir, but I'm afraid I can't see what else the *Triton* can do either!'

'Forget the *Triton* for a moment and try to guess at what point the privateer's virtually defenceless!'

'Just as she's going out through the entrance!' Jackson interrupted promptly.

'More than that,' Gorton corrected. 'From the time she passes us until she gets to the entrance, sir? That's about three hundred yards.'

Ramage nodded, feeling embarrassed at his earlier pomposity.

'Yes, and from where she's anchored now to here is a good six hundred yards. So if the *Triton*'s waiting hove-to six hundred yards off the entrance and gets under way at the same time, she can beat in . . .'

'And catch the privateer in the entrance and either drive her on the rocks or blow her to pieces with a broadside!' Gorton said triumphantly.

'Preferably both!' Jackson added.

'Preferably both,' Ramage repeated. 'Now listen, Gorton, the *Jorum*'s cable isn't likely to help this time—they might see it and panic, but I doubt it. Yet for the *Triton* to have the best chance—she's going to have trouble weathering the headland if the wind doesn't shift—the *Jorum*'s going to have to make a diversion; just enough to stop the privateersmen from concentrating too hard!'

'We didn't do too badly last time,' Jackson said.

'No—but that was in the dark. How many rockets left?'

'Only two,' Gorton said, 'I counted 'em just now. Plenty of powder and shot for the swivels and musketoons, and we can make some smoke with false-fires.'

By now Ramage was hardly listening. He'd been putting off the decision for some time, but now he had made up his mind. Whoever was commanding the *Triton* if she hit a rock or was put aground, so the privateer escaped, would face a court of inquiry and probably a court martial. It was not fair to leave Southwick to face that.

But—and this was the reason for delaying the decision—Southwick would be very disappointed if Ramage resumed command now. Yet Ramage knew he should: the chances of intercepting the privateer without damage were—well, slender. Southwick might hesitate to ram, for example; but losing the brig would be a small price to pay if it finally squared the privateer's yards.

'Gorton, I'm returning to the *Triton* and you'll——' he broke off, remembering for the first time since they'd escaped from the lagoon that Gorton was by no means under his command, and corrected himself. 'I propose leaving some Tritons on board here, and I'd like you to remain with your men and take command of the whole party.'

'Fine, sir!' Gorton exclaimed excitedly, 'we'll do the best we can!'

'Very well. I'll take Jackson, Stafford, Evans and Fuller. How many Tritons do you want?'

★

Twenty minutes later Ramage was standing on the quarter-deck of the *Triton*, relating to Southwick everything that had happened since he'd boarded the *Jorum* off Grenada, and then hearing the Master's report of what he had done with the *Triton*.

Southwick rounded off his report with a reference to the usefulness of the bonfires on the headland and then added:

'Two seamen under open arrest, I'm afraid, sir.'

'What charges?'

'Fighting, sir.'

'*Fighting?*'

'Yes sir—while at quarters.'

Ramage sighed. Seamen fighting with each other while the ship was cleared for action . . .

'What were they fighting about?'

'We had the grindstone up on deck to put a sharp on some of the cutlasses, and the men lined up for their turn. Seems these two started arguing about who was in front of which . . .'

'Not fighting with cutlasses, for Heaven's sake?'

'Well, in a way. One punched the other who fetched the first man a clip on the side of the head with the flat of his cutlass.'

'Drunk?'

'No, neither of 'em.'

'Hmm. Well, that can wait.'

Ramage picked up a telescope and looked at the entrance to Marigot. On the southern side of the outer bay he could see the *Jorum* quite clearly, with the first privateer grounded on the north bank opposite. Beyond them the gap in the palms where the raft had been smashed aside gave him a good view of the second privateer on the far side of the inner bay, directly in line with the gap. It wasn't quite light enough yet to distinguish men moving about.

Southwick joined him. 'Having a look at the lie of the land, sir?'

Ramage nodded. 'I was just thinking how the raft of palm trees fooled us.'

''Twas a good job young Stafford told me about it when he came on board: if I'd seen that gap in daylight I'd have wondered why the hell we never sent a boat in to look when we were up this way last week.'

'I still don't know why we didn't spot there was something odd.'

Southwick chuckled. 'Don't fret over *that*, sir. I had a good look at the chart. What happened is our chart's a bit out—it shows the lagoon smaller than it really is. And both those sandspits have each grown out another ten yards. The chart's fifteen years old . . .'

'Where did we get it from?'

'Master of one of the frigates in Barbados gave me a sight of his and I made a copy. Original survey was by the *Jason*.'

'I wish there'd been time to get my father's charts before we left England.'

'Yes,' Southwick growled, 'but it's time Their Lordships started issuing charts. We'd have been in a mess if I hadn't been able to copy that one. And this damned coral sometimes grows a foot a year, so if the chart's fifteen years old a shoal can have fifteen feet less water over it.'

'We need an Irish pilot,' Ramage said dryly, and Southwick laughed at the memory of a story well known in the Fleet of a frigate bound for an Irish port several miles up a river. The pilot seemed such an odd fellow that the captain asked if he knew the river well. Just as the pilot assured him he 'Knew every rock in it,' there was a thump that shook the ship, and he'd added: 'And that's one of 'em, sorr!'

After telling Southwick to shift the *Triton*'s position by five hundred yards, keeping her hove-to farther to the north so that she could lay the entrance with the present wind, and call him the moment there was a sign of movement on board the privateer, Ramage went below to his cabin for a brisk wash and shave and change into clean clothes.

One look in the mirror startled him: the reflection showed a stranger with bloodshot, wild-looking eyes, cheeks sunken with new wrinkles slanting out down either side of the mouth. This stranger staring at him had the look of a man hunted—like a fleeing privateersman who'd stolen the tattered and dirty uniform of a King's officer.

The steward came in with hot water. He refrained from asking how it had been boiled since, with the ship at general quarters, the galley fire had been doused. An hour ago on board the *Jorum*, he mused, the idea of clean clothes, hot water and a sharp razor seemed remote, just a memory of a way of life led many years earlier. Now, vigorously brushing the lather on his face, the hours in the *Jorum* seemed equally remote. Opening the razor and nestling his little finger under the curved end, he took the first stroke and swore violently as the blunt blade seemed to be ripping the skin from his face. The damned steward—he could get boiled water without a fire, press clothes splendidly, serve at table so unobtrusively

331

as to seem invisible. But stropping a razor was beyond him.

Angrily Ramage hooked up the leather strop and hurriedly stropped the razor first on the coarse side and then on the smooth. Gingerly he tried it. Not much better, but thank goodness he had a full set, seven ebony-handled razors, each with a different day of the week engraved on the heel of the blade. In future, he decided, six days shalt thou labour and the seventh thou shalt not shave! He stuck out his chin for the last few strokes when there was a shout from on deck :

'Captain, sir!'

He went to the skylight and answered.

Southwick called down excitedly: 'The *Jorum*'s hoisted a blue flag—looks more like a shirt, sir!'

'Very well—she's spotted activity on board the privateer. Acknowledge it. When it comes down it means the privateer's weighing.'

'Aye aye, sir.'

The comfortable tiredness Ramage had felt soaking into him as he shaved had now vanished. But the rest of the lather was drying on his face, tightening the skin unpleasantly, and Southwick was still standing there, waiting for orders.

'I'll finish shaving, Mr Southwick.'

'Aye aye, sir.'

Just as Ramage turned away Southwick called down again: 'Blue flag's coming down, sir!'

'I'll finish shaving, Mr Southwick.'

'Aye aye, sir,' Southwick said with as much disapproval as he dare register.

As he finished the last few strokes with the razor Ramage reflected it was a crude way of calming Southwick. Despite his original grumbling the old man had obviously enjoyed his brief hours in command of the *Triton* and was now thirsting for action. But Ramage knew that in the next half hour he needed every man on board the *Triton* to stay as calm as possible: one slip through excitement and the ship would be wrecked and the privateer allowed to escape. Then, in the mirror, he saw his own hand trembling—tiredness, of course. He looked himself in the eyes and grinned. Perhaps not tiredness but, thank God, not fear.

And that dam' fool steward had put out his second-best uniform, as though it was Sunday, and there wasn't time to get out an old one. Hurriedly Ramage pulled on the silk stockings, dragged on his breeches, tucked in his shirt and looked round for the stock. Hmm, perhaps not such a dam' fool—the silk was pleasant against his neck. Boots—another pair, highly polished, and he had changed the throwing knife over to them.

Pistols—newly-oiled and re-loaded. That'd be Jackson. He tucked them into the waistband, put on his coat and slipped the cutlass belt over his shoulder. A seaman's cutlass looked out of place—he should have an expensive, inlaid sword—but a cutlass was more effective. Jamming his hat on his head and ducking to dodge the beams, he went up on deck.

Southwick handed him the telescope.

The privateer was under way with her foresail and mainsail set. Men at the bow were catting the anchor and a jib was being hoisted. They had little more than a breeze; hardly strong enough to flatten the creases in the flaxen sails. Bow waves rippling over the flat water in ever-lengthening chevrons reminded Ramage of sailing a model boat across a village pond. Two knots? She was about level with the jetty, which meant she was two hundred yards short of the sandspits and five hundred yards from the *Jorum*.

Ramage looked across at Marigot Point on the north side of the entrance, and then at the south side. A line joining the two was four hundred yards from the *Jorum*.

'It'll be like a horse race with a starting line at each end and the finishing line in the middle!' Southwick commented.

'Brace up the foretopsail, if you please, Mr Southwick.'

Southwick bellowed orders, the yard was trimmed round and the brig gathered way.

'Full and by, Mr Southwick.'

'Aye aye, sir,' the Master said, turning to the quartermaster. With the chance of eddies from the hills, keeping the brig sailing as close to the wind as possible was going to be difficult.

Ramage walked over to the binnacle, looked at the compass and then at the windvane at the mainmasthead—east-north-east. Hhh ... It was going to be close. To succeed, Ramage had now to sail into the bay with the *Triton* hugging the north shore, forcing the privateer to keep on the south side and passing close to the *Jorum*.

Close-hauled the *Triton* could sail six points off the wind; in other words she could steer south-east, which meant she could just about sail parallel with the north shore—and a glance showed him she was already doing that. But if the wind veered a few degrees, just fluked a little to the eastward, she would have to bear away into the middle of the channel. And then God alone knew what would happen.

If she couldn't immediately wear round and sail out of the bay again, she'd run aground. Indeed, once she was halfway into the bay there probably wasn't room enough to wear round whatever happened, unless he boxhauled—juggling with the sails so she went astern to bring her bow round, or club-hauled, letting go an anchor over the lee side so that it suddenly dragged the brig's bow round. Then, by cutting the cable and leaving the anchor behind, the *Triton* would be able to sail out again.

But although either would be a close-run thing, neither would be necessary if he timed the manoeuvre correctly. Southwick's simile about a race, with the privateer starting at one end of the course and the *Triton* the other, wasn't a bad one; but Ramage knew success depended on him making sure both sailed the same distance . . . The privateer would be three hundred yards from the *Jorum* as she passed between the two sandspits, and the *Triton* would be the same distance from Gorton's schooner, approaching from the opposite direction, when the cliff on the south side of the entrance bore south-west.

And Ramage suddenly saw the privateer was that very moment in the channel between the two spits. He twisted round to see the bearing of the south side of the entrance. South by west—so he was already fifty yards or more behind in the race.

Damn and blast; he always seemed to be daydreaming. The sky over the hills to the south was pinkish now: it'd be sunrise in fifteen minutes. But he realized fifty yards didn't matter too much—they'd meet that much this side of the *Jorum*, and by then Gorton and his men would have done their best. And the cable might have scared them . . .

Southwick said: 'Shall I start the lead going, sir?'

'No point; we're committed to this course. But I'd be glad if you'd go forward and keep a lookout for isolated rocks.'

The privateer was past the spit now and running before the breeze: a soldier's wind with her booms broad off, her sails tinged by the pinkish light of the rising sun.

The leeches of the brig's sails fluttered and Southwick turned on the quartermaster:

'Steer small, damn you.'

Must have been a back eddy off the cliffs because the fluttering stopped even before the men began to turn the wheel. And the cliffs were close. No wonder Southwick wanted a man in the forechains heaving a lead—it wasn't often that one of the King's ships drawing eleven feet forward and nearly thirteen aft sailed so close inshore!

The privateer was bearing up a few degrees now to follow the slight bend in the channel.

Was her captain left-handed or right-handed? It might make a difference, Ramage suddenly realized, since in the next few minutes he had to guess which side the man would try to dodge past the *Triton*: had to guess moments before the man gave any indication by altering course or trimming sails. A right-handed man would tend to keep to his left, to the south side of the channel. And the *Triton* hugging the north side might decide him. If he was right-handed.

At each of the *Triton*'s ten carronades the crew stood ready: each gun was loaded with grapeshot; each had the lock fitted in place with the captain holding the trigger line in his right hand, the second captain standing by ready to cock it at the last moment. There'd be no last-minute traversing because they'd fire as the privateer passed. And a seaman was peering out of each port, quietly reporting to the captain of his gun the privateer's position.

And near each gun the high bulwarks bristled with cutlasses, pistols and tomahawks tucked into any fitting that would hold them, ready to be snatched up the instant Ramage gave the order to board.

Gracefully—for she was a rakish-looking schooner with a sweeping sheer—the privateer followed the curve of the channel, keeping to the south side. She had perhaps two hundred yards to run before she reached the *Jorum*. So far so good, Ramage thought—unless the *Triton* hit a rock. And there wouldn't be time to avoid one, so Southwick was wasting his time. He called the Master back to the quarterdeck.

Southwick had just arrived aft when the dull boom of a gun echoed between the cliffs, followed by another, then several at once.

As Ramage looked over at the *Jorum*, cursing Gorton for opening fire too soon, he was startled to see there was no smoke from her swivels and Southwick exclaimed:

'It's that damned grounded privateer!'

So the survivors must have gone back on board! Smoke was drifting away from her, towards the *Triton*. And because she had turned to starboard before she went aground, her larboard-side guns covered the entrance; covered the approach *Triton*, with the range decreasing every moment.

'Poor shooting, all fell short,' Southwick said disgustedly. 'Still, up fifty yards and the next broadside should get us.'

'Give 'em a hail and tell 'em.'

More gunfire—coughs rather than the heavier thumps of the grounded privateer's guns. And now smoke was drifting away from the *Jorum*. Then a curious popping, six distinct shots. Gorton had fired his swivels, then the musketoons, to harry them.

'I hope he re-loads in time for our friend,' Southwick commented.

'He will, but anything that distracts our friend is a help.'

She was half-way between the spit and the schooner: 175 yards.

'Second broadside's due now, sir.'

Out of the mass of cordage that made up the *Triton*'s standing and running rigging—it weighed more than seven tons—only half a dozen pieces were really vulnerable; but if even one of the half dozen was cut by a stray shot the *Triton* ... quickly Ramage dismissed the thought.

By now the second broadside should have arrived, but it hadn't. Did that mean Gorton's swivels and musketoons, sweeping the deck almost as effectively as if raking her, had killed or wounded enough of the men working the guns?

Nor was there a second broadside from the *Jorum*. Gorton was saving that for the second privateer, which was close now and bearing away a few degrees to stay in the deepest part of the channel.

Along the *Triton*'s larboard side the cliffs were receding and becoming less vertical, the bare rock hidden by bushes.

The privateer was obviously making a knot or so more than the *Triton*, and Ramage was thankful. He'd misjudged the point where he intended meeting the privateer: the whole bay was closing in, and there was less room to manoeuvre than he thought. The fact the privateer would be well past the *Jorum* before he intercepted her was to the *Triton*'s advantage. Nice of the enemy to cover up one's mistakes.

Unwittingly emphasizing it, Southwick said conversationally: 'Reckon you've timed it nicely, sir. He's still got that cable . . .'

And Ramage realized he'd forgotten that, too.

'I hope so, Mr Southwick,' Ramage said cautiously, wondering what else he had forgotten.

The *Triton*, was, if anything, losing the wind. Since it was blowing the length of the two bays, maybe the northern spit was blanketing it. Or perhaps the privateer was bringing the breeze down with her.

'Wind's puffy,' Southwick said. 'We'd look silly if we ran into a dull patch and she sneaked by us!'

Ramage, busy calculating distances and with the thought already nagging him, snapped: 'If we do, you can lead the boats towing us round.'

And the privateer was nearly up to the *Jorum*: thirty yards —twenty—hard to judge from this angle. Gorton's men would be carefully training round the swivels; the musketoons resting on the bulwark capping. Had the privateer spotted the cable?

A puff of smoke right aft in the *Jorum* as one swivel fired and a moment later he heard the report. Smoke at the privateer's bows—she had swivels too. Then Ramage heard the sharp double crack of two more of the *Jorum*'s swivels.

Smoke was spurting from the privateer's larboard side now: she must be almost abreast the *Jorum* for her broadside guns to bear. One—two, three—four—five: the whole broadside. And steadily the schooner's swivels and musketoons puffed smoke, the noise of all the guns reaching the *Triton* as a roll of thunder.

Then suddenly the privateer turned hard a' starboard, apparently heading straight for her grounded consort, the smoke of her guns still streaming from her ports and the big foresail and mainsail crashing over. Southwick swore softly, excitement in both his voice and choice of words.

But Ramage was not sure. Was it the cable? Or had one of the *Jorum*'s swivels killed everyone at the tiller, leaving the privateer out of control for a few moments? Would they wear round again?

The *Triton* was barely two hundred yards away from her now and, snatching up the telescope, Ramage could see the holes torn in her bulwarks by the *Jorum*'s grapeshot. He swung the telescope over to the schooner for a moment and it confirmed his fears. The *Jorum* was a shambles; it was a miracle she'd been able to fire the remaining swivels after the privateer's single broadside.

Then, the telescope trained back on the privateer, he saw several men running to the tiller—although there were two men at it already—while other were frantically hauling at the foresail and mainsail sheets.

It'd been the cable. She'd hit it and her captain, feeling the bump, must have instinctively ordered the helm down. But the privateer had shot so far across the channel that— no! The cable was no longer there!

'She's parted the cable!' he said abruptly to Southwick. 'They're trying to wear round.'

'Shall we board or ram, sir?'

'Wait and see!'

With the privateer now only 150 yards ahead and no indication whether she would be able to wear round before running aground, Ramage was tempted to add 'I wish I knew.'

'She's turning, sir!'

Slowly at first. They'd been able to see her long profile, from the end of her bowsprit to her taffrail, as she'd swung across the channel—but now it was shortening as she turned towards the *Triton*.

Ramage could see they'd managed to haul in the mainsail almost amidships: in a few moments, if they were lucky, it'd swing across and spin the privateer round on her heel, her bow heading for the entrance.

Ramage suddenly ran to a gun port and looked over the side. One glance showed him there wasn't enough depth of water between the *Triton* and the north shore for the privateer to squeeze through; in fact, it was a miracle the brig hadn't gone aground herself. As he came back to the binnacle he found he had made up his mind.

Up to that moment Ramage had felt strangely calm and detached—perhaps because the *Triton* could only continue sailing full and by—but now he was getting excited at the prospect of quick decisions; of sudden gambles, heavy stakes slammed down to profit from an opponent's mistake.

But, tugging at the pistols in his waistband to make sure he could draw them easily, Ramage fought the excitement.

The privateer's main boom crashed over, followed by the foresail, and almost at once she began to turn faster.

'She'll make it!' Southwick called, watching the shoals close to the beach.

'Now you'll get a run for your money!'

Me too, Ramage thought to himself: the privateer was turning as fast as a soldier doing an about-turn. Round she came, bowsprit sticking out like an accusing finger, pointing momentarily at the *Triton* with both masts in line, but as she continued swinging the masts opened up again. Hell, she was swinging fast now.

'Looks as if she's going to run ashore on the opposite bank!' Southwick called.

If she did she'd be only a hundred yards to seaward of the *Jorum*; but she wouldn't. Southwick could be very stupid at times.

One broadside from the *Triton* wouldn't do the job; Ramage was certain of that.

'Mr Southwick—we'll be turning nine points to starboard in the next few moments!'

'Aye aye, sir!'

Picking up the speaking trumpet, Ramage shouted: 'Larboard-side gun captains, fire without further orders as soon as you bear!'

To the quartermaster he snapped: 'Stand by now!'

And the privateer was now darting diagonally across the *Triton*'s bow, picking up speed every moment.

Ramage, rubbing his brow, tried to judge the precise moment to order the helm hard over to turn the *Triton* on to an almost parallel course and precisely placed so her broadside guns would bear. Almost parallel—converging just enough to squeeze the privateer so she had to choose between running ashore or crashing alongside the *Triton*.

Turning a moment too soon would let her suddenly bear up and slip by under the *Triton*'s stern: a moment too late would let her slip out ahead. If she managed to get a fifty-yard start there'd be no catching her . . .

Quickly he changed his plan: there'll be no sudden turn: he'd do it slowly, slowly . . .

'Quartermaster, starboard a point. Mr Southwick, smartly now with the sheets and braces!'

The *Triton* turned almost a dozen degrees, bringing the privateer dead ahead again for a few moments and a hundred yards away. Then, as the brig steadied on the new course, the privateer continued passing diagonally across her bow.

Southwick was beside him now, speaking trumpet clenched in his hand. Ramage saw Jackson watching him rubbing the scar and took his hand away.

'Quartermaster, a point to starboard!'

Southwick bellowed more orders to the men trimming the sails.

Once again the *Triton* was, for a few seconds, heading directly for the privateer, until she straightened up when the turn was completed. Seventy-five yards away—less in fact.

Ramage knew Southwick must be puzzled why he didn't wait and then make one quick nine-point turn to bring the *Triton* alongside the privateer immediately. But this way Ramage knew he was forcing the privateer farther and farther over to the south shore; cutting down the only chance the enemy had of suddenly bearing up under the *Triton*'s stern.

'Quartermaster—another point to starboard!'

Once again the sails were trimmed as the wheel was put over; once again the *Triton*'s bow pointed at the privateer for a few moments.

Fifty yards, and the old Master was giving Ramage an anxious look.

One man from each of the larboard side carronades was peering out of the port, keeping his gun captain informed. The pinkness had gone out of the sky; it was getting light fast. The privateer had splendid lines; a beautiful ship with raking masts.

Then Ramage saw a wind shadow coming fast down the bay—it'd catch the privateer first in a few moments and give her another knot or so: just enough to let her slip through.

All right!

'Hard a' starboard!' Ramage bellowed. 'Smartly now!'

The quartermaster leapt to the wheel as the men spun it; Southwick shouted encouragement to the sail-trimmers. Slowly the *Triton* began turning. Too slowly—Ramage swore softly as he watched the end of the jib-boom swinging against the land: it was moving so slowly that—ah, faster now: the *Jorum* dead ahead for a second, then the privateer. And, as the *Triton* continued turning, she was suddenly almost abeam.

'Larboard guns, stand by!'

His heart was pounding in a hollow chest; it had been sheer luck.

'Quartermaster—steady as you go! Come on to the same course as that devil!'

Both the *Triton* and the privateer were now sailing almost side by side, steering a course which converged on the beach and, inside a couple of hundred yards, would put them both ashore.

A crash from forward made both Ramage and Southwick swear; then a spurt of smoke, the rumbling recoil of the forwardmost carronade, the reek of powder drifting aft to catch in their throats, warned them the first of the *Triton*'s guns had been brought to bear.

A flurry among the men grouped round the privateer's tiller showed it had been well-aimed. Then there were flashes along her side, followed by the dull thumps of the guns firing.

The double crash of the *Triton*'s next two carronades firing was followed by fifteen feet of the privateer's bulwark abreast the quarterdeck disappearing in a shower of splinters and dust, with screams echoing over the water. Those splinters had been flung across her deck like wooden scythes, cutting men down with dreadful wounds.

More flashes from the privateer's guns, and this time splintering wood and the clanging of metal against metal in the *Triton*'s bow. Ramage saw the forwardmost carronade had been slewed round by the impact of the shot and every man in its crew flung across the deck like stuffed scarecrows.

The *Triton*'s fourth and fifth carronades crashed out; both tore into the privateer's hull almost on the waterline, splintering the planking, and leaving rusty-coloured stains in the wood.

The smoke was making him cough and his eyes were watering, but he could see the privateer would run aground any second now unless she put her helm down in the next twenty yards. And if she put her helm down she'd crash alongside the *Triton*. Then he saw there was no one standing at the privateer's tiller, and a startled glance showed why: the *Triton*'s second and third rounds had also smashed away the tiller: the privateer was steering herself and was bound to go aground!

'Mr Southwick! I'm going to wear round, shoot up into wind, let go the larboard bower anchor and drift back. We may need a spring on the cable to get our broadside to bear.'

'Aye aye, sir.'

The old man's white hair, fluffed out like the head of a mop, made him look like a benevolent parson taking an early morning stroll towards the church rather than a man itching to board an enemy ship and deal out death and destruction with the enormous sword whose scabbard was banging against his leg at every step.

In a few moments the Master had given the necessary orders: half a dozen men ran forward to prepare the anchor; the men at the sheets and braces acknowledged his warning to 'Step out smartly when the Captain gives the word!'

And the moment Ramage saw the privateer's bow lift as she hit the sandy beach, he shouted:

'Quartermaster, hard a' starboard! Hands stand by to wear ship!'

And swiftly the brig began turning, her jib-boom pointing along the cliffs on the south side, right across the entrance, then along the cliffs on the north side. Finally, as she came round to the closest she could sail to the wind, Ramage glanced over at the privateer and continued his stream of orders for trimming yards and sails with:

'Quartermaster! Shoot her right up into the wind. Forward there—are you ready with the anchor?'

An answering hail told him the cable was free to run.

'Starboard-side guns—as we drift back, fire as you bear without further orders!'

The *Triton* was now past the grounded privateer and shooting up towards the sandspits into the wind's eye. Already the sails were pressing against the masts as the wind blew from ahead, although Ramage kept the yards braced hard up.

Quickly the brig lost way and Southwick, peering through a gun port, called:

'No way on, sir.'

'Let go, forward!'

The anchor splashed into the sea.

'Mr Southwick, brace up the foretopsailyard!'

With yard and sail square to the wind the brig would drift back faster and Ramage prayed the wind direction wouldn't change: he wanted to continue veering more cable, letting the brig drop back until she was abreast the privateer.

As soon as the yard was hauled round, Ramage told Southwick to keep on veering cable until they were in position.

Suddenly the brig's stern began to sheer over to the south shore, yet the wind hadn't shifted. Then, glancing at the men at the wheel, Ramage roared:

'Quartermaster! Helm amidships, you blockhead!'

The quartermaster had kept the wheel over from the sudden turn with the result that as soon as the brig started to go astern the rudder began to get a bite on the water and push her stern round.

An explosion, the splintering of wood, the whine of grapeshot, and splinters right behind him showed the privateer had managed to train a gun round. The full charge of grapeshot had smashed into the larboard side of the *Triton*'s taffrail, ripping away a good deal of wood. But not a man was wounded.

And yard by yard, like a bull being driven backwards, the *Triton* was easing astern, Southwick watching and gesticulating to the men.

Ramage walked over to the aftermost carronade and, with a grin at its crew looked through the gun port. The carronade was already trained as far aft as possible. Another twenty yards would do it.

The gun captain moved over as Ramage knelt behind the gun and peered along the sight.

In a moment or two the gun would be aiming directly at the foot of the mainmast, round which was grouped at least a dozen privateersmen.

'No need to worry about rolling!'

The gun captain, a white strip of cloth round his head

showing he had been one of the party in the *Jorum*, grinned. 'There'll be a hit with every one sir: won't waste even one of them grapes!'

As Ramage stepped aside the man looked along the barrel, took up the strain on the trigger line in his right hand, glanced round the gun to make sure every man was clear, looked along the barrel again and jerked the line.

The carronade leapt back in recoil, smoke spurting from the muzzle; but without waiting to see where the shot had gone the men hurriedly began sponging out the barrel and reloading.

Ramage looked out through the port, keeping clear of the rammer. Not a man had been left standing by the privateer's mainmast—which was now pocked with what looked like rust marks, showing where the grapeshot had hit it. Then he saw two red eyes winking from the privateer's forward gun ports.

There was no time to jump back behind the bulwark. Splintering wood all round the port, clanging metal, the whining of ricochets, and he felt blood soaking his face and uniform. No pain; no report for Admiral Robinson that his orders had at last been carried out; a vacancy for the Admiral to promote a favourite; not to see Gianna again; Southwick sailing the *Triton* back to Barbados. Thoughts ran helter-skelter through his mind as he reeled back from the port.

A man was holding him, preventing him falling; a man with a cockney voice, anxiously repeating the question: 'You all right, sir?'

Stafford—he recognized the voice. Eyes stinging, head hurting—not much, numbed perhaps. No pain elsewhere. And, as he glanced down, no blood either.

He realized he'd been soaked with sea water thrown up by the shot. He rubbed his head, but the pain was at the back. He must have banged it against the top of the port as he'd jumped back.

He reassured Stafford, feeling foolish until he realized no one else knew the wounds he'd imagined. The *Triton*'s next carronade fired, then the third, fourth and fifth in quick succession.

Now Southwick was standing beside him, his first words

drowned by the thump of the aftermost carronade firing again.

Then a thud as more shot hit somewhere forward.

'Damn and blast 'em,' Southwick roared. 'There goes the jib-boom!'

Again a carronade fired—the men were keeping up a high rate of fire: must remember to mention it later.

Just as Ramage went to the nearest gun port someone hailed:

'Captain, sir! The Frenchies are shouting and waving a white flag!'

'Check fire,' Ramage yelled. 'Southwick—speaking trumpet!'

Through the port he could see a group of men right up in the bows of the privateer gesticulating. One was waving a white cloth. His shirt?

Reversing the trumpet and putting the mouthpiece to his ear, Ramage listened.

An English voice shouting. An agitated, frightened voice cracking in the effort to be heard. And shouting that the privateer surrendered.

'Mr Southwick, send away the boarders. Guns' crews stand fast.'

Was the old Master disappointed?

'And Mr Southwick—after you've taken the surrender of this one you'd better go over and secure the other one. And bring Gorton back with you . . .'

'Aye aye, sir!' Southwick exclaimed gleefully. 'Taking the surrender of two prizes in five minutes—not many can claim that, sir!'

'No,' Ramage said and, remembering the chances he'd been taking among the rocks and reefs in the last half an hour, added mildly, 'and it's an honour I'm willing to forgo in the future!'

CHAPTER TWENTY-FOUR

As the *Triton*, with the *Jorum* in tow, followed the two privateers for the last two miles down the coast to St George, Ramage listened to Southwick speculating why *La Merlette* should be anchored in the Roads.

'Anyway, shows the Admiral did buy her in,' the Master concluded more cheerfully. 'That means we'll all see a bit o' prize money—if those thieving agents don't get up to their usual tricks.'

With a new mainmast, *La Merlette* looked a fine ship, he added. 'And a nice command for one of the Admiral's favourites.'

Ramage nodded. A nice command, and a fast ship. Ideal, in fact, for carrying orders between the islands. And he had little doubt that her new commanding officer had, locked up in his desk, a letter for him from the Admiral.

'Must say they look nice,' Southwick said, gesturing to the *Triton*'s two prizes ahead. 'Still plenty of work for the shipwrights 'afore they're really ready for sea!'

Again Ramage nodded. It'd taken two days to re-float the two privateers and the *Jorum*, and he was thankful none was leaking. Two days' work had repaired them enough to be ready for sea but the *Jorum*'s foremast had been too badly damaged to repair, so it had been hoisted on board and the *Triton* had taken her in tow.

Southwick chuckled. 'I'll take a small bet that Gorton never reckoned he'd ever be doing this!'

Ramage glanced up. 'Doing what?'

'Well, acting as prizemaster to two prizes. Not bad, considering.'

Had the old Master guessed?

'Considering what?'

'Come come, sir,' Southwick chided. 'He's got "Run" written all over him!'

'Maybe, but I've left my spectacles in England. He's been more useful to us than twenty extra petty officers.'

'Oh I wasn't criticizing, sir,' Southwick said hastily. 'In fact it was a good idea on your part making him prizemaster. I can just imagine their faces in St George when Gorton sails 'em in and goes alongside the careenage!'

'It's about the only reward he'll get,' Ramage said.

'It'll be more than enough. He as good as told me so.'

'Good—and I'm glad Appleby understood. Anyway, I had to put him in the *Jorum*—she could whip *our* masts out if she started yawing around!'

Half an hour later, for the wind was light in the lee of the land, the two former privateers tacked in through the harbour entrance and, at a signal from Southwick, the *Jorum* cast off the tow and anchored. As soon as the hawser was hauled on board the brig she anchored to windward.

As Southwick made sure the yards were square and ordered the boats to be hoisted out, the Marine sentry at the gangway reported a boat leaving *La Merlette*. A few minutes later Ramage was greeting her commanding officer as he stepped on board. He'd guessed correctly—it was Fanshaw, the Lieutenant who'd been bustling around in the Admiral's cabin on board the *Prince of Wales*.

Fanshaw was proud of his new command but obviously embarrassed that Ramage would guess why he'd been given it. Ramage led the way down to the cabin.

'How does she sail?' he inquired.

'Well enough,' Fanshaw said, his tone implying he was speaking from a wealth of experience of all types of ships.

As soon as Fanshaw was seated on the settee, Ramage inquired: 'And what brings you from across the water?'

'From the Admiral.' Fanshaw produced a letter, and his voice told Ramage all he needed to know about its contents.

Putting it carelessly in his pocket he said: 'I have to go on shore to see the military commander. Would you care to come?'

When Fanshaw nodded cautiously, Ramage picked up the report he'd written for Admiral Robinson the previous day, outlining how the privateers had been captured, and led the way on deck.

Colonel Wilson had been watching from the Fortress and was waiting on the battlements when Ramage arrived, his face flushed with pleasure, and before Ramage could say a word exclaimed:

'I knew it, I knew it! So they're the villains, are they——' he pointed to the two privateers, which Gorton had now secured alongside in the careenage below. 'Well, I hope old Fishpot's watching from Government House! Now, come along to my office and tell me all about it!'

Glancing at Fanshaw occasionally, Ramage told Wilson the whole story, and while the Colonel frequently slapped the top of his desk with glee, the Lieutenant's face was getting longer and longer. As Ramage finished, he said to Wilson, 'I wonder if you'll excuse me a moment—Lieutenant Fanshaw brought me a letter from the Commander-in-Chief.'

'I know he did,' Wilson said sourly, 'he's been pestering me for the past couple of days to find out what's been going on.'

Ramage broke the seal and began reading. The letter was curt, telling him of the Admiral's extreme displeasure at not having received a report from Ramage indicating that he was carrying out his orders to find and destroy the privateers, and giving him—Ramage hurriedly recalled the date—another five days. If the orders were not carried out by then he was to sail at once for Barbados and report on board the *Prince of Wales*.

Knowing his reaction would be reported to the Admiral, Ramage managed to keep his face impassive. He folded the letter slowly and put it in his pocket, taking out his report.

He tossed it to Fanshaw.

'You'd better get under way at once and deliver that.'

Fanshaw glanced at the superscription and said without thinking:

'That's for me to decide!'

'Do you have orders to the contrary from the Admiral?' Ramage demanded.

'Well—no, not exactly.'

'Then you'd better sail at once or give me your reasons in writing why you refuse.'

'But——'

'What's your seniority?'

'Oh, all right. But I'll have to——'

'—Tell the Admiral you refused to sail with an urgent despatch? Yes, do that by all means.'

Fanshaw stood up, said a stiff good-bye to the Colonel, nodded to Ramage and left the room.

'Pompous young ass,' Wilson commented as the door shut. 'Isn't *La Merlette* the slaver you captured?'

Ramage nodded.

'And I'll bet that lad was fetching and carrying for the Admiral, waiting for a plum to ripen and fall in his lap.'

Ramage grinned. 'You seem to know a lot about the ways of the Navy.'

'Hmm,' Wilson growled, 'favouritism's not the Navy's monopoly. By the way, the Fishpot's very cross with you.'

'I guessed as much.'

'Hardly a surprise to me, either. Gave him your letter and he stamped and shouted. Reckoned he should have been consulted before you sailed. Told him I couldn't agree.'

'Thanks.'

Wilson waved a hand. 'Pleasure was mine. Anyway, he wrote a report and sent it off to Admiral Robinson—hired one of Rondin's schooners. She must have passed *La Merlette* on the way.'

'Fine—he's done me a good turn!'

Wilson looked puzzled until Ramage said: 'Fanshaw brought me a stiff reprimand for not having caught the privateers yet and giving me another five days. Then I must report on board the flagship. So with the Admiral already angry, Sir Jason's letter will make him livid. Then Fanshaw turns up with my despatch!'

The Colonel laughed, his whole body shaking.

'Well, your next orders should be more to your liking, anyway.'

'Why?'

'My dear chap—he was all ready to make you the scapegoat. Suddenly you succeed in doing what he thought was impossible. He'll make sure he gets the credit in London—that's the prerogative of a Commander-in-Chief. But he'll be anxious to make sure that no one saw through his little scheme. And in case you had any suspicions you can be sure he'll give you new orders that'll leave you happy—and grateful!'

'I hope you're right, sir.'

'Well, I suppose we'd better be getting up the hill to tell Sir Jason his Golden Fleece is safe from moths and free-booters.'

'I was wondering——'

'I have the letter here,' Wilson interrupted, opening a drawer. 'She's well and still staying with us. I don't think she's had a proper night's sleep, worrying and fretting, but the minute your armada was sighted I sent word to her.'

He slid the letter across to Ramage who looked at it nervously.

'I should open it,' Wilson said banteringly offering him a paper-knife, 'it won't explode.'

Dudley Pope

'Takes over the helm from Hornblower . . . Dudley Pope knows all about the sea and can get the surge of it into his writing.' *Daily Mirror*

'An author who really knows the ropes of Nelson's navy.' *Observer*

'The best of the Hornblower successors.' *Sunday Times*

RAMAGE £1·25
RAMAGE AND THE DRUM BEAT £1·25
RAMAGE'S PRIZE £1·75
RAMAGE AND THE GUILLOTINE £1·50
RAMAGE'S DIAMOND £1·25
RAMAGE'S MUTINY £1·35
RAMAGE AND THE REBELS £1·50
THE RAMAGE TOUCH £1·25
RAMAGE'S SIGNAL £1·50

FONTANA PAPERBACKS

Fontana Paperbacks

Fontana is a leading paperback publisher of fiction and non-fiction, with authors ranging from Alistair MacLean, Agatha Christie and Desmond Bagley to Solzhenitsyn and Pasternak, from Gerald Durrell and Joy Adamson to the famous Modern Masters series.

In addition to a wide-ranging collection of internationally popular writers of fiction, Fontana also has an outstanding reputation for history, natural history, military history, psychology, psychiatry, politics, economics, religion and the social sciences.

All Fontana books are available at your bookshop or newsagent; or can be ordered direct. Just fill in the form and list the titles you want.

FONTANA BOOKS, Cash Sales Department, G.P.O. Box 29, Douglas, Isle of Man, British Isles. Please send purchase price, plus 8p per book. Customers outside the U.K. send purchase price, plus 10p per book. Cheque, postal or money order. No currency.

NAME (Block letters)

ADDRESS
